OPTIONS

Stephen J. Dempsey

The sins of some men are obvious,
reaching the place of judgment ahead of them;
the sins of others trail behind.
I Timothy 5:24

To my wonderful family, whose love and encouragement gave me inspiration throughout the many hours working on this project.

Author's Note

The primary source of compensation for many top corporate executives is share price appreciation of their company's stock. A highly popular method is the use of executive stock options. Under these plans, senior managers are granted rights to purchase a specified number of their firm's shares at a fixed price once a required vesting service period is attained. The exercise price is set equal to the market price of the shares on the date of grant, which incents managers to increase firm value over the requisite vesting period. Compensation ultimately comes to them by selling their shares for the difference. While almost always resulting in goal-congruent behavior, such option plans occasionally entice opportunism by a few to artificially manipulate a higher stock market price.

Although this novel is a work of fiction throughout, meticulous effort has been made to ensure all financial, scientific, medical, and historical details depicted are accurate as to the time periods and settings described.

I hope you enjoy the story.

Stephen J. Dempsey
Burlington, Vermont
January 2017

PROLOGUE
(1993)

Saturday, August 21, 1993
Lake George, New York

A hot sun baked off the last of the silvery mist that had formed over the lake's surface during the night. For the two men aboard their dive boat, the calm morning conditions couldn't have been more ideal. It was their last dive of the season and their second day in search of a curious relic—a horse-drawn carriage rumored to be in the vicinity, some 100 feet below. Lake George entombed several such artifacts of the previous century's means of travel over the winter's ice. Fur trappers who misjudged the ice's strength would more than likely survive, but their horses and carriages wouldn't. Blanketed deep beneath thermocline layers, in anaerobic pressures, organic remains of the like would be preserved in remarkable condition.

If they were really there.

The pair studied their photocopied map one more time, confirming their position as best they could from shoreline references. It was by line of sight only. Instruments would have done no good since they were told the map's marked location was only an educated guess anyway.

They entered the water and adjusted their dive gear. Purging the air from their buoyancy compensator vests, they descended slowly, clearing their ears frequently of pressure as they followed the tethered anchor line with their underwater lanterns. At forty feet it was colorless. At eighty feet it was black. If not for the heavy wetsuits they wore, the frigid temperatures would have been intolerable. As it was, the cold moderated only bearably as the water seeped beneath the thick neoprene rubber of their wetsuits and warmed from their body heat.

Scott, 20, relished these times with his father. They had taken up freshwater scuba diving three years earlier, logging many hours together in the spring-fed lakes of the Adirondacks. The local dive shop owner told them the carriage was recently discovered by one of his customers. Unfortunately, there was no return address on the envelope he received in the mail, and the typed name on the letter was one he didn't recognize. The marking on the map contained in the envelope was casually drawn—a free-form 'X'—making the carriage's precise location impossible to discern with certainty. Hence, the father-son team's second day in search for it.

Jerry, Scott's father, led the way, Scott to his right and rear. The pair swam concentric sweeps of the area, variously 90 to 100 feet deep, making successively larger orbits as they paid out line from their penetration reel fastened to the boat's anchor.

The pressure at this depth meant they had no more than 30 minutes of bottom time.

They directed their lanterns into the darkness surrounding them. A large catfish scurried from their path and into the shadows. A few sunken logs and an occasional boulder were the only objects breaking the lunar-like monotony of the lakebed. Nothing else of significance presented itself. Nothing other than an old rusted spoon lure and span of attached steel line lost by a lake trout fisherman.

Drawing out the reel's last few meters of line, Jerry signaled to his son that they only had about five more minutes remaining. Their arc of travel went deeper now, 110 feet.

Gradually, in the distance, an irregular shape appeared in the path of their lights. Softly contoured in the muck, it measured about four feet long and two feet wide. Not their hunted object, they were sure. Scott approached it and gently brushed the sediment with his glove. A cloud of silt obstructed their vision a few moments. When it settled, it became apparent that what lay before them was a canvas bag—possibly an army duffel bag—obviously resting there a long time.

Jerry found the end tie of the sack and cut at it with his knife. Scott aimed his lamp to provide better lighting as his father carefully scooped away some rocks at its opening and peered inside. The stirred muck guarded the bag's secret another several moments. When it dissipated, Jerry reached into the bag and pulled out some small bits, which he studied with his flashlight. Rotted cloth. Then some firmer chalky white fragments, which he rolled in his gloved fingers. More curious, he reached in again and pulled out a femur.

A guttural shriek exploded through his regulator. Dropping his flashlight, he kicked against the bottom, away from the bag. Scott flashed his light at his father, but its beam was quickly swallowed by the thick cloud of stirred muck. He continued panning his light around him, unable to make out anything.

Then, just faintly above, he detected movement.

His father was finning for the surface.

OPTIONS

Ascending too quickly from these depths was lethal, Scott knew, and he swam hard after his dad. By inflating his vest a little, he was able to close the distance, but just as he was about to grab hold of his father's leg a flailing fin dislodged his facemask. Blinding ice water flooded his eyes.

With his buoyancy now increasing on ascent, Scott knew he had to stop for his own safety. He purged some air from his vest. Still holding his flashlight, though unable to read his depth gauge without a mask, he tried to neutralize his plane. His pulse and respiration were running dangerously fast. He forced restraint, trying to maintain calm and not to hyperventilate through the last of his air supply.

A faint current brushed his face. Sensing movement there, he directed his lantern and reached out. A searching hand was reaching back to him.

Rejoined and relieved, the pair eventually made an orderly ascent to the surface.

It took a New York State Police dive team two full days to locate and retrieve the bag. Early forensic analysis revealed it contained the skeletal remains of a young woman, 20 to 25, submerged perhaps fifteen to twenty years earlier. Edipocere had turned body fats into soaps, leaving only pasty patches of gray flesh on the bones.

The bag also contained a damning piece of evidence …

PART I
MIDDLEBURY
(1977-1978)

Chapter One

"HEY, Sands! Wait up!"

Recognizing her voice, Jonathan turned around. Dead leaves scattered in her trail as she ran across the stretch of campus green to catch up with him.

"I thought you were going home for the weekend!"

She hooked her arm around his, panting. "I am. I just had to pay that stupid parking ticket before I left. *Five minutes!* I left my car for *five* minutes and they got me. Can you believe it?"

"Just Middlebury's finest maintaining law and order, Sue."

She swatted his shoulder as they started walking together.

Susan Cabot was a perky cute blonde, always a lot of fun to have around. Her fur-collared leather jacket and flushed tone gave her a rich, healthy look.

"So what happened with your car?" he asked.

"Got it back." She veered him off the sidewalk and onto the lawn for a slight change in direction. "Cost me another fifty bucks. 'Welcome Back Students,' right! What a racket."

Sands smiled at the comment. Larson's Mobil in town hung a large 'Welcome Back Students' banner from its signboard at the start of each school year. The service station also had the contract with the College for towing away illegally parked cars. It was a perennial question among students whether the station's proprietor had some sick sense of humor or was just a plain moron.

Susan squeezed his arm. "So, Jon, tell me what you think of Karen."

He hesitated at the question. Though not because it was a surprise. Karen Wyman was Susan's roommate and best friend. His roommate and best friend was Decker Moss, Susan's boyfriend. Their not-so-subtle attempts to make the match over the past couple months had become a frustrating failure to date.

"Jon?" Susan prompted again.

"Oh, *Karen*? She's very nice."

"No, you know what I mean," she said, swatting his arm again. "What do you *think* of her?"

"Come on, Sue, you know how it is." He kicked a small stick from their pathway. "I'm just too busy to get distracted with this stuff."

"Distracted?" She laughed. "*Stuff?* Are you crazy? She's gorgeous, and you know it."

This was true. Karen Wyman was striking. Sculpturesquely figured, yet always smartly dressed, she wore her long dark hair down the full course of her back. Something Jonathan found tastefully provocative.

"I don't know," he said finally. "It's just that we're all getting close to graduating and she's set on going to law school. Why get something started when we'd just have to part ways in a few months?"

"Plans can change, Jon. Besides, who knows? You could both end up in Boston."

This was also true, although Susan didn't know about his fresh job offer. All she knew was that he'd received an earlier offer from a national accounting firm in Manhattan, and had attended a second interview with another national firm in Boston. Karen Wyman had been accepted into Harvard's Law School. The letter he received in the morning mail—a distraction that happened to preoccupy his day—contained an offer from Boston. A very generous offer.

Frustrated by his silence, Susan broke their pace and planted herself in front of him, drawing him to a stop. "She really likes you, you know. You're a fool if you let her slip away." She cocked her head at him, as if offering him a warning he'd better heed.

Sands averted the stare-down by eyeing a fat maple off to their side. Its denuded branches stretched high overhead like gnarled skeletons, bare fractal expanses silhouetted against the gray late afternoon sky. He shivered and reached for his shirt collar. "I ... don't know. I'm just not sure it's the best thing for now. I'll have to think about it."

"Right, like you have to think about everything," she chaffed. She gazed at his shirt. "Looks like you didn't think much about wearing a jacket today."

"Yeah ... well, it was nice this morning when I left, and I had a lot on my mind."

OPTIONS

Susan frowned at him, arms folded tight in a stoic look of perplexity. "Okay, Sands, you go on and think hard. It must be terribly difficult to say yes to the most perfect girl you're ever going to meet in your life." Her goading blue eyes stayed on him searchingly another several moments and then went down to her wristwatch. "Look, I've got to run. It's supposed to snow and Albany's a two-hour drive. Want a ride to your apartment? You'll freeze walking in this weather."

"No, that's okay. I have to head over to the bookstore and pick up some typing paper."

Evaluating him further with a curious squint, she said: "You're a real case, Sands, you know that?" Then she hefted up on her toes and kissed him on the cheek. "Keep an eye on Deck for me while I'm gone, okay?"

"You know me, Sue. I'll tie him up with a rope until you return."

"Thanks, Jon. Love ya!"

Susan bounded off to her Camaro, which Jonathan noted was illegally parked at the curb.

She rolled down her window. "Karen has the apartment alone this weekend!"

He wagged his head at her as she drove off.

A gust of cold air filled his shirt and it began to drizzle. Picking up his earlier direction and pace, he clutched his shirt collar with one hand and firmed hold of his books with the other.

Earlier when he arrived on campus, it was bright and pleasant. Now, somehow during his long afternoon hours holed up in the library stacks working on a research project, the day had turned foul, a gusty gray portending rain or snow or both.

It wasn't that Jonathan Sands was unaware of Vermont's turn-of-the-season tricks. Having grown up in the state, he was certainly acquainted with its temperamental fall days. The distraction, he knew—no, he allowed himself—was his new job offer ...

Certainly enough reason for not attending to such small bothers as a weather forecast.

And with his library research now finished, he wished to use the time to savor the good news. But after only a few minutes into that, his effort to dismiss the conversation about Karen Wyman eluded him.

Chapter Two

JONATHAN and Decker's apartment was on the second floor of a large Queen Anne Victorian, set back and aloof on a quiet side street on the northeast side of town. Its ornate architecture was decidedly out of place for a pair of college students: copious slate-covered roof lines with steep-pitched gables, ornamental scalloped accents in earth-tone pastels, and a prominent corner tower that went the full height of the house. Their landlord, a widowed professor emeritus, spent the summer months living on the first floor of the house but chose to winter in Florida. Fortunately for the two student tenants, the old snowbird interpreted winter as starting early October and ending late April, resulting in only a few weeks of the school year when they all lived in the house together. In return for their maintenance of the place, a deal was cut on the rent. Jonathan, and to a far lesser extent, Decker, were pretty faithful keeping their side of the bargain, their occasional lapses dutifully reported to the landlord by a meddlesome neighbor. Sands supposed his roommate would be able to live in high style even without such an arrangement, coming from the money he did. Decker Moss's parents contributed the majority of the rent for the place. And insofar as Jonathan's own funds were nearly drained from a maturing scholarship, he chose not to make an issue of his roommate's marginal efforts.

"Hey, Sandman," Decker greeted when Jonathan walked in the door. He was reclined on the living room couch, wearing a Yankee's baseball cap, a tie-dyed tank top, and a fermented smile on his face. A *Mr. Ed* rerun was playing on the TV. Three beer bottles sat atop the coffee table, two of which were empty.

"Starting kind of early, wouldn't you say, Deck?"

Jonathan placed his books on the kitchen counter that looked out over the living room. He grabbed a soda from the refrigerator and popped the can's tab. "I take it you flunked your stat exam."

"You got it, brain-boy," Decker retorted. "What a bunch of crap. Latin squares, Chi-squares, least squares, R-squares … it's all a bunch of squares crap. Who the hell gives a damn?"

Jonathan walked over to the TV to turn the volume down a bit. "I thought it was an open book exam."

OPTIONS

"It was, but you have to know what page to look up. Give me a break."

Sands saw the opportunity to sermonize a little about the need for test preparation, but chose to drop it. In Decker's case it was probably too late. Jonathan's attempts to tutor his friend over the past couple years had, for the most part, turned out to be a colossal waste of time.

"I swear to God, Ridley's a rattlesnake" continued Moss from his lounged position, raising his beer bottle. "He slithers around the room and makes these hissing sounds at the blackboard as he draws Greek symbols all over the place. Then he peers back at us with his beady little eyes, like ready to strike when we can't answer his ridiculous questions! It's too much!" Decker jabbed the air with fork-pronged fingers as he spoke.

"Slithers and hisses?" asked Sands dubiously.

Decker turned up to him. "No, Jon, it's the G d's honest truth. The guy belongs in an aquarium!"

Sands smirked. "Face it, Deck. You're mesmerized by him. That's why you can't concentrate."

"Screw you, Sands."

Jonathan retreated to the bathroom down the hallway and removed his shirt, drenched from his walk home. Standing in front of the vanity mirror drying his hair with a towel, he called out: "You won't believe what came in the mail this morning."

A yeasty belch from the other room was the only reply.

After changing into a sweatsuit in his bedroom, Jonathan retrieved the letter from among his books on the kitchen counter. He set it in Decker's lap. "Check that out, my friend."

Sands took a seat in the facing recliner and watched Decker's face slowly take on a contorted expression as he read. "From MM&P now? Man, this is two grand more than the offer you just got from New York!"

"Shows you what a little work will do," Jonathan replied smugly. "I must have really impressed the guys."

Decker whisked the letter onto the coffee table. "Well, you may get a job, but you sure lack class. Anyone with class would snatch up a girl like Karen Wyman in a second."

"Oh, so now I'm going to get it from you, too? At least I'm not married. Your little wife hit me with that not an hour ago."

Moss looked sideways at him. "You saw Susan?"

19

"Yeah, she was up at campus paying that parking ticket she got. Almost got another one today." Jonathan took a sip from his soda. "You better teach your wife where she can park."

"Cut it out with the wife crap. She knows we're parting once we graduate."

"Oh, does she really?" Jonathan asked with sarcastic inflection. "Then it wouldn't be news to her if I were to tell her about that?"

"You better not, you crafty bastard." Moss knew he was caught and gave up.

Jonathan got up to reclaim the letter from the coffee table and sat down again. He thought it ironic to be called a crafty bastard by the supreme artisan himself. Decker's ability to manipulate situations and people was the stuff of Great Men. On more than a handful of occasions he had been able to convince a professor of some story or excuse that led to a due date extension, a recorded grade adjustment, extra-credit, or some other such exception.

Although Decker would never admit it, he was using Susan. Oh, he liked her well enough, Jonathan knew, but he told her he loved her. And she thought he did indeed, with a capital L. The problem was that Jonathan was aware of cases when Decker cheated on her. Loyalty to his best friend had to supersede any sense of accountability to Susan of course, but for her part Susan had to know the type of character Decker was. They had been off and on for three years now, and his exploits out with the guys every Friday night had to get back to her sooner or later. Middlebury was a relatively small place.

"So, I guess your exam performance today gives you a good excuse to tie one on tonight," Jonathan offered.

"Yeah, that was my thinking. It's necessary, you know." Decker downed the last bit from his bottle and nodded in his roommate's direction. "I don't suppose you'd like to join us."

"No, not tonight. I finished my research on that tax project and thought I'd type it up. Get it out of the way."

Moss laughed. "You're the biggest loser I know, Sands. Thousands of students in this town and I have to room with the likes of you. The one guy who could get his kicks sitting at a typewriter on a Friday night cranking out tax returns. Here we are in our senior year and I haven't seen you get wasted the whole time I've known you."

"We don't need to get into that again," Sands replied dolefully.

Decker looked over at his roommate. "My God, Sands, that was back when you were in high school. *Years* ago. Get over it!"

Jonathan chose to ignore the comment.

"You're a machine," Decker said, still staring at him.

"No. I'm just not a hedonist like you."

"A what?"

"A hedonist."

Moss's face went blank. "Well, whatever the hell that is, I'll take it as a compliment relative to yourself." He got up, went to the kitchen and uncapped two more bottles from the fridge. "Here, have something frothier to drink, my friend. I bought a twelve-pack."

Decker set one down on the side table next to Jonathan's soda can and returned to his reclined position on the couch.

Their mutual razzing was as typical as it wasn't. It also wasn't unusual for their banter to get testy at times. But Jonathan sensed something was different tonight. He had long suspected it was a bad semester for Decker grade-wise. Worse than usual. Perhaps the econometrics exam posed a bigger concern to him than he was willing to let on.

"I wouldn't take that crap," Decker offered out of nowhere, his attention fixated on the TV. "Wilbur should just shoot that smart-ass talking horse and be done with it."

Sands regarded his friend lying on the couch like that. *Cyrus Decker Moss.* Decker hated his first name; and his vanity wouldn't take him the distance to actually use it. Something Jonathan could fully understand—although he occasionally took advantage of the fact. And while Decker's parents wished to honor his grandfather with a namesake, they had to accept his adoption of the chic, abbreviated version of the name: 'C. Decker Moss.' It was a potent kick-start to one's potential in the world to have a name like that, thought Sands. More than once he found Decker with pad and pen practicing signatures of it. Of course, no matter the horsepower, one had to have gas in the engine to get anywhere, and Jonathan hadn't witnessed much in the way of gas in Decker's engine. Not unless hops and barley qualified.

"Check this out, Sandman!" Moss blurted from the couch. "Mr. Ed's wearing a party hat. He's a party animal!" Decker thought this was funny and laughed by himself.

Yet despite all their differences, Decker was a free spirit Jonathan felt drawn to, a curious contrast to his own more assiduous personality. Dirty blond hair, dirt brown eyes, and superbly outgoing, Moss was a quintessential frat man. From what he told Jonathan early in their friendship, he was some kind of high school football star in his hometown of Irvington, New York, a swank suburb on the Hudson, north of the Big Apple. Fortunately for his grades, though, average as they were, Decker blew out his knee in an end-of-season game, making it impossible for him to play college ball. Being his father's *alma mater*, Middlebury proved the logical choice. Now Decker's only body-punishing diversions were weight lifting and rock climbing. His degree program, like Jonathan's, was Economics, which suited his love for money, but whose course requirements he found a general nuisance. *They go too deep*, he would say. *Just show me the tricks of turning a buck and I'll turn it into a million.* Jonathan wondered whether Decker's use of the term "tricks" contemplated whatever means necessary, ethical proprieties aside.

Decker Moss's wealth—his *parents'* wealth—flowed from both sides. His father's was self-made in a warehousing and distribution business that served the New York-Montreal corridor. The money on his mother's side ran deeper. Cyrus Schoen, Decker's grandfather, owned a highly profitable chemical company that enjoyed a growing national presence. The elder patriarch suggested he would be happy to take his grandson on with the firm, conditional on a B average upon graduation. It was a condition Jonathan suspected as probable of fruition as kiwi in Vermont.

"God wound you up too tight, Jon-Boy," Decker muttered from the couch, his expression still fixed on the TV. "You should really get out with us tonight and air out a little. To celebrate."

After investing a wasted moment on the campy sitcom, Jonathan said: "I don't know how you can watch this trash."

"Trash? How can you say that? It's a classic."

"Classic? Right. This from a guy who bellows on the floor at *The Three Stooges*."

"What? Are you suggesting *The Stooges* aren't classic?" asked Decker. "Where's your sense of culture? At least I have an existence outside the books, which is more than I can say about a certain geek in the room." Moss smiled over at his friend, but their eyes didn't meet. Instead, Jonathan spent the next several minutes in silence, staring out across the bland space of the apartment they called home the past two years.

OPTIONS

The place was sparsely furnished in the manner of coarsely matured college men. No homey wares or accoutrements, like wall hangings or table knickknacks. The curtains and major furniture pieces came rented with the apartment, albeit all quite plain and wearing considerable mileage.

Jonathan's eyes drifted to the folded letter in his hands. Without knowing why, he felt his mood slide ... what his accomplishments really meant; what the future would be; with whom he might share it. Perhaps it was only disappointment at Decker's reaction—his *non*-reaction—to his job offer. Aside from Jonathan's mother and grandfather, Decker was the only one whom he felt close enough to share such things.

Sands turned his gaze to the window beside the recliner. Pulling aside the dusty drapery, he looked out at the murky scene beyond, a featureless gray that diffused darkly through the drizzle-coated panes. It had been a long week, a long semester. A long three-and-a-half years. And now a very bright prospect for his future rested securely in his hands.

He grabbed for his can of soda, and then, looking at it, diverted his hand to the beer bottle resting next to it. Taking a swig, he exhaled a sigh. "Maybe you're right, Deck. I should probably get out and celebrate a little. I've earned it, right?"

Moss looked askance at his roommate.

"The tax project's not due till Monday, and I can type it up tomorrow." Jonathan raised his beer bottle, squinting through it to the bended light of the TV screen. Then he took a fuller swallow. "Where's everyone meeting?"

With bottle in hand, Decker lifted himself from the couch and genuflected with overdone exaggeration. "Ah, the great Jonathan Sands will grace us with his presence this evening! The man of virtue won't be disappointed!"

Decker chimed his bottle against Jonathan's and went into the kitchen to rummage around for some chips. Returning to the living room with a party grin, he said: "We were going to play some euchre up at the house and then head on over to Smitty's." The first reference was to Decker's fraternity house in town. The second was to a dingy bar. "What's your pleasure?"

"Smitty's?" On hearing of their intended destination Jonathan felt less optimistic about having a good time. It was a country tavern located on the outskirts of town. Walking distance from their apartment but far away from the bigger crowds attracted to bars closer to campus. Decker's friends liked the place on Fridays because it ran a special on pitchers and the peanuts were free. Of course, a place that had to run beer specials on Friday nights said something about its virtues in other areas.

"Tell you what," said Sands, "I'll go for my run, shower, and meet you at Smitty's at eight-thirty. Given your mood I wouldn't want to wipe you out at euchre."

Decker burped. "You don't have enough money to wipe me out, Sandman."

* * *

Surrounded by Vermont's verdant farmlands, with views of the Green Mountains to the east and the Adirondacks to the west, Middlebury was a small college town whose only token traces of commerce orbited campus life and student money. Jonathan's daily run covered a five-mile perimeter of the town. He was dedicated to the regimen, rarely missing a day. Although he hadn't ever experienced what others referred to as the 'runner's high,' he always felt a pained sense of accomplishment when it was over. And if he were honest about it, the more pain the better. His best runs were thus on cold, drizzly days, like this one.

His first thoughts focused on the offer from Marsh, Mason & Pratt. The two-thousand-dollar premium was significant. Not so much because of the money itself, but because of what it conveyed. New York should pay more than Boston, he knew, not the other way around. He suspected a tangible message was being sent about his desirability as an employee. Moreover, New York didn't hold the convenience or ambiance of Boston. He'd be closer to home and there'd be a smaller intimidation factor. Manhattan, he knew, could swallow you and never let you go.

Less important—though more pleasant to think about—was Karen Wyman. He had kept to himself his feelings about her for months. Yet, in spite of himself, they only grew stronger with his indecisiveness and silence. Clearly if there were more to look for in a girl he didn't know what it could be. And the prospect of a job in Boston now made that a possibility.

But as quickly as the enticement formed, he felt compelled to dismiss it from his mind. *No needless distractions until the CPA was in hand.*

It was the type of conflict that stitched the patchwork of Jonathan Sands's character: tacit interplays between emotion and conviction that invariably sided with the latter. Always purposed goals for the future's best—at least insofar as he could determine that future to be. Yet, despite Decker's quips about him, the "geek" stereotype didn't fit. Aplomb, six-foot-two and with raven dark-haired good looks, Sands was one of the top-seeded collegiate downhill skiers in the Northeast. Prominent among his facial features were his eyes. Outlined by bold thick lashes, they were a crystalline blue, the penetrating kind that could captivate and intrigue at the same time. Like the quiet dominance of an eagle's gaze. As for friends, his reserve held to only a few. And as for "girlfriends," there was simply nothing longstanding enough to comment. Timing was everything, and now simply wasn't the time.

It was a lesson he took from his parent's tragic example.

He turned up a residential road along the eastern edge of town. Street lamps kicked on in response to the lengthening shadows, offering better lighting to his strides.

Sands's upbringing began simply enough on a dairy farm in northwestern Vermont. With over 400 acres of pastoral hills and fields, it was by all appearances an idyllic setting to raise a young family. Unfortunately, the few sentient memories he had prior to the age of about four or five were disturbing, and became sharply painful thereafter. His probing questions to his mother left her uncomfortable. Her hurt ran too deep to recount the story, he was later told by his grandfather. Indeed, it was his grandfather who eventually felt inclined to do so when Jonathan reached his early teens. The soliloquy replayed often in his mind during his runs, etched there with repetition and the permanence of time.

From the day your grandmother died, Jon, your mom and you have been all I have. I'll share with you what you want to know, what you need to know, just so you never make the same mistakes. But if what I tell you ever causes you to look down on her, I'll never forgive myself. Nor you. She feels responsible. It wasn't her fault. Do you understand? You should never use what I share for anything but your own good.

The gray-haired sexagenarian spoke in a throaty Quebecois accent, one that turned upward at the end of each sentence, like always a question was being asked. The two were sitting on the front porch of his grandfather's hip-roofed bungalow, the house which had become home for Jonathan and his mother after the death of his father.

Your parents married young, Jon. Too young. Tom and Cheryl were a couple throughout high school. Your grandmother and I tried to convince her to see others, but she wouldn't listen to us. I guess the two of them just figured they were meant to be together. As it happened, you were … well, they married soon after graduation. Here in town, at St. Christopher's, where we attend.

Just before that time, your dad's uncle decided he had finished his days on their family farm up in Fairfield. He had back problems. He wanted to pass it on but had no sons of his own. And Tom was in need. It was a lease thing, not a sale. Your parents paid a small rent and also paid the property taxes. They kept whatever was left, which wasn't much if any. Still, they were happy at first.

But the pressures of fourteen-hour days on the farm without much in the way of financial payoff were the sort that wore your dad down. That's when his drinking started. At first your mom said she felt it was his way of getting his spirits back. He wasn't a drinker in high school, she said, and I suppose she was just willing to overlook his evening bouts in the early days of adjustment to full time farming.

As time passed, though, he would come in for dinner with the smell of liquor on his breath. Cheryl said he rarely came back to the house in the afternoon, so she figured he must have kept a stash outside somewhere. She made a search one day when he was in town. Eventually she found some bottles in the barn. Confronting him with it was a mistake. He reacted like a crazy man—near strangled her, she said. After that she felt she couldn't do anything. She wouldn't even speak to us about it. Not till much later.

The smell of booze became thicker and the farm income became thinner, and the bills and debts piled up. In time he'd often get drunk before lunch. She worried about your safety as even the smallest things led to outrage. He blamed her for his misfortune and the one who stole his promise from him. She would take you out of the house when she felt danger, but apparently many of the episodes had little warning. He would … do things to her, and then in the mornings claim he had no memory of it. But Cheryl had the scars and bruises to prove it.

They call it 'blackout.' The drinking and abuse got worse and went on for several years.

The end came when you had just turned five. It was winter. A huge rainstorm hit during a January thaw. I remember that storm well. We didn't get it as bad here in Montpelier, but the news reports covered it. The ground was frozen and the run-off caused flash flooding: ice dams blocked the rivers; knee-deep ice water covered the fields. Unfortunately, your dad's cow barn was set in a depression at the foot of surrounding hills. Not steep slopes, but still ones that acted like a giant bowl. The run-off had nowhere to go.

When evening came the temperature dropped sharply lower and the water began to freeze. The overflow in the barn turned to ice, sticking to the legs of the animals where they stood. As far as your dad could see there was no way out for them to higher ground. It was covered by sheer ice, and he couldn't get his cows up and out of it without them falling over each other. The temperature continued to fall—near twenty below that night—and the ice rose and thickened on their flanks. Their legs began to give way to the cold. Long hours went by as he ran around confused, wavering in desperation over the situation.

He was pig-headed, Jon, like most us old-time Vermonters. But he wasn't rational. Cheryl's pleas to him to call his uncle for help were stubbornly ignored. He told her he wasn't going to go cry for help from no one. Then he hit her with the flat of his shovel and warned her to stay inside and leave him alone.

He worked out in the barn all night, picking at the ice, trying what he could to keep his cattle moving around. I suppose it was a combination of things: the disorienting effect of the booze, the crazy cold, and his own mental rundown. But in the end he must have thought there was no hope of rescuing them.

Cheryl said it happened just before dawn. He made his way back to the house, near frozen to death himself. He grabbed his deer rifle and several boxes of rounds and trudged through the pond of ice that covered the barnyard, falling several times. She followed him from a distance, too scared to do anything.

That's when he did it. She screamed for him to stop, but he just went on like a crazy man. One by one he shot them. When it was all over, he stood at the end of the barn looking back at her and out over what he had done. Nearly a hundred head lay slaughtered—floating in the ice water—their steam filling the air...

Jonathan knew the rest. His father opened his mouth, drew in the barrel, and with an arm's-length shove of the trigger, left his torment behind.

Misfortunes in one's past could be dealt with. Childhood memories dulled with age. His mother's anguish would be cured with the years, and if coping with it on her own was her desire, then he would certainly honor that. But what remained for Sands was something worse than memories. It was a fear of what resided in his blood—an atavistic bent towards violence that could turn on him at an instant, as he found out about himself when he was sixteen.

The event concerned a girl he had befriended in the tenth grade. Obviously bright, she had a guarded though pleasant personality once you got to know her. They came to enjoy their daily study hall sessions talking about the various books they had read, their favorite music groups, history, politics and the like. Her family was poor. Poorer than his own, Jonathan knew from comments she made about her father's trouble finding good work. And also from what was obvious from the lack of variety in her dress: the same frayed plaid pleated skirt and yellowing white blouse every day. Peppered in their conversations were hints of her insecurities, especially about the "lookers," the popular girls who needed not vie for attention, and who had the clothes and looks and personalities to match.

Unfortunately, she also had a facial disfigurement: a repaired cleft palate that left her upper lip severely scarred, which caused her words to blend together in a nasal strain. Teens are naturally self-conscious, Jonathan knew, girls perhaps especially so. Her attempts to cover the scarring with makeup or with her hand embarrassingly when she laughed suggested as much. But she didn't bring it up, and he surely wouldn't.

The incident took place at a high school dance on the Tuesday before Thanksgiving break. Sands chose to go with a few of his friends in what they called "observation mode." In those days it was an easy matter with the help of an older brother or friend to make a beer run at a local convenience store. They sat out the first hour of the dance in the school's parking lot, downing Millers, listening to Frampton and Zeppelin blaring on the car's cassette deck, getting out every so often to 'drain the vein,' as they put it.

When they eventually entered the school building, Sands's attention was diverted by laughter down a hallway alongside the gymnasium. A couple of guys were taunting her, asking her to dance with them, choreographing their mocking overtures with lewd hip motions. A few others watched and jeered from the side, egging them on.

Jonathan's reaction was immediate. He charged through the on-lookers and slammed the two guys to the floor. The smaller of the two scrambled off in a daze, but the other Sands shoved hard against the lockers, pinning him with a tight-fisted throat-hold. His fingers squeezed the guy's gullet like talons, causing his face to engorge crimson. Sands threw vicious blows to his head and gut. Blood and saliva spewed all over. A growing mob of students tried to break them free, but this only increased Sands's fury further. The brutality went on for long moments, and if not for several adult chaperones that were eventually able to restrain Jonathan from behind, it would have likely gone on to a tragic end.

Charges were filed, yet despite his claim that he was only helping a friend in trouble, Sands was convicted of drunk and disorderly conduct, assault and battery. They were only misdemeanor charges, but the severity of the assault led to a relatively harsh sentence for a juvenile: ten weekends in detention and sixty days of community service. Fortunately for him, the mother of the brawler stopped short of a lawsuit. Mired in divorce proceedings of her own at the time, she considered also what she knew of her son's part in the blame. Nonetheless, under the court's restitution terms, Sands's mother was remanded to pay for medical damages.

With much time for reflection after the event, Sands remembered walking into the building, but literally nothing thereafter. What he learned about it he gathered only from others.

There was a dark irony to it all. *"You should really get out and socialize a little. Have some fun,"* he had suggested to his study hall friend. *"Heck, people go to dances by themselves all the time. Besides, I'll be there."*

The episode and its aftermath engendered an epiphany for Sands that branded his consciousness. It wasn't about *what* he was capable of doing—drunkenness and violence often go hand in hand—it was about *who* he was. A far more serious matter. But as deep into himself he sought an answer to that problem, it was completely inaccessible to him. One cannot simply offer oneself to alternative predispositions. And no further introspection or self-analysis could present any more prescriptive insight about how to overcome what he knew to be his blood legacy. Besides, he eventually came to conclude, people don't change. Not really. Not on the inside. Nature's sovereign wiring can always veto frailer vows of the will—that vulnerable software that so easily entangles and crashes at hardware's capricious convenience.

Yet, in the end, forced to terms, resolve was all he had. It was a resolution for his mother as much for himself. She deserved it. Life for both depended upon it.

The father of the man must never be allowed to show himself again.

A simple plan indeed. And drinking or mistimed romance played no part in that plan.

Chapter Three

THE cold drizzle turned to a slushy rain now, soaking through Jonathan's windbreaker as he ran. The sun had set, but with the thick cloud cover there was no hint of twilight, only soot gray turning inexorably coal black.

He turned onto Spring Street, the last leg of his course. Susan and Karen's apartment was just ahead on the right. It was a small two-story complex, new and tastefully designed with a brick face to suit the recently rezoned residential neighborhood. With the growth of the college, the town-gown relationship was in a constant state of flux.

As he got closer he saw a lone figure, a girl, rushing from the building toward the row of parked cars in front. She opened the driver's side door and rolled up the window.

From the car's interior dome lighting he recognized her.

"*Karen!*"

She lifted up in the direction of the voice, scrutinizing the approaching figure. "Jonathan?"

Sands emerged from the dark street and bent at the waist to grab his knees, attempting to suppress his heavy breathing.

"I knew you were a nut, but I didn't think you were stupid!" she needled. "What are you doing running out in this weather?"

"I'm stupid, too, I guess." His panting began to subside. "What'd you do, leave your window down?" He knew it was a stupid question as well, but passable in the circumstances.

"Yeah, they've been down all day. It was nice this morning but—" She circled around the car to the other side and rolled up the passenger window. It was a green Ford Pinto hatchback, nothing fancy like her roommate Susan's Camaro. Closing the door, she folded her arms, peering at him, seemingly oblivious to the rain. "Would you like to come inside to warm up? Hot chocolate or something?"

"Hot chocolate?" he repeated with a smile. "Sure, I haven't had that since I was a kid."

"Then, let's go!" Karen bounded toward the door stoop with Jonathan in tow.

OPTIONS

The apartment smelled, well, feminine … sweet scented, like spiced candles. Only a floor lamp was on, next to it a recliner with several open books spaced out on the floor. Karen turned on some lights and disappeared down the hallway. Coming out with a large bath towel, she threw it to him.

Sands removed his soaked windbreaker and began to dry his face and tousled hair while Karen walked off to the kitchen and rummaged around in the cabinet for a pot. After pouring some milk to heat up, she returned to the living room doorway where he was standing. "Give me a minute." She headed off to the bathroom again. Moments later he heard the hairdryer.

In her absence Jonathan surveyed the apartment, noting the touches girls add to make a place comfortable. There was a quilted tapestry hanging above the couch, colorful with soft lines, which he took to be homemade. Potted houseplants adorned the area in front of a sliding glass door that led to the backyard. He went over to the recliner and picked up one of the books lying on the carpeted floor. *Social Costs and Corporate Accountability.*

A jazz album was playing on the turntable.

A few weeks earlier Decker and Susan arranged for the four of them to attend a concert that was playing on campus. It was a popular fusion jazz band with an excellent sax player, out of Buffalo. Jonathan thought the music was excellent, and although he and Karen both felt a bit uncomfortable with the arrangement, they all had a good time. Afterward they went to a popular dessert house in town. Jonathan was relaxed, and, Karen thought, humorously entertaining in a self-deprecating sort of way. It was a defining moment for the evening when he was trying to cut the stubbornly chewy brownie to his hot fudge sundae and his fork went through to crack the glass plate beneath it in half. The four of them couldn't stop laughing.

Karen emerged from the bathroom. Her long dark hair, parted in the middle, draped over her shoulders and fell to the waist of her jeans. The two regarded each other for a moment. Each surmised the figurative space between them was about to close.

She smiled. "I've seen you run by from time to time, but I never thought it would take the rain to make you stop by and visit."

Jonathan laughed.

"Here," she said, reaching, "give me your stuff and I'll throw it in the dryer."

Jonathan removed his sweatshirt and handed it to her, along with his soaked jacket. He draped the towel over his bare shoulders as she exited for the building's utility room in the common outside foyer to tend to the task.

When she returned they sat at the table with their mugs, making small talk at first, mostly about their respective courses and the pressures of school. She was interested to learn more of what it was he was studying.

"When I first came to Middlebury I had no idea what I wanted to study," he said. "I liked my economics classes enough, but I was hoping for something more practical, something to help me get a job. Then last year I got an internship with a CPA in town and just kind of fell in love with it. Middlebury doesn't have an accounting program, but this is where my scholarship is, so I've had to make do." He paused. "I'm doing an independent study now in corporate taxes."

"Taxes? Do you actually like that stuff?" she asked.

"No, I hate it."

She laughed. "Then why do you want to be a CPA?"

"Auditing, not taxes." He took a sip of his hot cocoa and folded his arms, thinking of the miserable time he had researching his tax assignment in the library that day. "There's a good reason they call it the tax code. Lifetimes have been wasted trying to decipher it. Anyway, auditing is what I did for my internship. My CPA friend just helped me get a job offer from Boston."

"Boston?" she asked surprised. "I thought it was New York."

"How did you know about New York?" Sands asked, raising an eyebrow.

A snared expression crossed her face. "Well, maybe just a little snooping," Karen answered with a pursed smile. "Susan told me it was in New York."

The record album that had been playing quietly in the background ran through its side about five minutes earlier. She got up to turn it over.

He listened for a moment. "That's beautiful. What is it?"

"Chuck Mangione. *Bellavia*. He won a Grammy for it last year."

She returned to the table and he went on to explain about the new job offer he received that morning, along with his plans to sit for the CPA exam. It turned out they had both taken a class in business law, and both had the same professor. He was a practicing attorney out of Rutland, a real character who brought in actual case stories of farmers that painted 'promissory notes' on the backs of cows, and breach of contract cases involving skiers who sued resorts for being stranded in malfunctioning chair lifts.

The subject shifted to their backgrounds, where they grew up, what high school was like. Jonathan already knew that Karen lived in Potomac, Maryland, an affluent suburb north of Washington, D.C. But he didn't know her father was a consulting attorney on international law for the State Department.

"He's always had the ears of the higher ups," Karen said, "at least as long as I can remember. I don't get involved much, but apparently there's some work he's doing for the Carter Administration on a peace agreement between Egypt and Israel. He had lunch with Cyrus Vance a few weeks ago."

"Vance?" asked Sands incredulously. "Your dad actually consults with the Secretary of State on this stuff? Do you get to talk to him about it?"

"Not much. He has to keep things private for security reasons." Karen took a sip from her mug. "But he sure was excited about that lunch meeting, I can tell you that. They think Carter will be able to pull off a summit between Sadat and Begin. Maybe even mediate an actual peace agreement."

There wasn't any arrogance in her comments, only justifiable pride in her father's achievements. Still, Jonathan found the subject a bit intimidating, so he shifted the conversation back to their closer world. "So, how did you come to choose Middlebury, way up here in Vermont?"

"Well, my family used to come up here to take ski vacations at Killington. Unfortunately, my mother was diagnosed with multiple sclerosis several years ago, which put an end to that."

"I'm sorry to hear that." Jonathan traced his finger over the rim of his mug. "Will she be okay?"

"As well as can be expected, I guess, although it's getting tough on them. She's in a wheelchair now. She tries to stay busy with her volunteer work—charity telephone canvassing, that sort of thing. The worst part is that she had to put down her oil painting. She was very good at it."

"She sounds like a great person." He didn't know what else to say and he gazed down thoughtfully at Karen's hands, which were squeezing hold of her cup. There seemed to be some pain in every family.

She in turn coaxed a smile and returned to the original question. "Anyway, I always knew I wanted to go to college here in Vermont. Even as a kid. It's so beautiful ... and peaceful. Nothing like D.C. Middlebury has the best pre-law program in the state, at least according to my father, and I fell in love with the place."

"Are you close to him?"

"My dad? Very."

"Tell me about him. As a father I mean."

She looked a bit self-consciously at her cup. She knew from Decker that Jonathan's father died when he was young, but she didn't know the details. "As a father, he's always had a lot of respect for us kids. Firm-handed but never domineering, you know? Most of my friends had parents who were either overly protective or totally out of the picture. Dad and Mom just seemed to have a knack for how to connect, when to hold on, when to let go. I suppose there's never been any question I would eventually study law. My two older brothers as well. I guess it runs in the family."

"Is there a particular area you want to go into?" Jonathan asked.

"Environmental law," Karen answered. Responding to his blank look, she clarified: "You know, pollution controls, toxic waste disposal, that sort of thing." She pointed at the floor next to the recliner. "That's what those books are about. I'm working on a research paper for my environmental studies course. Congress just passed an act last year that's going to make a big impact on business. Don't get me wrong, I'm not anti-business or anything, but sometimes the bottom line can get in the way of the larger good, don't you think?"

"No question," Jonathan answered. "Power requires accountability, which is what I find interesting, I guess. Law and accounting have that in common."

There was a stint in their conversation, for which she took the time to enjoy his deep blue eyes. "So what about you?" Karen asked. "How'd you come to Middlebury?"

Sands chronicled some of the story of his childhood, yet tried to keep it suitably brief. It wasn't that there was any concern about her trust; he just felt no compulsion to share details that might make the two of them feel uncomfortable. Decker was the only one with whom he confided the whole story, and that was only after their friendship was well seasoned.

34

OPTIONS

"After Dad died we moved to Montpelier, to live with my grandfather. Mom had to take on the role of both parents, watching my track and ski meets, giving me advice. She was always there for me ... in many ways my best friend. I worked hard in high school. Not that I didn't have a good time, but I wanted to get into a good college, and Middlebury came up with the best scholarship. I can't really say I thought much about leaving Vermont. Now, however, I'm kind of looking forward to getting out."

She smiled at him, taking the final sip from her mug. "So do you think you'll take the job? In Boston, I mean."

"Well, I did a lot of thinking about it during my run and I guess ... yeah, I'd be foolish not to. You never know what the best decision is, of course." He downed the last bit of his hot chocolate and cradled the mug in his hands. "Boston just seems right to me ... in every way." His blush must have been obvious but she didn't give hint of noticing.

Her eyes fell to the gold necklace he was wearing. "That's pretty. Was it a gift?" she asked, pointing.

Sands grabbed the coin-sized medallion. "Yeah, a high school graduation present. Saint Christopher." Turning it over, he read the engraved inscription: "*To Jonathan Sands, the man in my life.*" Taking a moment to enjoy the quizzed expression on her face, he continued: "*Love, Mom. 6/74.*"

"That's so sweet." She placed her elbows down on the table and folded her hands beneath her chin. Then with a bold glint in her eye she said: "At least now I know who my competition is."

He held her look.

"So, Mr. Sands, where do we go from here?" The query came as casually as one remarking about the weather. At which Jonathan discomfited. She obviously wasn't concerned he knew where she stood with her feelings, and he rather than she found it disarming ... as if she somehow knew there was no other strategy she could take to provoke the only response he seemed unable to muster himself.

"You're definitely going to be quite the lawyer, Miss Wyman."

"You think?" Karen got up from the table and took their cups to the sink. Rinsing them out, her back to him, she said: "Actually, a good lawyer has to be better than I am at hiding things." She turned around and leaned against the counter as she dried her hands with a dishtowel. "We're not supposed to be so transparent, you know."

"Then again, transparency can be an effective lure."

"Not for such a zug it can't."

"A what?"

"A zug," she said again, crossing her arms.

"What's that?"

"A person who doesn't act how he feels. Thorne Smith … from *Topper*."

"Oh, I see." Not knowing about zugs, or Thorne Smith for that matter, Jonathan groped for something clever to say, some witticism. "I …"

"I what?" she challenged. "Have to leave?"

"No, I …" He glanced about awkwardly.

Karen laughed. "Jonathan, would you just please say what's on your mind?"

"I'd like to see you again."

"Yeah? When?"

"Tonight." There was no benefit to be gained by giving it more time. The words just came out anyway. "If that's okay with you."

He stood up from his chair and Karen came over to him. Meeting his dubious expression she gripped both ends of the towel that hung from his bare shoulders. "And for what purpose, may I ask?"

Sands softly brushed her cheek with his thumb, seeking to steady the quiver in his fingers as he cupped her face, combing a tendril of her dark hair just behind her ear. She leaned up into him and they kissed.

A yearning long due, their lips eventually parted, and save for the quiet ticking of the tonearm's stylus immured in the album's terminal groove, a comfortable stillness filled the room.

"I have to meet Decker and the others at Smitty's at eight thirty," he whispered. Her face rested against his chest as he held her. "Why don't you stop by at ten or so to rescue me? I bet I'll need it."

"I'll be there," she said, with matching softness to her voice.

And with that, Jonathan Sands's life changed.

Forever.

Chapter Four

SMITTY'S was, for all intents and purposes, a dive. Even without intent or purpose, it was a dive. If an instrument were invented capable of measuring ambiance it would have scored in the negative territory. Thunderclouds of tobacco smoke hung from the ceilings and the stench of stale beer emanating from the floor was palpable. A din of chatter and laughter mixed cacophonously with the noise of booming bass from distorted speakers and the raucous hooting and howling of drunken pool players in the back room. The type of patronage attracted to the place was self-selecting—the leather crowd and those who ventured down from the hills of rural Vermont—to make their weekly pilgrimage. Without, it had to be said, bath or deodorant. Toothpaste wasn't as much of an issue since many in the place lacked much in the way of teeth to brush.

But the beer was cheap and the peanuts were free ... so went Decker and friends' qualifications for a good time.

Sands sat by himself, fighting a headache, waiting for the others to show up. He patted at his wet hair, wet from the walk from his apartment, hoping for somebody he recognized to arrive through the front door.

How could anybody want to spend a conscious moment in this place?

Just then they bounded through the doorway. The 'they' were Decker Moss, Peter Roy, Matt Schulman, and Carl "Catman" Johnson. Johnson's sobriquet arose from his uncanny feline appearance: small almond-shaped eyes, narrow nose and fanged teeth. The nickname stuck when, one night out on the town having several drinks in him, he got down on all fours and started purring and pawing at the ladies.

"Hey, Sandman," they all said in unison, as if rehearsed. The ridiculous nickname Decker had come up with was relatively new. Jonathan hoped it would die a quick death.

The four frat men removed their jackets and sat down at the table with Sands. Decker was the only one who didn't live at the fraternity house. But as he'd often say, a frat isn't about *where* one lives, but about *how* one lives.

Whatever that meant.

37

A couple pitchers were quickly ordered, which Jonathan thought was unnecessary since they were obviously already well-lubed when they walked in. All except for Matt Schulman. Being a loyally 'dry' member of the football team, he was the designated driver for the evening.

"So who scored the night's winnings?" Sands asked.

"How can you ask that?" Decker carped. "Just look at these idiots. Do you really think they're capable of beating me?"

"Yeah, well you cheat, asshole," Peter Roy sniped back. Roy was a slightly-built, fair-haired, boyish-looking sort, scarce of eyebrows and lashes. Despite possessing a chronological misplacement of facial acne, he had been fashioned into a cocksure rake from nearly four years of fraternal order. Jonathan knew he was Decker's closest friend in the fraternity—his 'little brother' as he referred to him—which was an attraction Jonathan never really fully understood.

"Cheating's only cheating if you get caught," responded Decker. "Besides, I wouldn't even have to know how to play the game and still beat you, you bastard. What was that trumping my left bower when we were partners? I could have slugged you right across the table."

And so it went. Jonathan surmised table conversations among these guys could rarely amount to any constructive good.

He knew he had an obligation of sorts to down a beer or two, so he took to it directly. He enjoyed a cold glass as much as the next guy, but since his high school days he held well within his conviction-forged constraints. And while moderation was a personal issue for him, he still could never comprehend why so many in the college crowd ritualistically guzzled the stuff down on the weekends just to get wasted.

Their mutual drumming about the euchre game droned on and eventually fizzled out.

"Hey, boys, check this one out," Peter Roy said in a whisper. He pointed furtively at a loner sitting at the bar who was gazing trancelike in their direction. Wearing a mechanic's uniform laden with a career's worth of grime and grease, the guy's face was covered with pea-sized Recklinghaus tumors—seemingly hundreds of bumps and lumps as unsightly as warts on a toad, if a toad were human.

"Gee, Sands, I think he's looking at *you*," snickered Decker. "Why don't you go buy him a drink? You can hatch eggs together."

OPTIONS

"I can't believe you guys," Jonathan said below his breath. "*You* picked this place. It's unbelievable. I feel like we've just arrived at the watering hole for the carnival crew."

This drew overdone laughter from the frat men, the length from which Jonathan nervously refilled his glass from the pitcher.

"I wonder if he knows Ridley," said Peter Roy, who had also taken and flunked the econometrics exam that day. Before the others could respond, Roy craned his head around and hollered over toward the bar: "Hey, Lizardman, do you know Rattlesnake Ridley? Professor Ridley? *Statics?*" The word 'statistics' was hard enough to pronounce even when sober, so Roy let it go without a second attempt.

"I can't *believe* you," Sands muttered again, his eyes cornering side-to-side, looking around the place as if one seeking escape. For a guy whose acne problem was little better, Roy sure had nerve.

The loner broke out of his trance and bounced around with his eyes a bit. Roy resumed his sally: "C'mon, man, didn't I see you two baking out in the sun together on the rocks a while back?"

The guy turned around on his barstool and faced his drink.

Decker kicked back in his chair and pulled his arms behind his head. "Now you know why we love this place so much, Sandman. Beer's cheap, nuts are on the house, and nuts are *in* the house!"

There was another chorus of guffaws from Decker's frat brothers. They obviously found this hilarious, something Jonathan dismissed altogether by taking another large gulp from his glass. He felt for the guy. Excursions like this were probably the high point of his week.

Then the topic turned to football, a subject Jonathan really deplored. Although he liked the game well enough, it was one of those areas of fruitless discussion among men that could literally continue on *ad nauseam* for hours and leave no one better off in the end. To be a worthy participant you had to have under your fingertips volumes of arcane facts and stats going back ten years about every game, player and play, not to mention the myriad rules governing the game itself. Strangely enough it reminded Sands of the hours he spent in the library earlier that day studying the corporate tax code.

"So, Jon, who's gonna make the Bowl?" The question came from Catman Johnson.

"Huh?" Jonathan's consciousness had been diverted about five minutes earlier, thinking of Karen. His mental reverb replayed the question for him. "Oh, the Bowl? I guess I like Dallas," he responded, thinking it safe since the "Cowboys" was the only team having any prominence to him. Or maybe it was the cheerleaders who were prominent. Either way, liking Dallas was a safe bet.

"Yeah, you might be right. No money there, though," responded Catman.

Sands gathered Johnson must have been referring to betting odds and let it lie. The beer was now somewhat full in his stomach and it began to play with his senses. He looked at his watch. *Nine o'clock*. He popped a couple of peanuts. He hadn't had the chance to eat dinner after his stop at Karen's, and he felt his gut soaking in the beer like a sponge …

"I have to take a leak," he said, excusing himself.

After an inordinately long time at the urinal he went to the faucet and brushed his face. The sink's porcelain was covered with brown and blue stains. He looked up at the mirror—nothing but a stainless steel sheet—and made out his dull reflection. He wanted to leave, but he fought himself. Just take it easy, he said to himself. Can't let Decker down this time. Gotta celebrate.

Returning to the table, Sands found their banal conversation had evolved to school and that his beer glass had been refilled. Decker was animated.

"The jerk gave an exam that was twenty pages long. The whole thing was a bunch of crap. He didn't have to do that. I know the stuff. I just didn't have time to show it."

"It was truly a true masterpiece of shit," agreed Roy.

Catman chimed in: "Don't you see, guys? It's not about *what* you know. It's about what they *give* you. It's rigor they're after, not relevance. We could just as well be studying Einstein's relativity theory or Homer's iambic pentameters."

"Homer didn't write in iambic pen … pentameter," injected Sands, trying his best to fight the slur in his voice while making the point. "Homer was Greek. Iambic pentameter's an English invention, thousands … years later."

This elicited barking laughter from Peter Roy, who was seated directly across the table from Sands. "What a geek! What a fuckin' geek we have here!" He stared at Sands, his head wagging, mouth open wide in the form of a mordacious WOW expression. "Irregardless, Sands, what the Catman's saying here is that you just have to swallow down the shit they feed you and puke it back up on their tests. College's nothing but a money-making scam."

OPTIONS

Sands rolled his eyes, "It's not 'irregardless,' it's 'regard—'" He stopped, choosing not to debate the idiot.

"Yeah, well, whoever or whatever's relevant here, you two just better get your acts together, and fast," said Catman Johnson, directing his comment at Moss and Roy. "Finals are coming up, and if you're too shamed to put your GPAs down on your résumés you may as well use your diplomas as reefer paper." He chomped down some peanuts.

Schulman, the only sober one of the bunch, turned to Jonathan and gestured to him with his can of soda: "What do you think, Jon?"

"Yeah, tell the boys what you think," said Moss, looking at Jonathan wryly.

Sands didn't want to touch the question. He took another swig of beer. Was this his third or fourth? "What do I think?" he repeated, backing up in his chair. He stared at the glass palmed in his hands, and he attempted to clarify his murky thoughts. "I think it's pretty neat we're all here, thas' what I think. I know that prob'ly sounds trite, but it's true. I grew up on a farm here in Vermont and I know my dad didn't have this chance. I can make something of myself. You've all come from families that've already done that. I didn't. I have this one chance to make it happen." He took in their expressions, trying to surmise if what he was saying made any sense to them. It didn't look like it. The words flowed easily enough, though it was probably the beer. He took another gulp. "We have it good. I like where I am and I like what I'm studying. Most of it anyway. The work is painful. Kinda' like running. I can't honestly say I enjoy the pain of running every day, but I feel good afterward. It's the sense of accomplishment I feel when it's over. What I come out with in the end."

Roy erupted with mirthful laughter again. "What a fuckin' truckload of shit! Spoken like a true P-H-D … piled higher and deeper! What else would we expect from a shit-kicking farm-boy?" He looked around at his friends.

Sands tried hard to force calm. He didn't like the guy. Not one bit. He didn't like guys who thought they knew everything and knew nothing. He also hated gratuitous vulgarities spoken by obnoxious jerks just to garner attention.

Decker smirked at his roommate, knowing what he was probably thinking, and drew down on his elbows. "The problem, Jon-Boy, is that what you're saying doesn't answer the problem of teachers like Ridley. You can't tell me professors like him actually have something to say that's worth listening to. He gets his kicks by sticking it to his students."

Jonathan swallowed another gulp. "Can't tell you about Ridley … never had him. All I can say is that he's prob'ly here because he likes what he's doing, passin' on what he found interesting himself. Who knows? A lot of professors could be making more money doing something else. Lots more. Take Davidson, for example. The guy's a genius." Gene Davidson, a regular contributor to national media interviews, was an economist who specialized on the impact of federal fiscal and monetary policies on employment and inflation.

"He's an Uncle Milton Friedman ass-wipe," blasted Peter Roy. "An anti-Keynesian, probably like you, Sands, right? Fuck-the-government Republican? Mister flag-waving all-American personal-responsibility preacher? I bet you wouldn't feel that way if you didn't have that fat scholarship filling your back pocket to pay your full load!"

"*What the—?*" Sands stood, anger building within him like lava.

"So, Jon, Decker tells us you got quite the job offer today." The complete change of subject came from Matt Schulman.

Jonathan glared down hard at Decker. "Nice going, *Cyrus*."

"You didn't say your job offer was confidential. It's good news! That's why we're here. To celebrate!" Decker peremptorily gestured at Jonathan's chair. "Now settle down, Sandman. Little Bro Roy was just funnin' with you … like I do."

"Yeah, Jon-Boy," added Roy, "just having some fun is all. It's how we show our love for one another, right guys?" He laughed with a nod to the others and downed the rest of his glass.

"Can't hide success, Sandman," Catman said, raising his beer toward Sands in tribute. "You're the man of the evening. Besides, we were hoping you might spread the secrets of your success around here a little bit; you know, give us some interview pointers."

Jonathan slowly regathered himself and sat down.

Decker yelled over his shoulder at the bartender: "Hey, Smitty, we're celebrating over here. Bring on a round of chasers! *Schnapps!*"

Sands sensed the evening taking a turn. "Hey, guys, no need to call over the hard stuff. I don—"

"Hard stuff?" boffed Decker, "*Schnapps?* It's a ladies drink."

OPTIONS

"What a pussy," Roy muttered under his breath. Although Sands couldn't hear it, he could clearly see it in his mouthed words.

Decker leaned forward on his elbows again. "So, Jon, listen. I've admired you for a long time. Remember back when we first met in our freshman English class? Remember that? We were tight right off. I knew you were gonna be something special someday. A hick from Vermont, yet I smelled success, you know? So look at us now, three years later, celebrating exactly what I knew back then. It's something. New York? Boston? Name your price. You've got to let loose and enjoy the fruits of your success."

"That's right, Sandman," Catman inserted in agreement. "Always felt like you must be a great guy to be such good friends with Deck here, but you never showed it, you know? I can tell you that now, though, right?"

"Right, like there's a lot of us who wanted to get to know you better," added Roy, "but you always acted too good for us. Too good for the frat when you were asked to join; too good to party with us on the weekends; too good just to hang out. Anyway, no time like the present for a prick to make some new friends." Roy laughed and hefted his glass to Jonathan in toast.

"*Prick?*" said Sands.

Peter Roy set down his glass. "Yeah, you know, stuck on yourself. Like you don't shit like everyone else." He laughed again.

Sands was feeling woozy and he didn't know quite how to respond. Whether he liked it or not his body was responding without him, and what his body felt like doing was throwing a fist directly into Peter Roy's face. "I hope you guys don't take me wrong. I'm just not into partying. Anyway, I don' thing you have to call me a pri—"

"Say no more, Sandman," interrupted Decker with a raised hand. "Here comes the Schnapps."

A stocky barmaid, several days between shaves, set down five full shot glasses. "Here's a Jefferson for you, my pretty lady," said Decker as he offered the bill to her. "Keep the change." She took it with a smile and sauntered off.

"Now, there're two ways to put this stuff down, Sandman," Decker instructed. "One way is to chase the shot with beer. The guys here will demonstrate for you. But first I wish to make a toast." Moss raised his glass toward his roommate, and the others followed suit. "To the greatest mind in this place ... no, that ain' saying much." He laughed and regrouped. "To the best mind at

Middlebury, best roommate, and best all-around nice guy, except lacking class when it comes to women."

Taking the pause that the toast was over, Peter Roy and Catman Johnson downed their shot glasses and then quickly gulped down their beers, all in the space of seconds. After which Decker imparted further: "The other way to do Schnapps is like this." He dropped his shot glass into his beer glass and then drank the whole thing in what appeared to be three gulps, nearly swallowing the shot glass as well. When he came up he wiped his face with his arm sleeve.

With the cue and a bit of time to prime courage Jonathan opted for the first method. After completing his two drinks in respectable time, cheers followed.

He felt like he was in another place, as if sitting in a Western saloon being held hostage by outlaws to do their bidding. The room began to swirl. He looked at his watch with a wobbling arm: *9:20.*

Decker extracted a fat cigar from his shirt pocket and lighted it with quick draws, proceeding to blow smoke rings up toward the ceiling. Sands tried to make sense of what was left of his vision. It started as a massively thumping haze in his head, becoming blurrier as it passed through his scratchy eyes and then finished with near total absorption by the pall of smoke filling the room. The figures and sounds all seemed surreal. He needed to pee again. Badly.

Angling up out of his chair, groaning as he did so, he staggered to the men's room. Though he was aware of their laughing as he tried to straighten his shuffled line, the sound degenerated in what little of his consciousness he had left.

There was a queue at the urinal, so he waited, leaning against the sink, forced to breathe the malodorous gasses left from an overflowed toilet. The rank surroundings didn't seem to matter as much to him now. He had become part of it. Once his turn came he relieved himself at the porcelain, quietly mouthing the word 'prick' over and over to himself until his bladder drained away. He brought his watch to his eyes and focused on its reading: *9:35.*

Not long.

Rejoining the group at the table, Sands found that another round of shots had been ordered, this time whiskey. And their beer glasses had been replaced by quart-sized beer mugs.

"These are called boilermakers, Jonny," Decker informed. "By the looks of you, we thought you might need something to clear your head a little. The boys and I figured this would be just the thing."

Jonathan piled into his chair. "Don't know how you guys do it, but I'm finished. No way. Gotta stop."

"*Finished?*" exclaimed Decker. "You've only been with us an hour. How can you be finished?"

"Don' be such a pussy, Sands." Roy sat back with his arms interleaved across his diminutive frame. "We're just getting to know you, is all. You haven' even shared with us how you did it."

Sands's head bobbed around like a spring-necked dashboard doll, eventually fixing a focus on Roy. "Did *what?*"

"Get such good grades. A shit-kicking farm-boy? You must have quite the scheme going is all I can figure." Roy guffawed and Sands stood up clumsily from his chair, which fell over on its back. Wrath rose in him again, flushing his face deep red.

"You calling me a *cheat?*"

"Calm down, Jon-Boy," Decker said, "Like I said, Roy's just joking around. No need to get in a huff."

Sands just stood glaring down at Peter Roy. He pointed. "I've had it with this guy. *Prick? Pussy? Shit-kicker?* Take it back."

Decker gestured his stogy at Roy, the quick movement causing an ash to fall into Roy's space. "Come on, Jon, he didn't mean it. He's just playing like me and you do."

Matt Schulman righted the fallen chair and Sands slowly sat down again, grabbing its arms tightly to steady himself.

"Tell you what," said Decker. "You give us some interviewing tips and then you can swag off. But only after you celebrate like a man." He grabbed his shot glass, lifting it toward Sands. "Down the hatch." The three drinking frat men downed their shots and then chased them with their mugs.

Jonathan, not knowing whether it was the challenge to his manhood or the need to quench the volcanic anger now raging within him, felt pressure to comply. Perching the shot glass in his fingers and tipping it to his lips, he felt the liquor course his throat, searing his insides as it went down. Before the reflexes of his gullet could be activated, he gulped down a large mouthful of beer.

Following that was a long time before he made contact with his senses again. Not sure whether the foul stuff would stay where it was or come back up, he sat there with his eyes closed, his upper half swaying like a blade of grass in the breeze. There was little awareness anymore. He couldn't talk … didn't want to talk if he could. His head swam and felt too heavy to hold up, so he rested his chin on his chest. What took place after that would have to take place without him.

It was his last thought before nodding off.

"Well, guys, I guess the man of the evening has bowed out." Moss eyed the others around the table with a victorious grin. "Sandman's first time getting wasted since coming to Middlebury."

"Nice going, Deck," said the sober Matt Schulman. "Great friend you are."

"Right. Like you don't think he'll have to wine and dine the big boys in order to make partner? Of course he will. The way I see it, we just did him a huge favor by breaking him in. It's his night of passage." Decker laughed, but the others completely missed his play on words.

Then Moss drew forward to gain their attention. "So listen, guys, not that Jon-Boy here would care to hear my idea anyway, but I know how we can snag some aces on the finals. I've been thinking about it and I think it's brilliant."

Jonathan's head bobbed up and down occasionally, but it was only a reflex. The others tuned in as Decker continued.

"Ever notice how Avery Hall has those drop ceilings? Well, I checked them out the other afternoon during a faculty meeting when everyone's out of the office. There's a good two feet of crawl space above them. The partitions to the professors' offices only go up as far as the ceilings, and it would be pretty easy to go up and over from above …"

* * *

"… Sounds like a plan then," concluded Moss. The frat brothers clanked their glasses in agreement.

Jonathan's head popped up at the word 'plan.'

"Ah, the pussy wakes up from his catnap!" said Roy, noting the slits of Sands's eyes had pried open.

Taking hold of where he was, Sands uttered a belch. "Yeah … gotta go. Got plans."

He stumbled up, looked at his watch, and fighting the blur, noted the big hand nudging against the twelve. "Got plans."

The four watched as the besotted man-of-the-evening struggled out of his chair and swagger to the front door, trying to find the arms of his jacket as he did so. But before he opened it, he turned around to glare back at Peter Roy.

OPTIONS

Roy met his look with a cocky grin and shot him the bird. "Good night, pussy-prick, shit-kicker!" he yelled out with a laugh.

Which did it for Sands. Like an exploding grenade, he sailed across the room and bowled Roy backwards over the fallen chair. Pinning both of Roy's arms down with his knees, Sands's fingers went around his throat. *"Take it back, Roy! Li'l-Bro Roy? Acne-boy Roy!"* he yelled with mocking inflection. Peter Roy was writhing and choking and couldn't get anything out. Sands socked him hard in the face, catching a knuckle across Roy's front teeth.

The others leapt out of their chairs and grabbed Sands from behind, but his hands wouldn't relent. They were clutching Roy's neck firmly in a death-grip. *"Take it back!"*

"STOP!!" yelled Smitty from behind the bar. The proprietor raced out with a baseball bat and swung it at Jonathan's shoulder, shy of bone-breaking force but strongly enough to knock him off of Roy.

"Get the hell out of here before I call the cops!" he commanded Sands. "I saw it all. I don't know who the hell *you* are, but I know these guys and they've never given me any trouble before!"

Sands slowly got up, grabbed hold of his smarting shoulder and straightened his jacket. The entire place was looking at him. Then he floundered to the front door, kicked it open, and exited.

"He'll be all right," Decker assured the owner. "The rain'll sober him up."

* * *

Sands wasn't sure what to do or where to go, so he just stumbled around the gravel parking lot looking around. He took his bleeding knuckle to his mouth and sucked on it. The weather had turned worse. The precipitation was falling harder, seemingly indecisive about which state of matter to assume, liquid or solid. Although there was little accumulation, it was the ice-cone variety that wasn't good for driving.

His head spun and he found it difficult to stand.
Better sit down.

Backtracking in his steps he moved to the right of the tavern's entranceway, just into the shadows and under the protection of the building's overhang to try to stay dry. With his back against the wall he slid down next to some juniper bushes. There were no gutters and the drain-off from the eaves pelted his lower half. The spinning intensified and his stomach couldn't hold it in any longer.

47

He retched.

Then he lost consciousness.

* * *

"Jonathan?"

It was faint.

"Jonathan, is that you? Are you okay?"

He peered up. "Karen!"

"What are you doing here!" She knelt down beside him, and, seeing the vomit that ran down his mouth and chin, she scooped some cold water from a puddle to wipe his face. "It's a miracle I saw you before going inside."

"I … I guess I drank too much. Decker jes' kep' ordering more … couldn't let him down."

"We've got to get you home."

Karen placed his arm around her shoulder and struggled to pull him up. Her car was idling in the parking lot. As she guided him into the passenger seat, slipping some as she did so, he stammered: "You're a nice girl, Karen. Jes' like Mom … much more beautiful though." He gurgled a laugh.

"And you're a great second date, Sands. I can't wait for our third." She shut the car door behind him and then got in herself.

"I'm a good guy. Really." Every word he spoke was drawn out and slurred.

"I'm taking you to your apartment. Where's your key?"

"Oh … right." He pulled his apartment key from his pants pocket, the knuckle of his hand hurting as he did so, and gave it to her. "Here's my key." He slouched against the door. "I don' feel well—" and then he immediately dry-heaved. What little came up dribbled from his lips and onto the door. Then he was out again.

A few minutes later Karen pulled into the driveway that ran alongside the Victorian. She parked in the rear, in front of the detached garage. Grabbing her keys she circled around to the passenger side to help Jonathan out. She struggled as they slipped and skidded through the slush.

The stairway to his apartment ran along the inside of an unheated vestibule that was located on the backside of the house. As they entered he tripped on an iron doorstop, which sent him sprawling headlong into the newel post. Helping him up, she led him up the treads carefully. A single low-wattage ceiling bulb faintly

OPTIONS

illuminated the steep narrow staircase. He carried most of his
weight but she provided most of the balance for the short climb.

"I don't think I've ever seen anybody so drunk before. How
much did you have, anyway?"

"Six … nine? … Should've eaten."

"You drank all that on an empty stomach? In such a short
time? No wonder you got sick!"

"Don' … don' wanna talk … too dizzy."

At the top of the stairs she opened the apartment door with
Jonathan's key. "Where's your bedroom?" she asked him firmly
once they were inside.

"No … I'll 'mall right. No need to…"

She led him through the living room, deposited his apartment
key on the kitchen counter, and then continued guiding him down
the hallway. He was conscious of her full breast rubbing against his
side. "Dragged away by a woman … isn' that funny?"

"A riot."

"Thiz's the bathroom … here's Deck's room … and … here's
mine." His arm swung like jelly at each. "Nice pad, huh?"

"Okay, now listen, Jon. Try to listen to me." Waiting futilely
for his assent she said: "You're soaked to the bone. You have to
get—" He swayed across the room and fell down hard on his bed,
which was actually nothing more than a mattress atop a box spring
on the floor.

"Jon, you have to get out of your wet clothes. Can you do
that?"

No answer.

"Jonathan?"

He was out again.

"Oh, please, don't make me do this," she pleaded.

His breathing was heavy. With only the scant light spilling
from the hallway Karen removed his jacket and shoes and socks,
and set them on the floor next to the bed. All soaked. Then she
undid the buttons of his shirt, which she pulled off from his
shoulders. "Jon?"

"P'ssy pick," he muttered softly.

"*What?*"

The room felt cold. Karen knew she had to remove his soaked
pants as well. She undid his belt and unclasped his jeans at the
waist. Unzipping them she went to the foot of the mattress and
drew them off his legs. After setting his pants on the floor she

49

noticed his briefs were also soaked. With the back of her hand she felt the skin of his thighs. Freezing. Looking down at him in the dim light she contemplated her next move.

He'll be all right.

Another pause.

I couldn't sleep like that.

She grabbed the elastic of his underwear and slid them off as well. Then she fumbled for the quilt to cover him.

About to exit the bedroom door she peered back at him. His stertorous breathing was loud and uneven. The clock radio on the floor next to the mattress read *10:28*. Relenting, she shut the door and returned to his bed, lying atop the quilt with her arm around him. She kissed his forehead and whispered: "It's still early. I'll stay with you for a while just to make sure you'll be all right."

He didn't feel her kiss and he didn't hear what she said.

His sleep was deep.

Chapter Five

THE splatter against the windows sounded like drums in the distance, pounding softly ... softly ... then louder. Muffled cracking and splintering.
No, rain is gentle and soft.
But it continued pounding.
The rain fell in sheets and the flooding rose. She pleaded for him to stop.
It came from outside ... from the barn ...
Dad, it's okay. We'll be all right. Please be good!
The steam rose above the water and the bellows of the animals echoed in the air. "Don't!" Mom screamed.
No, Dad, don't! We'll be good. Mom and I will be good for you!
She slipped and fell. The apparitions twisted and the cows fell in the frozen pool.
The pounding of the pelting rain turned louder.
He was hurting her. Dad, stop! ... Please leave her alone. You're drunk. You don't know what you're doing!
Then he struck her ...
And she slept.
Deeply.
"We'll be good for you."
They all went down.
Down deep where the cows were.

* * *

The jolt to consciousness came in a rapid succession of realizations.

Realization he was in bed.

Realization he was dreaming.

Realization he was yelling.

No ... someone else was yelling ... calling him ... banging on the door.

Jonathan pulled himself off the mattress and struggled to stand, tripping over a pile of clothing and shoes on the floor as he staggered across the dark room to the doorway. Feeling his way along the wall he found the doorknob and turned it. The door opened only the few inches permitted by the chain lock, but enough to yield a slice of backlight to Decker's silhouetted frame.

"Are you okay?" Moss asked, alarm in his voice. Decker reached between the door's crack for the light switch along the inside casing.

Jonathan shielded his eyes against the bright ceiling light and moved his lower half behind the door to cover his nakedness. He didn't remember getting undressed. He peered weakly out at his roommate. "Yeah, fine," he managed to answer, "never better."

"You were pretty wasted tonight," Decker chuckled. "I thought I should check on you before hitting the sack myself. Why'd you lock the door?"

"Yeah, thanks for the great time," said Sands. "G'night."

As Jonathan was about to shut the door Moss's eyes widened at what little he was able to make out through the opening. Just visible was a stockinged foot. "Sorry, Jon," he whispered. "I thought you were alone."

The words didn't register. "Mmhh?" Jonathan looked vapidly through the door's crack at his roommate, and then, fixing on Decker's line of vision, he turned around.

The room held its breath. It was confused at first, but the sight gathered speed ... horrific speed. The room—the truth—screamed back at him like a sky-shattering lightning bolt, electrifying every nerve in his body. It knocked him hard backwards against the door, slamming it shut.

"Jon?"

For Decker there was nothing but the sound of Jonathan slumping along the door's backside. He pushed against it but it didn't budge. "*Jon!*"

Coughing gasps.

Decker banged hard. "*Open up, Jon!*"

Then a hideous retching sound.

Decker shoved his shoulder against the dead weight, managing to budge the door open again as far as the chain.

"*Damn it, Sands! Unlock the door!*"

Jonathan crawled quickly away to the adjacent side of the room. Decker yanked the door against the chain but it didn't give way. Then he stood back and kicked it full strength, sending the chain bolt free, shattering a good portion of the door casing with it.

"*MY GOD, SANDS!*"

OPTIONS

There Karen lay on the hardwood floor at the foot of the mattress, partially propped up against the wall. Her eyes were open, dry, and glazed over. Jonathan's belt was wrapped serpentinely around her neck. A large streak of blood stained her cheek. The maroon sweater she wore was pulled up over her exposed breasts, and except for socks, she was naked from the waist down. Her head was angled down to the side. The long dark-brown hair Jonathan had stroked only once was in gnarled skeins—matted and wet at the underside temple. Its full tresses draped over her shoulders and onto the bed in a cascade of absurd elegance.

Sands was now curled beneath the window of the adjacent wall with his arms around his knees. Staccato breaths mimicked the undulations of his heartbeat. Trembling, he reached for the St. Christopher medal that drooped from his neck, pleading in his mind ...

"*My God!*" Decker exclaimed again. He came over and knelt down beside his friend. "*What happened?*"

Sands didn't respond. He just sat shaking, staring at Karen in shock.

"*WHAT DID YOU DO?*"

Jonathan looked down at his trembling hands, inventorying himself, feeling the soreness in his knuckles and along his side and shoulder. He reached for his forehead where he felt a welt and more dull pain. "I didn't ... *Oh, God, I don't know ... I don't remember!*"

Decker got up to fully close the blinds, first the window above Jonathan and then the window over his bed. He made his way to Karen. Carefully, he pulled her fully onto the floor and covered her with the bed sheet. "I just wanted to check up on you, you know? And when you didn't answer with the door locked, I—I thought you might need help."

"*I don't know what happened!*" Jonathan yelled. He grabbed his face in his hands. "She helped me! She drove me home, but that was ... I don't remember anything after that!" He folded his knees tight against his chest and gazed through his fingers at the sheet-covered figure lying on the floor. Her pants, panties, shoes and jacket were mixed with his wet things alongside the bed. "*I don't know!*"

Decker sat down beside him and rocked the back of his head against the wall. The wind howled outside. He took his hand to Jonathan's knee and then to his arm, which was shivering. His skin felt cold as ice. The room was drafty, something Jonathan customarily didn't mind for sleeping, and Decker looked at the door along the opposite wall that led to the poorly insulated attic above. Puffs of chilled air seeped through its threshold crack and washed across the floor with the pulsating wind outside. He got up, steadying himself against the wall for balance, and grabbed the quilt from the bed to cover his friend.

Tears welled from Sands's eyes as he looked up beseechingly at Moss. "She can't, this can't be … *Oh, God, help me!*" His crying intensified, with sobs turning to convulsing howls that went guttural as the air depleted from his lungs. All the while Decker's gaze remained fixed on the clock radio that sat on the floor next to the mattress. It had a dimly-lit scrolling screen, currently reading *2:46.* He became mesmerized by it, and in the minutes that scrolled by he tried to deal with his own muddled thoughts, trudging through the horrific scene before him with only disjointed comprehension of what to do. He wavered on his feet, knowing he was still very drunk.

Finally, he broke the long silence. "Jon, if you turned yourself in …"

Sands looked up at him through mucose fingers. "What, Deck? Would they believe me?"

Moss clutched his hair between his fingers, trying to sift through his imaginings, confused as they were. "I don't know. We certainly have to do *something*." He knelt down next to his friend. "I just can't believe you could *do* this."

"But I didn't do it! I didn't! *Please tell me you believe me!*" he pleaded.

Decker didn't reply.

"Deck!"

"It's not important what *I* believe," Moss said gloomily. "It's what *they'll* believe."

The statement seemed to prompt a new line of comprehension for Sands, one, which for him, had even more dire consequences. "*NO! My mother! I can't turn myself in! She—*" Sands grabbed at the air. "You've got to help me, Deck! Please believe me! *I don't know what happened!*" Then, without warning a deeper pain coursed within him, deeper than before, coming from a cavernous part he didn't know existed. He cried out as it crushed his insides like a vice. His body heaved into a jackknife and he vomited whatever was left of his stomach onto the floor.

Moss had to lie down. He chose the hardwood floor. The feeling was poisonous, adrenaline mixed with alcohol. For long minutes he struggled to think it through. The crisp air wafting through the room mixed with the stench of puke and death, making the moribund space feel all the more like the sepulcher it was.

Eventually, Decker got up. He exhaled the dizzying nausea he felt and made his way to the bedroom door. Staring down the hallway his eyes narrowed. Slowly, he turned back around and peered down searchingly at Sands. "Did anybody know you were with her?" he asked.

Jonathan's catatonic stare passed beyond him, unseeing.

"*Jon, listen to me.* Did anybody know you were with her tonight?"

Sands shook his head. "No ... no, I don't think so."

"So, what happened? She met you here? Met you at Smitty's? *What?*"

"I was running. I saw her. We talked at her place. I ... I really like her. She's ..."

"So what happened? You saw her at her apartment? She picked you up at Smitty's? Is that what you meant by 'plans'?"

"She picked me up. We were going to spend some time together. I ... I never wanted to go to Smitty's."

Decker bent down next to his roommate. "Jon, listen to me. After you left us at Smitty's you never saw Karen tonight. *Never.* Do you understand? You got drunk with us, you walked home and you *never* saw her."

Jonathan didn't respond. He just stared cataleptically at the rumpled mound on the floor.

Decker quickly exited the room.

Several minutes passed before he returned with a large canvas duffel bag. It was an Army surplus bag he used for his laundry. "Grab some clothes," Moss commanded. "Go into the kitchen and make us some coffee. We're going to need it."

Jonathan's expression didn't register. His wet eyes just drifted, reflecting the overhead light. Snot purled down his lips and chin as he caressed his St. Christopher's medal between his fingers, seemingly in another world.

Decker came down and grabbed Jonathan's arm. "*I said get up!*" The chain snagged in Decker's movement, causing the medallion to break away and roll across the floor. "Get dressed! We don't have much time!"

The sharpness of Decker's tone and action propelled Jonathan to his feet. He pulled some underwear and socks from his bureau drawer and gathered a pair of sweatpants and a sweatshirt from his closet. Managing his way through the hallway and into the kitchen he washed his face and put on his clothes. And then some water to heat up. Grabbing the counter to steady himself he stared desolately at the stove console clock: *3:20.*

The teakettle's whistle eventually returned him to task.

The sound of Decker dragging the bag along the hallway floor prompted him to glance over at the kitchen's entrance. The top of the bag revealed a portion of Karen's stockinged foot. Jonathan ran to the sink and vomited again.

"Pay attention, Jon. I don't see any other way out for you. You've got to get yourself together or you'll ruin it for both of us. Do you understand?"

Sands didn't reply. Another spasm shot through his bowels and he bent over in pain.

"We've got to get her down into my trunk and we have to do it without making any noise. Do you hear me? Now, grab an end." Decker reached for his coat on the living room floor and put it on, along with his leather gloves.

Jonathan wasn't moving.

"I said grab an end!"

Sands fumbled for what he could of the canvas sack, trying to manage a grip. Decker snatched his car keys from the kitchen counter and then the two of them hefted the bag through the living room and out into the vestibule. Tread by tread they lumbered down the steep creaky staircase. Then they carried her out across the snow covered driveway to the stand-alone, single-car garage where Decker's BMW was parked. Karen's car was parked in front of it. Jonathan noticed the mass of footprints in the snow along both sides, and he imagined her as she must have struggled to get him into the house.

After placing the bag in Decker's trunk they quickly retreated back to the cover of the vestibule's doorway. Fortunately, tall arborvitae hedges fenced in the entire dooryard, obscuring any view from the neighbors' houses.

"Where are her keys?" Decker asked firmly.

Sands wavered clueless.

OPTIONS

"Where are her car keys, *dammit*? We have to get her car out of here." His breath reeked of alcohol.

"I don't know," Jonathan answered. "She must have had them."

"Well, they weren't in your room. Not in her clothes or your clothes. Think, Sands!"

Nothing was forthcoming.

"I'll check her car." Moss grabbed Jonathan's arm. "You head back upstairs and search the apartment. Look everywhere!"

Jonathan responded as best he could. He didn't know where to begin. He looked in the obvious places where she might have set them down: the living room coffee table ... the kitchen counter. He saw his apartment key there but that was all. There was a faint memory of falling down somewhere. He checked the floor of the living room and beneath the furniture under the off chance she dropped the keys and they fell out of view while she was helping him in. Failing, he made his way down the hallway and into the bathroom.

That's where his search ended. Though not for success. There was no way he could go back into his bedroom to look further, if he could ever go in there again. Instead, he squared his back against the hallway wall and sank to the floor, sobbing.

Decker searched the car again with methodical precision. Not in the ignition ... ashtray ... dash ... floor ... He checked under the seats and between the seat cushions. Her purse rested against the hump of the transmission, which he carefully fingered through one more time under the car's dome light. Nothing.

Where could they be?

Tracing a wide swath back to the house, he peered closely at the driveway, also now a second time. The fresh accumulation on the asphalt was heavy, like schoolroom paste. The sparse light he had to work with was limited to the throw-off from their apartment's windows. He got down on all fours and felt through the snow, looking for dimples or impressions ... anything that might stand out. Again, nothing.

In the vestibule he scoured the floor and stairs again. The low-wattage bulb high in the ceiling made for poor lighting. The BIC lighter he used didn't help much, and they didn't own a flashlight. He was beginning to panic. The stair treads were wet with foot tracks and splotched with wet leaves. He took the steep flight of stairs and removed his gloves, feeling each tread one by one with his fingers. The top landing was blanketed in shadows cast by the baluster spindles. Kneeling, he felt the wooden planks with the sides of his hands, turning up only the moist grit of the floor. Then he trotted down the stairway again, stopping halfway in his tracks. The vestibule door remained open—as it usually did—against the inside wall. The old antique iron the landlord used as a doorstop was lying tipped over just to the side of the stairway. His eyes lingered there a moment, as if transfixed.

Both of them were careless about keeping the door closed from the weather, and a season's worth of dead leaves formed a pile in the shadowed corner to the right, next to the landlord's back entrance. Taking the remaining stairs down with deliberate steps he carefully culled through the leaves, palming them. Just as his hand went against the baseboard, there was a slight clinking sound.

He exhaled a gasp of relief and snatched up the ringed set of Ford keys, shoving them into his pocket.

Contemplating for a moment what to do with her purse and the other item, Moss concluded they had to go with her. After tending to the task he was back in the apartment.

"I found them!" he shouted in a whisper. Jonathan stumbled into the living room from the hallway. "They were buried in the pile of leaves in the vestibule," Decker said. "She must have dropped them when she helped you in."

Jonathan now had a faint memory of falling down at the stairway.

Trying to stifle the excitement in his voice, Decker continued: "Here's what we're going to do. You drive Karen's car and follow me out of town. Can you do that? We go slowly. You leave her car on that dead-end road, to the quarry. You know the one." Decker pulled one of Jonathan's jackets from the hallway closet and handed it to him.

Sands put it on and hesitantly accepted the keys.

"Then we drive to Lake George, to my family's summer place."

"*New York!*" exclaimed Sands.

"Quiet down! I don't see any other way. It's only an hour away and nobody's around. You know the lake's deep."

"We can't do this!" Jonathan pulled his jacket sleeve to his eyes.

"Jon, you have two choices. Either you do this or it's all over. I don't see any other way out. Nobody's going to understand.

Karen's father is a powerful man. You get implicated in his daughter's death and you fry. You think they'll just let you off without ruining you? *Think!*"

"I—I can't go through with this! Why don't we just leave her in her car somewhere!"

Moss grabbed his shoulders "There'd be way too much evidence. We *have* to go through with this, Jon. We have no other choice."

"But—"

Decker slapped him. "*Listen, Sands, get with me!* I'm sticking my neck out to save yours, do you understand? There's no other way. And once we start there's no turning back."

Moss walked over to the stove, grabbed the hot teakettle and poured two cups of instant coffee. Black. "Here."

Jonathan was barely able to control the trembling in his fingers as he took the mug and sipped what he could. Decker downed his cup in quick gulps, burning his mouth.

"No," Decker said, reconsidering, "I better drive her car. You're too drunk for a standard shift."

Moss snatched the keys from Jonathan's hand and opened the back door for him to exit. After he did so, Decker returned to the rooms, made a final check, turned off all the lights, and exited himself.

Chapter Six

THEY ditched Karen's Pinto on the shoulder of the quarry road without incident. It was a dead-end gravel road with no houses around and no cars in sight. Moss was now at the wheel of his BMW, trying to ignore Jonathan's incessant sobs. Although traffic was sparse at this late hour the heavy wet snowfall made for difficult driving. Moss directed bead-eyed attention to the highway, struggling to make out the faint glow of the pavement through the snow's assault on his windshield.

They had to return to town to pick up the main highway west to New York. At a red light a police cruiser pulled up at the intersection opposite them. Seemingly endless minutes went by as Decker impatiently tapped the steering wheel.

"Why doesn't it change?" he uttered through clenched teeth. *"C'mon ... move!"*

The green light finally glowed and ushered them through. As the cruiser passed by them Decker peered into his side-view mirror. The cop kept going and he exhaled his pent up nerves.

A few moments later Decker's eyes caught the reflection of brake lights in his rearview mirror. The cruiser, a quarter mile back, stopped and turned around with grill lights flashing.

"He's coming after us!"

Jonathan craned his neck to look around.

"*No!* Get down! Pretend your sleeping!" Decker slowed and veered over to the shoulder.

The cop bore down upon them quickly. It continued fast on their tail and then passed by, continuing on the road in front of them.

Moss let out a deep sigh of relief. *"Thank God!"*

Once a safe distance out of town he pulled the car to the side of the road and the two relieved themselves in a stand of trees. Jonathan took the opportunity to empty his churning bowels. Dead wet leaves had to suffice.

Five minutes farther down the road the reason for the cop's speedy dispatch became apparent: an overturned car rested in the embankment. Passing the flares in the road and the flashing lights of the cruiser, Decker remarked: "Probably just a Friday night drunk."

Jonathan offered no acknowledgement of the scene, nor the irony of the comment. "We have to go back," he said in a monotone.

Moss didn't respond.

"I'm going to turn myself in, Deck," Sands said. "Turn around."

"Quiet, Sands."

"I said turn around." Jonathan grabbed the steering wheel.

Decker threw an elbow against Jonathan's side. "*Dammit Sands!* You want to get the both of us killed?"

"We have to turn around." Jonathan cried in protest. "We can't do this to her!"

"*I'm* not doing this to anybody. *You did it!* And you're too drunk to even know what you did or what you're saying." Decker wiped his face with his hand to draw focus. "This is the only way out for you, Jon. Why don't you see that? We have to go through with this and there's no turning back."

Jonathan coiled against the passenger door. "She's back there in the trunk like some … piece of garbage …" His words trailed off as he mouthed the words *she can't* repeatedly, as if in hopeful incantation for an earlier time. *She can't.* A folding back of time like a metaphysical bend in space—wishing it were all only a pitiful joke by a playful God: *Everything's okay, Jon, none of this really happened. You can laugh about it all now. But I had you going there for a while, didn't I? Wasn't that funny?* His thoughts went to that very short period earlier in the day … to the letter he received in the mail, the talk with Susan, his time at Karen's, their kiss, his excitement about a new beginning, their future … and then the drinks. The drinks and Smitty's and Peter Roy.

And then oblivion.

All a heinous whirl. Zenith to nadir, in less than half the time of a single rotation of the planet.

They drove on for miles without another word spoken between them. It was mostly flat and straight through remote farmlands.

Eventually it was Decker who broke the silence. "Jon, I believe you when you say you can't remember anything. Your dad and everything. I … feel some responsibility for what happened."

"I just don't get how I have no memory of it. Absolutely nothing," Jonathan said emptily. "I thought it was all a dream."

Decker silently stared ahead, trying hard to maintain his fix on the road.

"It was a nightmare ... of my dad beating my mother," Jonathan continued. "I've had them before, but never where I actually acted anything out."

Decker glanced over at his friend. "You mean you think you were dreaming what was taking place?"

Jonathan wiped his eyes with a corner of his sweatshirt sleeve. "Right before you woke me. But it wasn't me beating her; it was my father beating my mother. And it was far away. I must be ... insane." It was a word usually spoken in sarcasm, but here he used it literally.

"No, Jon, booze can do crazy things to people. Most of us get happy, but others, they completely lose it. Belligerent. You had a lot to drink and that was my fault." Then he glanced sideways at Jonathan again. "I thought you were far enough away from the past, but I guess I was wrong. You told me that's why you don't drink much, but I've always thought you were just being overly paranoid about it."

The shock was beginning to subside, yet the stupor was still there. Nausea, headache, and profound despair were also still there. "I just wanted to celebrate. But then the booze came over me. The anger just kept building up inside. I wanted to kill Roy. And I could have. I felt his scrawny little neck in my hands and it felt good. I didn't want to let go." Jonathan stared out through the blur of the passenger window and noticed they were passing a dairy farm. Without speaking he mouthed the words: "Just like my dad."

The two of them remained quiet the rest of the way through Vermont, heading westward on Highway 125. A couple times Jonathan opened his window, seeking fresh air, wishing to empty his churning guts again. But his insides were dry and returned only fire to his throat. The weather was beginning to clear with patches of moonlight, now in its last quarter, showing through breaks in the clouds.

"Once we go over this bridge we'll be in New York," Decker said. "The Adirondacks are right in front of us."

It was well after four in the morning. They only had another two hours of darkness or so.

* * *

62

OPTIONS

The bridge to Crown Point, New York, crossed at the southern narrows of Lake Champlain. From there, the pair traveled south for a number of miles on Highway 9N, which by day was a pretty road that carved the mountain along the western edge of Lake George. Any appreciation for the views surrounding them, however, was precluded by the darkness of the night, to say nothing of the macabre circumstances governing their trip. And the curves in the road, unanticipated by Jonathan, served only to enhance his nausea.

Slightly more than half an hour down the highway a modest routed wooden sign hanging from a post marked a driveway on the left: *Mossy Rocks*. The gravel access road graded downhill from the highway and wound through tall standing conifers, leading to a magnificent log home on the water's edge. Jonathan remembered the place well from his visit with Decker and his parents the previous summer. The property consisted of over twenty forested acres, much of which stretched along private shoreline. Actually more of an estate than a summer home, the lodge sat on the rocks in luxurious rusticity. Massive rough-hewn log timbers joined with wrought iron supports formed trusses that buttressed towering rooflines. Large picture windows spanned the entire lakefront side of the house, and save for a few trimmed mature hemlocks along the shore, the view of the lake was unencumbered. Interspersed in the surrounding woods were several outbuildings, also in log theme, which provided guest quarters and storage.

Decker pulled into the dooryard and turned off the engine. He ran to the rear entrance of the house and unlocked it with his key. Locating the circuit breaker in the utility room, he hefted the main switch and found the key ring he was looking for on a hook just below the panel.

"Come on," he said to Jonathan when he returned to the car. "We don't have much time."

"I can't."

"Dammit, Sands. It's *you* who should be doing this dirty work." Moss moved around to the passenger side, pulled the door open and grabbed Jonathan by the arm, yanking him out onto the gravel driveway. "Now get with this thing! It's *your* life I'm trying to save!

Jonathan peered up from his knees. His vision blurred through tear-filled eyes. "I can't do this, Deck, please," he pleaded. "It's all wrong."

Moss glowered down at him. "No, *you're* all wrong, Sands!" He circled around to open the trunk and hefted out the sack. Then, steadying the bag with his hold, he said grimly: "Let me tell you like it is. You raped and killed this girl. Do you really think they'll listen to some crazy story about drunkenness or temporary insanity? Some excuse about what you got from your dad? I'm telling you, your life will be ruined. Do you hear me!"

"*Rape?* You mean I raped her?"

"What do you think, Sands? My God! She was naked. You were naked."

"But you don't know—?"

"Of course I don't know… Who could possibly know? Certainly not the great Jonathan Sands, who was too drunk to even know he was with a beautiful girl or what he was doing!"

Then Decker repented of his anger and let loose of his hold on the bag. He squatted down. "Look, Jon, what I'm saying is—" The bag fell stiffly on its side, momentarily catching their attention, and Decker turned back to Jonathan again. "What I'm saying is any autopsy would show it if you did. Rape and murder will get you a minimum of life. You know Karen's father is a powerful man. You want to face that? You want your mother to face that?"

Jonathan knelt silently in the pool of wet gravel, cogent enough to know the truth of Decker's words. All along he had been thinking of his mother. Either way he went from this point his life was over. No amount of time could cover over what he had done, and no act of restitution could bring her back. And his mother must never know any of it.

Bankrupt, Jonathan slammed his arms into the sharp stones of the driveway and wept bitterly.

Decker glared down at him for several moments. Frustrated, he returned to the sack and hefted it into his arms. The relative ease with which he was able to manage the sack confirmed *rigor mortis* was beginning to set in. Then he took the dark path through the trees down to the boathouse.

It sat a stone's throw to the south of the lodge in a secluded bay. The whitecaps on the lake were visible; a waning crescent moon snuck in and out of the scattering clouds that still lingered from the storm. Waves from a strong southeast breeze crashed against the shoreline.

Moss keyed the boathouse padlock, pried open the door and flipped on the light switch. Inside, hoisted above the water by block and tackle were two boats: a 23-foot cuddy cabin Sea Ray and a 13-foot Boston Whaler. Knowing the larger boat's inboard-outboard engine had been winterized for the season, Decker went around to the side of the runabout and worked the block and tackle chains to set it into the water.

After making the battery connection and checking the fuel supply, he pumped the primer bulb and turned the key at the console. The outboard engine sputtered at first, but then fired. He climbed out and carefully lowered the duffel bag down from the dock onto the open bow.

The creaking sound of a plank caused Decker to look up. Jonathan stood in the darkened doorway. Decker stared at him a moment and then sidled out past him.

When he returned a few minutes later he carried some large rocks. "Come on, Jon, give me a hand. We need the weight."

"I can't."

Moss deposited the rocks onto the bow seat area and turned toward Sands. The wind howled through the few inches below the boathouse lift gate. "Maybe you want to see your mother's life ruined a second time." He moved over to the gate winch and worked its crank, increasing the level of his voice to overcome the wind and the waves. "Is that what you want? We come here with nothing and we leave here with nothing. You have a choice to make!"

Decker sidestepped the taciturn figure and exited again. He eventually returned cradling more rocks and dropped them into the boat with the others. Then he fixed his eyes on Jonathan and said coldly: "Maybe you *are* no different from your father."

At that Sands threw a punch, but Moss reacted faster with an undercut that connected with Jonathan's jaw. He reeled back from the blow and grabbed his chin. Decker peered up from bended waist. "In time, Sands … in time you'll realize I saved your life tonight."

Decker jumped into the idling boat, unfastened the tackle chains, and pulled the gearshift forcefully into reverse.

* * *

Lake George is deep. The section off the Moss property shoreline went down to depths as much as 150 feet or more. Massive glacial movements ten millennia earlier scooped out the

65

basin, and the mountains that cupped the lake fed it continuously with pristine spring water.

When Decker judged he was out a safe distance he shut off the engine. Opening the drawstring to the duffel bag with his gloved hands, he loaded it with rocks. Then he closed the fold and knotted the tie, sliding the canvas sack against the boat's hull.

He took the seat on the open bow and watched the rolling swells in the passing moonlight. The precipitation had stopped altogether and he looked up at the moving cloud currents. A couple of times the waves shook his balance, prompting him to hold the gunwale to steady himself.

"I'm sorry, Karen, you sure didn't deserve this." The apology fell silent to the wind. Holding the gunwale he stroked the rigid form beneath the canvas with his free hand, struggling on the edge with where he was, with what he was doing ...

Will I ever be able to live with it?

He knew he was probably still too drunk to fully appreciate his acts, which were now almost fully committed. Yet he sat furious at his friend for not coming out with him. He turned to face the shoreline a half mile away.

Don't you realize what I'm doing for you?

There were no lights there. There was no sign of life along the lakefront for miles. He knew Jonathan was out there, though, probably on the shore watching him, and he feared a moment about his friend's loyalty.

A large wave rocked the boat. Decker clenched the gunwale, feeling in the quick movement Karen's car keys poking through his pants pocket. He wondered what to do with them beyond the obvious. Then he looked down at the sack. With only slightly more reflection, he hoisted the bag enough to straddle the gunwale where it rested in his hold. There were no more alternatives to think through; only a simple act remained and he wanted to get it over.

He shoved the bag into the water. It floated atop the swells and away from the boat, gradually disappearing from his sight in a gurgling shadow. When the bag became soaked and gave up its air, it sank.

"Damn you, Sands."

* * *

Jonathan stood on the shoreline watching the low-riding runabout travel slowly out into the night. Once Decker stopped—

midway to the other side, Jonathan judged—he sighted two hazy reference points across the lake that he recalled from his summer visit: a bald-faced mountain and a jutting peninsula.

He didn't know why, but it was a triangulation he wished to remember.

Chapter Seven

THE pair chased dawn, arriving back at their apartment just as a
pallid sunrise showed in their facing horizon. The trip and entire
next day went by without more than a handful of words between
them. Jonathan couldn't face going back into his room, so he
spread out on the living room couch—the couch that just a few
hours earlier Decker reclined upon as Jonathan shared his letter for
a bright new future.

Now all nothing but a forlorn casualty of ruins to hopeful
imaginings.

He lay there in a 24-hour marathon of gloom, weeping
inconsolably when he had the breath to do so; locked up in
motionless misery when he didn't. For the most part, Decker left
him alone, yet made him a couple sandwiches. They sat uneaten on
the coffee table.

Sands always went for a run early Sunday mornings. Today,
after a second sleepless night, he concluded had to be no different.
It was a decision from beyond his being, a struggle to get outside of
himself. And outside of the infernal apartment.

The day was cold and cloudless. He chose an altogether
different route from usual, south beyond campus and then east
along the outlying country roads. The mountains were freshly
glazed with snowy peaks. It was all a death knell, a forewarning to
those in the lower elevations that they had but another couple of
weeks before the season kicked into full hold. When it did, it
wouldn't let go for five months. Five more months of death. And
then the cycle would repeat itself ... winter turning to spring ...
denuded trees returning their leaves ... death coming back to life.

Oh, if it were only so.

"I didn't know what I was doing, Karen. I didn't want to, but
they ..."

*No, they didn't make you, Jonathan. You got drunk yourself. You and
your celebration. Great time?*

Hell.

68

OPTIONS

The chill in the air and steep inclines burned him. He wanted it to burn away everything … to incinerate his miserable filth to ash.

How is it possible to literally remember nothing of it?

But he had experienced it before, at the high school dance. Like the effects of an anesthetic after surgery, the booze left him with no recall of his maniacal rampage. And from his grandfather's description, it was certainly possible for a drunk to have no memory of his actions. 'Blackout,' he called it—beating someone you supposedly loved with no recollection afterward.

Could intoxication really have such an amnestic effect?

Jonathan wished he could speak to his mother about his questions. He just wanted to talk to someone who would know. Trying to psychoanalyze one's own behavior was a bit like asking a dog why it messed on the floor. It can't analyze. It simply reacts. Some through reinforcement, yes, but mostly to what just comes naturally. Had the drinking reduced him to such a primal state? Some perverse reaction to sleeping with a girl he loved and feeling so guilty about it afterward that he strangled her for being the source of that guilt? Had his adolescent resolutions, his self-imposed prohibitions, become so inviolate, so venerated a taboo that when profaned by booze and sex they aroused the father-animal hibernating within? Perhaps provoked further by the rage he fell victim to earlier that evening?

Was that all too incredible a theory?

His father beat his mother for being the one who stole the promise of his life from him. Did Karen pose that kind of threat to him? At least somehow in his drunken subconscious?

For two hours Jonathan ran and walked the country roads, his mind tearing into himself, weeping and tormented by a self-encounter that left him in the end with nothing more than in the beginning. Discarding any hope of reconciling what he knew with what he could piece together about the night, Jonathan circled back.

People don't change. Not really. Not on the inside.

* * *

While Sands was out for his run, Decker spent the morning giving the apartment and vestibule a thorough cleaning. Focusing first on Jonathan's room, he changed and washed the bedding and vacuumed and scrubbed down the floor and walls. Then he went through the rest of the apartment, removing and washing away any

69

evidence that could have been left behind. He did his best with the shattered door-casing using some small finish nails and a hammer he found in the garage, but it was a haphazard job.

Afterward, he set about switching his larger room for Jonathan's, exchanging their respective belongings: clothes, furniture, stereo equipment, typewriters, poster hangings … all of it neatly rearranged. Jonathan wouldn't sleep in his own room again, Decker knew that. The move was necessary for his friend.

A little past noon the phone rang. Alarm was in her voice.

"Sue, what's wrong?"

"Karen's missing! We can't find her."

"Missing? What do you mean 'missing'?"

"Just that, Deck, we can't find her! The police found her car on the side of a road out of town and she's missing. Her dad and mom are frantic."

"What are you *talking* about?"

"*Karen's gone!*" Susan shouted. "There's no note or anything. The police found her car early yesterday morning, so she must have been gone since Friday night. They contacted her father down in Maryland this morning. It's not good. She'd never do this."

"But, how—?"

"I don't know! She's just … disappeared!" Her breathing was heavy. "Listen, I have to keep the line clear in case there's any word. Say a prayer, okay?"

Decker didn't reply.

"I'll talk to you later."

"Do you want me to come over?" Decker asked.

There was a pause. "It is pretty creepy being here alone."

* * *

Susan greeted Decker at the door. From her flushed face and red eyes he knew she had been crying for a time.

"I just know something terrible has happened," she said, holding him.

"Come on, Sue, nothing's happened." Decker stroked her back. "She'll probably walk in the door any minute and we'll all be laughing by the end of the day."

"But her car—she would have had it towed if it broke down. And on a dead-end road? Besides, she wouldn't be gone this long. You know she wouldn't."

Decker traipsed over to the recliner. Stepping over the books sprawled out on the floor, he sat down. "What about the cops? What do they say?"

"I haven't talked to them yet. Mr. Wyman did. Just that they found the car and wanted to find its owner, so they traced the Maryland plates back to him."

"Are they out looking for her?"

"I don't know. I don't know what they do when someone's missing."

Decker glanced down at the books on the floor. "And there's no hint where she might have gone?"

"None." Susan sat down on the couch across from him and palmed her face in her hands. "Mr. Wyman had me go through the entire apartment, describing everything I saw to him over the phone. Her bed's made and her jacket and purse are gone. Everything else looks normal, except maybe the chairs over there." Without looking up, Susan gestured toward the dining area.

"Why, what's wrong with them?"

"Well, they just look like two people might have been sitting there, and there are some footprints in the carpet that seem too big to be ours."

Decker got up and started over to the area.

"No, don't go near there. Mr. Wyman said to leave it all just the way it is."

"That's ridiculous. What does he think, that some Jack-the-Ripper came in here and carted Karen off?"

"No, Deck, I'm serious. He said it's important not to go near them. He's a lawyer, you know."

Frowning at her, Decker squatted down at the edge of the dining room area trying to make out the prints in the carpet. A couple appeared to be large. *Jonathan's running shoes?* He concealed his concern and returned to the living room. "Those are probably my footprints," he suggested.

"Not unless you were here since Friday. I vacuumed before I left."

"Well, it doesn't mean anything," contended Decker, "I can tell you that. Karen probably just had some guy over."

Susan looked up at him with a challenging glare. "What guy would she have over? You know she only likes Jonathan."

"How should I know? Hell, maybe it was a Jehovah's Witness or something. Who knows? It doesn't mean anything."

71

"She wouldn't go serving hot chocolate to some Jehovah's Witness, Decker!"

"Hot chocolate? What are you talking about?"

"There are two mugs and a pot in the sink, and cocoa mix on the counter." She gestured in the direction of the kitchen.

Moss shook his head in frustration. "I can't believe this. For all you know she made that for herself before she left. I'm telling you, Sue, you're making way too much out of this thing."

"I don't care what you think. I know Karen. She wouldn't use two cups for herself. You know she's a neat freak. She must have made it for someone else. And probably pretty soon before she left."

Moss sat back down in the recliner, gently rocking as he thought things over. Jonathan must have had hot chocolate with Karen, and his fingerprints would be all over the cup. Identifying carpet shoeprints was less of a problem, though still something had to be done.

"She's either been kidnapped or murdered."

"My God, Susan, I agree it's bizarre, but nothing like that. You don't have to get so melodramatic."

"Well, then, you tell me what you think happened to her!" she said with a rise of anger.

Decker regrouped. "Look, I'm sorry. Let's not fight. I just don't think you should get yourself all worked up about this … not yet, anyway." He patted his knees. "Come over here."

After a moment Susan got up and went over to sit on Decker's lap, setting her head against his shoulder. He ran his hand beneath her sweater and rubbed her back. Then he drew her chin to his and kissed her. "You need rest. Let's take a nap."

She frowned at him. "How can you think about that now?"

"C'mon, Sue, it'll help you get your mind off things. We'll both take a nap and feel better afterward."

She lay in his arms in silence for several minutes. Then she rose and headed down the hallway to her bedroom. He followed and closed the door.

* * *

Half an hour later she was asleep. In slow animation Decker lifted himself from the mattress, closed the bedroom door behind him, and headed for the dining room.

OPTIONS

It was a new apartment with new carpet, which left discernible prints in the fibers. He got down on his knees. Squinting through the light from the patio door, he traced the back of his hand over the shadowed prints that he could see, just enough to blend their edges—artfully, subtly, yet in a parsimonious way that didn't take more than a minute.

Then he went into the kitchen. A dish towel rested on the counter. He used it to carefully wipe the cups clean, one at a time.

The phone rang.

Damn!

Susan exited the bedroom, finding Decker standing in the middle of the kitchen in his briefs with a caught-naked expression on his face.

"What are you doing?" she asked, reaching for the phone.

"No, Mr. Wyman, I haven't," she said in response to the phone caller's question.

Decker came over and leaned into the handset.

"I didn't think so," came the voice on other end. "Look, Karen's mother is beside herself with worry, and so am I at this point. Travel for us really isn't possible … not that we'd be able to do anything anyway." There was a perceptible struggle in Wyman's voice.

Susan thought of Karen's mother being confined to a wheelchair. "Yes, I understand."

"I've been able to arrange for an agent up in the Albany FBI office to check things out," Wyman said. "He should be there shortly. I hope that's okay."

"Why, yes, of course," returned Susan, realizing Karen's father probably had the Washington connections to make such a speedy arrangement with the feds possible.

Decker quietly uttered some words to her about the police.

"But shouldn't the police here be doing something?" Susan asked.

"Karen's an adult and a missing person's report can't be filed yet. Not without some evidence of foul play or imminent danger. But given the work I've been doing for the Administration, I just worry …" Wyman didn't finish his sentence.

Susan's imagination filled in the void. "*Kidnapping?* Oh, my God!"

"Let's just try to stay calm about this. I'll be in touch in a couple hours, okay?"

"Sure, that's fine, Mr. Wyman."

She hung up the phone and turned to Decker. "The police can't do anything yet, but he's getting the FBI involved."

"I heard." Decker turned his back to her. "This is really getting serious, isn't it?"

"That's what I'm trying to tell you, Deck. It's as serious as it can get!"

* * *

"We have to get our stories together, fast," said Moss, nervously gulping a swig from his beer bottle. Jonathan was sitting next to him on the living room couch.

"The more we do the more trouble we're going to get into. It's no use. I told you, I should just turn myself in and take the consequences. I'll tell them I did everything myself. You don't have to be involved."

Decker moaned. He set his bottle down on the coffee table and wiped his face with his sleeve. "You don't understand what you're saying, Jon. You can't do it alone. Not now." He turned toward his roommate. "How could you explain taking her to Lake George by yourself without my help? I would have had to know about it. It was my car, my summerhouse, my boat. And how could you have ditched her car alone? You have no choice but to involve me."

"I'll think of something," Jonathan suggested unconvincingly.

"Please, Jon, let me give you this chance with your life. We're going to come out of this. She's gone. There's nothing you can do about it now. She liked you … she wouldn't want you to do this. Wherever she is now, she wouldn't want you to throw your life away. It was an accident."

"An *accident*? I raped and killed her! Are you telling me she'd want me to just get away with that?" Jonathan stood up and paced the living room floor.

"I'm just trying to speak some sense to you," Decker appeased. "You've got so much in front of you. You can't just throw it all away."

"I have nothing in front of me. I might have had a lot a couple days ago, but my life is nothing but hell now." Jonathan's pacing took him into the kitchen where he grabbed the counter's edge. "And it's going to get worse if I just go on covering this up."

OPTIONS

The grip of his fingers went weak and his head fell to the cushion of his arms. "She brought me home and helped me. She thought I was something great. Then I killed her, and we dragged her out of here like some piece of trash. No burial. No place for her ..." His sobbing choked off further words.

Decker came off the couch and into the kitchen. He brought his arm around his friend. "Jon, this hurts now ... a lot, and it's going to hurt for a long time ... for both of us. But we're going to heal. Time will take the edge away. We have to be strong for each other so that we can get over this. We'll grieve. We'll honor Karen's memory. But whatever we do, we have no choice but to do it together." Moss drew his hold tighter around Jonathan's shoulder. "And you didn't really do this to Karen. Not the *real* you. If anybody did it, it was me. I forced you to drink and that makes it as much my responsibility as it is yours. Don't you see?"

Jonathan didn't say anything.

"I need you to stay strong, Jon."

Sands lifted his head from the counter. "Strength is about doing the right thing, Deck. It's not about hiding or running away from what you've done. We did the wrong thing and I have to put it right. I may end up going to jail for the rest of my life. I'm offering you a way out."

"A way out? So, you think it's okay to lie about my part in this so you can get me off? Is that your definition of strength? Because if it is, then I can be just as strong and lie about your part as well. Can't you see the inconsistency? You love me as your friend and you want to protect me. I want to do the same for you."

"But *I* was the one who was responsible, dammit. I did it, not you!"

"No, Jon, the *booze* did it. And I was the one responsible for getting you drunk. That puts us in the exact same position. You've got to see reason."

Decker's palm ran firmly across Jonathan's shoulder as he tried to catch his friend's eye. "And your mother, Jon. If you turn yourself in you know it would destroy her. You're all she has."

Sands attempted to wipe away the wetness from his face, but it didn't do much good. Decker grabbed a couple pieces of paper towel and handed them to him. "Together," he said, "if we hold together we don't have to lose ourselves ... or your mom. Together we can get out of this."

"There's no way. I just don't see how."

"Because they'll never find her, and there's absolutely no evidence—other than for those cups and the carpet. And I took care of those for you. We were out drinking when she disappeared. We have an alibi."

"I don't have an alibi," Jonathan said, looking up at him. "I left Smitty's."

"But you were dead drunk. I'll vouch for that. The guys will vouch for that. Hell, you barely made it out of the place. Nobody saw Karen there. You walked home alone."

"They didn't see her car in our driveway when they dropped you off?" Jonathan asked.

"No way that they could have. Matt dropped me off out in front of the house. It would have been impossible to see her car parked in back. Besides, it was pitch-black that night."

Jonathan turned off to the living room and settled heavily into the recliner. He sorted through all that had been said, all his feelings, his future, as much as he could. And if not for one thing his thoughts would have led to an inevitable choice, the only right choice. But turning himself in would do more than ruin his own life—he didn't care a damn about that now—it would destroy his mother as well. She didn't deserve that.

At long length Sands asked plaintively: "Why are you so determined to help me, Decker? I killed her, you didn't. Why risk all this on yourself?"

From the kitchen, Decker Moss looked down at the counter and then over at him. His mind took him through places he hadn't yet taken time to explore, and he wondered if any of it was likely to sound satisfactory to his friend, no matter how he phrased it. "I reacted, Jon. I simply reacted. I didn't see any other way. I was drunk, and maybe if I weren't drunk I wouldn't have done it. I saw you there like some kid's pet that had just been hit by a car, and I did what I had to do. I felt responsible."

Moss walked around to the living room and took a seat on the couch. He grabbed his beer bottle from the coffee table and rolled it between his palms. "I suppose for me it's like when we first met. Here's a guy who has success written all over him. It wasn't really jealousy because you were such a hick and such a machine at the same time, and I thought that was funny." He stared in thought toward the living room window. "But I know it's more than that. Something deeper maybe I'm not even sure about."

Setting his beer bottle down, Decker glanced at his hands, as if studying them. Introspection was foreign territory for him. Like well-marked landmines, the hurt had always been better left undisturbed. "I know I always wanted to amount to something, that I could if I really worked hard enough at it. Yet it's always been just out of reach. My father seemed to have this way of holding me off unless I achieved something. It's like there was just no place in his head for me. He always had money, lots of it, but never the time. Not that he'd give that away, either."

Decker paused for several moments.

"I was good at football, Jon, really good. My senior year, I threw thirty-eight touchdown passes and over four-thousand passing yards. They were both division records. And then I got hurt. But he never showed up for my games. Not once. He always worked on Saturdays. That's when he bought me the BMW. And Mom was a closet drinker. In the afternoons, I'd come home from school and she'd be locked up in her room sleeping it off. My father would come home late and she'd be sober by then with his dinner ready. He'd talk to me for a few minutes but I always felt like the clock was running, you know? I'm not blaming him for anything. It's probably not relevant. I mean, you didn't even have a dad growing up and yet you accomplished so much. Your mom was there, though. She really cared about what you were doing. She rooted for you whether or not you would succeed."

Swallowing the final remnants from his now warm bottle, Moss stared at it meditatively. "I'm just someone who was there for you, Jon ... who's here now. I want you to succeed. For yourself as well as for your mom."

Decker's words were uncharacteristically sensitive. It was a vulnerable side Jonathan hadn't witnessed before.

"You sound as if you think I'm really innocent in all this."

"You *are* innocent," said Decker, turning up. "You didn't know what you were doing. That's innocence in my mind ... isn't it a valid defense in court? The fact nobody else would understand, especially some powerful Washington lawyer, doesn't make you guilty. And I sure doubt your mom would be able to afford the kind of lawyer who could convince a jury as it really happened."

"I'm not innocent, Deck. No matter how much you say it, the booze doesn't make me innocent. You can't blame gravity for a bad fall. I killed her. I wanted to kill Roy, and if I could have finished him off I feel I might have killed the bastard, right there.

He just kept pushing me, taunting me, like he wanted to see what I'd do if I got worked up enough. Why did he *do* that?"

"I don't know why. After you left, Schulman and Johnson both acted as if it was somehow my fault, getting you drunk when you're not into partying. But Roy, God, I have no idea what got into him. I know he was trying to be funny, cutting up with you the way I do, but he went way overboard. I suspect he's always been jealous of you. You know, your grades, your looks, your job offer … that comment he made about your scholarship. I've always thought he had an insecurity problem. You know, about his small size and all. I suppose that's why I've always been there for him, too. Like a big brother." Decker's words trailed off as he thought the matter over more thoroughly. "Why? Do you think your fight with Roy had something to do with what happened with Karen?"

Jonathan's answer didn't require thought. "Of course I do, in some crazy way. I'm certain of it. The anger I felt in Smitty's just possessed me; it took over me like I was some kind of madman. It must have still been there when I was in bed with her. God … my belt was around her neck. Blood on her temple and smeared on her face." Jonathan started crying again.

"Jon," Decker pursued softly, "you never answered the question I asked that night. Why did you lock your door?"

"I have no idea. I told you, I don't remember anything. Karen must have locked it."

"But, if that's the case she must have thought you were going to have some time together. She must have felt you were sober enough for that, right?"

Jonathan looked up at Decker, whose look was imploring.

"I … I guess so. It doesn't make sense, but I guess so."

Decker just continued studying his friend. "You really have no memory of having sex with her? Touching her? Anything at all?"

Jonathan stared morosely into Decker's eyes, which in turn betrayed doubt. Jonathan just shook his head in response.

Decker's wary expression then gave way. "I'm doing this for you, Jon," he whispered.

The late autumn sun hung low in the sky, making for long shadows in the room, and there was a prolonged period of silence between the two. Jonathan then looked over at his best friend. His only friend in the world.

"Are we together on this?" Decker asked.

OPTIONS

The question negotiated a presence of reason that, despite challenge, had only one possible answer. Finally, and with hesitant resolution, Jonathan nodded.

Chapter Eight

STATE trooper Kenneth Nolan stood with his clipboard in hand while FBI agent Edward Fitch studied Karen's abandoned car from the driver's side. They, along with Susan Cabot, arrived together in Nolan's cruiser shortly after four in the afternoon. The three of them had just completed a brief walk of the woods on either side of the road, but it revealed nothing. A more extensive formal search was being arranged.

"So how long do we have to wait before we can file a missing person's report?" asked Fitch, uncertain of Vermont's state requirements.

"I think we should do so right away, sir. She's been missing now for more than twenty-four hours. We just wanted to be sure we weren't hunting for ghosts." Nolan regretted his use of the metaphor as soon as he said it, but let it lie. He had been making notes of the location of the car and the details of its contents. There didn't appear to be any unusual items, and there certainly wasn't any sign of violence. "We can do a dusting, but in my experience cars contain so many prints that it's probably not going to yield anything useful."

"Still, I'd like you to do it," said Fitch.

"Of course," replied the trooper dutifully. "If nothing else, we can keep them on file."

Edward Fitch was a tall, clearly fit black man in his mid-30s, wearing a gray business suit and blue wool overcoat. He was sitting in the driver's seat. He turned to Susan who was standing next to him at the car's open door. "Would you have any idea why Karen might have come out this way?"

"Not at all," she answered. "It seems far too spooky a place out here for me." Susan Cabot struggled in her imaginings about a possible romantic interlude between her roommate and Jonathan, but it was cold on Friday. Besides, Karen had the apartment to herself. "She wouldn't have come out here on her own, I'm sure of that much."

As Fitch glanced a final time around the car, he asked: "So, you don't see anything out of the ordinary? Anything at all?"

Again Susan poked her head into the driver's side and panned the interior carefully, considering his question with fuller evaluation. "Well … maybe that," she said, pointing across to a small whitish stain on the passenger door, just below the window. "Karen's a neat freak and I'd think she would have cleaned it up."

"Neat freak?" repeated Fitch. He came around the car, opened the passenger door, and studied the congealed stain Susan indicated.

"It's a running joke between us," Susan responded. "We both are. We try to outdo each other."

Fitch's first impression was that it was milk. "Which explains why you vacuumed the apartment's carpet before you left." It was a statement, not a question. Fitch examined the spot and drew his nose to it, taking a sniff. "Officer Nolan, could you get what you can of this into a sample bag?"

"What's that?" Nolan was standing at the front of the car.

"This here," Fitch pointed. "It looks fresh."

The State Trooper walked over to them and studied the spot. "You know how cars get over time." He thought the FBI man was stretching.

"No, it still appears a bit moist. It might be emesis residue. Get all you can of this."

"Puke?"

"Yes, puke," answered Fitch with slight annoyance.

"I'll try." Nolan took out a plastic bag, and using the blade from his pocketknife, scraped what he could into it. "I'm not sure what it'll reveal, but we'll check it for substances." He labeled it and placed it under the clasp of his clipboard. "One sample barf bag."

Fitch ignored the officer and asked him: "Would you mind taking us down the road to the quarry?"

"Not at all."

The three of them got into the cruiser and headed to the end of the road. "The quarry's become a regular hangout," commented Nolan. "It's part of my rounds, which is why I was suspicious when I saw the deserted car. We had a drowning here four years ago. Tragic thing. Teenaged boy goofing off too close to the edge of the cliff." He turned to the FBI agent. "Of course drinking was involved."

At the end of the road was a path that led under a portion of bent chain-link fence. The trail was well-traveled and continued beneath oaks and maples around rock ledges. The oaks still held

81

their dead brown leaves. Looking around the place, Fitch could certainly understand the attraction of the place to the younger crowd. Quiet, out of the way, romantic. He and Nolan walked the path to its conclusion at the cliff wall.

"A person falling from here the wrong way wouldn't make it," said Nolan. "There's ledge down there just below the water line that juts out about five feet and then goes straight down. That's where the boy landed. Broke his neck and continued on down."

"How deep is it?"

"Sixty, seventy feet. A lot of junk submerged down there, too. Even an old washing machine from what the divers found."

The two lawmen scanned the area carefully, poking around the scattered debris, picking up various items and looking for anything out of the ordinary. Susan stood off to the side for the most part. Fitch was just about to conclude they weren't going to find anything when Nolan called out from his right.

"Hey, come take a look at this!"

The FBI agent quickly made his way in the direction Nolan was pointing.

"Panties. Not too old either from the looks of them." Nolan snagged them up with a stick. "Could they be hers'?" he asked Susan, who had joined them.

"No," she said almost immediately. "No way. Those are far too large to be Karen's."

Nolan placed them in a second plastic bag. "Crazy what things you find up here. A girl doesn't miss her underwear?"

As they made their way back to the cruiser, Officer Nolan said: "Sorry we couldn't be more productive. We'll have the car dusted for prints and then get it back to you. Do you want it delivered to Karen's apartment?"

"That'll be fine," returned Fitch. He pivoted around to the backseat where Susan was sitting. "Earlier you told me Karen didn't have a boyfriend. But was she close friends with any guy, or guys, that I should know about? Someone you think she might feel comfortable enough to meet at the apartment for hot chocolate and then come out here with?"

Again, Susan's only private thought was Jonathan, though she struggled with herself about sharing it. She simply couldn't imagine him having anything to do with Karen's disappearance. Yet, the circumstances required her voicing the connection anyway.

"Well, there is a guy she *likes*, if that's what you mean. His name's Jonathan Sands. They went out on a double date with my boyfriend and me. But he's about the most unlikely person I can think of that would be involved in anything …"

"Of course," said Fitch. "Still, would you have his number or address?"

"I can do better than that," Susan answered. "He's my boyfriend's roommate."

* * *

The meeting Susan Cabot was able to arrange for that evening at Jonathan and Decker's apartment was for "informational purposes only," Fitch assured the young men. In attendance were Jonathan Sands, Decker Moss, Carl "Catman" Johnson and Matt Schulman. Peter Roy declined the invitation, his stated reason being that he had an exam to study for the next day. This was Decker's idea. The truth was that the bar fight between Sands and Roy was an irrelevant detail that obviously had nothing to do with Karen's disappearance, and Roy's facial injuries could only provoke unnecessary questions and suspicions. The other frat brothers agreed to the need to cover for Roy. No mention whatsoever was to be made about the altercation, "either directly or indirectly," Decker emphasized again to all before the meeting.

They sat around the kitchen table as the FBI agent sought to gain a fuller understanding of the events for those who had been at Smitty's the night of Karen's disappearance. Alternately sipping from their cans of soda, the college men listened while Fitch explained what he knew, at least the facts insofar as they needed to know. The stale bag of Fritos Decker placed on the table sat uneaten.

Special Agent Edward Fitch approached things in what he regarded to be a natural order. From his training and experience an investigation traveled more or less a heuristic path, starting with the initial report, the trunk, and then proceeding to the various connecting branches in different directions, until all the thick foliage of data was gathered for interpretation. It was both a science and an art—cues and clues coming together to form a cohesive picture, hopefully one that gave a convincing portrayal of the truth. The art came into play when the branches didn't seem to connect. From there intuition, inference and instinct had to take over—or, as one of Fitch's academy instructors often referred to them, the visceral INs of investigation.

"Jonathan, you say you left earlier than the others. What time would that have been?"

Sands was fidgety, visibly uncomfortable about the meeting. "I think it was about ten."

"And you left because …?"

"I was too drunk to go on. I knew it was time for me to get out. Get some air and get home to bed."

"Jon doesn't usually go out with us," Decker inserted. "He's not a partier."

"Not a partier?" asked Fitch of Jonathan.

"No, I have a beer from time to time, but never like that. I had a bad experience in high school."

"Yeah," added Carl, "we were celebrating the great job offer he got that day. He was pretty wiped out by the time he left."

"Job offer?" asked Fitch.

"Yes, from Marsh Mason & Pratt … in Boston," Sands answered. "It's a national CPA firm."

"I've heard of it," said Fitch, "very prestigious. Nice going." Resuming, the agent directed another question at Jonathan. "And, how'd you get home?"

"The same way I got there: I walked. It's not that far from here—just a mile or so. I was starting to pass out." Jonathan gestured to the others. "They'll tell you."

"Yeah, he barely made it out of the place," Decker said. "It was probably my fault. I seem to remember ribbing him some about his manhood."

"But it was cold with precipitation that night." Fitch's statement implied a question.

"That's right, it was miserable outside," said Jonathan, "but I had no choice but to walk, and the rain probably helped. I really don't remember how I did it though, to be honest."

Fitch turned his attention to the others. "And then after that, when did the rest of you leave Smitty's?"

Carl, who seemed at ease, looked over at Decker. "Another few hours. I'd say one, one-thirty or so, wouldn't you say, Decker?"

"I thought it was a little later than that, but you might be right."

"So, you were all pretty drunk when you left?" asked Fitch.

"Well, we had a good time," Moss replied. "We played a bit of pool after Jon left, but I wouldn't say we were nearly at the point he was. We ate beforehand, and then, of course, the peanuts while we were there."

"And you all left by foot that night?" asked the agent.

"Oh, no, I drove," Matt Schulman explained. "I was the designated driver. We got home safe."

"So, you didn't drink that evening?" Fitch asked.

"Not a thing," Schulman answered. "I can't because I'm on the football team. I dropped Decker off here and then we went home. We live at a fraternity house in town."

Ed Fitch took down the note that Schulman was the only sober one in the group. He turned to Decker. "So, what did you do when you got home?"

"Well, I was really too wasted to do much of anything. Jonathan's bedroom door was locked, so I figured he was sleeping it off and I just hit the sack myself."

"Locked?" Fitch asked with a raised eye.

"Yeah, I thought I should check on him before going to bed myself, and it was locked. I thought I should just let him sleep it off."

Jonathan couldn't understand why Decker would volunteer such an unnecessary detail. Then Decker covered with a lie: "He usually locks his door."

The FBI man looked over at Jonathan and squinted at his bruised jaw. "When did you get that injury, Jon?"

Sands grabbed his chin self-consciously. "Friday night. Like I said, I was blasted. I remember tripping and hitting the post down on the stairway. I scraped my finger as well." He gestured toward the vestibule. The knuckle of his middle finger was wrapped with a bandage.

Fitch wrote another note and then peered over at Johnson and Schulman. "And the rest of you?"

"Pretty much the same thing," said Carl. "Some of the other brothers came in a little while after we got back. We hung out watching TV a little and made some popcorn. After that we all went to bed."

"I had to hit the sack a bit earlier than the rest," inserted Schulman. "We had football warm-ups in the morning for a game that afternoon."

"What about earlier in the day, before you all got to Smitty's?"

Decker responded first. "Peter Roy and I had a brutal exam that afternoon. I got back to the apartment here a little before three. Watched some TV until Jon got home. What was that, Jon, about four-thirty?"

Sands nodded and Decker continued: "Then we all got together at the frat house to have some pizza and play euchre."

"Everybody but me," Jonathan clarified. "I took my run and got here at about six-thirty. Then I showered and worked on my tax project a bit." His rehearsed version of the story had kicked in.

"And after that you walked to Smitty's?" pursued the agent.

"That's right."

"Do you own a car?"

"No, I can't afford one. But the town's small enough to get around on foot for the most part, and Decker lets me borrow his occasionally if I need it."

Fitch looked alternately at the two roommates. "Do you both have keys to the car?"

Decker was somewhat uncomfortable now with where the questioning was going. "No, I'm the only one with a key to my car."

"And you had the key with you Friday night?"

"Yes, of course, my key ring has my apartment key and my car keys on it."

Fitch quickly glanced over at Jonathan. "What about dinner, Jonathan?"

Sands was caught off guard. "Dinner?"

"Yes, the others said they had pizza but you didn't mention anything about having dinner."

"No, I don't think I had dinner that night. In fact, I know I didn't. That's why I got so drunk, I guess."

"Is not having dinner typical for you?"

"Well, no, not really. I got into my tax project and then before I knew it, it was time for me to head off to Smitty's. We agreed to meet there at eight-thirty."

Fitch made a note *J: no dinn. Tax pjct. Smitty's 8:30.* "Which is consistent with you so drunk that evening." He penned a few more notes. "Your run," asked the agent, "where did you go?"

Jonathan straightened in his chair. "I cover pretty much the same course every day. Leaving from here I head east of town, and then up around, all east and north of the campus." He drew the course on the table with his finger, mentioning the street names he commonly traveled. "I don't remember exactly which route I took that night."

"You don't remember?"

"Well, I run every day, with different routes, but I'm pretty sure I headed directly back down Washington Street that night. It cuts a quarter mile off the run, and I remember the roads were getting slippery."

"That would take you close to Karen's apartment building, wouldn't it?" Fitch had some familiarity with the geographic layout Jonathan described, having traveled around the small town that afternoon.

Jonathan stared at his interrogator. Whether his expression showed frustration or nervousness, the FBI agent wasn't sure.

"Yes, to answer your question. It would take me close. But everything's close in Middlebury."

"So you didn't run past Karen's apartment or see her that afternoon?"

"No, I didn't. I certainly have run by her apartment in the past, but on that night I took Washington Street down closer to our side of town." Jonathan gave the street names again, this time more definitively, but this time also with a very discernible tension in his voice.

"What's your shoe size, Jonathan?" asked Fitch.

Sands's expression went tight. "Ten and a half."

"And you, Decker?"

"Size ten. Why?"

"We just want to rule out that the carpet imprints Susan saw around the dining room table weren't from one of you. She said she vacuumed the floor before she left but it's certainly possible she missed that area. She said they looked to be about a size ten or eleven. In any case they aren't clear anymore."

"They could have been mine," suggested Decker. "I told Susan that."

"But it doesn't fit because whoever made the tracks also had hot chocolate with Karen Friday night, or appeared to. Would either of you know who could possibly have been close enough with her to do that?" The agent looked individually at the four of them. They, in turn, all just shook their heads. Jonathan knew his face was flushed, but couldn't help it.

Decker decided to take on the question. "Karen is a pretty popular girl, Mr. Fitch, at least on campus. I certainly know that any number of guys would *like* to get to know her better. Maybe one of them just stopped by, you know, nothing to lose. I've done it myself with girls from time to time."

"You guys all have girlfriends?" Fitch asked them.

"Well, you know about me and Susan," Decker offered, who then looked across at Carl as if prompting him to answer next.

"Yeah, off and on," said Carl, "mostly off at the moment. You know how college is … girls aren't a problem." Catman Johnson had an overly flattering impression of himself. The nose he countenanced was clearly too long for his face, and his small mouth could barely conceal his fanged teeth, even when tightly pursed. "Are you wanting names?"

"No, that's not necessary. What about you, Jonathan?" Fitch asked.

Sands swayed at the question. He wondered if the man had somehow found out about his interest in Karen, but concluded it wasn't possible. Did he know of her interest in him? Clearing his throat, he said: "Mr. Fitch, I don't have a girlfriend. I know from Decker and Susan that Karen liked me, though, if that's where you're heading." He glanced around the table, noticing Schulman and Johnson's eyes raised a bit at the revelation. "We went on a double date a few weeks ago. I really like her, but only as a friend. That's all, really."

Ed Fitch quickly pursued the point. "But she's obviously a very beautiful girl. And from what I hear, the two of you have a lot in common. Both very bright, studious, ambitious?"

"No, that's right, we do. And if it were another time and place I would definitely be interested." Jonathan fingered one of the stale Fritos from the bag at the center of the table, and with slightly quivering fingers broke it in half, swallowing a bite. "It's just that I have goals." His look shifted upward to the clock mounted on the wall, eying it blankly, as if considering how to answer the question in a way that would be understood yet delivered in a brief amount of words. "My parents met too young. It's a long story, but they ran into a lot of problems because they didn't take the time before getting married. I decided long ago I didn't want to make the same mistakes."

"You're obviously a very disciplined young man. So you're not the type to date?"

"No, not really. Not much. I want it to be the right time. People cut up about me, I know, but it doesn't matter."

"I appreciate your being forthright with me, Mr. Sands. I hope you understand my need to ask certain personal questions."

"Well, yes, of course I do. I really like Karen, and I hope—" Jonathan's voice trailed off. Looking up at the clock again, tears began to well up in his eyes.

The FBI agent couldn't help noticing the apparent sincerity with which Jonathan had responded. It certainly seemed convincing—too spontaneous to be contrived. Unless, of course, he happened to be an excellent actor.

After taking down some more notes, Fitch's eyes circuited the men around the table a final time, sensing there wasn't much more to be gained by further questioning. "I want to thank the four of you for meeting with me tonight." He extracted several business cards from a pocket in his notebook and dealt them out. "If anything else crosses your memories that might help me piece together the reason for Karen's disappearance, please contact me. No matter how small it might be."

Matt Schulman felt he had to speak up. He had been holding it back, but he knew it might be relevant despite his friends' feelings around the table. "Sir, I've been sitting here debating whether to say anything about it, but there is *one* thing…"

"Yes, Matt?" asked Fitch.

"Well, I completely vouch for the fact Jonathan was drunk— totally wiped out that night—but there was something he said just before he got up to leave the bar that's been hanging in my mind …"

"Go on," said the agent, very interested. Decker looked over at Jonathan. Fitch caught the eye connection and then turned in Matt Schulman's direction.

"He said he had plans," Schulman continued. "Right before he left, that's what he said. 'I have plans.'"

"What are you talking about?" challenged Decker. "I don't remember him saying anything like that."

Schulman rebounded. "No, don't you remember? We were talking about some plans we had, and Jonathan said, 'Yeah, I got plans. Gotta go.' Don't you remember that?"

The table went quiet. Fitch, who found Schulman's statement particularly significant since he was the only one not drinking that night, turned to Carl Johnson with a questioning eye.

"He might have," said Catman. "I don't remember it, but he might have."

"No he didn't," countered Decker. "Jonathan was completely wiped out. What plans could he possibly have had?" Over to Fitch, he added: "I may have been drunk, but I sure would have remembered if he said that. He barely made it out the front door."

Schulman shrugged his shoulders. "Well, that's what I remember him saying," he muttered.

There was an uncomfortable silence that followed, which Jonathan finally broke. "Mr. Fitch, I'm not telling you I didn't say it and I'm not saying I did. I honestly don't remember. But if I had any plans when I left that night, it was to get outside as fast as I could so I could puke my brains out. Which is what I did."

A bit more silence—and then Fitch closed his notebook, pocketed his pen, and nodded to his hosts. "Again, I want to thank you gentlemen for letting me meet with you on such short notice. If you can think of anything else, or happen to remember any information that might be helpful to the investigation, please call me." He gestured at his cards on the table and lifted from his chair.

The frat men rose likewise but Jonathan remained seated.

"Sure will," said Decker. "So, do you have any ideas what could have happened to her?"

Fitch shook his head. "No more than you might have at this point. But it's really too early to tell. We'll have a lot to do over the next few days. One thing you guys can do is to keep your eyes and ears open on campus. It's very possible this has a school-connection. Tell Peter Roy the same." The young men nodded in understanding and Fitch turned to Decker: "Do you mind if I visit your facilities before I leave?"

"No, not at all." He pointed down the hallway. "First door on the right."

Ed Fitch entered the bathroom and locked the door. He immediately saw what he was looking for. On the counter were two hairbrushes, one with strands of blond hair and the other with dark brown. He extracted two plastic bags from his coat pocket and placed within them a sample of each.

A minute later Fitch flushed the toilet and rejoined the others in the kitchen.

"Thanks again, guys."

Decker handed the FBI agent his coat, who then exited the back door.

"I have to go, too," said Schulman uncomfortably. He turned to Jonathan, who was still sitting at the table. "Sorry, Jon. I know it was nothing, but you did say you had plans. It wouldn't have been right not to tell him." Trying to gauge the others' reaction to his stance, yet failing, Schulman grabbed his coat off the chair, stepped out the door, and shut it.

* * *

Moss, Sands and Johnson stayed silent as the sound of Matt Schulman's footsteps down the outer vestibule stairway fell to silence.

"What do you think, Carl?" asked Decker, retaking a seat at the table.

"I think this is really something. Karen Wyman. *Man.* But why is the suit asking *us* so many questions? We had nothing to do with it."

"Because he has to start somewhere, and she's my girlfriend's roommate," said Decker. "It's a logical starting place."

Jonathan got up and removed the soda cans and bag of chips from the table.

"You sure got shook up there, Jon." Carl's fingers tapped the tabletop as he turned in Jonathan's direction behind him. "But I can see why." He then winked at Decker. "If a girl like that had it for me, I'd sure be shook up if she just up and disappeared."

Jonathan stood at the sink with moisture in his eyes. Decker noticed it but Carl didn't.

"It's really something. Someone so beautiful?" Carl looked at Decker. "And nice tits and ass, too."

Jonathan's reaction was immediate, so quick nothing could have stopped it. From the sink to the kitchen table he charged for Carl's throat. The table fell over with a crash. The pair writhed back and forth with Jonathan clinging Carl's neck tightly, his fingers tension-filled. Carl's legs kicked, causing the table chairs to fall and slide across the kitchen floor.

"*How dare you!*" Jonathan screamed.

Carl Johnson couldn't get anything to flow from his windpipe. Decker recovered from his fall and flung his arms around Jonathan's, grabbing for his friend's hands, trying to pry them apart. "*Stop it, Sands! My God, you're going to kill him!*"

"*You Greek bastards are all alike!*" Jonathan yelled.

In the tumult Decker was finally able to get a firm hold of Jonathan's wrists and pinched them tightly in the center raw spot.

91

His strength was the greater of the two, and his words finally started getting through. "*Stop it!*"

Jonathan's fingers came away slowly. Then he stood up and stared down at his hands and what he had done. Tears filled his eyes. A moment later, without saying a word, he grabbed his jacket from the closet and stormed out the door.

Decker took a towel from the counter and ran it under cold water. Kneeling down beside Carl, he placed it under his chin and around his cheeks.

"He's crazy," Catman muttered, coughing. "The son-of-a-bitch is crazy."

Chapter Nine

BEACHLIKE warmth filled the soccer field on the sunny afternoon marking Middlebury's commencement. Flowering crabapples and ornamental shrubs were in full bloom, and the spring foliage was of the deep lush green for which Vermont was renowned. Indeed, the two times of year when promising benefactors were most likely to be on campus—mid-spring and early fall—were conveniently also those in which nature's performance was most jubilant. It wasn't a fact lost on the College's Board of Trustees. Their annual appropriation to the campus grounds budget ensured generous funding during the spring and autumn months.

The string and horn octet played a repetitive round of Elgar's *Pomp & Circumstance* as the graduates marched in alphabetic procession up the field, past the attending audience of family and friends, and to the reserved front seats they were to occupy for the ceremony. The surrounding bleachers were filled. In all, nearly four thousand were in attendance.

Jonathan searched for his mother in the rows of guests as his procession advanced, but he didn't see her. He didn't really expect to. She told him earlier she worried about being able to make the ceremony because Jonathan's grandfather, whose prostate cancer metastasized into the lymph system, had severely declined in health recently. Her portent apparently proved true.

The commencement speaker was a 1955 alumnus who had built a successful empire of theme steakhouse restaurants along the east coast. His message was forged from insights gained during his illustrious career, concluding with the predictable *carpe diem* sermon for the graduates. Unpredictable, however, was its unlikely source: Dr. Seuss's *Yertle the Turtle*. It was all a decorous affair.

Yet Jonathan felt none of it. None of the nostalgia; none of the celebration; none of the excitement for what lay ahead. Like a Sisyphean boulder lashed to his back, interminable guilt remained heavy upon him. Time did little to weather away the asperity of its surface, and less to wear away at its weight.

Distraction had become his only solace the past several months. He quit the ski team, and during his final semester he spent around-the-clock hours in the library studying for the CPA exam. With little of its contents actually covered in his formal coursework, he had to master the lion's share of the material through self-preparation. And this he did with what Decker thought fanatical absorption.

The black academic regalia adorned by faculty and students soaked in the rays beating down on them, and they wriggled restlessly in their seats as more than an hour was taken for the diplomas to be presented. Most of the time was devoted to individually recognizing graduates earning academic honors. Jonathan's degree was presented *summa cum laude*, along with Middlebury's top ceremonial award, the highest scholastic recognition given. The applause he received, however, fell deaf to his ears. Without his mother present the public acknowledgment meant little.

Following the ceremony, a big-tent reception was held on the campus green. Sands came to wander the crowd by himself, fidgeting with the sliced-vegetables and dressing on his paper plate, greeting some friends and their families, but feeling self-conscious and alone. After a few minutes standing idly off to the side, his favorite professor approached him with an outstretched hand.

"Way to go, Jon. Our shining star. I always knew you would be." The sagacious-looking man grinned, cradling a briar pipe in his hand.

"Thank you, Professor Hawthorne," said Sands appreciatively.

"No, no more of that 'professor' stuff. You can call me Bob."

"Well, thank you very much … Bob." Sands doubted he would ever do so again. A deferential respect seemed lacking by addressing a professor by his first name.

"So, are you planning to take the exam in November?"

Jonathan nodded, knowing he was referring to the CPA exam. "Yes, I am. I know it's going to be tough, but I want to get it over with."

"And you'll pass it, for certain." Hawthorne drew some quick puffs on his pipe, but it was dead. He tapped its bowl against the palm of his hand and let the ashes fall to the ground. "Any thought about going to grad school? After being out in practice for a while?"

"I can't think that far ahead right now. School's been a firefight the whole way."

"Think it's any different out there?" Hawthorne asked with a brimming smile, his hand waving past the crowd of parents and students milling about, as if in some appeasing reference to the outer universe itself. Then he pulled in closer to Jonathan with a whisper. "We do that on purpose, you know. It teaches you about hell."

"*Now* you tell me." Jonathan grinned and took a bite of his cookie, which had a musty institutional taste, and he set it down.

"Jonathan?" Her immediately recognizable voice came from behind.

He turned around. "*You did make it!*" Jonathan wrapped his arms around his mother, accidentally catching her sleeve with his diploma, causing it to fall to the grass at their feet.

"Don't do that, honey," she laughed. "You worked too hard for it!"

Sands reached down to pick up the rolled certificate. "I thought for sure you weren't here."

"I wouldn't miss this for the world, you know that. You must be ecstatic. Did you hear them cheer for you?"

Sands placed his arm around his mother's shoulder and faced his professor, who immediately noticed the resemblance between the two. She was a slender woman, attractive with deep blue eyes and mid-parted dark-brown hair.

"Professor Hawthorne, this is … my mom." Jonathan stumbled at the proper introduction of one's mother to a professor. "Cheryl Sands."

"Wonderful to meet you, Mrs. Sands. You must be incredibly proud."

"Beyond words."

"I have to say, in my thirty-plus years here I could count on one hand the number of students I've had like him. He could *teach* my courses. On top of everything else, he's one heck of a nice guy."

"You obviously haven't seen him when he first wakes up in the morning," Cheryl Sands said smiling, turning to her son with a wink.

Just then Decker and Susan sauntered up. Their respective parents followed. An elderly gentleman trailed further behind.

"Excuse me, but I wanted to shake the hand of the man of the day," said Decker. His gown was unzipped in the front.

Susan arched up on her toes and gave Jonathan a kiss. "Way to go, Jon." She pulled back with her Polaroid camera and took a shot of Jonathan and Decker with their arms wrapped around each other.

Jonathan turned to Decker's parents in greeting. "Good to see you again, Mr. and Mrs. Moss. I bet you never thought you'd see this day," he quipped.

"Yeah, isn't it something?" replied the elder Moss. "He's been racking up quite a tab since he was a baby." He turned to his son. "You better get to work, my boy. It's payback time."

The trailing elderly gentleman turned out to be Decker's grandfather, Cyrus Schoen. He heartily congratulated Jonathan for his recognition. "You'll do very well for yourself, young man. Hard work got you here, and hard work will take you wherever you want to go."

"So, what about you, Decker?" asked the professor. "Where are you off to?" He had refilled his pipe and was proceeding to light it.

"I'll be working for my grandfather's firm, in Manchester. Ever heard of Schoen Chemicals?"

"Schoen? Of course I have," said Hawthorne. Turning to Decker's grandfather he said: "I'm sorry; I didn't make the connection. So it's all in the family?" The professor turned back to Decker. "But I didn't know you had a science background?"

"I don't. My work will be in their finance department," Decker clarified, "cooking their books, not the potions." They all chuckled.

Professor Hawthorne's attention was diverted then by a group of students and parents who were about to disband. "I hope you folks will excuse me. There are so many to say good-bye to and such little time before they all leave. I wish the three of you my very best." Then the academic looked imploringly at Jonathan. "And you'll be sure to stay in touch, right, Jon?"

"Of course," replied Sands.

They shook hands again, and, as Hawthorne walked off, Decker turned to Jonathan and his mother. "So, what are you two doing for dinner? We have reservations at the Dog Team Tavern and thought maybe you'd like to join us."

"Well, thank you very much, that's very nice." Jonathan turned to his mother, but her furtive expression depicted a desire to decline. He turned back to his roommate. "Unfortunately, Mom has to get back to be with my grandfather."

"And pick up some last things at Jonathan's apartment before I go," she added.

Moss senior played it with a diplomatic smile. "Of course. Well, we just didn't want our *summa cum laude* to get off without celebrating a little." He turned to Jonathan with a smile. "After tonight, you'll find it's all downhill."

The proverbial adage that college offered life's best.

Sands feared if it were the truth.

Chapter Ten

DECKER had obviously graduated, and while certainly not with honors, he did so respectably enough through the success of his exam-pilfering scheme. It had gone without a hitch for the most part, employed for their fall semester final exams, and then for several exams in their last semester. Owing to his small size, Peter Roy was the one sent up over the ceiling tiles to gain access to the professors' offices. Decker's GPA went up a full point, pushing his overall average to a B-minus—acceptable enough for his grandfather to offer him a position at Schoen Chemicals. Carl Catman Johnson's went up three quarters of a point, Matt Schulman's a half point, and Peter Roy's only marginally. Apparently, even with the benefit of knowing an exam's contents beforehand, Roy's memory failed him under pressure.

Things eventually cooled down between Jonathan and Johnson, mostly at Jonathan's insistent apology. He blamed it on the stress of the evening of interrogation about Karen's disappearance by the FBI agent. But nothing changed one iota between him and Peter Roy. Their mutual hatred was a bitter poison without antidote—which neither would be inclined to partake even if it existed—and both clearly avoided being in Decker's circle of common company thereafter.

Karen, of course, was never found. The Vermont State Police search was extensive, covering the entire wooded area surrounding the quarry road, and divers searched and dragged the quarry for days. Fingerprint dusting of the car yielded nothing of significance. The hair samples Fitch took from Jonathan and Decker's bathroom yielded a match in Karen's apartment only for Decker's blond hair. No match for Jonathan's they could find. News of the disappearance played in the media for weeks. But the kidnapping angle never materialized.

In the end, Fitch focused on Jonathan as a suspect, momentum increasing slightly with his discovery of Jonathan's prior record for misdemeanor assault and battery. But the evidence and motive were simply altogether lacking. The cups showed no fingerprints, consistent with Karen having washed them out beforehand in the sink; the congealed vomit from the car door showed significant, albeit trace amounts of alcohol, but there was no way to identify its source; and the carpet impressions, if they were ever clear at all, showed no definable prints by the time they were examined by an expert. Without evidence and a motive, to say nothing of a body, there was no place further for Fitch to go. The investigation eventually turned cold, relegating Karen Wyman's disappearance to the unsolved missing person's list. She was, however, presumed dead.

* * *

Following their celebration dinner at the restaurant, the Cabots went to Susan's apartment and the Mosses dropped Decker off at his. After filling their car with what they could of Decker's remaining things and saying their good-byes, his parents left for their return trip to New York.

The power company had shut off the electricity to the upstairs apartment that afternoon. Jonathan and Decker worked into the early evening to complete their last bit of cleaning and packing. The latter was minimal as they had arranged for their larger belongings and inessential items to be moved out earlier in the week.

The day's heat actually worsened into the night, and without a fan the two were now dripping wet. When it became too dark to do any more, they headed downstairs to convey their final farewells to their landlord, Martin Freedman. The emeritus professor had returned from his winter hiatus in Florida to summer in Vermont.

His vestibule door was propped open by a kitchen trashcan.

"If it isn't my all-time favorite student tenants," greeted the landlord as he welcomed them at the doorway. He moved the trashcan out of the way for their entrance. "Black fly season isn't here yet so I like to keep the door open for a cross-breeze. You come to hate those constant air conditioners down in Florida. Come on in." He was a frail old man, blind in one eye and losing vision in the other. The two genuinely liked him. Although he had returned earlier in the month, they hadn't yet taken the opportunity to visit with him.

"Usually when I return it's a big question what I'll find. Of course, now with my macular degeneration, I can't see much anyway," he chuckled. "But Ricker's been feeding me good reports." Bob Ricker was the 'meddlesome neighbor' who kept an occasional watchful eye on the place in Freedman's absence.

"So, you like the paint job on the outside trim?" asked Jonathan.

"From what I can see and what Ricker tells me, it's a fine job. You and Decker have been good men."

"Our pleasure," said Decker.

Jonathan glanced over at his roommate, hiding his irritation since it was entirely Jonathan's work. Decker didn't do a bit of the painting.

Freedman made iced tea and they sat together in his living room. "I take it your studies went well, seeing how you've both graduated. Congratulations."

"Thanks. It's been a long year," said Moss. "Now we can get on with our lives. Onward and upward," he said, lifting his glass.

Jonathan drew a sip of his iced tea and rolled the cool glass across his forehead. "You're looking good, Professor. Still enjoying your swimming?"

"Oh, still enjoying the swimming, though the ladies down there seem to like to keep the condominium's pool water at bathtub temperature. I guess it goes with the territory in St. Pete. I have to say it would be a much cheerier place if it weren't for the sirens in the night. More of my friends pass on every year."

"That's very sad," said Decker. He pulled an ice cube from his glass and chomped it down. "I guess you've probably heard we had our own loss this year."

Jonathan was surprised Decker would bring it up.

"You mean that missing girl?" Freedman asked. "Nothing like that has happened around here in my memory. Did either of you know her?"

"Yes, we both did," Decker replied with a nod. "Actually, she was my girlfriend's roommate."

"*No!* How terrible!"

"They share—or shared—an apartment over on Spring Street," said Moss.

Freedman set down his glass. "I'm so sorry. It must have been unbelievably tough on you both. On all of you."

"Very. Karen had everything going for her. And she was very pretty as well." Decker looked over at Jonathan and his words trailed in pitch. "But I suppose I shouldn't speak of her in the past tense. There's always hope I guess."

"Yes, I suppose there is," said the man. "Such a sad thing."

OPTIONS

The three of them sat in silence for a few moments. Freedman eventually changed the subject. "So where are you two heading from here?"

The two filled him in on their respective plans, and generally made small talk for another half hour. When the landlord drained the last of his iced tea and withdrew his pocket watch, the young tenants took the cue that it was time to say their good-byes. Before leaving they shared their new addresses and assured him they'd visit whenever they returned to Middlebury.

"Go with good hope, young men," he said to them as they exited up the vestibule stairway.

* * *

At a quarter to ten, Decker returned back to the dark apartment with a cold six-pack of beer and a bag of chips. He wanted to commemorate their last night in the apartment together. A lone candle on the coffee table cast a dim glow across the room. The two sat on the living room couch. The hot evening filled their salty shirts.

"Well, it's been a long haul, my friend," declared Decker, raising his bottle to Jonathan's paper cup of water. "And life in all its fullness stands before us. As the man said in his speech today, we have to live for the moment. Cheers."

Jonathan returned the toast. Setting his cup down, he asked: "Will you be able to give me a ride over to the bus stop before you leave tomorrow?" Jonathan's mother had to get back to her failing father, and a bus ride was the only workable arrangement.

"Sure thing, Sandman. And my taxi rates are lower than market price."

"Such a nice guy." Jonathan leaned back into the couch with a smirk on his face.

For Decker there was an unspoken sadness to the moment. He would be leaving the comfort of their friendship, a friendship that had soured from events and which could probably never be repaired to its previous state. Both had changed as a result. But among men, feelings didn't have to be spoken. Instead, Decker downed his beers and reminisced about their times together, the crazy first year in the dorm, the classes they shared, their rock climbing and skiing excursions, and the mutual ribbing they inflicted on each other.

101

Jonathan forced himself to give their last evening some of its older conversation. "So, what's going to happen with Sue?" he asked. "Are you two going to stick it out?"

"Sort of, but we decided it was okay to start seeing other people. Albany's a couple hours from where I live, so I should be able to see her some this summer. But when I start work in New Hampshire, I don't think it'll be worth holding together."

"Any chance of getting married?"

"*Married!* My God, Sands, I'm only twenty-two!"

"She's a spunky girl. She'll be able to keep you in line." Jonathan reconsidered. Susan hadn't been able to tow Decker's line yet. It would be a rare woman who could do that.

A barely perceptible breeze drifted through the open window, puffing at the candle whose shank held only another inch or so of light. The faint sound of peepers could be heard outside in the distance. The hour was late and they were both tired from the fullness of the day.

Just as Jonathan was about to get up and declare an end to the evening, Decker's voice turned somber. "Jon, I have to tell you something ... before we leave tomorrow."

"What's that?"

Moss stood up and walked across the room. "I'm not sure how to say it." His words were slow and low, almost like a confessor's prayer. "It's not that easy."

Sands waited for him to continue, but he didn't. "What is it? You can tell me."

The silhouette of Decker's broad build paced slowly across the backdrop of the wan candlelight. He stopped and looked out the window over the driveway that ran along the side of the house. "You know what an option is, right?"

"Yes, of course," Jonathan replied.

"You buy an option, and then depending on which way things go, up or down, you can either exercise it or let it expire. A hedge."

"Yes, I know how they work. What're you getting at?"

"Well, let me just say that a while back, I had to take out an option," said Decker, selecting his words carefully. "To cover myself in case our friendship, you know ... in case it didn't hold up."

A shiver ran down Jonathan's spine. "Decker, just tell me what the hell you're talking about?"

OPTIONS

Moss turned around and looked over at his roommate. "The night we did what we did. I didn't know if you were going to stay with me or not, you know? And I had to have some insurance that you wouldn't go off and accuse me of what happened. If you, if down the road ... things really changed between us."

"*Dammit, Decker!*" Jonathan exclaimed. "*Tell me what you're getting at!*"

Moss pulled in a long breath. "It's your Saint Christopher medal, Jon. The engraved one you asked me about after I switched our rooms the next day." He looked at Jonathan's profile in the soft flickering candlelight, trying to gauge his response. Unable to do so, he finished what he had to say.

"The reason you couldn't find it is because I placed it in Karen's hand."

PART II
THE TAKEOVER
(1992)

Chapter Eleven

Saturday, July 18, 1992
Camden, South Carolina

FORTUNATELY, the night was tar black. If there were another soul around the persistent tapping of his rubber mallet might be heard. An observer would have to be fairly close, however, since the wind and drizzle did a lot to drown out the noise. But there was no other soul around, of that he was certain. Miles from any clusters of civilization the farm field sat very much by itself on the farthest stretches of town, accessible only by a private dirt road. The added shroud of the murky weather was, in fact, a bonus Elwood Darby hadn't counted on. And he was glad for it. That is, except for the fact that it was a constant assault on his cigarette.

Presently he relit the soggy fixture in his mouth and inhaled the smoldering stub. Small matter that there was little tobacco to take the light. The craggy-faced, stoop-shouldered man was known for taking his butts down to the filter and beyond. As long as it produced smoke, that was all he cared about. And the harsher, the better.

Off a ways, about seventy-five yards closer to the access road, was a seven-acre parcel of field that was cordoned off and secured by a chain link fence. It was the location of Elwood Darby's "day job." Once farmland, it was now called a Superfund waste site, something he had only marginal understanding of. Apparently, back in the 60s and 70s, the farmer engaged in a bit of shady work of his own, burying companies' chemical wastes. When a real estate developer purchased the property and discovered the buried drums while doing site work for a new housing project, the EPA was called in. Being a local excavator who worked cheap, Darby was hired to do the grunt work, exhuming the buried containers.

Muck now caked to his boots with the density of concrete as he schlepped through the soupy trench. He had been at it all night. He sucked deeply in vain on his dead cigarette and threw it to the ground. He wiped his forehead with a drenched flannel sleeve. Only five more lids to go and he would be finished.

Most of the drums—just over a hundred of them—were quite empty, their chemical contents having seeped through the rusted metal long ago. The new lids were Darby's creation. When shown proudly to his anonymous contact, they passed inspection with flying colors. The go-ahead was given and he pocketed the fastest five grand he had ever earned. Another ten would be his soon enough.

It was two months earlier, while moving earth for fill-dirt with his heavy equipment, that he came upon this unexpected discovery. He was able to make out the name on the rusted lids—Columbia Chemicals—the same name as that on dozens of others he had unearthed at the main site. Smelling an opportunity, he covered them up again.

"C'nnect me to the top man," Darby said with a nasal twang. He was speaking into the 7-Eleven payphone he tripped to during his lunch hour. "I got information 'bout that Sup'fund site he'd be int'rested knowin'." The "top man" was at lunch, the Columbia Chemicals receptionist informed him. She took Darby's name and home phone number.

It was some time into the bottle later that evening when he got his return call.

"You've done well to contact us, Mr. Darby. We'll see to it you're rewarded for that. A representative of ours will be in touch with you soon." The unidentified caller on the other end told him to keep his information strictly confidential.

Over the ensuing two-month period the representative met with the excavator several times to arrange the details for Darby's "moonlighting job."

His six-volt lantern was now on its third battery and dying again, struggling to cast even faint light across the freshly dug pit. It was the depth of a grave. He had dug it out the previous day with his backhoe, thankful the EPA supervisor didn't make one of his unannounced site inspections. The man had never done so on a Friday in the past and fortunately held to custom this particular week.

After firming down the final lid, Darby walked the two rows of retrofitted drums and admired his labor with the dull lantern, chuckling proudly to himself in the dark. They were truly a work of art, he thought. The representative had provided the supply of old lids and Darby stenciled on them a new name at his home shop. Then he replicated the look of subterranean aging using various strengths of sandblasting and saline dunking solution. Even under the closest scrutiny the distressed look of his finished product gave them a genuinely mottled, earth-worn appearance. The new company insignia was made to look old, and the subtle patchiness of simulated wear and rust rendered the name difficult to make out. Fortunately, the flange rings had all rotted of strength and didn't need replacement. That could have easily doubled his work time.

Darby strained uncomfortably as he climbed out of the muddy trench. His injury from a tractor accident a decade earlier acted up in the rain; the limp was something he always carried with him. Rounding up the old lids that lined the perimeter of the trench, he stacked them into the back of his pickup. Then, taking a final look around to make sure he hadn't forgotten anything, he got into his truck and idled off the field for the access road.

A red sun nudged the horizon. Monday morning he would call the EPA supervisor to report his 'find.'

* * *

Friday, July 24, 1992

The man veered his car off the country gravel road and into the cover of a stand of fir trees. Grabbing the attaché case and bagged bottle of Jack Daniels that sat on the seat beside him, he got out and headed to the lone decrepit trailer up some distance on the right.

Darby's dog howled with the shrill sound of lunacy.

It was pretty country, but even in the twilight the excavator's place was a repugnant affair, thought the man. In the front yard were two wrecks on blocks: a Chevy Nova and another he couldn't make out—both aborted of their engines and rusting in tall weeded overgrowth. The single pathetic attempt at landscaping was a plastic flamingo, impaled by a thin metal rod and stuck bent into the ground. The threadbare dog was chained to the house and looked as ugly as roadkill. A thousand miles had been worn out of the yard by its lousy existence, filled with clawed holes and piles of smelly turds.

"Shut yer trap, you fuggin' an'mal!" yelled the homeowner at his pet as he greeted the bearded visitor at the doorway. A cigarette bobbed up and down on Darby's lips, glued there by pasty saliva. His breath reeked of liquor.

The man noted that the stench of the place was no better inside than out. Although no cat was apparent it smelled like there were a thousand. Dirty dishes and rank food scraps cluttered the counter and sink area. He set the attaché case and brown bag on the wobbly kitchen table, one of whose legs was broken and wound slapdash with duct tape.

"Perty hoochin' holler, fine stiff'n shine," declared Darby with a chuckle, pulling the bottle from the bag.

Elwood Darby always chuckled when he talked. The representative hated that. He hated it when people chuckled when there was nothing to chuckle about. Or hummed or whistled all the time, especially the 'random-noters,' those who had no tune but chirped out notes on the fly like some dumb bird. "I thought I'd bring you a celebration gift," the man said politely in his guttural voice.

"Well ain't ya nice to do that. Have a seat, Mister Rep'sentive."

The man did so, though he hoped he would be able to make it a short stay. Darby limped to the counter, took two cloudy glasses from the stack of filthy ware there and ran them under the faucet.

"Oh, no thanks. But help yourself."

"Not a drinkin' man? Wazzat? Missin' out da best pert a life." Darby returned to the table and sat down with his guest. "So, ya got ma r'ward?"

"Right there in the case, Mr. Darby." The representative undid the latches and opened it. "Want to count it?"

"Naw … jes' wanna lookit it." The rheumy-eyed man turned the briefcase around and shoved it to the edge of the table so he could view his bounty. In it were neatly bundled stacks of well-worn twenties. He poured himself a tall glass of the bourbon, raised it to his guest in toast, and downed a generous gulp. "Not oft' I get to drinkin' Jackie Dee."

"Our way of saying thanks, Mr. Darby."

Darby kept chuckling, which caused his cigarette butt to dance precariously on the cusp of his lips. The representative knew he was already hammered, and no amount of further drinking would likely make him farther gone. Liver-weathered boozers like him could put it away all night long and then just simply fall asleep.

Looking around the place, trying to breathe through his mouth so as not to accost his olfactory senses, the visitor considered any family Darby might have had at one time was understandably absent. There were no pictures, and the only thing he saw evidencing any social connection whatsoever was a bowling trophy on a dusty cabinet in the corner. He got up and went over to it.

"You a bowler, Mr. Darby?"

"Used t' be. Got hurt in a tract'r accident years back. Ain't done none since."

"That's a shame. Good at it?"

"One-ninety a game," boasted the excavator with a sloppy smile.

"That's pretty damn good. I bet you get kind of lonely out here by yourself. You told me you're not married?"

"Lef' years ago. Bitch 'a woman. Rather be by m'self and m'dog." Darby downed his drink with the ease of Kool-Aid, and then poured himself a refill. He raised his glass. "Sure ya don' want some?"

"No thanks. Enjoy the gift." The representative walked over to the kitchen counter, to Darby's behind, and fixed a look out the window above the sink. He was able to make out the Quonset shed Darby used as a workshop. Heavy equipment littered the backyard. Peering over his shoulder at his host, he extracted a pair of thin leather gloves. "So, no family at all?"

"Jes' m' brother, Murray. Ain't seen 'im in months. Lives way 'cross town."

The representative wondered how visiting one on the other side of Camden could be a time-consuming task. He returned his gaze to the window and changed the subject. "You did a good job on those lids I gave you. Disposed of the old ones like we agreed?"

"Buried 'em out back and cov'ed the spot with an old car wreck. By God, iffa man was meant t' work at night he'd been born with headlights 'stead of eyes."

"Neighbors?"

"You see any houses aroun'? No fuggin' neighbors 'roun here. Could dance ass-naked out in the yard if I had the mind."

His back still to Darby's behind, the man pulled a .38 revolver from his jacket pocket. "I bet you have some nice plans for that money, don't you, Mr. Darby."

"Sure do," he chuckled. "Buy m'self a nice woman for one thing. Do some travelin'." He turned around. "Ain't never done no travlin' befo—"

In a single movement the representative pivoted, drew the pistol to the right side of Darby's skull and fired. The excavator fell heavy to the floor, taking his glass and the rickety table with him.

The head of Drexel-Pace security placed the gun in Darby's right hand and gathered the attaché case and paper bag from the floor. In a moment he was out the door.

The mangy dog howled.

Chapter Twelve

THE early morning rush hour had been brutal.

Again.

How the term "rush hour" ever came to be associated with the slowest traffic of the day eluded Decker Moss entirely. Not that the size of the city merited it. Population only a hundred thousand in the city proper, Manchester, New Hampshire's metro area was nonetheless one of the fastest growing in New England, metastasizing like a cancerous tumor from Boston's feed to the south. A few token high rises poked above the midtown section, with manufacturing represented by an increasing number of commercial and consumer product firms along the city's outskirts.

C. Decker Moss occupied the chief executive suite of Schoen Chemicals Corporation, located in an industrial park just south of the city. Its new four-story headquarters complex was constructed in a handsome black marble motif and laid out on a gently sloping lawn that overlooked the Merrimack River. Although he had always envisioned himself in a grander city, Decker's work was here, and here, thus, was his home. He made the best of it.

A sour mood was typical for Monday morning. Weekend withdrawal, hellish traffic and a new week's set of problems customarily brought it on. This particular Monday morning, however, he hoped would be different.

The phone call he was expecting came before his executive seat was warm. Answering it, Moss got no reply but white noise. Another few minutes passed and the incident was repeated, this time with dial tone. Irritated, he rang his secretary.

"What's going on, Jean?"

"Sorry, Decker, it didn't transfer." She was sure she had followed the protocol that was printed on the quick sheet of instructions given her by the telecom outfit hired to install the company's new phone system. "They were up here a few minutes ago to warn me about some switching problems they were having

113

over the weekend. The bugs should be worked out by the end of the day." She stammered. "At least that's what they said."

"And they think that's acceptable? Thousands for this tin-cans-on-a-string crap? If you see them again tell them if they can't get it working properly by noon I want our old system back, and I'm not shelling out a dime." Decker forced composure. "Who was it that called?"

"Larry Carpenter, of Drexel-Pace in Atlanta. I wrote down his name but I didn't get his number."

"Well if he calls again, get his number and I'll call him back if I have to. I sure can't afford this. Not with him." Moss replaced the handset with a curse.

The originator of the call, Larry Carpenter, was CEO and Chairman of the board of Drexel-Pace Pharmaceuticals. He had tried the previous Friday but Decker was out of town. The recorded message on Decker's voice-mail was brief yet poignant: Drexel-Pace was interested in a possible merger deal and Carpenter wanted to discuss a "win-win situation," in his words. He would call back Monday morning.

As head of Schoen Chemicals for two years now, Decker Moss was accustomed to the occasional call from a corporate suitor. But most of those queries never got out of the block for lack of fit. And of the few that held promise, ensuing negotiations broke down for lack of an attractive offer price or favorable board sentiment. Lamentably, Decker's board tended to be overly provincial, holding stiffly conservative on the issue of business combinations. This was despite his repeated attempts to convince them of the benefits of diversification, particularly in the increasingly competitive chemicals industry. Drexel-Pace could very well turn out to be different, Decker hoped. It was a marquee pharmaceutical giant whose revenues ranked it in the Fortune 100. Already a major customer of Schoen's chemical products, it also happened to hold nearly five percent of Schoen's stock.

Moss had become the epitome of the good-old-boy version of American enterprise—a maverick product of nepotism. Following his unremarkable record at Middlebury College he took a position in the finance department of Schoen Chemicals. It was a privately-held company at the time, owned by his grandfather, supplying the chemical needs of a fast-growing ledger of manufacturing clients along the east coast. Raised rich didn't mean one would stay that way, as Moss soon discovered, and he became a fervent worker as a result. With one part savvy and one part smarts—the latter a gene endowment he hadn't the time nor inclination to exploit during his college years—he was rewarded the position of departmental manager of finance in four years.

He learned well the rules of the game insofar as financial performance was concerned: cost control and research productivity. If bringing new chemicals to market ensured viability of the industry, then biochemical research was going to be its life-blood. And the business aspects of this he studied with the hunger of a starving graduate student. He hit a home run with his suggested improvements in research productivity by employing a team approach to innovation. Scientists, he quickly learned, basically lived in their own world. The problem was that one side of the research house had little knowledge of what the other side was doing. His idea was to formalize weekly brainstorm sessions. Scientists maintained their creative independence but also found that the information flow provided by the sessions increased their research output. He was promoted to chief financial officer in the space of only eight years with the company.

Largely through his ability to convince his grandfather of the need to grow its specialty chemicals business, the firm was taken public. Sizeable investments in research and development were made possible by the influx of new shareholder capital. Pharmaceutical raw materials—'intermediates' as they were known in the industry—became the company's focus. A majority of this business was to drug firms whose research and manufacturing requirements involved critical processes, skills, and special technologies to produce. Biochemicals fast became the emphasis of Schoen's research efforts and resulted in an impressive pipeline of proprietary know-how. The patented technologies made it possible to produce synthetic amino acids, phospholipids and peptides from readily available and inexpensive ingredients. All at monopoly scale profits. The firm reported impressive bottom line growth and Schoen's shareholders were happy.

When Cyrus P. Schoen, Decker's grandfather, stepped down for retirement two years earlier, Moss was voted President and CEO. The old man retained his place as board Chairman, but Decker considered it little more than a titular role. Schoen appeared to greet retirement with the same unwavering commitment he gave to his work, seldom involving himself in the operating affairs of the company. Thus, at the impressive age of only 36, C. Decker Moss sat firmly at the helm of a highly profitable, publicly-traded corporation that was on a fast clip upward.

The phone rang again. "Larry Carpenter's on the line."

"Thanks, Jean, put him through." Thankfully, Decker heard the sound of a successful connection. "Yes, Larry, glad you finally got through. I have to apologize. We're going through a telecom upgrade here that unfortunately hasn't made the grade yet."

"Sorry to hear that, Decker." Larry Carpenter's southern accent was jovial. "We've certainly gone through our own share of snafus down here with these so-called cutting edge advancements. I've often thought the term 'telephony' says it all."

"That and more I'm afraid," returned Moss with a low laugh. "So, how may I help you?"

"Well, it's no secret we like what you're about. Schoen's put on a class act the last several years, no doubt largely due to your young talent."

"Thank you." Decker leaned back in his chair. "I like to think we're doing things right. It's a fast-changing business, of course." He knew he was speaking with a man significantly his senior in the corporate food chain, yet he spoke with ease.

"Sure is. In fact that's some of what I was hoping to talk to you about. Do you think we might be able to get together?"

Decker paused, fingering the coiled cord. "That should be possible, although it may help if I were to hear a bit more of what you have in mind."

"Yes, yes, of course," concurred Carpenter. "As I said, we like what you're about, clearly on the face of things. We thought there might be a good fit between Schoen and Drexel-Pace. Without getting into details at this time I can say we're becoming increasingly concerned about some of our supplier relationships. The bottom line is we desire a tighter partnership with a chemical firm that has synergies with ours. Our research thus far suggests Schoen's a good candidate. Our top candidate."

"Well, we're very appreciative of the business you've given us."

"Likewise." Carpenter's voice trailed a moment before resuming. "Do you play golf?"

"Love to, although I don't get out as much as I'd like." It was a stereotypical aspect of business Decker Moss found to be true; a great deal of it was indeed conducted on the golf course.

OPTIONS

Carpenter finessed: "I'm a hacker myself, which is embarrassing given the years I've spent playing the game. Tell you what, I have a place in Hilton Head and we can play a round or two. You can meet some of my management team."

"Sounds like fun." Decker quickly scanned his desk calendar. "Unfortunately, I'm pretty full this week."

"Understood." Larry Carpenter didn't want to sound too anxious, but time wasted was opportunity's threat. He gently pushed: "How about a weekend trip?"

Decker considered the question. One of the benefits of being single was flexibility. "Saturday should work I guess. Given the distance with layovers I'd probably have to make it an overnight stay."

"No problem," agreed Carpenter. "I'll make the arrangements here and have the tickets couriered up to your office."

With details suggested and niceties shared, they said their salutations and rang off.

Decker smiled at the phone that just minutes earlier he had cursed.

Chapter Thirteen

THE golf course was the nicest on the island, among the nicest on the East coast, with fairways meandering through thick woods of oak and pine, and beautifully sculpted greens carved out onto protruding oceanfront peninsulas. A quiescent surf moved and shimmered from the bright cerulean sky.

"You might as well use a low-powered cannon, Larry," said Moss wryly. "A small Howitzer would do the job, I think."

Larry Carpenter was using an oversized driver. Decker Moss hated anyone's use of an oversized driver. He also objected to oversized tennis rackets, heavy pound-test fishing line and seven-foot basketball players for the same reason. They all cheapened the challenge of sport.

"Too noisy, Decker," retorted the Drexel-Pace CEO. "It would disturb the wildlife. This is the next best thing."

The broken breeze played with Carpenter's wisps of gray hair as he lifted his golf cap to study the down-angle of the fairway. Deep facial lines and not a modicum of male-pattern baldness evinced the man's sixty-three years, though his flushed cheeks showed the healthiness of a child coming out from the winter's cold. His lithe frame currently sported a blue sleeveless mohair sweater draped over a yellow Polo golf shirt. Clearly a well-appointed man, thought Decker.

Carpenter carefully addressed his ball. Winding back slowly, his abrupt swing went rotten in a half-arced disaster, yet sent his ball sailing straight down the fairway, a good 200 yards. Picking up the snapped tee with a wink he moved to the side. "I'll take that. Have at it, Joe."

Joe Moran was next up. He was Carpenter's chief financial officer. A red-haired man of gargantuan waist proportions, he was already showing signs of a sweat despite it being only the second tee. The guy actually won the first hole, scoring a par, which Moss thought had to be a fluke. The man's grunts and panting gave concern to Decker he might suffer a cardiac on the back nine. Fortunately, they were driving golf carts.

Wack! The wood connected squarely, heaving the ball all of 250 yards dead on.

Decker swallowed his frustration. "Great shot, Joe." He motioned his club at the men. "So, tell me guys, is this your idea of how to schmooze me?"

They laughed.

"You're up, Deck. Want to try my driver?" asked Carpenter, holding his Big Bertha by its shank.

"No thanks, Larry. I'm a diehard purist." Sporting a grin, Moss teed his ball, went through a trial stroke and then corked it, hooking the shot 175 yards into the rough.

"*Damn.*"

"That's okay," consoled Joe. "I packed a gas trimmer in my golf bag."

Moss shared in their mirthful laughter and looked around. "Thanks, but it might take a chainsaw. Things look to grow pretty healthy down here. Any snakes around?"

"Some nice ones," answered Kent Shaughnessy, who rounded out the foursome. "Watch your head though. The cottonmouths like to hide in the Spanish moss that dangles down from the trees."

"Thanks for telling me." Decker firmed down the brim of his cap.

Shaughnessy towered over the rest of them at a statuesque six-foot-three. In his early forties, he had a full cropping of prematurely graying hair, deep-set eyes and an aristocratic Roman nose. His position in the Drexel-Pace chain of command was chief operating officer and President of the company. His drive was strong and respectable, a couple hundred yards, but slightly to the right.

Moss liked these guys. He enjoyed men who could cut up with each other. For the most part their conversation on the course focused on the game, the ongoing '92 presidential bid between Clinton and Bush, and general small talk. Fortunately, Decker's game began to kick in after the second hole.

It wasn't until the sixth fairway, however, when driving the golf cart, Larry Carpenter cut to subject: "I can tell you'd fit right in, Deck. You're a good sport."

"Three shots behind you, Larry. Not much of a sport today, I'm afraid."

"No, but I'll erase some of those hash marks if you like," Carpenter quipped, pointing at the scorecard clipped to the center of the steering wheel. "That is, provided you take a good word about us to your board." An obligatory chuckle by both was quickly followed by the elder man's more intent regard. "Seriously, though, have you given any thought to our interest?"

"Some," answered Decker. "It might make for a nice play, but I would certainly have to know more to assess the idea. You'd have to make it compelling."

"Oh, we'll certainly do that." Carpenter stared off at an egret poking around for lunch in the marsh along the paved cart path and explained: "As I hinted on the phone, Drexel-Pace wants a lock on our raw materials requirements, our drug intermediates. We don't care much about your generic stuff. It's your specialty chemicals production we're interested in. You're enjoying a nice little game of Monopoly up there. More and more of our prescription products are dependent on the type of processing technology you have. And very promising new drugs are coming down the pipeline all the time. Your patent portfolio is strong, the strongest and best-fitting of any of the candidates we've looked into. Our idea is that we can combine your knowledge assets with ours and be the top force in the market."

Larry set the floor-brake where Decker's ball landed and the two dismounted from the cart. Moss pulled a nine-iron from his golf bag, sighted and swung, lofting his ball over a facing hillock to the edge of the green closest to the pin.

"Nice shot." Larry's ball required him to reverse course about twenty yards. His customary half-arced swing produced acceptable distance but set his ball in a bunker to the left of the green. He mouthed a silent curse as he strode back. "Talking business, especially when I'm excited about the topic, can get my focus off the game." They re-mounted the cart and motored off towards the hole.

"Anyway," Carpenter resumed, "where possible we've diversified our supply sources. But very few chemical suppliers exist for the type of exotic ingredients required in many of our products. It takes a lot of time working with a supplier to get the specifications right for an increasingly sophisticated set of raw materials. And then once you do, you're pretty well dependent on them. In many cases a single supplier is all there is."

OPTIONS

"Just so I'm clear, you're talking about the whole shop. You're not just interested in purchasing our specialty chemicals unit or licensing our patents?"

"No," replied Carpenter quickly. "We considered all that, of course, but it doesn't give us what we need in the long run. Besides, licensing agreements, I've come to learn, are always rife with holes."

Larry Carpenter steered the cart to the side of the green where the other two members of their party were waiting. Just out of their earshot Decker took the opportunity to clarify further: "Your hope, then, is to boost your ownership in Schoen to a holding large enough to gain control? What's your target?"

The Drexel-Pace CEO stopped and looked at his companion with curiosity, as if surprised by the question. Then he said squarely: "All of it, Decker. We want *all* of it."

* * *

Wrenching all or most of Schoen's shares out of the market would require a hefty premium over the current stock price, Decker knew. Otherwise Schoen's board wouldn't be willing to approve it and the shareholders wouldn't be willing to let it go. How much would the offer have to be over current price? Thirty percent? Forty percent? He thought of the implications on the value of his stock options. They would be worth a small fortune.

His spirits buoyed by Carpenter's comments, Decker's game took flight. He shot par on ten holes, birdied two, bogied three, and double-bogied two. His only triple-bogey occurred on the fourteenth hole, a singularly bizarre event. A three-iron shot off the fairway sailed into a reed marsh to the left of the green. From a survey of the scene up close, the four of them looked down in amused astonishment.

"What are the odds of that?" Decker asked, kneeling down at the lip of the marsh where his ball landed.

"Is it dead?" asked Larry.

"I'd say quite. Looks like I hit it in the head." An egret, which fell victim to Decker's ball, lay disheveled, its legs locked upright in the water and its neck forced into the muck of the bank from the ball. It looked very much like a tripod.

"I'd say that qualifies for a mulligan," bellowed Moran with a full gut of laughter. "That's got to be the craziest luck I've ever seen."

Moss stood up from his kneeling position with a grin. "I wonder what these things taste like."

"Probably like chicken," speculated Carpenter, "like everything else other than beef and fish."

"Great. Southern-fried egret. What do you say, guys?" asked Moss jokingly.

Roundly rejecting Decker's suggestion to cook the fowl for dinner, the men took irons and hastily scratched a furrow in the bank of the spongy marsh to inter the bird.

"A gator will get it," said the Drexel-Pace Chairman as they walked away.

* * *

Larry Carpenter's spread in the Sea Pines Resort was exquisite and modern. It was also a generous corporate tax write-off. Too tired for another outing, the men opted to cook Porterhouse steaks on the grill. Portabella mushrooms, potatoes, garlic, onion, and a prodigious amount of beer were also carried into the sea-side villa.

A salty breeze mixed in the air with the smoke of the sizzling steaks. They stood around a massive, custom-designed, charcoal-grill on the back terrace that looked out over the Atlantic.

"So what's your secret, Joe? You sure pack a wallop." Decker gestured with his bottle of Heineken over to Moran, who won the day's round with a four over par. Decker's score placed him second in the low eighties, notwithstanding his triple bogey.

"It's really pretty scientific," replied the red-haired fat man. "I just pretend the ball is Clinton and I blow it away."

The reference drew a laugh from the others. It was no secret what Bill Clinton intended to do to the drug industry if he were to win the election. His pledge for health-care reform and restraints on drug price increases had sent stock prices in the sector on a nervous pitch for months. Price controls, they feared, would put an end to the profits that made the U.S. the key innovator and supplier of drug products in the world.

Attending to the barbecue, Carpenter called off in Moss's direction: "How do you like your meat, my friend?" The olive oil he was making a point of pouring over the steaks was causing a genuine conflagration.

"Well, Larry, if you intend to burn those much longer, I'm heading back to the course to grab that bird."

"In that case it's dinner time."

OPTIONS

They took turns pulling their cuts of meat off the gridiron. Joe Moran forked two steaks onto his plate, placing one on top of the other. Decker pointed at the curious stack as they strolled over to the teakwood patio table. "I've never seen anyone dish up steak like that, Joe."

"I'm twice your size so I thought I'd make it a 'Double-Decker'!" Moran laughed and then made like a whisper. "Besides, it's all on Larry. I like to make sure he takes a loss on me."

With their company now together at the patio table, Carpenter suggested: "Why don't you fill Mr. Moss in on some of the details, gentlemen? I shared our general idea with him on the course but I'm sure he'd be interested in more specifics."

Dutifully, Moran and Shaughnessy looked at each other, and, with a beckoned nod, Kent went first. "Decker, these are interesting times in our business, as you're well aware. Things are extremely competitive and it's the first mover who's going to have the advantage. With the fear of government price controls the survivors are going to be the ones who have strategically placed themselves on the supply and distribution ends, with aggressive cost management in between. Larry gave you our general take on how you, Schoen as a supplier, would fit in. But what may not be obvious to you is this. You have a great deal of technology we can use." Shaughnessy brushed away a mosquito that lighted on his nose and took a swig from his beer. "I'm not a scientist but I'll do my best to explain."

Moss studied Shaughnessy a moment, and then hefted his beer bottle as indication for the President of Drexel-Pace to do so.

"We're a leader in the development of active antibodies for therapeutic applications. These are designed to act through the immune system and potentially offer greater effect with lower toxicity than is typical of existing drugs—for immune system cancers, such as lymphomas and leukemia, and autoimmune diseases, such as multiple sclerosis and rheumatoid arthritis. We have some promising new research in the works that's in initial clinical stages. A big problem that remains for many of our drug candidates, however, is that they still appear to result in too much blood toxicity. Much too high for FDA approval."

"You sure sound like a scientist to me," observed Moss, who was laconically working his plate, though listening intently.

"Just enough to hold my own. I'm a good parrot." Kent skewered some mushroom and steak onto his fork and mouthed it.

Washing it down with a gulp of beer, he continued. "Your firm holds some key patents on a number of biochemical compounds and processing technologies, many of which are important developments in the field that could be vital to our efforts. One product, for example, you call Threonatrix."

Decker nodded recognition. "It's been receiving quite a bit of attention lately," he responded. "Looks like we'll soon pass muster with the FDA." Threonatrix was a chemically altered vitamin C metabolite, which when added to aspirin, appeared to greatly increase its absorption into body cells. Much smaller doses of aspirin could thus be taken with the same medicinal effect, thereby reducing substantially the gastrointestinal side effects of the drug. The FDA human trial results were uniformly promising.

"Decker, our research suggests the delivery properties of Threonatrix are instrumental in lines far more extensive than just aspirin. We've found that certain modifications of it reduce the toxicities associated with a great number of drugs. Ours as well as others: antibiotics, antihistamines, anti-inflammatories, even vitamins."

Moss slowly set down his fork. "You're kidding."

"Not in the least," said Kent. "Our research has been extensive. We'd like to partner with you in these discoveries."

Surprise held on Moss's face. Thinking it through further he asked: "Why not just seek a licensing agreement with us for Threonatrix? Why are you interested in the whole shop? It would seem a far less risky proposition for you."

Shaughnessy expected the question and was prepared for it. "Frankly, that wouldn't be good enough. It's only a matter of time before others discover what we've found, and there'd be nothing to stop them from entering into similar licensing arrangements with you. As I said, in the competitive state of this industry we need first-mover advantage. FDA approvals can take years, which opens up too much possibility for encroachment on our research. If we soloed the advancements, the regulatory hoops could be jumped through much more easily. There'd be far less confusion all around."

Kent wanted the points to stick, so he paused a moment to look out at the vista. The gentle lapping of the waves gave quiet sequestration to their conversation. The sun had just about expended its light for the day, and with the drop in temperature the breeze had settled to an intermittent stir.

"Besides, it's not just Threonatrix," resumed Kent, "not at all. Tying back to what I said earlier, your biochemical production includes a number of state-of-the-art advancements we feel we can capitalize upon. Your science is top-notch. There's too much to go over tonight, but we feel Schoen's proprietary knowledge and manufacturing methods would integrate very nicely with ours."

Larry Carpenter cleared his throat and interposed with emphasis: "We like what your firm is about, Decker. We've done our research. After all, we've owned a sizeable piece of Schoen since you went public."

Decker mused over the words, yet held back. He wanted to hear the rest.

In the silence that followed the four men put finishing touches on their plates and drained their beers. Joe Moran handily finished his two steaks several minutes before the others finished theirs. The T-bones on his plate were picked clean, like they had been sun dried.

Carpenter gathered his shirt collar and stood up. "Gentlemen, why don't we head inside? Joe can cover more of the specifics of the deal as we see them, which I'm sure our guest would like to hear about."

After clearing the table and grabbing another round of beers from the refrigerator the group came to lounge in the living room. It was comfortably furnished in clove-colored nubuck leather: three large armchairs, matching ottomans and a full-length sofa. A stone fireplace climbed the full height of the cathedral ceiling, which currently burned a low gas fire. Overlaid on the yellow birch wood floors were brightly colored oriental rugs. African wall hangings and figurines of sculpted ebony and mahogany accented the eclectic décor of the room.

Joe Moran, whose sanguine complexion lit up from the glow of the fire, began: "Decker, we'd be talking about a cash transaction. We're sitting on a sizeable amount from the recent spin-off of our hygiene products business to Bentway & Sons. You may have read about it."

Moss hadn't and sat forward in his chair. He didn't want to miss anything. "How would you intend to structure the deal?"

"Ideally?" asked Moran. "An outright purchase—board approvals, stockholder approvals, everything. We've been given the green light from our board and we were hoping to get the same from yours."

Decker thought of the fifteen percent of Schoen's shares held by his grandfather, Cyrus P. Schoen, himself. The old man was still the board Chairman and he still had clout. How much, Decker didn't know, yet it was still a concern. "And in the possibility of my board's opposition?" he asked.

Joe Moran's bulk shifted in his chair. Carpenter interjected: "We hate to think in the negative, Decker. We think our offer will be difficult to turn down. Of course, we can't predict your board's sentiments with certainty either, which is some of why we wanted to meet with you first."

"Cyrus Schoen's identity is pretty tightly wrapped up in the firm, Larry," said Decker. "He's got this funny idea about a loyal shareholder group—'family,' he calls them. And I can't predict my board's sentiments either. The onus would be on you to make your case attractive enough."

"And, as I told you before," Carpenter hastened in reply, "I think we can do that." He was stretched rakishly out on the couch, one leg vaulted over the other. Lifting his beer bottle he squinted at its contents and asked casually: "How does a fifty-percent premium over current market price sound to you?"

Decker controlled a gasp. He didn't have a chance to respond before Kent Shaughnessy chimed in: "I believe your bylaws state a two-thirds vote is needed for a friendly buyout. Isn't that right?"

Moss knew his corporate bylaws were a matter of public record. "Yes, it was a recent change we made. A supermajority of the board."

"So, two-thirds of your eleven directors, eight votes," said Carpenter, not a question.

Decker turned to the elder man and nodded. "That's correct. And I have to tell you they've been a tough nut to crack in the past. We're a young firm—young at least in terms of public ownership—and the board feels strongly about the return potential for our shareholders. I do too, of course, but I've tried to convince them of our need for a more diversified position, to spread our business risks under a larger umbrella."

At this Joe Moran flapped: "Well, for them to turn down a fifty-percent premium bid over current market price would just about amount to a dereliction of fiduciary duty to their shareholders."

"Besides, diversification's only a small part of it," supplemented Carpenter, who wanted Decker to be sold on the more substantive economic reasons for the proposed marriage. "It's a match that's got gold written all over it."

Decker reflected on this over another swig of beer before reverting to an earlier question he had. "Given what you've told me about your strategy against your competition—your desire to get a lock on our patents—have you considered antitrust concerns?"

"Competition?" asked Larry.

"Yes," Decker answered, gesturing to Shaughnessy. "Kent said something about blocking licensing rights from your competitors."

Joe Moran cleared his throat, furtively seeking Larry's approval to take on the question, who in turn nodded his consent. "Well, Decker," said Moran, "it's true that if we held your patents we'd be able to channel them to strategic advantage. But as far as antitrust issues are concerned, we've thought them all through very carefully. We certainly don't believe it will be any problem with the feds. In fact, we're ready to submit our notice at any time."

The Federal Trade Commission and Department of Justice had jurisdiction over whether proposed business combinations would substantially lessen competition. Potential acquirers of another firm had to notify the FTC of their intentions.

"There's no need to advertise our competitive motivations, of course," Moran continued, "since that's only a strategic matter. However, on the face of it, a drug company buying out a chemical firm shouldn't raise any eyebrows. There are too many chemical companies out there, and very few vertical combinations such as this are challenged on antitrust grounds anyway." The rotund CFO chugged his longneck. "The fed review can all take place during our negotiations."

Larry Carpenter raised himself from the sofa. "Gentlemen, I'm about to burst. Don't say too much without me."

"I could use a break myself," said Kent, who also got up.

Carpenter caught Decker's eye. "We have three bathrooms in the place. The powder room's over by the front door. Another bathroom's up the stairs, first door on the left. There's also a master ensuite if you happen to fancy a bidet."

Moss chortled. "Thanks, Larry. I'll keep that in mind."

When the men regrouped, each clutched a fresh bottle from the refrigerator. Joe Moran grabbed an orphaned morsel of portabella mushroom off a plate resting on the counter.

"Any chips, Larry?"

"Should be, Joe. Check the pantry over there in the corner."

Moran returned chomping from a bag of cheese puffs. A frown on his face evidenced displeasure. "These taste like parmesan-sprinkled packing material, Larry. What gives? Every time I come here I can't find a decent after-dinner snack."

Carpenter rolled his eyes. "Sorry, Joe. I'll make a note of it on my to-do list."

Moran sank heavily into his chair. The air in its leather cushions was expunged by his girth like vacuum-packed trail mix. Decker was reclined in his, very much enjoying the warm glow of the beer and the fire and his prospects.

Suddenly affecting a more serious expression, Joe Moran addressed Decker. "I want to cover two more things with you: first, how our proposition would benefit Schoen; and second, how this would benefit you personally, along with your executive management team."

"I was hoping you might get to that. Not that I wouldn't enjoy this little party without it."

The corpulent Moran set his snack bag down in frustration. He wished there were chips and dip. Folding his hands over his mountainous belly, he went on: "Schoen is set apart from its competition. The large chemical firms will continue to do their own thing. Oh, there will be more merger activity, but mostly offshore plays. The small domestic ones will fade away unless they find a niche. You guys, however, stand out there pretty much on your own. You have the best of both worlds: the flexibility of smallness, yet many of the characteristic advantages of larger firms. Your plants are FDA approved, you have the research power to succeed in performance chemicals, and you also have some of the most modern production facilities in the industry. Schoen's profitable generic chemical business wouldn't be affected whatsoever by our proposal. We like all those attributes. A lot. But critically important to you, what you'd get from us is the most valuable asset a specialty chemicals firm like yours could have—information. Our research on new drugs would feed you millions you haven't begun to tap. And no pharmaceutical company has a more extensive behind-the-scenes market research team than we have. We know where our competition's going with their product development efforts. You'd have access to all that." Moran hefted his beer bottle.

Decker crossed his legs, a signal he was waiting for more.

"For example," went on Moran, "we have a number of alliances with other drug companies and universities for joint research that would eventually result in new business being directed your way. Access to opportunities and markets that will give you a sizeable lead in the development of new intermediates and biochemical compounds. Schoen will become a horizon firm."

Joe Moran appeared to be finished. Decker sat back with his hands clasped behind his head, silently excited about the prospect, yet left wondering. "What's the bottom line, Joe?" he asked.

"The bottom line?" Moran replied. "The bottom line is that by integrating our two firms we combine our respective advantages and eliminate our redundancies. Together we sell a superior product with shared advantages in house. The competition gets clobbered and it's a win-win on both sides."

The guy was good, thought Decker. There was no question about the economic benefits of combining. It was now a matter of hammering home those benefits to his board. Moss's expression, however, remained a guarded blank.

Carpenter came forward. "I think what Decker might be getting at, Joe, is what *his* future might be with us, *personally*."

Business combinations often brought about a change in upper-level management, which was always a fear of those being targeted.

"Oh," said Moran, coming forward in his chair with a backhand brush of his nose. "Yes, yes, of course." He took a cheese puff from the table dish and broke it half. Peering disappointedly at its plastic-looking composition he flung the thing into the coffee table ashtray. "Decker, here's what we're prepared to offer you. You'd remain as head of Schoen, a wholly-owned subsidiary of ours, but we'd double your salary. Whatever management team you wanted to keep would be yours. No questions asked. Your stock options, whether vested or not, would be cashed in full upon our fifty-percent-premium buyout." Moran paused. "Those alone would amount to over two million."

Decker swallowed his adrenaline. He knew Joe Moran would be able to properly calculate the figure since his option holdings were a matter of public record in Schoen's SEC filings.

"Finally, Decker," added Larry, "I'd make you a member of *my* board."

Decker Moss stared at the three men, matching their eyes, betraying no reaction in his own.

Then, with a savory glint, he said: "Gentlemen, I think we can do business."

* * *

Sunday, September 20, 1992

Flying at thirty-plus thousand feet, Decker reclined in first-class sipping a Scotch. The complimentary drinks were a nice amenity, but he especially enjoyed the legroom. Coach was a cow-train.

The thought of yesterday's events forged a smile on his face as he regarded their implications. He appreciated the forthrightness of the Drexel-Pace team's proposition. He had been involved in preliminary negotiations with other firms before, but more often than not he found them to be a fruitless exercise. Like playing with one's ingrown toenail, sensitivities overwhelmed sensibilities, and instincts for self-preservation prevailed against the need for extraction. The end result was that nothing ever ended up getting done.

Not so in this case. Carpenter and company had very succinctly and persuasively presented what they wanted in the deal, and they had clearly laid out what they were willing to pay for it. It was an offer nearly impossible to reject.

From his standpoint anyway.

He hoped his board would see likewise. Pondering on that some more, and then further about his grandfather, the smile on his face momentarily dissipated. But then he forced the negative out of his mind. The old man was a collapsing fossil.

The men had finished their evening together playing poker at the villa's kitchen table. Always the epicurean, Moss felt it was like college days all over again. With their continued downing of beers the games became increasingly inventive: black threes became wild and winning hands were made on the basis of the fully left-peering Jack of Hearts. In the end, a series of "high-low" games was played for lack of ability by any to concentrate much longer. Decker took home the winnings for the night, netting ninety-three bucks.

He now stared out the window at the Chesapeake Bay below. The Delaware River and New Jersey were just off to the east.

I've finally made it, he thought.

* * *

OPTIONS

Simultaneously, the Drexel-Pace executives cruised northwest in the comfort of their corporate Gulfstream jet from Savannah to Atlanta. Shaughnessy sat next to Carpenter, who in turn sat with his attaché case open on his lap. Joe Moran was in a back seat sleeping.

"So, how'd you think it went, Kent?" asked the CEO.

"I think we've got him, Larry. He's hungry."

"My thoughts as well. I got a little nervous when he brought up the licensing issue, like maybe we weren't getting through to him about the bigger picture. And that antitrust crap. You did a good job on it, though, both you and Joe."

Kent nodded. "Not a hard sell." Shaughnessy stretched his legs and leaned back into his soft leather seat. "I just hope his board's not going to slam us."

"Mike Reilly tells me he thinks they're now pretty much behind Decker."

Riley was a good friend of Carpenter's and an outside director on the Schoen board, among several others he served on. He and Carpenter had met early in their careers at Procter & Gamble. Both grew through the ranks to move on to executive positions at different firms. The nexus of relationships among those high in U.S. corporate echelons made for a number of small worlds.

"In that case we wait," said Kent.

Carpenter said: "I've begun a draft of my letter of intent outlining the parameters of our offer. I want you and Joe to meet with me and some of our counsel in the morning. Can you do that?"

Shaughnessy pulled out his pocket calendar. "Yeah, I have a meeting at ten, but I can push it back if I have to. It's important what goes in that letter. It has to have enough meat so he has something strong to bring to his board ... but weak enough not to tip them off about anything."

"Agreed," said Carpenter. They were actually willing to pay a much higher premium than fifty percent, if necessary. He turned his gaze to the window and stared out at the red Georgian fields below. It was deceitful, he knew, yet it was for a far greater purpose. Months earlier the three chief officers had concluded that it was the only way. And telling Decker or anyone else outside their inner circle would jeopardize their plans.

Carpenter resumed in a staid tone: "It's time for you to meet with our friend, the doctor. I've had enough of those cryptic fax reports he's been sending. I want more hard data and I want you to get it in person. No later than the end of this week. We have to be absolutely certain of what we have before taking this thing any farther."

"I'll have to do some reshuffling" said the Drexel-Pace President.

"Do it, Kent. Plan on a couple of days for travel."

It wasn't merely the synergies they had spoken about to Decker that motivated the Drexel-Pace executives. Those were important, to be sure. And very persuasive reasons quite on their own insofar as external parties needed to be aware. Indeed, they were convincing enough reasons to persuade Carpenter's board to move forward with negotiations.

But the more critical issue at hand was that Schoen held vital trade secrets and worldwide patent rights on mass production processes for novel synthetic amino acid peptides. In combination with Schoen's patented Threonatrix product currently under FDA review, one of those peptides, which Schoen called HX413, appeared to possess a special property—a very *valuable* property. And seeking to purchase Schoen's patents and trade secrets individually risked their separation. A buyout of the company was the only way to ensure the imperative outcome.

An outcome they believed held every promise of becoming one of the greatest medical breakthroughs of all time.

Chapter Fourteen

THE black wooden shack was no more than three square meters. Its contents were primitive: a single mattress, a stove, some pots and pans, and a paraffin lamp. Where the walls met the rusted corrugated metal roof, rags were stuffed into the gaps. It did little good. The rats easily nosed their way in during the night. Large rats—some the size of housecats—scurried up and down the rickety walls in the dark, eating their food supply of maize provided by a local Christian charity. Twenty kilos a month, and when that staple was gone, the rats ate the soap.

The Zimba family resided in Mbare, a high-density area just a few kilometers south of the capital city of Harare. Formerly known as townships, "high-density areas" had become a Zimbabwean euphemism for the impoverished, largely black-occupied, suburban slums.

Another bleak day ran its course for the five children who lived in the hovel, doing what they could of their schoolwork, cooking and cleaning, and for the youngest, playing on the dirt floor. Mafuta, the ten-year-old breadwinner of the family, was out as usual panning for money on the streets or pick-pocketing unsuspecting tourists in the Mbare Marketplace. In Zimbabwe, school fees, like food, required cash, and the nearly-orphaned children never attended.

A soft knock sounded at the door. The eldest of the five siblings greeted her visitor with a broad toothy smile.

"Hello, Nomsa," said Millicent to the twelve-year-old girl in English, the official language of the country. "Is your father doing any better today?"

"He looks the same I think. His coughing is bad, but not as bad as it was. He still doesn't move much."

Nomsa led Millicent outside to a smaller shack in back. The two of them looked in on the emaciated form that lay motionless on a mattress on the floor. Boils and herpes sores covered his leathery ochre-colored skin; loose excrement covered the sheets.

133

Blood that had dribbled from the man's lips congealed darkly down his cheek. It was near the end, Nomsa feared … very much like the death of her mother little more than a year earlier.

Millicent took a fresh sheet from her satchel and worked to replace the soiled bedding. "Honey, will you go get some water while I tend to him?"

Nomsa complied. It would take a while since fresh water was scarce. In this township an average of seven families shared a single toilet.

Donning latex gloves over her fingers Millicent extracted a vial and wrapped a rubber tourniquet around the man's upper arm. Long seconds went by before an ample vein surfaced. She poked him gently, watching the blood trickle slowly, gradually filling the tube. After labeling the specimen she withdrew a syringe from her bag and filled it with the required dose of special medication from a vial. She dabbed his upper thigh with alcohol. As she administered the 100 mg injection, the sick African man wheezed with the sound of fiberglass in his lungs.

Nomsa returned with a wooden bowl of water. She set it down on the floor and stepped back outside, not wishing to observe the undignified work to be done on her father. Millicent poured a cup and fed the man several pills for his tuberculosis. With what water remained she did her best to clean him, working carefully, patiently, around his sores. The blood and fecal matter on his skin had hardened like clay.

When finished, Millicent quietly exited the hut's doorway.

"I'll be back again the day after tomorrow," she said to Nomsa. She pulled out a Zimbabwean dollar—a small fraction of its U.S.-denominated equivalent—and gave it to the young black girl, who displayed a wide grin. Then her large coffee-brown eyes turned down and she began to tear.

Millicent caressed her cheek. "What is it, honey?"

"Poppa's going to die. Isn't he? Like Momma?"

"Nomsa, you and I will pray really hard. God's got your daddy in His hands. Your mom didn't have this new medication. With only what I gave him the other morning his temperature's down and I think his breathing is better. Do your best to keep him clean, though, and keep feeding him, okay?"

Nomsa nodded.

OPTIONS

The hospice nurse bent down to kiss her forehead and gave her an affirming hug. She then departed to tend to her next charge down the road.

Millicent's rounds, like those of nine others under her supervision, covered an average of fifteen AIDS patients a day. Picking up the specially formulated antiviral serum in the predawn morning, she returned to the lab with the day's blood samples in the secretive dark of night.

Her operation was now routine.

A more fruitful setting for covert HIV research didn't exist elsewhere in the world. The AIDS pandemic in sub-Saharan Africa was of biblical proportions. Unlike in the U.S., where the disease affected principally those in the homosexual community, here it was a more universal scourge. These were societies whose political upheavals, migrant working conditions and male-dominated cultures all steered toward profligate heterosexual sex. Women without economic control, including bereft teenaged girls forced or coerced with money by older men, had little say in sexual relationships. Rape rates were nowhere higher in the world. So-called "dry sex" was the preferred mode for many African men. Women douched with household detergents or herb concoctions to eliminate natural lubrication during intercourse, which created ripe conditions for blood transfer infection. Other sexually transmitted diseases were similarly rampant, and the sores and inflammation they brought on increased the likelihood of HIV transmission by two to ten times.

Zimbabwe's distinction among the sub-Saharan African region was that it had the fastest growing incidence of HIV transmission of all. Experts estimated fully one in four was in the class of HIV-infected, and the rate was increasing.

AIDS had struck Zimbabwe with a disease progression not seen since the Medieval Black Death. And interestingly, the most promising medical research in the country happened to be covert, all sponsored by private American funding. Whose source—if one could possibly dig deep enough—would ultimately lead to a behemoth of American enterprise: Drexel-Pace Pharmaceuticals.

* * *

Stephen J. Dempsey

Harare, Zimbabwe

The clandestine laboratory was located in an industrial park on the south side of the capital city, hidden below a distribution warehouse. Construction of the subterranean chamber was recent. It was situated beneath the rear quarter of the building, accessible only by a phantom wall in a back office closet.

Presently the wall traversed upward into the ceiling by what reminded Kent Shaughnessy of a quiet garage door opener. He had to admire the wall's carefully engineered workmanship. Only the closest scrutiny would reveal anything unusual about it.

"So glad you could finally visit my lab here, Mr. Shaughnessy," said Dr. Graham Woods. His South-African accent resonated as they traveled down the elevator to the bottom. It was a cultured accent that matched his stylized comportment. "I've got marvelous things to show you."

"I'm looking forward to it, Doctor. Larry Carpenter wanted me to see first hand what we've got in terms of details and specifics before taking this to the next step."

"Of course." Woods smiled and raised a welcoming arm for his guest as the elevator door opened. "I've got plenty of details and specifics."

The room was bright and well-ventilated, approximately thirty-feet square, optimally configured for the operation. Modern white-cased equipment and refrigeration units took up two entire walls, and in the middle of the room was a large counter area filled with customary lab ware: instruments, test tubes, beakers, decanters, microscopes, and the like. Another wall was covered with graphs, diagrams and computer printouts. Along the fourth wall, where they had entered, stacks of plastic tubs stood in rows, containing drug vials, blood samples, and Schoen's intermediate compounds. The latter were processed by Woods to make the antiviral serum according to the special recipe provided him.

Following the serendipitous discovery made by a Drexel-Pace scientist on one of Schoen's synthetic peptides, a lid was placed on further stateside research pending strategic review by "upper management." Having experienced them before, Larry Carpenter knew the dangers of leaked trade secrets and corporate espionage in pharmaceuticals research. He and his two trusted corporate officers also knew that preliminary tests on HIV therapy candidates had to rely on *in vitro* models of HIV for safety and practicality

136

reasons. Unfortunately, the virus behaves quite differently in a test tube than it does in the human body, and no animal models had been found to replicate HIV's effects in humans. Moreover, FDA approvals for clinical trials on human subjects would take years ... precious time wasted in bureaucratic hoopla when the firm needed to know right away.

The classified operation in Harare was the brainchild of Kent Shaughnessy. Zimbabwe's subject base was unequaled, and being a developing nation rife with more distracting socio-economic concerns, it also happened to benefit from near-perfect obscurity.

Graham Woods was a fair-haired man in his mid-thirties. He had been recruited to head up the study from Somerset Hospital five months earlier. Somerset was a teaching and research facility in Cape Town, South Africa. His research in immunology—disease latency, specifically—served as important credentials to Carpenter and company. Of course, filling such a position wasn't as easy as placing an ad in the help wanted pages. Yet locating and coaxing the researcher to take on the assignment with Drexel-Pace turned out not to be too difficult. A human-interest article about him and his research appeared in *Transformation*, a high-brow quarterly journal covering contemporary South African issues. He was HIV-positive himself, self-inflicted from an accidental needle prick while working with tainted blood samples at Somerset's clinic. When approached by the Drexel-Pace men with a lucrative pay package, modern lab facilities, and an unfettered research budget, the scientist couldn't turn it down.

"Let me show you these first," Woods said to Shaughnessy. He turned the computer monitor on the counter for his guest to view and opened a file. "These are historical T-cell counts for our subjects. Take this one for example, a female patient in the suburb of Mufakose. We first logged her in on the third of June. If you focus on this column, labeled CD4+, watch the pattern as I trace downward." His index finger moved through the computerized log.

"They go up," Shaughnessy said. He knew it was good news but he didn't know what else to make of it.

"That's right," agreed Woods with a smile, "they go up. Magnificently. Any one of these patients I could point to either go up or hold steady, depending on their stage of disease progression." The man then stepped over to his wall of charts with the joy of a child in front of a Christmas tree. "Up here are several time-series plots, each representing a large group of patients with initial CD4+ counts within plus or minus twenty-five."

"So each group is roughly equivalent in the stage of disease at the onset?" asked Shaughnessy.

"That's right. Let's take the extreme cases here. This is a scatter plot for those in very advanced stages of AIDS—CD4+ counts of 175 to 225. The red jagged line represents the average count for the group over time." The scientist retraced a line that traveled markedly upward from left to right. "This solid horizontal line in the middle of the graph represents the boundary for statistical significance. In other words, if the medications did no good in achieving an increase in CD4+ you would expect the red line to fluctuate randomly, even drifting downward, but it would tend to stay well below this line."

He looked at Kent and then back up at the graph. "You can see that that's not at all the case here. They're off the chart. Never in my life have I seen field experimental results like this before."

Shaughnessy corralled his optimism. "How pervasive—I believe you scientists like to use the term 'robust'—are your results?"

"Unequivocal. I haven't seen a single exception. In fact, from what I've been able to gather from my sample it works for every class of HIV I've studied."

"Class?" asked Shaughnessy. "You mean there are various versions of the disease?"

"Absolutely. One of the biggest problems with the virus is that it happens to possess an uncanny ability to mutate—faster than any other virus known to man. Different classes exist in different geographic regions. Here in southern Africa we have no less than five classes, more than any other part of the world."

Kent reflected on the explication, thinking that the statistical conclusions sounded convincing enough, though not their practical importance.

"What does all this mean in terms of the lives of these patients?" he asked. "What exactly is CD4+?"

Woods regarded his guest a moment before answering. "Well, Kent, I don't know how much you know about AIDS, or immunology for that matter, but CD4+ counts are critical. Where would you like me to begin?"

Shaughnessy took a seat on the swivel stool next to the counter. "You've been sending faxed reports to us on this favorable progression, but those of us who are reading them aren't experts in the area. We're few in number and we've been relying on your qualitative conclusions for the most part. They're certainly impressive, but as you know we've had to keep a very tight lid on all of this. We've believed it wise not to yet share any of your data with our scientific team at home. Not even the 'inventor.'"

From the outset Woods knew the extremely classified nature of his field study. He also knew it was miraculously blind luck for them to even have the primitive form of the drug he was experimentally dispensing. But until now he didn't realize he was the only scientist even privy to the data. "Such limited manpower and tight reporting protocols aren't typical for such a complicated scientific endeavor. You show perhaps too much faith in my abilities." Woods paused with his words. "Otherwise I would have seen more of your people down here."

It wasn't a question, but Kent nodded anyway.

"So, would you like a brief primer on the disease, Mr. Shaughnessy?"

"I think that would be helpful. I obviously know the layman's basics, but it's time I became more acquainted with your specialized science down here. We'll bring more folks into our fold when it's time."

Kent pulled a dictation recorder from his suit coat pocket and set it down on the counter. Zimbabwe's telephone system was notoriously unreliable. And the number of switching connections and operator interface required for overseas transmissions meant that confidential conversations could be monitored. Even satellite transmissions had the potential for interception with sophisticated enough equipment.

"Try to keep it as understandable as possible, Doctor. No embellishment or hopes on your part, just the facts as you know them. And don't be too pedantic. I'm suffering from jet lag."

Woods acknowledged Shaughnessy's meaning with a nod and smile. He sat down on the stool next to him and drew some figures on a pad of paper as he spoke.

"The immune system is a fascinating machine, Kent. Antigens are the enemy—the term given to invading foreign substances in the body—such as proteins produced by a bacterium or a virus, and other toxins. The system produces various cell types that work together in concert to kill these off. It also makes antibodies for possible future infections. Two of these cell types develop in the bone marrow: white blood cells that we call B-cells and T-cells. We're particularly interested in T-cells since these are the cells the HIV attacks. In other words T-cells are needed to kill the HIV microbe, but the HIV wins out eventually and kills off more T-cells than the body can reproduce. When the override becomes extreme, usually after several years of so-called latency, there are no longer sufficient T-cells to ward off disease. That's when the patient is said to have AIDS, or immune dysfunction. If you had no T-cells whatsoever you would die from exposure to a simple fungus. But of course AIDS patients succumb to more serious invaders long before it gets to that point."

Kent took it all in, most of which he had heard or read about before. "Yes, I get all that. Explain to me why our medication seems to work when all the others they've tried have failed."

"It's actually quite simple. Simple conceptually, but anything but simple chemically. Keep in mind that T-cells are the Achilles heel of the problem. Now there are actually two types of T-cell: CD4+ and CD8+."

"The CD4+ counts you have on the charts?" asked Kent, gesturing to the wall.

"That's right. The HIV focuses its attack on those particular T-cells."

"Why don't the other surviving T-cells, the CD8+, do the job?"

"Because they perform a different function. Think of the CD8+ cells as the 'killer' T-cells, the ones responsible for attacking and killing virus-infected cells. The CD4+ cells are referred to as 'helper' T-cells. They manage the process and provide signals to various other cells in the immune system to perform their special functions. If not for the CD4+ cells the whole immune system fails."

Woods illustrated by drawing an oblong circle with his pencil on the pad. "This represents a CD4+, or helper cell. Now here's what happens." At the top of the circle he made a dark point. "This dot represents a CD4 receptor molecule, which resides on the surface of the CD4+ cell. That's why we give the cell a plus sign. We know the HIV cell attaches itself to this molecule, binding tightly. Once fused the HIV releases its poison—genes—into the T-cell, which either kills it or disables it. After doing so the HIV cell multiplies rapidly. Billions of new virus particles are created in the body every day."

"Sounds sinister."

"Very. And extremely efficient, because if the HIV doesn't end up killing the infected helper T-cells, then the killer T-cells will do the job. What's more, infected helper T-cells can infect other *un*infected helper T-cells. The immune system literally kills itself off."

"Incredible." Kent swiveled in his stool and looked over at the rows of containers along the wall where the Schoen ingredients were stored. "So, what is it in those chemicals that works?"

"Well, Kent, I'll say this. Your researcher was a very lucky chap, that's for sure. Nobody could have dreamed this up in a million years. All other efforts have focused on discovering a vaccine that trains the immune system to produce antibodies to fight against infection. This is *no vaccine* you have here. This actually modifies the structural DNA of HIV cells."

Woods eased off his stool and went over to the wall of computer printouts again, stroking his chin. Then he turned around and faced his guest. "Earlier you told me he just happened onto this discovery ... that he wanted to see if Schoen's Threonatrix product could be used to deliver a peptide he was experimenting on?"

"That's right. We've found it reduces the toxicity of a number of other drugs. It's a unique vitamin C metabolite, whatever that means."

"I'll tell you what it means," said the scientist. "As a delivery agent for Schoen's synthetic peptide compound, HX413, Threonatrix does more than reduce toxicity. It's what makes the delivery of the peptide into the bloodstream even possible. Without a means of coating the peptide it would be instantly killed off by the immune system. In other words, Threonatrix shields the peptide so that it can attack a very important protein."

"Protein?"

"Yes, Kent, it's called glycoprotein 41. GP41, for short."

"What's that?"

"Well, remember how the HIV cell fuses to the helper T-cell?" Woods came back to the table and placed his finger on the dot he had made on his drawing. "GP41 is the protein embedded in the surface of the HIV cell that makes that fusion possible. Its entry point. I've conducted a binding assay. HX413 binds to GP41—bloody unravels it."

Graham Woods's eyes soldered onto Kent's, which in turn slowly registered comprehension.

"What you've stumbled onto here, Mr. Shaughnessy, is a drug that appears to make HIV as harmless as bread mold."

* * *

Following his meeting with Woods, Kent Shaughnessy had a few hours to kill before his next appointment. He wouldn't see the scientist again on this visit since the doctor's afternoon schedule buried him in sample results, serum preparations, and various dosage experiments he was conducting on the drug.

Driving was on the left hand side of the road. Consequently, Shaughnessy opted for a taxicab over a rental. He requested a tour of the city. Welcoming the fare, the cab driver happily extended his radius from the city proper to the outlying high-density slums. At an intersection the cabby warned him about the risk of "smash and grab." Street punks would target foreigners in stopped taxis by breaking the windows and seizing their handbags or briefcases right off the seats.

At its center, Zimbabwe's capital city of Harare appeared as modern as any other Shaughnessy had visited. Actually, it was quite beautiful, he thought, with wide thoroughfares and spacious parks and colorful gardens. He had expected to see something different, though what that was he wasn't sure. It was indeed a country of sharp contrasts, possessing some of the most magnificent scenery in the world, yet also home to some of the most squalid places on earth.

As his taxi drove through the littered ghettos he reflected on the significance of the experimental results contained in the briefcase resting upon his lap. He wished he could just broadcast to the pedestrians along the filthy shanty-lined rows that there was hope indeed.

His four o'clock appointment was at the Parliament Building with Zimbabwe's Minister of Health, James Tsumbia. He was a charismatic man who often took to the spotlight as an outspoken campaigner for AIDS education. They were media stunts for the most part: sit-downs, head shavings, and hunger fasts choreographed to enhance public consciousness of the role risky sex behaviors played in the spread of the disease. As a result of his national celebrity, Tsumbia wielded influence beyond his office among the true power brokers in government.

OPTIONS

The black Minister greeted Kent with a flashy smile. "It's not often I get to meet such a high-ranking executive of a multinational pharmaceutical company, Mr. Shaughnessy. Come right in." The man gestured to a desk-facing chair in his office.

"Thank you for making the time to meet with me, Mr. Tsumbia."

"Welcome to Harare."

Kent had no difficulty setting up the meeting earlier in the week. He purposely left his intentions vague, stating only that he wished to discuss a possible arrangement between his firm and the Zimbabwean government. For Tsumbia it was both a curiosity and a welcomed twist. Insofar as the AIDS issue was concerned it was invariably at the behest of motivated southern African governments to initiate discussions with U.S. drug companies, not the other way around. And company representation had never been at Shaughnessy's level. He was Big Pharma in the flesh.

Their introductory exchange was amicably chatty: Kent's long flight, the hotel at which he was staying, the location of his briefly lost luggage. He shared with the Minister his favorable impressions of the city during his tour, yet also of his shock at the poverty-stricken townships.

"The AIDS epidemic has completely devastated my country," said the Zimbabwean. His full cropping of wool-white hair looked very much like an aureole against his charcoal-black skin. "Since gaining our independence from the Brits twelve years ago we've been literally mired in it. Our people are dying like flies. Orphans are filling the streets and our economy has ground to a halt. There's no one to work the fields. Inflation's rampant, and sadly, the only ones making any money are in the funeral business."

The official grabbed a thick file from the side of his desk and held it up as if in evidence. "And our efforts to educate the public are apparently having no effect. I just got this report yesterday. Some of the worst infection rates are among our schoolteachers, the very ones we had hoped would carry the horrible truth about this disease to our children!"

Kent observed the fierce desperation in the dignitary's eyes.

"We sit here in virtual oblivion, Mr. Shaughnessy. Those who can help—the wealthy governments of the world and the corporate drug lords—have turned their backs on us. I can understand there's no profit in it for them. Our people can't afford the drugs. But we've tried negotiating better prices for helpful medications, such as AZT, without success."

Tsumbia paused, appraising his visitor. Then, more as a question than a statement: "I hope that's the reason for your visit."

"In a manner of speaking, yes. You can certainly understand the nature of this disease and this market don't align as well as we'd like. AIDS therapy drugs are extremely expensive, for those in our country as well." Kent briefly glanced about the room. "With regrettable irony AIDS happens to strike the poorest nations hardest. You are, of course, aware that offering differential drug prices across borders would create a huge black market. In order for our industry to survive we have to recoup our research and development costs, and it has to be on a rigid pricing schedule. It's really not a matter of exploiting those in need. In the end I think you'd agree the world's state of affairs would be far worse if we weren't able to afford the continuous development of new and better drugs."

"Yes, yes, I've heard all that before," Tsumbia responded with irritation in his voice. He had indeed heard it all before. Nor did he wish to surrender to it. The heartache of watching his country hurtled into ruin obsessed him, and he vowed not to let its engines falter when they hit against the brick wall of the almighty American dollar. He leaned forward, resting his arms on his desk. "So how may I help you?"

Kent appreciated the man's forthright manner. "I'm going to lay my cards face-up, Mr. Minister. Our firm would like to approach your government with a novel approach to the problem. But before we do, you and your government will have to assure us absolute confidence until further notice. Without that confidence I will just take my leave."

The dignitary eyed his visitor with a look of curiosity. "You're asking me to maintain confidence before I even hear what you're proposing?"

"I certainly wouldn't ask for it following my proposal."

Tsumbia stood up from his chair and ambled over to his office window, gazing thoughtfully through its panes. "It must be very novel indeed. If it weren't for who you are I would think this is some kind of absurd prank."

"Then do I have your confidence?"

Tsumbia turned around. Kent Shaughnessy stood tall even in his chair, a commanding élan not easily dismissed.

OPTIONS

"I suppose I really have no choice," said the Minister finally.

"Good. In that case, I suggest we take a walk. That bustling marketplace down the street will do nicely."

It was a cloudless, azure sky day in September, springtime in this part of the world. Streets were busy with tourists meandering flower stalls and open market tables, seeking deals with merchant peddlers. Africana, small enough to fit in a suitcase, was what was most in demand: tribal artifacts, carved figurines and colorfully-woven textiles. Shaughnessy was taken by the display of culture and artistry throughout.

"In the past your talks with drug companies have no doubt stalled for lack of resources—product prices and volumes prohibitive if the bulk of the cost were to be borne by the sick, correct?"

"Well, yes, of course," answered Tsumbia. "What other reimbursement scheme would you propose?"

Shaughnessy's attention was diverted by a craft stall. He picked up a set of hefty mahogany bookends, smoothly carved elephant busts with honed tusks of genuine ivory. "May I call you James?"

The Minister nodded. "James is fine."

Kent asked the child tending the merchant's table the price for the carved set. He dickered with the boy a bit, driving the purchase price down next to nothing. In a few minutes Shaughnessy cradled the newspaper-wrapped artifacts as a memento of his visit.

The men resumed their walk through the pedestrian crowds. "Let's talk economics, James. What would you say is the dead-weight loss to your country supporting medical treatments for one quarter of your population, those dying from AIDS?"

Tsumbia turned to the American, stupefied by the question.

But Kent went on: "To support your orphaned population? The empty fields, the loss of workers, their destitute families? No hope of economic recovery because you can't educate your youth. How much would you say your nation's economy suffers each year from this disease? And then continued devastation sightless into the future?"

"That's incalculable."

"Precisely. It's incalculable. But they're all very real costs you, your people, and your neighboring countries face." Kent raised an eyebrow as he looked at his companion. "The point is, whatever those costs are, your government would be willing to pay anything less to avoid them. Simple economics. Pay less than a dollar to save a dollar, right?"

"This is beginning to sound like bribery," Tsumbia said with edge in his voice. "What are you getting at?"

"What I'm getting at is a solution to your problem."

"Well you better start making sense, Mr. Shaughnessy. I'm sorry, but I'm finding this meeting a little too unorthodox for my liking."

At Kent's leading they crossed the street to a large park that presented a coruscating kaleidoscope of color as brilliantly chromatic as Shaughnessy had ever seen: scarlet *poinciana*, mauve and white *bahhinia*, and purple *jacaranda*. The native flowers gave off a pungent, exotic smell. Kent sat down on a bench near the entrance. He placed his package and briefcase down next to his side and gestured for the government official to have a seat next to his other.

"This is absolutely beautiful."

"Please, Mr. Shaughnessy, I'd really appreciate it if you would get to your point."

"And I told you I wasn't going to waste your time." Kent squinted out at the lush green lawn and then spoke with ponderous weight to his words: "Mr. Tsumbia, Drexel-Pace believes it has a cure for AIDS."

"*What?*"

Kent's gaze persisted outward, his voice almost a monotone. "I'm not talking about therapeutic treatments that only address its symptoms. Our experiments have been convincing on all known strains and groups. The drug doesn't kill HIV but it renders it completely harmless. As a result the virus doesn't infect the immune system, so the immune system kills the disease off naturally."

The Minister simply stared at the man aghast, unbelieving.

"My reason for secrecy is complicated but very well-intentioned, I assure you," continued Shaughnessy. "Let me just say we presently don't have regulatory approval for the drug—even for experimental purposes—and we probably won't have it for years. As you're certainly aware, FDA approvals can take as much as a decade. And they require extremely expensive clinical trials, costing hundreds-of-millions of dollars. Lacking that, it is very unlikely foreign regulatory agencies would grant carte blanche approval for us either. That is, if we were forced to stick to status quo protocols."

Kent turned and looked sidelong at the man. "That's more time and lives and money wasted, Mr. Tsumbia. We can do all that in parallel, and in time we'll get it. But we want to share our knowledge with your government now and with as many developing nation governments on this continent as we can. We will do so with all the proofs of efficacy our experimental data permit and your governments require."

Tsumbia removed his glasses with nervous fingers. Beads of sweat formed on his forehead. "I simply can't conceive what I'm hearing. A cure for AIDS? That's unbelievable."

"Yes it is," said Shaughnessy. "Unbelievable, but true."

"But without approvals how could you possibly satisfy us in any official capacity that your drug is as effective as you claim. Side effects? Unknown long-term complications?"

"All very understandable questions, Mr. Minister. For now you'll just have to trust me when I say we have extensive human field tests from trials outside the U.S. that show absolutely no side effects. Of course, we don't have long-term results, but by the nature of the drug it is extremely unlikely there are any complications. It targets a protein unique to HIV. Nothing else we're aware of."

"But if not in the U.S., then where? Where are you conducting these experiments?"

"I'm not at liberty to discuss our field data."

Tsumbia bridled. "I'm troubled by the ethics of what you're suggesting, Mr. Shaughnessy. Secret clinical trials outside of your own country?"

Kent turned to him again. "Ethics, Mr. Tsumbia? These aren't Nazi-esque experiments I'm talking to you about. People on their deathbeds are being cured. Would you call that unethical? Five years ago the FDA itself changed its regulations to give 'investigational new drug' status authorizing treatment for seriously ill patients outside of clinical trials. The regulations only stipulate informed patient consent and prohibit promotion or commercialization *within the U.S.* We're simply suggesting that the spirit of those regulations be applied to your country. And possibly other countries on this continent."

The Health Minister took in his points, though remained guarded by the litany of questions that competed in his mind. "Still, you can't possibly expect me to say yes to such a thing as this. Not without proof."

"I'm not asking you to say anything. Not yet." Kent reoriented his seat position as he contemplated how to phrase his proposal in a prudent way. "I'm asking you to speak with those in the highest ranks of your government. No one else. Any indication of a leak and we'll play completely dumb. Do you understand? At the proper time you will have all the documented proof you need. Until then we have to get all our ducks in a row."

"Ducks?"

Kent smiled. "Sorry, an American idiom. On our side we need a couple months to work out our supply details. What I am asking you to do, though, sir, is to get the wheels started on your government's financing for this cure. It has to be a *quid pro quo*. We won't just give it away. I trust you understand."

The heavy beads of sweat that had formed on the Zimbabwean's brow were now following gravity's course, stinging his eyes. Removing his glasses again he wiped his face with his arm sleeve. "How much would you want?"

"James, seventy percent of new HIV infections and ninety percent of all AIDS deaths occur in sub-Saharan African nations, yet less than one percent of AIDS drugs are sold in this region of the world. How do we do it? How do we structure a mutually agreeable deal that's workable so that the people of your country who can't afford the medications get them? And how do you get them given our prohibition to export them? I think you can see as well as I do that it can't be a traditional solution. It requires some thinking outside the box."

"You Americans and your idioms." Tsumbia stared out at the lawn again. The rush brought on by the gargantuan prospect for his country flooded him. A thousand questions dotted in queue, not the least of which was what he might be expected to do at this point. "And what kind of thinking would that be?"

"We have a proposition. We think it's very workable. But it's ... it *is* unorthodox to use your word. Would you like to hear it?"

* * *

Later that evening, flying northwest to the neighboring country of Zambia, Kent Shaughnessy sat exhausted in contemplation. The idea was indeed novel, and he was happy that Tsumbia, too, found it a provocative one. There would be no way to make such a deal profitable otherwise. Not if it were left to the destitute to pay for it. A national income tax for AIDS-related funding was a very reasonable approach, and actually one that was currently under consideration by the Zimbabwean government. A modest rate targeted at those in the higher income brackets would also be a palatable solution. After all, they had the greatest vested interest in the economy's improved overall health.

Why a special deal with South African governments? The answer to that question was that the technology underlying a true AIDS cure wouldn't be protected in international settings where the disease was the greatest problem. Developing nation governments would likely "bust" the patents using generic copies of the drug, assuming they could reverse engineer it. Many countries, including the U.S., had constitutional provisions under national health emergencies that permitted them to do so. As long as the drug remained abroad, U.S. Federal law was powerless, and the FDA would be unable to prohibit its distribution.

Despite Tsumbia's persistent inquiries, however, the most intriguing part of the plan Kent had left unspoken.

"In time I'll share with you our ideas about supply logistics and compensation. All very legal and all very reasonable. For now, however, it will be up to you to satisfy me of your government's willingness to negotiate further. It won't be with Drexel-Pace. Not formally. We'll have to set up a quasi-autonomous entity right here." When asked how, Kent simply answered: "That's your problem, Mr. Minister. You're the politician."

The pilot's voice came over the loudspeaker. They would be touching down in Lusaka in ten minutes.

Chapter Fifteen

Tuesday, September 29, 1992
Manchester, New Hampshire

"WHAT the hell is this, gentlemen?" erupted Decker. "How can we possibly be saddled with this crap when we didn't even own the plant back then? It doesn't make sense." Moss's face was flushed and furious.

"Ownership status back then may not be relevant," replied his corporate lawyer. "Recent court cases have been interpreting successor liability pretty loosely in the environmental area. I don't know for certain, but that's probably the legal theory they're relying on." Everett Royce, Schoen's chief internal legal counsel, spoke with a peculiar idiosyncrasy in his eye movements. Frequently when he cogitated, his orbs rolled back behind his eyelids, which fluttered like a hummingbird's wings. Bald and white as an egg on top, but with long frizzy hair on the sides, the man reminded Decker very much of Larry Fine, the second Stooge. He, along with Charles "Cap" Satterfield, Schoen's chief financial officer, sat at the conference table in Decker's office trying to sort out the implications of the news.

It came in the form of a special notice letter from the Environmental Protection Agency. And it carried a ton of bricks. Schoen Chemicals Corp. was just added to a list of six other "potentially responsible parties" for disposing hazardous substances at a Superfund waste site. EPA's abbreviation for the dubious distinction was PRP. Not an accident, Decker surmised, since PRP could easily be read as 'perp'—as in perpetrator of a crime.

"Then tell me what you do know, Everett."

The lawyer leaned back in his chair with his hands behind his head. "According to our files we bought the South Carolina plant in a bank foreclosure back in 1983. Mullins Chemicals was a small firm with only a couple of plants at the time. Apparently they suffered financial problems during the recession of the early seventies. The oil crisis in the mid-seventies dealt them a final blow. We acquired one of their plants primarily for its chlorine production." The lawyer dabbed the prow of his nose and sat forward. "What especially troubles me is that we retained their workforce, leasing the facility from the bankruptcy trust until the final purchase went through. Unfortunately, that continuity of operations is the thing that might hang us, if anything does. Had we stripped the facility and started from scratch there'd be no way they could tag us with successor liability."

"You keep mentioning this 'successor liability,'" Decker interrupted. "The letter says the alleged dumping took place back in the sixties and seventies, years before we bought the plant. Mullins went bankrupt for God's sake. What's more permanent than that?"

Royce addressed the question with his rapid eye movement going again. "When it comes to hazardous substances, Decker, it's cradle-to-grave responsibility. Successor liability means subsequent owners can be held responsible for the acts of their predecessors in certain circumstances. Although a strict reading of the statutory law would limit successor liability to mergers and consolidations—where the entire predecessor company is acquired but continues to operate as it did before—environmental case law has evolved to impose liability even when only *parts* of a company are purchased. As in this case." Royce was referring to a 1990 district court decision whose reasoning had been applied to a number of recent court cases. His index finger tapped the table as he went on. "Even though we didn't own the plant at the time they disposed of the waste, we operated it continuously both before and after our purchase. Same workers, same plant management."

"So, in essence looking as if there was no real change in business," completed Moss.

"Exactly," affirmed the lawyer. "It's called a *de facto* merger. From a legal standpoint our purchase of the plant may be viewed as a purchase of its past disposal practices. Again, I'm only trying to anticipate the EPA's case, but they may claim that as purchaser of the plant we reaped the benefits of Mullins's old hazardous disposal methods."

"Incredible." Moss watched the legal man play with his hair. Androgynous in both voice and manner, Royce currently wore a salmon polka-dotted bow tie and wide-collared teal-green shirt. Decker suspected he may have a lighter pair of loafers in the closet, despite being married with two children. But he was brilliant when it came to the law, and that was all that mattered.

Moss picked up the letter again, trying to make out its full meaning. But it was too replete with legal jargon for his minimal understanding. He set it back down.

"What's more incredible about Superfund law," continued the lawyer, "is that back when Mullins disposed of their wastes they may have been in full compliance with the existing disposal requirements and laws at the time. We're not necessarily talking about midnight dumping here. Any connection with a site on the National Priority List, either as a chemical producer, waste transporter, or owner-operator of a waste site makes for potential liability. Fault isn't required."

"I simply can't believe this," blurted Moss, his volume working higher. "It's changing the rules of the game after the game's over. What the hell is this place, Everett?"

Royce did his best to fill in the gaps he could. "It's just north of Columbia, South Carolina. I've only had a little time to look into it, but from what I've been able to gather it was an industrial waste pit, converted to that purpose by a hungry farmer trying to make ends meet. He carved out a seven-acre parcel of his land and used his heavy equipment to bury whatever business came to him. Given Mullins's financial problems at the time, I'd say they found that hole a pretty attractive option. Hundreds of drums were discovered a couple years ago when a land developer bought the property for a housing project. Not exactly the kind of buried treasure I'd like to find."

"And the farmer?"

"Don't know. Probably long gone. Even if he were still around, the EPA wouldn't likely look to him unless he had a nice bankroll." Royce looked down at some paperwork in front of him. "The site was placed on their Superfund list because the groundwater flow moves in the direction of the source of the town's drinking water."

"What I don't get is that it's a good hundred miles from the Mullins plant," put in Cap Satterfield, his first substantive comment of the meeting. "For them to transport their trash that far, it must have been a bit shady."

Decker Moss considered his point. "You're probably right, Cap."

"I'm afraid it gets worse, Deck," said Royce hesitantly.

"What do you mean it gets worse? How could anything get worse than being cited for shit you had nothing to do with?"

"Liability is joint and several."

"Meaning?"

"Meaning we could be held responsible for cleaning up the whole mess. Ours as well as others'. Again, it's not necessarily based on fault. It's ability to pay."

Moss wiped his face with his hands. Hard. Wishing control he couldn't muster he managed to ask: "And what could all this boil down to, gentlemen, in terms of dollars and cents?"

Royce and Satterfield glanced at each other, neither wishing to be the one to tell him. Finally, Cap Satterfield responded. "The EPA's Record of Decision puts the estimate at between seventy-five and a hundred million."

"*What!* A hundred million? For some old rusted drums?"

"And liability can extend for years as they dig up new evidence in the cleanup," averred Royce. "We might be responsible for reimbursing the government for the remedial investigation study as well as the cleanup itself. And then the legal costs can amount to another quarter of that. It all depends on what we can negotiate with the other PRPs, and whether new ones will be named. Of course, I believe we can make a strong defense, at least pursue a *de minimis* settlement with the EPA."

Decker Moss gathered himself out of his chair and paced his office. Being named a 'perp' was typical in the chemical industry. Schoen had been fortunate to navigate the harbor cleanly to this point, but there was certainly much more at stake here he secretly knew of than just that. The Drexel-Pace negotiations could very well be derailed. Who would want to buy a firm with these kinds of skeletons knocking around in the closet?

"What about insurance?" Decker asked.

"Unlikely," replied Satterfield. "Most of our policies explicitly exclude pollution coverage. Those that don't—even assuming they'd cover an inherited problem like this—have a prohibitively high deductible. As a practical matter, we probably have to consider ourselves self-insured."

"I figured as much." Decker sat on the corner of his desk and folded his arms.

Cap Satterfield picked up the letter, as if scrutinizing it. "What I find incredible is that it's completely silent on what evidence they have … what types of chemicals were involved, quantities, nothing. How do we even know it was the Mullins plant?"

"They intentionally keep that kind of information vague," explained Royce. "It's a boilerplate letter that includes only the essentials. The old game of keeping us guessing about what they know so that we trip up and spill our guts. I plan to call them to get some answers, and if they don't want to cooperate, I intend to file a request under the Freedom of Information Act."

"Are there records of the plant's transports?" queried Moss. "Manifests perhaps?"

"That's a question I have as well." Royce's eyes twittered in thought. "I haven't researched it yet, though I kind of doubt it. Again, the transports took place back in the sixties and seventies, and any records maintained by Mullins were probably destroyed long ago. A bankrupt firm would have no need to keep them."

"What about drum labeling?" pursued Moss. "The EPA must have some evidence that Mullins was the source of the dumping. Would there actually be labels or other identification on the drums that would survive all these years?"

"I could check into it."

"Do that, Everett. And while you're at it, find out exactly what we're dealing with—the nature of the spills, the quantities and types of chemicals involved. Maybe there are some old timers still working at the plant or living in the area that remember something."

Royce jotted an action item down on his notepad.

"Who are the other parties involved?" Decker asked.

Satterfield, who still held the letter in his hands, referenced the pertinent section. "Six companies I've never heard of before. Another chemical company, a couple of trucking outfits, an electronics firm, a textile firm, and the other I can't make out from its name. Must all be small. Their names and contacts are listed here. The EPA wants us to get together with them to form a PRP steering committee."

"Right, I can only imagine why," blurted Moss. "So we can commiserate and blame each other and look for new PRPs to spread the cost, right?"

The other men didn't answer Decker's speculation, though they guessed it was probably on target.

Cap Satterfield addressed another matter of importance. "The Agency wants us to notify them of our willingness to participate in the negotiations and gather whatever information we have about the disposals. They give deadlines."

OPTIONS

"Expensive deadlines you don't want to exceed," injected Royce quickly, "twenty-five thousand dollars per day. You should know that a special notice letter like this is sent out only after the EPA has already done their homework. A general notice letter went out a couple of years ago to a larger list of firms they eventually pared down after some investigation as to likely involvement and financial wherewithal."

"Oh, now it all makes sense," said Moss with sarcastic inflection. "We're considered deep pockets, right? Why didn't *we* get a general notice letter?"

"I don't know, Deck" answered Royce. "Possibly because they had to track down who bought the Mullins plant."

"Or," postulated Cap, "perhaps they just recently dug up the buried drums bearing the Mullins Chemicals name."

Decker mused over these possibilities. "You said Mullins had more than one plant in operation at the time? Maybe it wasn't really ours that was involved. Do the drum labels actually identify the particular plant in question? Hell, it was twenty years ago." Decker's frustration grew with the growing list of new questions that went unanswered.

"Yes, they had one other, a smaller plant," answered Royce. "But successor liability doesn't necessarily concern itself with those inconvenient details, I'm afraid."

"Gentlemen, I have to know more about this, and fast. Do whatever you have to do to find out." He turned around and perused his desk calendar. "By Friday afternoon, in my office."

The two men dutifully lifted from their seats and collected their papers. Before they exited Decker issued command: "And don't share this information with anyone. Any work you do on this is to be done by you, completely on your own. Do you understand?"

The men nodded to each other and then to him, and left his office.

Decker remained sitting on the corner of his desk as he contemplated the Whats and Hows he would have to share with Larry Carpenter.

* * *

Friday, October 2, 1992

It was late afternoon three days later when Decker Moss concluded his scheduled meeting with Everett Royce and Cap Satterfield. The men had returned that morning from their reconnaissance work at the South Carolina Superfund site. Slightly relieved by having more information, though even more unsettled about its implications, Decker knew he had to speak with Larry Carpenter. Being named a 'perp' was publicly available information—at least information that could be obtained with a little research of EPA documents—and it would inevitably surface under the due diligence expectations of any ensuing merger negotiations.

Fortunately, the Drexel-Pace CEO was available to take his call.

"Decker, I was just thinking about you." Larry Carpenter's southern-toned greeting was customarily jovial. "Were you able to get the green light from your board on Wednesday's meeting date?"

"Next week's a 'go,' Larry. Most of my directors sounded quite interested in what you have to say."

"Happy to hear that."

Decker then shifted in his chair as he composed his words. "Larry, there's something I have to talk to you about. You're going to find out about it anyway if we move forward with our merger talks. A couple days ago I received news that would be of interest to you, unfortunate news that may affect your interest in us."

"What's that?" Carpenter asked, concerned.

"It's an EPA notice. We've been named a PRP at a Superfund waste site."

A pause. "Is that so?"

"I have to be honest with you, Larry, it doesn't look good."

"Nothing about the EPA looks good." Then Carpenter's voice lifted brighter. "So you're no longer a virgin, huh? Drexel-Pace and its subsidiaries are associated with no less than two-dozen sites. Some firms out there have close to a hundred. It goes with the territory."

"I suppose."

"So, what's the story?"

OPTIONS

In a few minutes Decker recounted the general facts as he knew them, beginning with the special notice letter and ending with the new information he just gathered from Royce and Satterfield's debriefing. "There's considerable legal question about our liability, but it appears they have us on the physical evidence. We just completed a brief investigation of the site. They're there. A hundred-plus drums with clear signs of our plant's name on the lids, corroded and leaked out over the years. The site administrator told my men a hired excavator discovered the drums a couple months back with his earth moving equipment, buried some ways off from the main area. I guess PRPs are responsible for hiring most of the bulk cleanup work under EPA's supervision."

"Yeah, that's typical. Once the containers are removed then the professionals come in to do the soil and groundwater remediation work. It's pretty sophisticated science. So, it's certainly not over once you dig up the dirt."

"I gathered that."

"Do you know what was in them?"

"Chemical soup," replied Moss flatly. "Volatile organic compounds, PCBs, mercury. You name it."

"Well, Decker, I agree it's not good news. And I appreciate your being candid with me about this before our meeting with your directors. Do you plan to tell them?"

"Of course I do. I have to."

"Yes, of course." Carpenter silently weighed the implications of the matter. Then in an upbeat tone he said: "It might actually work in our favor if you did."

"Your favor?" Decker asked, puzzled. He came forward in his chair. "How's that?"

"Well, I'm just thinking out loud, but wouldn't you expect they would be more inclined to negotiate with a buyer that had the financial wherewithal to assume that kind of liability?" Decker remained silent, intrigued by the statement, but Carpenter went on: "We'd have to assess the extent of your exposure and adjust our offer price accordingly, but I think it's still a workable prospect, don't you?"

"Larry, I have to say I find your lack of concern about this very surprising. I thought for sure you'd want to backpedal into the sunset."

"It's not a lack of concern, Decker. I manage my concerns. But this doesn't change Schoen's fundamentals. Not a bit. Like I said, following our due diligence we just reduce our offer price for the expected remediation costs."

Decker merged onto that last track of thought. "It might help if my shareholders were aware of this information, the potential liability, in order for them to entertain a lower bid."

"Yes, you may be right. Perhaps a news release of the EPA's notice would be in order."

Each quietly pondered the issues a moment longer before Carpenter concluded: "For the time being, however, I suggest you just share with your board what you know, and then we'll see how things go at next week's meeting. Don't let them know you've made me aware of this. I think they'd appreciate having the upper hand on how to dispense with that information. If they agree in principle to a deal, I'm sure we can work out the financial details and the media release later."

Moss digested the points in order, thinking them valid. "In that case, I'm happy I called."

"I am, too, my friend. Let's just keep this train on the tracks."

After hanging up, Decker looked at his phone, expressionless at first, then with a smile and a nod. The Drexel-Pace offer was still on the table.

Unseen by him, the party on the other end also smiled.

Chapter Sixteen

NOT unlike the signature boardrooms of corporations double or triple its size, Schoen's was an extravagant affair, decked out in mahogany from floor to ceiling, including its centerpiece conference table and chairs. C. Decker Moss's philosophy was that one wears a room much like one wears clothes: both create an amorphous impression, and both affected the quality of work that takes place inside. Consequently, he spared little expense in its design. A large oil portrait of Cyrus P. Schoen hung on the wall opposite the entrance, as if a constant reminder to those making decisions at the table that the company's founder, whether present or not, would always be looking down on them. But the old man was still very much alive. And, as Moss would soon come to find out, he was also regrettably very present at today's meeting.

After his trip to Hilton Head, Decker met with his board via teleconference. He outlined the basics of the Drexel-Pace proposal, along with his tentative endorsement. This was followed by an express mailing to his directors of the lengthy letter of intent Larry Carpenter sent him. Actually more of a report than a letter, it spelled out in considerable detail Drexel-Pace's motivation for the buyout and the parameters of their bid. Decker's board agreed the issue merited a special conference, which happened to coincide with the already scheduled third quarter board meeting. Phone calls by Decker over the weekend informed his board members of the recent EPA notice.

Today's meeting was attended by nine of his eleven directors. It was a quorum, though one whose makeup caused Decker some concern. The two who couldn't make it due to unavoidable calendar conflicts happened to be two of his more faithful.

The Drexel-Pace team was also present: Larry Carpenter, Kent Shaughnessy, Joe Moran, two stiff-suited men making up their legal counsel, and a partner from their CPA firm, Marsh, Mason & Pratt. Decker made cordial introductions, but as Chairman of the board Cyrus Schoen held prerogative to set the agenda and pace of the

159

meeting. The sallow-faced, baldheaded man offered the floor to the Drexel-Pace visitors to make their pitch.

Larry Carpenter began. "It's a pleasure for me to be in this boardroom with you today. I know some of you." He gestured to Michael Riley. "Mr. Riley and I go way back. What, thirty years, Michael? Procter & Gamble." He then looked over at a more casual acquaintance, Paul Richfield. "Paul, good to see you again." Richfield was a high-powered Wall Street investment banker who had worked with Carpenter on a few Drexel-Pace deals in the past. Such VIPs frequently sat on several boards, sometimes invited to serve more as figureheads than cerebral heads.

Carpenter's disarming eyes traversed his audience. "It is indeed rare for me to come across a prospect such as this, to feel as excited about a potential mix that offers this kind of promise. Since you went public a few short years ago we've been keeping a very interested eye on your noticeable achievements. Of course, we continue to be a major customer and have evidenced our backing by being a significant shareholder as well.

"Everything tells us our corporate cultures mesh comfortably and our operations are mutually synergistic. As for that matter, I'm speaking mostly of the major advancements you've been able to make in your intermediate processing and biochemical production. Major discoveries are being made each day in our understanding of molecular biology, to the point where it is now becoming possible to target drugs to the specific molecular processes that underlie disease. Knowledge of the binding properties of proteins, for example, is critical to the development of drugs for diseases such as cancer, AIDS and Alzheimer's." Carpenter paused a moment for emphasis. "For background, allow me to share with you more information about our research initiatives and the way we feel Schoen fits in very nicely."

The Drexel-Pace CEO went on to elaborate about some of the major recent breakthroughs his company was making in protein engineering, chemical compound formulations that mimicked the disease conditions of amino acid chains, and new targeted modes of drug delivery. He also expounded on the problems of relying on external chemical supply sources, and why Schoen, as a relatively small, technically advanced firm—"unhindered by the inertia of the status quo"—was such an attractive merger candidate. It possessed the manufacturing capabilities and scientific backing called for by Drexel-Pace's cutting edge research. Clearly a man comfortable in his suit, Decker thought, Carpenter didn't miss a beat. Moss was impressed.

"To sum up, our firm wants—no, it *needs*—the type of dependability, social consciousness and technology offered by your firm. In many instances outsourcing no longer makes sense for us, not for the increasingly complex chemical formulations we require. We're no longer talking about commodities; we're talking about very novel ingredients that involve mass production at cost-effective prices. We believe Schoen is optimally positioned to do that for us."

All in the room were attentive to Larry Carpenter's monologue delivery.

All, that is, except Cyrus P. Schoen himself. His bushy eyebrows crested over skeptical eyes, which leveled in on his guest: "Your letter implied there are certain existing formulations of ours that are of interest to you. Threonatrix you named, specifically."

He took the bait, Carpenter thought. "Yes, Mr. Schoen, that's correct. It's just one example of the type of research you've come up with that may very well have a number of important applications beyond your current understanding."

Schoen cleared his throat. "I'd be interested to hear you elaborate on *your* understanding."

Carpenter glanced at his teammate sitting to his side. "I'd be happy to. But Kent Shaughnessy is actually better-equipped to speak to that, so I'll defer to him, if you don't mind. Kent?"

The Drexel-Pace President and chief officer of operations lifted his pen and rolled it in his fingers as he contemplatively addressed the board Chairman. "Mr. Schoen, we named Threonatrix in our letter simply as an example. It's a good one, however. Your FDA tests have been focusing on its efficacy in reducing the toxicity of aspirin. That's a very understandable starting place, and one you've fortunately had success with. In the case of Threonatrix, however, we've found its toxicity reducing properties extend to a great number of drugs beyond that. Far more significant drugs than just aspirin alone."

The room quietly fanned surprise.

"Such as?" pursued Schoen.

"Literally hundreds: antibiotics, anti-inflammatories, vitamins, therapies for immune system diseases. Our new Holzipan product, for example, which barely made FDA approval last year for rheumatoid arthritis due to its toxicity rating, shows significant improvement with only slight modifications of your Threonatrix base."

Some energized chatter threaded around the table. Everett Royce spoke up over it. "Then why not just seek usage patents for those applications? That would seem a far less complicated way for you to get what you want."

Kent Shaughnessy turned in the direction of the eye-flittering man who currently wore an incongruous display: a gray double-breasted suit framing a purple shirt and yellow bowtie. "My simple answer to your question, Mr. Royce, is that usage patents aren't effective. Not in pharmacology. Again, the obvious example is aspirin. The discovery that it benefits blood circulation and reduces risk of heart disease can't be channeled into profits because it's a freely-available over-the-counter drug. Even prescription drugs under patent protection known to have medicinal benefits beyond that for their approved application can't be policed from being prescribed for that alternative use. It's a suit of paper armor."

Royce knew Shaughnessy was correct on the practical issue. Usage patents had a number of weaknesses nearly impossible to remedy under the law.

Kent then directed his attention to the larger board. "Our firm has poured tens of millions into drug toxicity research, which is a chief benefit of being large from a capital standpoint. Analogous to drilling thousands of holes rather than just a few, the chances of discovering riches are greatly multiplied. It's a way of diversifying against the risk of time, against having someone else beat you to the treasure. Again, Threonatrix is only one example. You've found one application, we've found hundreds. But I think you can see that sharing our discoveries in house as opposed to dealing with the obstacles of turf protection and legal loopholes in joint venture agreements is a far more efficient and effective approach. The whole in this case becomes much greater than the sum of the smaller parts."

The board sat silent in their ruminations. Decker thought Kent was a master, and he grew excited that this appeared to be going very much his way. To top it off, he hadn't yet had to say a single word in the meeting.

The Drexel-Pace executive team had planned their presentation very carefully. As risky as it was, the explicit mention of Threonatrix in their letter—or for that matter, to Decker early on—was a tactical decision on their part, not an accidental show of hand. They knew there had to be a very tangible jewel to put on the table, an example of the mutual benefits of their buyout proposal. And as legitimate as their claims about Threonatrix happened to be, it was still a red herring. Their upfront disclosure would quell later potential suspicions once the more explosive truths about the drug eventually surfaced. The argument would go as follows: Schoen couldn't have been exploited in the buyout negotiations since Drexel-Pace had been so forthcoming about their ongoing research on Threonatrix. Their willingness to share such valuable findings in board discussions with the patent holder could never be interpreted as bad faith negotiation.

Larry Carpenter caught Cyrus Schoen's eye, seeking permission to speak again. "May I, sir?"

"Yes, of course, continue Mr. Carpenter," said the withered board Chairman.

"I think it's important to add here—very important to add—that it's not your hard assets we're after. It's not your generic chemicals business, nor even your proven chemical advancements to date. We want them of course, but it's your *future* capabilities, *in combination with ours*, that excite us most. It would take years for us to reproduce your intangibles from scratch. You've assembled some of the most creative scientific talent out there. Schoen's intellectual property and proprietary manufacturing methods, whether patented or not, have the hidden potential of a Picasso in the attic. We know how that value can be discovered, directed and deposited. Your untarnished environmental record is virtually unheard of today; we want that type of goodwill behind the Drexel-Pace name. And the institutional flexibility that comes from your size and youth is something that makes our proposal very workable from a human resource standpoint. Too many business combinations fail for lack of corporate fit."

"Thank you, Mr. Carpenter," said Schoen with flatness in his voice. He climbed out of his chair, stretched his back with evident discomfort, and then sat down again with a sigh. "I understand you have some financial projections for us?"

"Yes, Joe Moran, our chief financial officer, has done some *pro forma* analyses that he'd like to share with you."

Moran got up and took center stage at the end of the table. A sharply tailored suit draped his massive body. More respectably packaged than on the golf course, he reminded Decker of a tidy though sprawling farmhouse. On cue, an automated screen un-scrolled downward from the ceiling and the projector came to life.

The presentation consisted of forecasted income statements, balance sheets and financial ratios, which if delivered by anybody else but Joe Moran would have put even a corpse to sleep. Most such presentations were like reading an eyechart, Decker thought, and he couldn't believe the guy could make the numbers come alive the way he did. Moran's projections focused on the large increases in revenue that would come Schoen's way, both in terms of what Drexel-Pace would give them directly as well as the expected throw-off business from affiliated partners. All marshaled to Schoen's revenue advantage, the halo effect would turn what was currently a "garden hose" into a "city water main."

When he was finished, the farmhouse sat down with his colleagues. Decker loved the guy. He couldn't imagine his board not feeling likewise.

"Mr. Moran," inquired Schoen, "you focused a good deal of attention on your revenue assumptions, but very little specifics on the cost side. Just what do you mean by 'cost economies' of the acquisition?" Cap Satterfield, Schoen's CFO, was interested in the answer to that question as well.

"I'm sorry, Mr. Schoen, I didn't intend to be vague on that. Typically, in our industry mergers result in a five to ten percent reduction in operating costs. In this case that is reduced somewhat. There isn't much there on the production side—I factored very little into my analysis—but on the administrative side we believe there's between a ten to fifteen percent range of savings in centralized services."

"What, precisely, would those be?" interrogated Schoen.

"You know, redundancies in support staff, procurement, legal and accounting fees, facilities ... that sort of thing."

"Layoffs?" Schoen probed further.

A chilly hush fell across the room. But Joe Moran remained unflappable: "Well, yes, impliedly some layoffs would be called for. Not many mind you, but I would be less than candid to tell you otherwise. They are incorporated in our fifty-percent premium offer."

"So, layoffs." Schoen peered individually at the occupants around the table. The tremor in the old man's countenance evolved into something of an exposed nerve being probed by a cold instrument. "Including, no doubt, some of our top-level management. I was under the impression that if we went along with your plan, giving it our blessing to our shareholders, you'd leave us alone. To continue much as we are, with the possibility of improving our revenue base."

"Qualitatively, that's absolutely correct. I assure you that we have no intention of coming in and redecorating your house."

"Redecorating our house?" Schoen repeated lowly. "Qualitatively? Mr. Moran, qualitatively, Mr. Carpenter, qualitatively, and Mr. Shaughnessy ... qualitatively ..." The old man looked at each of them icily. "Qualitatively, I think you're all full of shit."

Decker just about fell through his chair. The room went silent.

"Mr. Schoen, if I may offer a little levity to this discussion?" It came from Alan Pelleman, Drexel-Pace's CPA.

There was no acknowledgement from the board Chairman.

"Mr. Schoen?" Pelleman tried again.

"What is it?" came out Schoen with a scowl.

"I just want to add that the types of figures Joe Moran presented are actually quite conservative. In fact, in my consultations with him I thought there would be significantly larger cost reductions than he factored into his analysis. Not layoffs, but a great many tax benefits possible if we took certain joint research and development activities elsewhere, to our Canadian subsidiaries, for example. They offer nice tax credits."

"Oh, that makes it all very clear to me. Now we're going to play the taxman's charade. A little here, a little there, sum it all up and it isn't anywhere. Frankly, I'm tired of all that bullshit. I built this business from scratch. Buyouts, tax schemes, restructurings? It's all waxmen, witches and whores. Whatever happened to good old-fashioned bright ideas and hard work? We don't need your esoteric tax ploys, your dressed-up paper dolls."

Schoen's blood continued to flow upward to fill his skull until, with volcanic eruption, he slammed his fist down on the table. "Schoen Chemicals is, and will always be, just that: Schoen Chemicals! *Not for sale!*"

The crusty figure got up from his chair and sauntered out the door, slamming it with a reverberating thud.

* * *

Several uncomfortable moments passed without a formal word spoken in the room. There was a whisper here and there. A few glimpses up at the oil portrait of the man who had just taken leave. Others looked at each other or helplessly about, not knowing how to deal with the Chair's departure.

"I'd like to apologize to you for Cyrus's reaction," Decker said after a while. "He no doubt finds this prospect to be a daunting change, not unlike giving up one's daughter in marriage." The comment drew a few smiles from around the table. Then, as Vice Chair, he asked: "Is there any further discussion before we call for a vote?"

In the brief quiet that followed there was some awkward shuffling of papers and reorienting of seat positions.

"As a point of order, Decker, there's no motion on the table and no second." It was uttered by Helen Anderson, an external director and the only female member of the board.

"You're absolutely correct, Helen, forgive my oversight." He surveyed the table. "Do I hear a motion to entertain the Drexel-Pace bid?"

"We don't even have a Chair," exclaimed Nathan Peel, another outside director. "Are you intending to continue this meeting without a Chair?"

Decker gathered himself, trying to cover his lapse. With the departure of the Chairman and no pass of the baton there was no meeting. It was indeed bizarre. "In that case, I suggest we adjourn for lunch and reconvene at one o'clock. We've been at this all morning and I'm sure we could all use a break."

* * *

Decker found the company's founder sitting at his blank desk, in the office he rarely occupied, which carried the sterile cleanliness of one so absent. "I was afraid you might have left the building."

"I *should* leave the building. I might as well leave it for good," Schoen said bleakly.

"C'mon, Grandfather. You're making this into a far different thing than what it is. It's good for the company. It's the right thing at the right time."

"No it isn't, Decker. A lifetime of experience and hard knocks tells me it isn't."

"But it's a perfect fit. Can't you see that we'll continue to get chipped away by the competition without this kind of move?"

"Decker, let me tell you something. Competition is good. It disciplines you. Moves you, makes you stronger. They aren't offering us anything we can't do on our own. I know it might take more time and effort on our part, but we'd come out far better in the end. This way we simply get devoured and forgotten. There'd be no shareholder group to motivate us, which is the reason I agreed to your idea to go public in the first place. The shareholders are our boss. We're accountable to them."

"But we'd be offering them fifty percent over what they have now. You can't tell me that's not in their interest."

"It's whoring, Decker, witching and whoring. The shareholders get bought out and Schoen will become a prostitute of the great Drexel-Pace pimp. You don't think they'd just let the generics business I built all my life shrivel up and die? Of course they will. You heard them. They have no interest in it, only the high-tech specialty stuff."

"But that's where the market is, where our profits are. We're damn good at it."

"I know we are, young man, and I have you to thank for much of that. But the fact is, generic chemicals remain the manufacturing blood of this country. Foreigners are taking them over. Hell, U.S. manufacturing is going to be as dependent on other countries for its basic chemical needs as we are for petroleum and everything else. They'll hold us by the balls."

"We can't fight it, Grandfather. This isn't about patriotism, it's about business. The environmental costs are eating us up. And now with this Superfund issue we need to get ourselves under a larger umbrella."

Schoen turned in his swivel chair and stared out the window that overlooked the Merrimack River. "That's a crock and you know it. The EPA can't tag this on me. I've been clean all my life—that is, until this recent witch-hunt. And I'll beat this one, too." Then he turned back around with a pointed finger. "I've given command of this company over to you because I trust you. I can't let it lose the identity I've created my whole life. I've lost two wives and God knows what else for the years of time and sweat I've put into this. I'm asking you to hold to my interest in it. To the interest of all the employees who have given their lives to it as well. Don't just cave in to the first appealing offer. There will be plenty of them, and much better ones, in the future."

Decker studied his grandfather with a quartered look of admiration. There was an internal quest still driving the old man, which Decker found alien. It was a thirst that towered above financial payoff or self-recognition. Nothing as selfless or as virtuous as a humanitarian cause, yet it still represented goals that were measures beyond his own.

"Would you like to join us for lunch?" asked Decker.

"No. I think I just want to be by myself for a while. You go on ahead." Schoen swiveled back around toward the window. From the back of the chair his baldpate rose like a harvest moon, liver spots looking like lunar shadows. "When's the board reconvening?" Schoen asked.

"One o'clock."

"Then I'll see you then."

Decker was about to exit the door when his grandfather addressed him again, still with his chairback turned. "Decker?"

"Yeah?"

"Just remember: some of the most attractive mushrooms are the most poisonous."

* * *

The directors filed back into the boardroom in twos and threes according to their paired lunch groupings, and were all present shortly before the designated time. Decker and the company of men from Drexel-Pace made it a point to be prompt. He enjoyed lunch with the team despite the wave they rode out from the morning session. Afterward, he came to talk a bit with Alan Pelleman, Drexel-Pace's representative CPA partner from Marsh, Mason & Pratt in Atlanta. Larry Carpenter stood with them.

"I have an old college buddy who went with your firm way back," said Decker. "His name's Jonathan Sands. Your Boston office. Ever heard of him?"

"Sands?" Pelleman asked surprised. "My God, no kidding. Sure I know him. He's a senior partner in that office now. Two hundred plus employees and his client list keeps growing. He was under consideration for the managing partner position a while back but turned it down. I guess he enjoys his client base too much to give it up."

"I always knew he'd make it big." Decker thought of the closeness he once shared with his old college roommate. Although he had stayed fairly close with most of his old frat brothers, the relationship with Sands went cold once they graduated. "We used to rent an apartment together in Middlebury, Vermont. But I haven't spoken to him in years."

OPTIONS

"Is that so? Well, if this merger deal works out you'll very likely see him again. As our New England expert in high-tech manufacturing, he'd be perfect to head up the engagement."

Decker certainly hadn't thought about that. If the deal with Drexel-Pace went through there would likely be a change in auditors to the ones employed by the parent firm. He shelved it away in his thoughts.

Ten minutes went by without the Chair. Decker was about to get up to seek out his grandfather when Schoen quietly stepped into the room and took his seat at the head of the table.

"I want to thank the gentlemen from Drexel-Pace for their very informative presentation," he said in resumption of the meeting. It was the closest thing to an apology that would come from Schoen. "Now, if I can get a motion and a second for further entertainment of this offer, we can open the table up for discussion."

Without pause Michael Riley put in: "I make a motion that we go forward with our negotiations with Drexel-Pace."

Schoen immediately regretted the requirement that his directors take stock options in the company.

"Seconded," said Decker.

Schoen glanced over at his grandson, hurt but not a bit surprised. "In that case the table is opened up for discussion."

Howard Melnick, a business associate and career-long friend of Schoen's, raised his hand to be recognized. "Cyrus, given your obvious misgivings about this proposal, I think the board would benefit by hearing from you first. Perhaps the Drexel-Pace team can address your reservations directly."

"That's a sensible suggestion, Howard, and I appreciate it." Schoen folded his hands with a slight quiver of Parkinson's and looked around the room. In a much calmer voice than he displayed earlier that morning, he began: "I meant what I said about the Drexel-Pace presentation. It was well done and quite informative. Certainly it looks to be a very generous bid. I'm impressed these men have placed before us a plan as detailed and as clearly spelled out as it is. We've had our share of proposals that have left us with far more questions than answers, nothing nearly as compelling on its face.

"But to be honest with you," he continued, "I have more than misgivings about it. How many mergers have taken place the past decade where everything on the front end appeared ideal, only to fail in the end with millions, billions, of dollars wasted? The newspaper accounts are full of them. Despite what Mr. Carpenter said there will always be clashes in corporate culture, ones that can never be foreseen. A firm as large and as established as Drexel-Pace undoubtedly has ways of doing things that will run contrary to our wishes and methods. As they said, our key assets are our human assets. Those assets, unfortunately, have legs. And if our people become unhappy, as many surely will, there's nothing to keep them from walking out. Think about it. We acquired our portfolio of talent precisely because we are a young public firm with great upside potential. Most of them have enjoyed wonderful gains in their employee stock ownership plans. Do you really think once their shares are bought out they won't be looking elsewhere?

"Second, and relatedly, our small size and growth prospects have attracted a loyal shareholder base that is genuinely interested in what we're doing. The fat institutions that recklessly vote their shares, that couldn't care less about what we do as long as we provide the returns they're looking for, don't hold us. We're too small for them and that's a good thing. As it stands, we're accountable to our owners. Small stockholders ... socially conscious investors who hold us for our environmental record, as well as our profits. I've been clean my whole life. Not once have we run afoul of the environmental people."

At this, Carpenter directed an almost imperceptible glance at Decker.

Schoen went on: "What other chemical firm of our size can boast of such a record? That kind of discipline keeps us working harder. If we were to allow ourselves to be bought out by a mega-corporation like Drexel-Pace, that social responsibility and entrepreneurial spirit would go down the toilet. I've studied some about these people. They have dozens of EPA sites. They don't give a damn. Instead of motivations bred out of a quest for innovative excellence and social consciousness, they would be driven by unsympathetic lordship. We'd become slaves to their wishes."

Old as he was, Schoen was still very much with it and in command of his game. He held the faces of his board members, pleased to see from their occasional nods he was scoring points.

Decker could see that as well, causing his concern to rise. He raised his hand. Cyrus P. Schoen stared at his namesake. "Hold on, *Cyrus*, I'm not finished. You'll be given your chance."

OPTIONS

Decker withdrew his hand, not showing the embarrassment he felt. Schoen's use of his first name—bestowed by his parents in honor of his grandfather—was taken as the subtle chastisement for disloyalty it was intended to be.

The board Chairman stood from his seat and walked over to the projection screen that was still down. "A little while ago you were presented forecasted figures up here. *Pro forma* figures, whatever the hell that means. I may not know Latin but I know the chemical business. You heard these men. They said they weren't interested in our generic chemicals business. Quite frankly, that got me boiling. Fifty-two years ago I started this firm as a wholesale distributor of chemical products—products that are integral to the manufacture of goods that have made this country great. Goods we use and we eat and that help us win wars. More and more chemical production is now taking place overseas. Most claim they're cheaper to manufacture elsewhere, but I've proven them wrong. Our margins in generics are the highest in the industry. And we've done it by being clean, green and mean. Generic chemicals *have* to remain an emphasis of this company because they provide the fundamental by-product resources that make specialty chemical manufacturing even possible. Listening to these people, you'd think they would be an afterthought ... or worse, something to be spun off!"

The animated man walked back to his seat. He coughed to clear his throat and took a sip of water from his glass.

"We didn't say that, Mr. Schoen," countered Larry Carpenter.

"It's more what you didn't say, Mr. Carpenter," Schoen shot back proleptically. "You said you're not particularly interested in our generics business, which I take to mean you're not appreciative of the very core of this company."

"No, I—"

"I'm sorry, Mr. Carpenter, but you've spoken and you're not properly recognized." Schoen waved him off with a dismissive hand. He turned instead to his grandson. "Decker, you wished to say something?"

Carpenter's face flushed livid.

"Yes, I would like very much to say some things," responded Decker. "With all respect, Cyrus, I think you're reading this all wrong. I've been assured our generics business would be completely unaffected by the buyout." Decker looked at Carpenter and company, each in turn nodding. It was a way of sliding in their affirming input without going against the old man's sudden desire for proper parliamentary procedure. "Yes, we would be wholly-owned, but these men recognize the qualities that made us an attractive candidate in the first place, and they know it would be foolish to interfere with those qualities. Joe Moran said as much when he assured us they had no such intentions … to 'reorganize our house,' is the way I think he put it."

"The problem, Decker," broke in Schoen, shaking his head, "the problem is there would be no way to ensure that. What assurance could they possibly give us that we would be left alone to do what we do best?"

Decker knew no such assurances could be given, only faith. He chose instead to shift the subject to an area he wished to address earlier. "Your point about our employees walking out upon the combination can, however, be addressed. As can your fear of layoffs. I propose you take the matter as a point of negotiation that there will be no layoffs, and condition our board's approval on a profit-sharing plan in lieu of their current ESOPs. That way our employees would get an immediate fifty percent return on their shares and also remain devoted to the future profitability of the company."

It was, in fact, an idea worthy of consideration. ESOPs—employee stock ownership plans—made little sense if the shares were not publicly traded, as would be the case following a 100 percent buyout by Drexel-Pace. Maintaining comparable employee benefits would require them to be substituted for something else.

Schoen appeared modestly intrigued by the suggestion. "Mr. Carpenter?"

"I'd be happy to take it under consideration." Carpenter caught the eyes of his colleagues at the table. "Perhaps you would allow us to step out to talk it over?"

"Yes, of course. We'll continue our meeting and call you gentlemen back in to join us." Schoen looked down at his copy of the meeting agenda. "Would an hour be adequate for your needs?"

The Drexel-Pace team members nodded to one another. After the motion was made and carried for an agenda amendment, they lifted their papers and briefcases and shuffled out of the room. A secretary directed them to a smaller conference room down the hallway.

Once the door was closed Kent Shaughnessy said: "Things aren't going well."

OPTIONS

"I feel like strangling the old bastard," blared Carpenter. "How dare he twist my words like that? I'm just about ready to walk out of here and go with 'Plan B.' Screw the whole lot of them."

Joe Moran and Allan Pelleman sat at the conference table with their calculators out, poring over financial data Joe carried in his briefcase. The Drexel-Pace lawyers conversed quietly about the legal implications associated with Decker's suggestion that the buyout be conditioned on no layoffs. They toyed with the possibility of "tin parachutes"—employees offered the right to generous severance pay—but rejected it in favor of a temporary moratorium on unit terminations. There would have to be a reasonable expiration period, of course, but a clause could be worded to capture the spirit of the idea without offering what amounted to lifetime job tenure. Larry and Kent remained silent while the others went about their work.

Forty-five minutes later Moran lifted his head from his calculations. "Gentlemen, without having a computer my numbers are a little crude, but I've come up with something. Factoring in zero layoffs and a five-percent bonus pool—I'm assuming ten-percent constant profit growth for ten years and a two-percent growth perpetuity thereafter, with tax deductibility for profit sharing—"

"Shut up, Joe. I don't care about your algebraic gymnastics at the moment." Carpenter rolled his eyes at Moran's financial-speak, which was his custom when the fat man irritated him. "Just give me the damned bottom line."

"Well, in order to maintain parity with our initial offer, I don't see how we could go higher than forty-five percent over current price. And even that's probably giving them more than our board intended."

"Then that's as far as I'm going with these people." Larry stood up, resolve stamped on his face. "If they can't see what's plainly in front of their eyes then they're fools. And I won't do business with a bunch of fools."

Standing outside the boardroom entrance, they painted pleasant faces. But fifteen minutes of waiting stretched into a half-hour, then an hour, and their felicitous expressions melted with each passing moment. Ten minutes short of two hours, Decker finally came out to call them back into the room.

Larry Carpenter was given the floor again. Before speaking he caught Michael Riley's eye. Carpenter's old comrade furtively shook his head and mouthed the words: "No go."

Screw them, thought Carpenter. He stood up. "Members of the board, I want to thank you for the opportunity you've given us today to present our case, and by doing so to let us share our respect for the wonderful job you've done leading this company. Irrespective of today's outcome, please be assured that our respect is sincere regarding your firm's autonomy. Whether you caucus to become part of us or not, we will not interfere in any way with the recipe you've found so successful to date."

He shifted position in his chair and paused, carefully organizing his thoughts. "After giving the concerns you raised every benefit of consideration possible under the tight circumstances—that is, without further approvals from my board—we are prepared to modify our offer as follows. We will provide an eighteen-month layoff moratorium, provisional on customary employment performance, and offer a five percent bonus pool on Schoen's year-over-year operating income." He cleared his throat again. "However, by offering these concessions we must necessarily reduce our bid premium to thirty-five percent." Carpenter then sat down.

Joe Moran whispered in his ear: "I think you meant to say *forty-five* percent."

Carpenter peremptorily shook his head.

"Thank you, Mr. Carpenter," said Schoen. He then looked around the table. "Are there any further questions of these men before I excuse them for our final deliberations and vote?"

None was forthcoming.

"In that case, I thank you gentlemen very much. We'll adjourn for half an hour and then re-convene at three-thirty."

Decker hurried out of the boardroom to catch up with Larry Carpenter and his men. He quickly ushered them into his office down the hallway.

"I'm very sorry, Larry. Both for the way you were treated in there and for the way the board seems to be going with this. We need six out of the nine and I only count five for sure. There's one possible, Nathan Peel, and Helen Anderson's a long shot. Quite a long shot."

Carpenter nodded. "What seems to be their hang-up?"

Decker walked over to his desk and sat on its edge. "There was a lot of discussion about the timing; that we'd be selling out too soon after going public … a so-called violation of implied shareholder rights to invest long-term. I don't have any idea what that's all about, and I told them as much. But several of them also seem to be backing Schoen's concerns about corporate cultures and accountability to shareholders. It's all a bunch of crap as far as I'm concerned."

"What about the Superfund issue? Did it even come up?"

"I tried to persuade them along those lines, but Cyrus just argued with me, saying the EPA matter is no reason for selling. The other three uncertain votes seemed to agree with him—that it's no big deal, that we'll beat it."

"Well, we gave it our best shot, Decker. Let me know when you get the vote. We'll be in the hotel atrium for happy hour, and then in the restaurant for dinner. You're welcome to join us."

The men shook hands and parted.

Chapter Seventeen

THE dissenting directors were miffed about the huge reduction in the offer premium, and the "possible" vote Decker was hoping for didn't materialize. The ballot failed to carry and further negotiations with Drexel-Pace were henceforth terminated.

The balance of the day's board meeting was spent going over the draft of the third quarter financial statements and the EPA citation. Everett Royce discussed at length his research regarding the firm's legal exposure. Cap Satterfield, Schoen's CFO, elaborated on the financial reporting alternatives. He indicated there was no need to book a loss at this point since the extent of the firm's liability—if it was to amount to anything at all—was too uncertain. The directors agreed to provide at least some qualitative discussion of the Superfund issue in the footnotes to the financial statements. They decided to meet again the next day via teleconference to conclude the matter.

Frustrated, Decker left the building at 5:30.

He found Larry Carpenter, Joe Moran and Kent Shaughnessy sitting in the hotel atrium as Carpenter had said. All were smiling.

The Drexel-Pace CEO stood to greet him. "Don't tell me … five to four, right?"

"Exactly. How did you know?"

"Your face. Probably due to me pulling back so much on my offer price?"

"Again, yes."

Carpenter pulled out a chair for him. "Here, have a seat."

A cascading waterfall and pond of rock masonry decorated the foliage festooned atrium. Artfully adorned with ornamental tropical plants, it all reminded Decker of the type of scene one would find at Disney World. Despite the disappointing news, the men were in astoundingly good spirits, Decker observed. Certainly accounting for more spirits than they could have downed in the short time they were there.

"What can I get for you, Deck?" Kent asked cheerfully.

"A double Scotch please, thanks. On the rocks." Shaughnessy headed off to the bar.

"Where's the rest of your team—the lawyers and the CPA?" Moss asked Carpenter.

"They had to catch their flight back to Atlanta. The three of us booked a morning flight. We wanted to make sure we had the opportunity to speak with you some more."

"Larry, again I apologize for the treatment you received. It was beyond anything I've ever seen from the man. I think his crusted arteries must be choking off his brain cells."

A minute later Kent returned bearing his familiar grin and Decker's drink.

"I can't understand why you guys appear to be in such a good mood," said Moss.

"It's not over, Decker," said Moran, "you have no faith." A quart-sized beer mug sat straddled in his palms, dripping condensation from its sides.

"What do you mean? We lost the vote." Decker took a gulp of his Scotch, feeling the malt embalm his throat. "The way I look at it, even if my other two directors showed up we couldn't have done better than a seven-four split. Not the two-thirds we needed."

"Joe's right, Decker," Carpenter concurred with passive emphasis. "It's not over." He extracted some chunks of ice from his glass and chomped on them as he looked out across the grand space, as if monitoring the surroundings for security. "Not unless you want it to be."

Perplexed, Decker eyed the man with curiosity. "Why? Are you intending to increase your offer?"

"No way in hell." Carpenter sat forward in his chair. "I've been through these things before ... many times. Oh, never with the disrespect given me by your Chairman, I'll say that. But I've certainly had my share of disapproving boards. It's all part of the great mosaic of events and institutions we call American enterprise." Larry set down his empty glass, crossed his arms, and looked pointedly at the man who was only slightly more than half his age. "Are you still interested in seeing this happen? If so, we talk business. If not, we'll talk sports."

Decker thought the question, odd as it was, didn't need a reply. The morning's prospects had crashed headlong to the ground, taking his psyche along with the ride. The whirlwind of emotions he felt was just now beginning to fade with his drink.

But not the anger he felt at his grandfather. "Yes, very interested," he said.

Carpenter plucked an olive from his glass and mouthed it. "Decker, we don't need your board's approval. We never did. Things just tend to run smoother that way. We've been planning for this possibility all along—in fact, I've been expecting it—and it comes with my board's blessing."

Larry caught the waitress's attention with a glance and held up his glass to request a refill. Then he turned again toward Decker with a chess-move look in his eye. "I purposely undercut what we were willing to pay in the end when I gave them my revised bid. I saw from Michael Riley's expression that your people weren't going to be amenable to our proposal no matter what, which is what I suspected when I left the room. I don't like to throw my pearls before swine."

"Strong words, Larry."

"Nothing personal. Anyway, I knew at that point your board was too far gone in their vote to make a marriage work. I wanted to get my money off the table. If I looked too hungry, I might have tipped them off to our next move."

"Next move?" Moss shifted in his chair. "Sorry, but I'm not following." He downed more of his drink, waiting for the man to clarify.

"A takeover," Carpenter answered simply.

The liquor reversed itself halfway up Decker's gullet. "*Takeover?*" he coughed.

"Yes, a tender offer to your stockholders. Let *them* decide whether or not to sell their shares to us. After all, your board's vote today is arguably quite counter to your shareholders' interests. They didn't even get the chance to hear our good-faith bid."

"But a hostile bid, Larry? What if my board puts up a fight?"

"So what? There's no need for your board's approval here. It's a public announcement, a media proffer. Your stockholders simply take it or leave it. We only need more than fifty percent of the shares and we'll be in the control position we want."

Moss was drinking on an empty stomach and it had been a long day. He'd read about hostile takeovers, of course, but he had never been involved in one. Schoen had been public too short a time for anything like it to come up.

"I don't know, Larry. I'd need to know more about this."

"Well, if I can set you at ease, this is nothing unusual. It's done all the time." The pharmaceutical chief glimpsed blithely at his colleagues who nodded agreement.

OPTIONS

The waitress returned with Larry Carpenter's cocktail. All ordered another round. When she was off again Carpenter said: "What would you like to know?"

Decker's eyes wandered about the atrium, momentarily diverted to the retreating waitress's shapely backside. "Well, for one, if you're seeking to gain control of my board by owning a majority of the shares, then you'll have to wait a while. Our corporate bylaws require staggered director terms. In fact, my term comes up next go-around."

"We're very aware of that fact," said Larry in a soothing tone. "You, Schoen, Royce and Anderson are each up for vote at the next meeting. Not a problem, not now that we know *who* the dissenters on your board are. We vote two of them out at the next annual meeting and we'll have control. Following that, the next two meetings we'll dominate. That's one reason we wanted to face your directors with our proposal in person … to see who our sympathizers might be."

"Clever." Moss was quickly becoming aware of the shrewd minds he was dealing with. Although Carpenter didn't say it, Decker knew who those two ousted directors would be: Anderson and the old-man, Schoen himself.

"Oh, it's not so clever, Deck. Like I said, I've circled the sun a few times."

It wasn't uneasiness Decker felt. In fact, if he felt any unease whatsoever it was that he felt no uneasiness at all. His shareholders had been denied the right to even hear of the bid. The only recourse available to them was to elect directors who acted in their best interests, but with the blind faith they would do so behind closed doors. Moss genuinely doubted that had taken place today. Not with an offer of fifty percent over current market price on the table.

The waitress walked up with their fresh rounds. Decker winked at her, surprised that she returned it with a receptive smile.

What didn't yet make sense to him was why the CEO of Drexel-Pace was being so candid sharing his intentions with the CEO of his target firm. "So, why are you telling me all this?"

"Quite simple, my friend." Carpenter stirred the ice in his glass with his long bony finger. "We want you. You should be aware of that. Once we make our offer public we wouldn't want your board going off and writing you a golden parachute." As a takeover defense, executives of a target firm would sometimes be ensured severance at exorbitant pay in hopes that a would-be bidder would find it prohibitively costly and bow out. "Beyond that, however, your being on our side and the CEO of Schoen at the same time could work out very beneficial to us."

"I can only imagine," said Decker, pulling a long draw from his Scotch. On this point he knew he was skating on thin ethical ice. But the anger he felt at his grandfather and his three minions on the board took him there anyway. Besides, skating was easy if done with a bit of booze on an empty stomach.

"We're prepared to take good care of you for that," said Carpenter. "For that and your loyalty."

"Loyalty? I won't ask what that would be." Moss set down his drink. Then, draping an arm over the back of his chair with a tempted expression on his face: "Though, if you buy me another drink, you can whisper in my ear."

Joe Moran explained the revised terms of Decker's compensation. They remained what they were under the original proposal with the following important exception: "Whatever number of shares we take in from our tender offer, as long as we're above our fifty-percent threshold for control, we'll hold three percent in treasury for you ... for stock options."

The steady splash of the waterfall resonated brightly across the tiled room and Decker's mind went into a momentary whiteout. *There were over 40 million shares outstanding.* "Did I hear you right?" he asked.

"That's right," affirmed Carpenter. "Three percent of whatever we take in, as long as we retain a majority holding." He stared intently at the younger CEO, waiting for the point to stick. "We'd set the strike price equal to the market price that exists just prior to our public offer announcement. But we want your loyalty, Decker. Your *demonstrated* loyalty."

Decker knew he had to ask the question: "Which would mean...?"

It was Kent Shaughnessy who responded: "On certain matters that will help us pull off a successful buyout. The Superfund issue, for example."

Again Decker regarded the men with curiosity.

"When's your scheduled third quarter earnings announcement?" asked Joe Moran.

"We come out with our numbers next week. Thursday."

"Then I think you can see what needs to be done," said Joe. "Your third quarter earnings release ... The SEC would like nothing more than for Schoen to come clean in its financial statements about that environmental liability issue. And while it will slow things down a bit on our side, it would have to take place before we can make our bid public to your shareholders."

Decker sensed where the men were heading. It was a notable rarity for firms to recognize contingent environmental losses in their income statements. Doing so would rip their stock price. According to his legal man, Everett Royce, the SEC was beginning to tighten disclosure requirements in the area, suspecting many firms purposely hid their environmental exposure even when they knew full well they had a material liability. Those that disclosed the matter at all tended to do so with intentionally obscure wording buried deep within the footnotes to their financial statements.

"My board thought some qualitative description in the quarterly report would be appropriate," said Moss.

"No," objected Carpenter. "It has to be front and center, Decker. You have to *book* a loss ... a full hit to your earnings, no footnote crap."

Moran added: "And I wouldn't dance around with it. The more liberal your loss estimate the better."

Decker shifted his gaze across the room in reflection. He briefly caught the eye of the waitress again and then turned back to the men. "I only have a week. What about my auditors?"

"No green eyeshade crew is going to frown on you reporting a loss provision," assuaged Moran. "Besides, your quarterly results aren't audited, only reviewed. Believe me, a week is plenty of time for them to review your estimated write-off. Your CPA firm is some regional outfit, aren't they?" Moran knew they were.

Decker nodded.

"They're not going to give you a problem."

Moss suspected Joe Moran was correct. One of the accounting profession's most sacrosanct principles was conservatism—the CPA's mantra—and booking losses was subject to far less scrutiny than booking gains.

Yet, for Decker, the obvious question remained. "How do I get my board to go along with it?"

"Well," answered Carpenter, "whether it came up at your meeting or not, I know what they've got to be thinking at this point. Merger talks always have a way of leaking out, and that usually invites other suitors. They also have to be wondering if we might not be planning another play of our own, perhaps even a hostile bid like we're talking about here. What better way of insulating themselves than to announce a significant environmental liability? A firm that places such a heavy premium on social responsibility would no longer look as attractive as a target. Who'd want them if it meant taking on that kind of exposure?"

Decker's eyes widened with realization. "So *that's* why you didn't want me to let my directors know I told you about Mullins." He raised his glass. "You're a crafty man, Larry."

"Thank you."

Decker downed another gulp. "So how much of a write-off would it have to be?"

"What's the EPA's overall estimate?" asked Joe Moran.

"Upwards of a hundred million."

"*My God!*" exploded Moran. "*A hundred million?* What'd your plant do, stick its sewage pipe directly into the Washington reflecting pools?"

"Very funny, Joe."

"What percentage is your responsibility?" Kent Shaughnessy asked, slurping some ice.

"I have no idea. They dug up just over a hundred drums bearing the Mullins plant's name, but we haven't yet had time to determine their chemical contribution to the mess."

"That's understandable." Larry Carpenter leaned back in his chair and folded his arms against his chest. "How many containers in total? That is, everyone's combined?"

"A few hundred, give or take."

"So for now what's wrong with accruing one-third of the total estimated cost?" Larry looked alternately at the three men. "Add your legal costs in there. Forty? Fifty million? That's enough, I'd say. You can always revise your estimated loss provision in the future as you get better information. Your directors know how to play the game."

"I don't know," said Decker doubtfully. "That would be pretty extreme. There are six other PRPs."

"Yes, but they're small players," reminded Kent. "Don't forget the EPA goes after the big guys, the deep pockets. Going heavy with it your slate would be clean."

"Yeah, that along with my bank account," Decker tittered. He looked wistfully off to the waterfall again, thinking of his stock options. "So the stock price takes a dive and you pick up Schoen's shares at a bargain.

"No, not a bargain," Kent clarified, "the *proper* price. The market's discount for the environmental loss will make it the proper price."

The Drexel-Pace men watched Decker's contemplative expression evolve as he mulled over their points. It didn't take him long for one matter to rise to the forefront of his thinking. "My stock options will go underwater with the tumble. They won't amount to wet toilet paper."

"You didn't listen to me carefully," corrected Joe. "The exercise price of the options we give you will be correspondingly lower since it will be based on the market quote *after* your third quarter results are released—along with your Superfund write-off. Personally, you should make out very well. Extremely well."

Decker hadn't made that connection yet. Of course. He announces the environmental loss, Schoen's stock price takes dive, and he gets his options at the correspondingly low exercise price. Then when Drexel-Pace makes its offer at fifty percent over market, the share price soars, and he pockets the difference ... *on three percent of Drexel-Pace's purchased shares.* His existing stock options may not do as well but they were trivial in comparison. All that on top of a doubling of his salary and a position on the Drexel-Pace board.

Moss was in the rocket seat again. And his whiskey was working its magic mellow.

"As I said before, gentlemen, I think we can do business."

* * *

After the men imbibed a few more drinks in the atrium they had dinner in the hotel restaurant. Their subsequent conversation was largely auxiliary to their earlier discussion, a good part of which was spent educating Decker on the anatomy of a corporate takeover. They answered his questions about regulatory requirements and the timing in which ensuing events would take place. In the end, he found comfort in their request for him to just take it easy and "ride things out."

There'd be no remaining meetings among them until it was all over, they agreed—not even any telephone contact—for if Decker Moss were ever discovered as a turncoat his fellow directors would see him fry. The Drexel-Pace men did, however, leave Moss with a directive to return some important deliverables to them during the "blackout" period.

Following dinner Decker sat by himself in the atrium waiting for the waitress to finish her shift. She consented to have a drink with him. It was followed by a second and a third. Afterward, they left the hotel together for his place.

* * *

Monday, October 19, 1992
New York, New York

It was an up day on Wall Street.

That despite it being an October Monday—points on the calendar that seemed to hold an unaccountably bad omen for the market. Indeed, it was in spite of it being the five-year anniversary of the October 19, 1987 "Black Monday" crash—a day on which the market evaporated nearly 23 percent of its value, far eclipsing the 13 percent one-day slide that ushered in the 1929 crash and Great Depression.

The financial press had been capricious in its replay of remarks by so-called market pundits, commentators whose references to the anniversary led to wacky predictions of recycled doom. As if the stock market was driven by a mad mind of its own. As if what took place five years ago had anything to do with what would take place today.

As always, the commotion on the floor of the New York Stock Exchange was deafening: brokers yelling orders, specialists calling out commands to their clerks, floor traders running from one end of the room to the other with order sheets falling to the floor like Broadway confetti. One thing Jack Edmonds had learned about the New York Stock Exchange over the years was that where there was a lot of money there were a lot of brains. And those brains generally belonged to levelheaded thinkers.

As a specialist on the floor, Edmonds basically took the unfolding bid and ask prices as a product of market rationality. It was his job to make an "orderly market" for his seven listed stocks. Orders would come in from various brokerage houses around the country and ultimately be transacted at his post. If there were insufficient buyers or sellers within a reasonable bid-ask spread, the specialist was expected to fill the order from his own inventory. It was this function that differentiated the NYSE continuous auction market from the over-the-counter NASDAQ. Edmonds was proud of his role in the process, and with good reason. Being the only person in the world who had the "full book" supply and demand for his listed firm's shares at any given moment, he was able to earn for himself and his partners several million dollars in trading profits annually.

The newest of his seven listed stocks, however, was nose-diving at the moment. So much so that he called up the ticker symbol, SCHO, on his news screen. He had expected Schoen's third quarter earnings announcement to be made the previous Thursday. He knew a company's delay in release of its quarterly earnings often portended bad news.

And there it was:

> *PR Newswire*: MANCHESTER, NH, October 19, 1992. Schoen Chemicals Corporation (SCHO) announced today a third quarter net loss of $.39 per share, down $.72 from second quarter earnings and down $.68 from 1991 third quarter earnings. This was on sales of $83.75 million, compared to $75.1 million, year over year. Included is a one-time environmental charge of $50 million, or $1.13 per share, for estimated costs associated with its connection to a Superfund waste site.

> According to Schoen's chief executive officer, C. Decker Moss, the firm was recently named as a potentially responsible party (PRP) by the U.S. Environmental Protection Agency (EPA) for hazardous waste disposal at a site located in Camden, South Carolina. "This is the firm's first citation by the EPA, and the first blemish on an otherwise untarnished environmental record," reported Moss. "We have always been a responsible player in the environmental arena, and with that sometimes comes the responsibility to own up to conditions that might not go in our preferred direction." He declined to comment on the legal implications of the matter other than to say that Schoen intended to cooperate fully with

EPA, yet vigorously pursue all defenses available under the law. The write-off to earnings and hit to the balance sheet, he said, was being taken "in the interest of full disclosure to Schoen's shareholders and to comply with the SEC's efforts to get firms to record their environmental liabilities sooner rather than later."

"The site poses a serious threat to human health and the environment due to hazardous substances disposed during the 1960s and 1970s," commented Robert Elray, EPAs regional administrator. "We are ordering those responsible for causing the problem to design and perform the remedy."

EPA originally issued a Record of Decision (ROD) for the site on July 1, 1991, which prescribed the remediation measures to be taken. In that decision the cleanup was estimated to be between $75 and $100 million.

The newswire continued with various details concerning the site, including the fact that there were six other named PRPs.

It was a curious media release, thought Edmonds. Curious yet explosive. Voluntarily recording a contingent loss before a consent decree with the EPA had been issued? He had never heard of it being done before. And by a chemical company whose shares sold at a hefty multiple precisely because of its celebrated environmental record? What did Moss think would happen, that his stockholders would somehow reward him for his probity?

Several brokers now circled Edmonds's post representing sizeable sell orders. Buyers were nonexistent. He looked again at the loss estimate: *Fifty million.* It was half the high end of the EPA's ROD estimate, yet there were six other PRPs. The firm was essentially lying on its back, he thought.

He stared at Schoen's price on his trading monitor. It had already dropped three and an eighth from its opening quote of 341/3.

Jack Edmonds realized he was going to take a bath that day after all.

Chapter Eighteen

THE Tuesday edition of *The Wall Street Journal* sat folded and unread at the corner of his desk, which, when it happened, broke a comfortable routine. Arriving bright and early at the office and reading the *Journal* were two habits Jonathan Sands laid down for himself early in his career. Both yielded intangible payoffs: the first, uninterrupted time when he was at his mental peak; the second, an awareness of current affairs in the fast-changing world of business—always valuable conversational fodder when meeting with his audit clients.

Today's calendar, however, was simply too full to make room.

Sands spent the morning going over the files for a recently completed audit, TempQuest, Inc., a manufacturer of commercial heating and air conditioning equipment located in Lowell, just north of Boston. His morning preparation was for a meeting with their finance team at ten. It would be tight since it was now 9:15, and Lowell, even in good traffic, was a good half-hour away. Had it not been for some major inventory overstatements the company committed, he would have been finished with his review the previous afternoon.

The phone rang.

"Are you ready, Jonathan?"

He consulted his watch again. "Sorry, Jensyn, I'll be right down. Give me two more minutes."

"I'll meet you at the lift."

Her British accent prompted a smile as he re-cradled the phone. Upon giving the executive summary of her report one last read, Sands gathered up the stacks of TempQuest working papers he might need for the meeting and placed them in his briefcase. Then, stiffening his tie knot and grabbing the suit jacket off the desk-front chair, he was out the door.

Jensyn Chandler stood waiting, briefcase in hand, in front of the elevator at the end of the corridor. She was wearing a sharply tailored sable-colored dress suit, only a shade darker than her long brunet hair. An MBA from Harvard, she was one of the rising stars in the office. Having distinguished herself in the manufacturing and technology sectors she was now working increasingly with Jonathan as a new audit manager on a few of his major clients.

"I was afraid you might have forgotten," she offered apologetically. "I knew we'd be in a rush."

Sands smiled. "No, Jen, thanks for the call. I was just checking out your adjustments one last time." They stepped into the retracting doors and he hit the lobby button.

"Everything okay?" she asked.

"Yes, your report is right on. Great work, as usual."

She responded with a smile.

In the recent months working with her, Jonathan came to appreciate her commitment to detail. He also enjoyed her spiritedly good-natured personality. No airs of play or pose, no haughtiness, no insincerity in her nature at all, just authenticity. It was a refreshing contrast to many in the rising talent group, those who seemed to do only what they thought would please their boss. The obsequiousness of some of his subordinates was downright nauseating.

"So they hadn't properly written down their inventories?" Jonathan asked. The question was superfluous since the working papers he spent the morning reviewing made that abundantly clear.

"No, not by a long shot. I'm sure you read the consultant's report. Much of their warehouse stock was manufactured for Freon refrigerant several years ago, making it obsolete without some costly retrofitting. I'm recommending they do so."

"Clever of you to think of it." His previous audit manager of the engagement hadn't detected the problem the year before. "How did you know it was even a possibility? It's pretty technical stuff."

"The turnover ratios," Jensyn answered. "I noticed they were sluggish and I recalled an article I read about Freon being outlawed in the States a while back. It all just connected."

"Very impressive. We'll see how they react."

They exited the revolving doors onto State Street. Marsh, Mason & Pratt's CPA offices took up five floors of a building in the heart of Boston's financial district, on the wharf overlooking Boston Harbor. In an anachronistic display, the modern high rise buildings stood tall, flanked by colonial treasures such as Faneuil Hall, The Old State House, and Old Town Hall. The day happened to be bright and pleasant despite the late month of the year, and Jensyn tilted her head to take in some of the warm rays as they walked together to the parking garage down the street.

His black Mercedes 500 SL still had a new-car aroma—mixed scents of top-grain leather and deep varnished mahogany. "Pretty car, Jonathan. Have you had it long?"

"Just a couple weeks. I used to drive a Cherokee, but what do I need all that room for? Besides, it's great to drive out on the Cape with the top down."

"I bet."

Pulling out of the parking garage, he put on a pair of sunglasses that rested on the dash. "I'm probably just suffering from the proverbial middle-aged thing."

She turned toward him. "Middle-aged? You don't look much over what? Thirty-two?"

"*Thirty-two?*" he laughed.

"Thirty-two and a half?"

It was true that Jonathan Sands looked younger than his thirty-seven years, far younger than the other senior partners in the office. Much of his youthful appearance owed to a five-mile run after work each day. Running was certainly preferable to the many lonely alternatives. An empty house was the bane of bachelorhood.

They immediately hit traffic. The makeshift boundaries of what had come to be known as the "Big Dig" took them through a maze of detours. It was the largest metropolitan infrastructure renovation project in American history—engineering feats that were truly remarkable, though understandably underappreciated by Boston commuters. Already the project's cost overruns had been projected into the billions. And that didn't account for the hidden costs borne by businesses driven down or completely out as a result of the redesign of the city landscape. Collateral damage of the sort was rarely factored into the calculus of civil budgets.

Jonathan drummed his fingers against the steering wheel as they waited for a front-loader to lift broken pieces of blacktop into a dump truck. "You know they're not going to like this, Jen. A thirty percent reduction in their bottom line?"

"No, I don't imagine they will." Then she added with a capering smile: "But I have to say I'm looking forward to seeing the master explain it to them."

"Oh, it won't be me doing that," he countered with a gaming look of his own. "You're going to be the one to get the honors."

"Me?" she asked surprised.

"It's time you learned some of the more pleasant aspects of the job. You may be a new manager now, but we're honing you for partner, you know."

"And if they challenge me?"

"Oh, you can bet they will. Estimated write-offs like this don't go unchallenged."

A hardhat finally waved them through the gravel ramp that eventually took them out onto the freeway. The traffic thinned down, returning hope to him they'd make the meeting on time. He pushed a cassette into the tape deck, which quietly played the Latin jazz flugelhorn of Chuck Mangione.

She turned to him. "I've always wanted to ask a partner an honest question. With you I feel I can … would you mind?"

"No, of course not. Shoot."

"Well, being the one who has to sign the audit opinion, have you ever given in to a client?" She brushed a strand of hair behind her ear. "In a disagreement, I mean?"

He smiled. "Yeah, they don't teach us that one in school, do they?"

Her question was a good one. Companies were responsible for preparing their own financial statements and auditors served only as a monitoring agent, certifying company reports if they passed their audit tests. CPAs rarely issued a qualified or adverse audit opinion due to disagreement. There were simply too many gray areas in accounting that could be argued either way, and opposing views usually coalesced long before disagreement hit an impasse.

"Well, to be honest, I generally try to give my clients the benefit of the doubt. That is, as long as they have reasonable backing for their judgments. But I've never allowed my opinion to be bought if that's what you mean."

"And the pressure?"

"Getting worse. We're supposed to give an independent opinion about our client's financial reports, but our client also happens to pay our fees. I suppose I've lost a couple of accounts to other audit firms over the years due to us not seeing eye-to-eye."

Jensyn nodded agreement. "I've always thought that to be a conflict." She tugged at the hem of her skirt and adjusted her position in the low riding seat. Her legs were shapely, with the lathed lines of an athlete. A runner, Jonathan suspected.

"And making matters worse," he continued, "the profession's been moving more into consulting relationships with those same clients. You have to ask yourself how independent you can be as an auditor if your firm is also giving your clients business advice. I suspect the government's eventually going to put a clamp down on the industry."

"Really? How so?"

"Well, for one, I think it's just a matter of time before we're prohibited from doing consulting work for the same firms we audit. And, I guess for another, it's not that hard to picture a day when instead of audit fees companies pay a tax to the government, which in turn hires our services under competitive bid." He turned to her. "I'm not saying I'd like to see that kind of intervention, but the political pressures may move us there if we don't do a better job policing ourselves."

Jonathan saw that she was squinting in the glare of the sun. He reached over to the glove compartment and grabbed a spare pair of sunglasses. "Here."

"Oh, thanks." She put them on.

"So, what about you?" he asked.

"What about me what?"

"Do you think the government should regulate us?"

She thought on that a moment. "Well, I've always been a Tory I guess. Despite all the marvelous arguments and well-intentioned legislation they offer, in the end they just seem to sully things worse."

He nodded, thinking of the Big Dig they had just suffered through.

The traffic suddenly came to a halt. Several minutes of inching their way northward in the lane, it became apparent there was an accident up ahead. A fire truck, ambulance and several state police cruisers crowded the left lane. As they were finally flagged through, Jonathan could make out an overturned car, and what he took to be the driver stretched out on the median lawn, paramedics attending to him. "That doesn't look good," he said.

When he turned his attention back to the road, out of the corner of his eye he noticed Jensyn's head was bowed. He glanced over at her. She drew some hair away from her filled eyes.

"Are you okay?" he asked.

She didn't answer.

"Do you want me to pull off, Jen?"

"No, it's okay. I'm all right."

* * *

They arrived twenty minutes late for their meeting, which was quickly excused on account of the accident. Now, two hours later with the meeting over, Jonathan walked with Jensyn back to his car in the parking lot.

"You were superb," he said.

"No thanks to you," she chided.

"What do you mean, 'no thanks to me'? You had them eating out of your hand. 'They may be spanking marvelous compressors, Mr. Rombley, but they happen to be illegal.' I loved that one."

He unlocked the passenger door for her. She placed her briefcase in the back and climbed in. Then he circled around to the driver's side. Sensing coolness, he asked: "Are you mad at me?"

"Furious."

"Really?"

Jensyn gazed in the direction of her side window and then back over at him, not allowing the smile she felt underneath to show. "You're a cruel man, Mr. Sands. I kept looking over at you during the meeting but you just sat there, stone-faced. You wanted to let me get gobbled up, to see how I react under pressure. Am I right?"

"Not really. But ... if I did? You handled it wonderfully. I couldn't have done as well. And that retrofitting idea of yours— they loved it."

"Now you're just trying to appease my anger, right?"

"No, Jen, it was a perfect opportunity for you. You took ownership of it like it was your client. I just wanted you to see what it's like, that's all." He patted her arm and inserted the key in the ignition. "You really were terrific."

"So I earned my billing for the day?"

"Ten times," Jonathan answered as he started the car. "And you can charge consulting fees on top of that," he said with a grin.

Pulling out of the parking lot and onto the road in the direction of the interstate, he asked: "Do you want to stop for some lunch?"

"No, I have a bag back at the office. I really have a lot of work to do."

"Suit yourself."

She turned to him, finally letting her smile show. "I'm really not angry with you, Jonathan. I understand what you did."

192

He met her eye. "You're going to do very well for yourself, Jen. Probably better than any new manager I've worked with so far."

"Thank you. That means a lot to me."

With the meeting now over her anxiety began to subside. Shifting her gaze to the windshield, staring at nothing in particular, her thoughts returned to the accident they had passed earlier that morning.

Jonathan's hand rested on the console gear handle, which she came to study. The veins that ran beneath the surface ... the life and soul that flowed within them. It could all be taken away so quickly ... for anyone. She wondered why he wasn't married. Beyond a composed exterior—a certain enigmatic distance he placed about himself—he possessed an obvious sensitivity she found rare.

But he was her boss, she reminded herself again.

"Are you sure you don't want to grab a bite?" he asked. "On me?"

"No." Then turning to him, she compromised: "Not if it's on you, but I will if we go Dutch."

* * *

The off-interstate restaurant was a trucker's stop. Clean, comfortable and predictably austere. Hers was a chicken sandwich and his was a well-done cheeseburger.

"We should have picked a more expensive place," Jensyn said with a mischievous grin. "That way, if we stay on business, I could have stuck Rombley with a fat expense voucher."

"Sounds about right." Jonathan regrouped the lettuce and tomato that had slid off his burger. "Speaking of business, how do you like your new managing position so far?"

"Honestly?"

"No, dishonestly. Make it a good one." He took a bite.

As a new audit manager specializing in technology and manufacturing, she had been working under him on a few of his clients for slightly more than two months. Although she worked for other partners as well, Sands was by far her favorite. To tell him that, however, would sound too ingratiating.

"I guess I'm feeling good about it. Mostly, that is. It's a lot of travel, but at my stage in life I can handle it. I'm confident enough with the technical side of things, but, you know ..." She let the statement dangle as if he would fill in the blank, taking the moment to pull her sandwich to her mouth.

"No, I don't know."

Jensyn finished her bite. "I just hope I can deal with some of the blokes, that's all. Today for example."

"Jensyn, I told you, you did great."

"But you saw how he treated me."

"Yes, I did, and that's just the way it gets sometimes. Unfortunately, despite the times, men still have it a lot easier when it comes to dealing with certain men." He looked up at her over his burger. "You thought he was being condescending?"

"*Of course he was.* Calling me 'Missy'? Couldn't you tell how angry I was?"

"No, not at all. Again, you handled yourself perfectly. In a tactful way you put him in his place with your smarts, not your words. In front of his chief financial officer? Believe me, getting the best of a guy like that in front of his superior was the worst kind of punishment you could possibly inflict."

She paused a moment and then said more apprehensively: "They knew about those outdated compressors, Jon. They *had* to."

"Of course they knew. A large write-off like that to their inventory would devastate their liquidity position ... and result in higher financing costs demanded from their bankers. You just happened to be clever enough to catch them on it."

"I don't know," she said finally, taking another bite, "I just feel ugly about it."

"There's not an ugly thing about you, Chandler."

The words came out before he could consider their possible interpretation. For an instant he wished he could drench the statement with some clever add-on, some follow-up witticism, but he couldn't think of one that wouldn't sound even more awkward, so he just took a large bite of his burger and let it lie.

"Tell me about yourself," she asked, chewing.

"Tell you about myself?" he repeated, lifting a fry. "You mean the lunch version?"

"Yes, the lunch version," she said with a playful grin. She had a large mouth and wide smile. Her eye teeth crested slightly forward of the front row, which added allure to her smile, as only so-called imperfections can do. But hers was a welcoming kind of beauty, Jonathan thought—an easy aura about herself that set him at ease rather than on edge.

"Well, I'm originally from Vermont. I went to Middlebury College, then took a job with MM&P. Worked hard, made partner, and here I am."

"You're so deep," she said, her emerald-green eyes burrowing in on him.

"No, just boring. To save us both from falling asleep, why don't you tell me about yourself first?"

She sipped from the straw of her soft drink and gathered her hair behind her shoulders. "What would you like to know?"

"Well, for one, that funny accent of yours. I've certainly read your resume, but there's some space between the lines. After all, fewer than half of our people attended Oxford."

She chuckled. "The lunch version?"

"Yeah, the lunch version."

Jensyn tabled her cup. "Well, I grew up in Belsize Park, just north of London, on the tube. Pretty average life, really. Dad was a schoolteacher and Mom stayed home at the flat while I was young. When I was older she took a job in the city with Rank Xerox. I'm an only child. I grew up at a time when punk was still in. School was queer, though Dad always instilled in me the importance of a good education. Math came easy to me, and when I finished my exams they were good enough to get me into Oxford. They don't have a formal business program. You have to pick and choose."

Jonathan nodded, knowing firsthand what that was all about. "John Hicks used to teach there."

"Hicks?"

"Yeah, Hicks," she repeated. His blank expression told her the name didn't register. "You've got to be kidding."

"Never heard of him."

"John Hicks? *Sir* John Hicks? The genius behind ordinal utility indifference curves of consumers?"

"Oh, *that* John Hicks. Great guy. I loved his stuff." He had no idea whom she was talking about and swallowed a fry. "So how'd you end up coming here?" he asked.

About to take another bite of her sandwich, she set it down, considering how to answer. A more serious expression came to her face. "Let's just say I needed a change."

"Okay, let's just say that."

She caught the warmth of his expression, appreciating his not pushing it further. Even after five years the hurt still ran deep. Much of the fault for that, however, was probably her own, she knew. She had made the move physically, but had never done so inside. To do so would imply something of a betrayal.

"And Harvard? Did you like it?" he asked.

"How can you enjoy brutal torture?"

He smiled. "How about Boston? Do you like Boston?"

"Love it. There's so much to see and do. Not that I have any kind of private life with my twelve-hour days. But I get out and see the town when I do my run."

Jonathan's palm came down firmly on the table with a thud. "I knew it! You *are* a runner!"

She laughed. "Yes, how did you know?"

"Let's just say I knew." It was a replay of her earlier dismissive reply.

"Why? Do you run?" she asked.

"Every day. Five miles. It's the only thing that keeps me sane."

"And life outside the office?" she asked.

"About like yours, by the sound of it. I do a lot of reading."

"So you're me in ten years?"

"I thought you said I look like I'm thirty-two."

She simpered at the trap. "Well, you *look* young. I just *figure* you're older."

"I'm thirty-seven. Made partner six years ago. There, are you satisfied?"

"And do you enjoy it?"

"What, being thirty-seven?"

"No!" she laughed. "Being partner."

"How can you enjoy brutal torture?"

It was an odd conversation to be having with one's boss. Yet he made her feel at ease, almost as if he knew her without her having to share much.

"You don't really find it torture," she said after a moment, taking the last bite of her sandwich.

"No, and I bet you didn't find getting your MBA to be torture either. You actually found the challenge to be rewarding. Am I right?"

"It was good for me. Like I said, I needed a change and it kept my mind occupied." Lifting a fry from her plate, she deliberated whether to take a bite of it, then set it back down. "I find it rewarding now that it's over."

"See? That's how I feel about my run every day. Pain yields its own reward."

"You may be right," she smirked, "not to mention it keeps the waist down."

"Do you enjoy running?" he asked after a moment.

She paused. "I suppose I make companions with myself when I run."

She didn't say anymore. He didn't either. It was a comfortable silence that stole for each of them a small moment of time, a reprieve. The day would pick up its pace again, yet for now, neither wanted to pull away from the unfamiliar yet comforting connection they felt.

"I guess I run because it moves me," Jonathan said finally.

"Moves you? Where to?"

"Another place."

Jensyn looked searchingly at him. They were captivating eyes, she thought, ones possessing depth, and she wondered if he wanted to share more. She sensed he did. His gaze shifted above her without focus, as if to a place farther away. "The pain of it kind of gets me there." They were words heavy with meaning for him, though certainly uninterpretable by anyone else. He turned back down to look at her again. "But only until the next day."

"I know what you mean," she said plaintively.

He hadn't really expected an affirming response.

"I really do know what you mean, Jonathan."

He reflected on the emphasis of her comment, and the truth she intended for it. "…The accident today?"

She nodded. "It was five years ago. My fiancé."

"I'm very sorry, Jensyn." He reached for the top of her hand.

"Thank you."

Jonathan squeezed firmly. And then, as if realizing where he was and whom he was with, he picked up both chits from the table. "Ready?"

"I thought we had an agreement."

"No, *you* said Dutch. I never agreed to it. Besides, you don't need a receipt because we didn't keep it to business."

* * *

Back in the office at 2:15 Jonathan Sands stared emptily at his desk. Always one who existed on two levels—the inward real, the outward not—the burden felt heavier than usual. He had brushed away similar stirrings through the years, infatuations that drained with time or acquaintance, or a simple determination put to an end what wasn't even a discernible beginning. Perhaps it was only the fatigue of having to do so, but now he felt like he actually wanted to lose the war.

Much like the one he fought and lost many years earlier.

In a week and a day it would be fifteen years. Time didn't do what it was supposed to do ... the shrapnel of filth buried in his soul. The layers washed up like flotsam on the shore, never quite covering the carcass, and the remorse and grief just grew fouler with age. Always the guilt. An inexorable, stultifying guilt. It would always be there, prevailing upon his existence like a viper that made its home in the walls, forever seeking a way out.

How many mornings had he waked up hoping it was all only a terrible dream? The number of evenings spent alone to live the hell all over again?

The rainy night he happened to see her during his run.
The excitement they shared as they talked about their futures.

A full caseload of files sat on his desk requiring his attention, but he couldn't give them the thought they required. Instead, he picked up *The Wall Street Journal* resting on the edge of his desk. Reading was perfunctory, little of it absorbed. And it didn't take long for his mind to pull him back into the abyss.

The dried blood on her cheek. The belt wrapped around her neck.

It would have been preferable to enter hell through the front door ... to be inside with certainty rather than always peering in through the backdoor, wondering when the demons would finally drag him inside for their eternal companionship. The years of anguish, wishing he could turn himself in and be done with it, knowing with certainty he could never do so.

Earlier in his career his accomplishments had been for his mother. She was indeed proud at first, but beyond a point they no longer seemed to impress her much. Now there were only stale experiences, preoccupations, and loneliness. It was all a life sentence, only worse. At least a convict lives with the knowledge the wrongs he committed had been meted justice.

Twenty minutes into the paper Jonathan's consciousness repaired when an all-too-familiar name jumped out at him from the page: *C. Decker Moss.* The previous week he had read a bit piece in the *Journal* referencing that name as well—an environmental loss announcement. Jonathan flipped to the beginning. It was a tender offer by Drexel-Pace Pharmaceuticals for Schoen Chemicals at $43 per share. A hostile takeover bid. Strange that Schoen, such a small firm, would make for unrelated copy in the *Journal* twice in one week. Strange, too, that Decker Moss's name would stare back at him just as he was thinking of Karen …

Her body would never be found, Decker had assured him long ago. Jonathan concluded it was probably true. After a decade and a half, it had surely been lost to the workings of predation and decay. The bag, her remains, whatever was down there, would certainly be unrecognizable, or gone altogether by now.

All except for his damned gold medallion that went down with her.

Chapter Nineteen

"GREAT to see you again, Mr. Sands. Every year like clockwork, right?"

"And it's always nice you remember me the way you do, Jacques."

"Of course. You're always my last faithful customer of the season." Jacques Gaudette, owner of the marina in the small lakeside town of Hague, walked with Jonathan from the street-front office down to the dock at the waterfront. "Your boat's right over here," he gestured. "This year's model."

Jonathan looked appreciatively at the Four Winns bowrider.

"Someday I'm hoping to actually get you to buy one of these things," said Gaudette. "Surely you realize Lake George has a much nicer season for boating."

"I'll keep that in mind," Sands said, returning the proprietor's friendly smile. "And, Jacques, if I'm ever in the market for a boat, I'll be sure to give you first dibs on me."

Gaudette untied the lines as Jonathan warmed the engine. "Oh, here," the man said, handing Jonathan the long white box resting on the dock.

"Thanks. I'll be sure to be back by closing time."

"Take your time, Mr. Sands, I'll be here late. Lots of boats to put up and winterizing to do. Another few weeks and we'll have ice fingers forming in the bay."

Jonathan was about to wave off when he grabbed the dock plank, as if reminded. "Say, Jacques, you wouldn't happen to have a depth chart of the lake, would you?"

"Depth chart? Sure. Hold on." The man jogged up the bank to his street-side shop. In a minute he was back at the dock with a folded map. "It's a bit old, but the lake levels don't change much."

Sands unfolded the chart. It was a 1948 hydrographic survey published by the U.S. Power Squadron. "My, this *is* old."

"Keep it, it's only a copy. I've got a stack of others."

"Thanks," Jonathan said, noting the listed depths on the map as he scanned it south to north. "The lake looks a bit too deep for scuba diving."

"No, actually Lake George is quite popular for that. One of the clearest lakes in the country. Loaded with history."

"Dive shops?"

"You a diver, Mr. Sands?"

"No, but I've always thought I might give it a try someday."

"Well, we've got a small shop in town, mostly charter trips. Hold on." The man took off again up the sloped pathway. When he returned he was bearing a business card and a pamphlet. "They ask us to pass these around. Small town like this, we've got to support each other."

"Thank you very much." Sands took the materials and pushed the boat away from pier. When he idled through the moorings he accelerated out of the bay and then headed north.

His annual trip to Lake George was always only a brief afternoon excursion. Nevertheless, he had learned the northern part of the lake fairly well over the years, at least the shoreline and location of underwater hazards.

It was a raw gray afternoon, which was somewhat typical. Not that the weather mattered to him. Sun, snow, rain, wind—he'd seen it all on Lake George in early November. Rarely were there other boats on the water this time of year, and today was no exception.

When the landmarks came into view he slowed. It was a triangulation he had memorized long ago, from the shore that awful night fifteen years back. Just about midway between Blairs Bay and Slacks Bay, and then half again that distance to Anthony's Nose, a bald-faced mountain directly to the north.

He brought the throttle down to an idle. When he judged he was over the spot he shut off the engine.

It was quiet.

What there was of a breeze came from the south, lapping gently against the hull. He took a seat in the stern and looked westward. The sun would be setting in little more than an hour. Just below and to the right of its suffusing glow was the Moss family lodge.

It was right here.

Jonathan pulled his jacket collar tight to his neck and descended into himself. Something of a prayer for Karen Wyman, for her father and mother … and then for Susan Cabot, Karen's roommate. Sometimes he left without remembering Susan as well, mad at himself afterward for doing so. He hoped she had found a good life.

But Jonathan's contemplations of Decker Moss during these anniversary trips never transpired in prayer. Only doubts and uncertainty. Over the years recalling and rethinking the events of that night, Jonathan came to wonder even what little he thought he did know. The incongruities ... subtle things that didn't mesh ... details that became more curious the more thought he gave to them.

Cajoling hidden information out of a good friend was tough enough; inducing a confession from an estranged friend, based on unverifiable notions about what might have occurred a decade and a half earlier, was nigh impossible. Following Decker's revelation their last night together in the apartment about his St. Christopher medal, Jonathan chose to cut off the relationship altogether. It had essentially gone sour by that time anyway. Simple things, like not responding to Decker's Christmas cards after graduation, or returning his occasional phone calls, came to evolve into a definitive separation.

Was it justified? Sands wasn't sure. He only found his lingering questions forced him to stake a position on the more conservative side of speculation. Unfortunately, the break would never give him an opportunity to probe those questions further.

The full truth of what happened that night was thus as far removed from him as Karen was herself ... though physically just 100 feet below.

Jonathan reached for the box and removed its contents: a dozen long-stemmed roses. This time they were yellow. He liked to give Karen variety. Setting them in the water he sat down again. For long minutes he just sat in pensive contemplation, as he did every year, staring emptily at the scattered flowers as they drifted away on the surface.

"I'm sorry, Karen," he whispered again, for the millionth time.

As the sun was beginning to set Jonathan started the engine and pointed the boat south at idling speed. And again, he looked off at the shadowed western shore and the lodge sitting there, wishing he could somehow know what might be locked inside the mind of the one who still owned the place.

* * *

OPTIONS

Friday, November 13, 1992
Albany, New York

Senior FBI agent Edward Fitch was diverted to a much earlier past as he read with interest the Bureau's internal newsletter. Being a Friday and late in the afternoon he yielded to the rare luxury of actually getting through the stack of trivialities accumulated on his desk. The subject of the article was the recently commissioned DNA laboratory in Washington, D.C. Much of it described the various types of forensic evidence available from the new technology, emphasizing proper protocols to be used by agents when collecting DNA samples from a crime scene. The process was becoming increasingly probative, driving statistical error to tolerable levels for prosecution. Even the licked seals of envelopes provided enough genetic blueprint to nail a kidnapper.

Fitch noted the irony of the publication date: *November 4.* But it was probably the date that subconsciously prompted his thought. The mystery of Karen Wyman's disappearance from Middlebury, Vermont, on that date fifteen years ago never completely vanished from his mind. Perhaps frustration, perhaps challenge, self-esteem, whatever, the unsolved case was an enduring blemish on his otherwise exemplary record. He had, after all, achieved Senior Special Agent status early on in his career with a very commendable dossier, one full of investigatory accomplishments.

His mind wandered from the article as he tried to recall the details of the case, few as they were. But something seemed to snag him about it. Something now relevant.

He got up from his desk and went to the stand of file cabinets along the wall. Finding the relatively thin case folder, he went back to his desk. The folder was actually a copy of a more permanent record archived in the basement of the building. His photocopied notes were there, as was a copy of a photo of the young woman.

A beautiful girl, he thought again. Of particular interest to him were the interrogation notes he had made, and as he reviewed his scratchily-penned entries his memory was jogged. Decker was the boyfriend of Karen's roommate, Susan Cabot. She had gone home for the weekend, leaving Karen Wyman alone at the apartment on the Friday night of her disappearance. Karen liked Jonathan Sands, per Susan Cabot's testimony, but Jonathan showed no interest. Fitch had always found that part of the story difficult to understand. According to Sands, he liked her as well but felt the timing for a relationship was wrong. "Both graduating, heading diff. places. Didn't want repeat mistakes of parents," the penned notes stated. But Fitch knew that Sands had taken a job in Boston and that Karen had been accepted into Harvard's law school. Not different places at all.

He perused the other paperwork in the file. Karen Wyman's car was discovered by a state trooper Saturday morning on an outlying country road. There was no evidence of foul play. Fingerprint dusting yielded nothing of significance. Other than a bit of congealed sputum on the interior passenger door nothing out of the ordinary was found. The pasty saliva, however, turned up trace amounts of alcohol … significant enough to suggest that it probably came from one quite intoxicated at the time.

Edward Fitch initially suspected Sands. He just seemed overly nervous in the interview, like he was hiding something. That, along with the fresh bruise on his jaw and Fitch's subsequent discovery that he had a conviction for misdemeanor battery fueled his suspicions. Unfortunately, the hair samples he took from Jonathan and Decker's apartment the night of his interrogation—from their hairbrushes under the guise of a bathroom visit—turned out not to be helpful to the case at the time.

But now Fitch wondered.

He dialed the Washington, D.C., number that was provided in the tail line of the newsletter article. Given the lack of urgency, the lab technician informed him it might take several weeks to complete the test. But the evidence was possibly still quite viable.

Fitch then called the evidence room downstairs in the building to arrange for its shipment to the FBI DNA laboratory in Washington.

Chapter Twenty

DECKER Moss always thought he had a nice office. That is until he stepped into Larry Carpenter's. The first thing he noted was the view. Carpenter's aerie stood forty-five stories high, presenting a panorama of Atlanta's cityscape that played out for miles The second was the décor. Atop a colorful mosaic tile arrangement in the center of the room was a richly buffed mahogany meeting table whose edges were sculpted with fine dadoed lines, inlaid with ebony and ivory. The matching desk, file cabinets, bookcases, credenza, and wet sideboard—Decker always wished he had a sidebar in his office—were of similar design and rounded out the extravagance of the room.

"I've definitely been outclassed," remarked Moss.

"Not for long, my friend. You're with us now." Carpenter strolled over to the sideboard and pulled out a bottle. "I remembered you're a Scotsman from our meeting in Manchester." He pointed at its simple label. "Macallan 1926, single-malt Scotch. That's 'whisky' without the 'e.' Not bottled till 1986."

"Very gracious." Decker glanced at his watch. It was three in the afternoon. "I'd say the sun's well enough over the yardarm."

"Ah, a nautical man as well? We'll see how you do on my yacht tomorrow." Larry held the bottle and glass raised as he poured. "You'll want this stuff straight up." He then mixed himself a gin and vermouth martini with two Spanish olives. "I rarely take advantage of my little bar here before quitting time, but this calls for a special celebration." Carpenter came around to Decker, handed him his drink and offered a toast: "To a wonderfully long-lasting and profitable relationship."

"Here, here." Decker raised his glass. He took a sip and tasted the aged Scotch go down. "Beautiful. Has kind of a licorice after-taste."

"A couple thousand for that bottle. Only the best for my partners."

Impressed by the expensive show of generosity, Decker curled a smile as he brought the Scotch to his nose and sniffed again its punchy aroma.

"Kent and Joe should be here shortly. They had a late afternoon meeting." Carpenter set his glass down on the greeting area table. "I hope your trip into town went smoothly."

"Fine. Very nice limo." Decker gazed toward the floor-to-ceiling windows. "And I have to say, I welcome the warmer weather here. Manchester gets cold and gray this time of year."

"I'm sure you'll be making many visits." Carpenter motioned to his leather couch. "Here, have a seat."

Decker did. Carpenter sat in the facing armchair and crossed his leg, tucking the crease of his slacks beneath the cuff at his ankle. "I'm curious to hear how things have been going on your side. How's the reaction been?"

"You don't want to know."

"That bad, huh?"

"Only amongst those you'd expect," said Decker. "My board had an emergency meeting and a couple of teleconferences to put together our response to our shareholders. As you probably gathered from the SEC filing, the overall feelings on the board remain quite ambivalent." Moss was referring to a special schedule required to be filed with the SEC within ten days of a tender offer outlining the target firm's position. "In the end it was an obligatory statement. It's pretty tough to tell your shareholders to turn down a fifty-percent return on the heels of a devastating earnings announcement."

"It certainly lacked a negative tone. I'm sure I have you to thank for that." Carpenter gave an appreciative thumbs-up gesture.

Moss smiled. "Fortunately, I haven't heard any murmurings amongst the rank and file."

"And your grandfather? Schoen?"

"He doesn't get it. You blindsided him. Not too savvy about Fortune 100 finance, I'm afraid."

Larry Carpenter reveled inwardly. He hoped the old bastard had learned his lesson.

"To date we've pulled in more than two-thirds of your stock. At forty-three per share that's nearly one-point-two billion." Carpenter lifted his watch ceremoniously. "The tender period expires midnight tonight. I'd say we've certainly done what we had to do, wouldn't you, Decker?"

Moss held up his glass again. "Salute."

"Which brings me to a very lucrative point. Joe will fill you in on the details later, but your stock options look very good at this point. Schoen's price should remain about where it is, in the low forties. At the time of our bid it was at twenty-nine. The spread's yours. Several million."

Conservatively, Decker thought.

"Not bad for five weeks of little work on your part, right?" Then Carpenter added, as if reminded: "Did you bring those shareholder records with you?"

"Got them right here." Decker pulled out several floppy disks from his suit coat pocket and set them on the table in front of him. "Another present for you."

Moss had mailed a similar set of disks five weeks earlier. It was a clear benefit of his collusion with Drexel-Pace that Carpenter could acquire the records so quickly and with such little difficulty. As a hostile bidder Drexel-Pace would probably have had to obtain a court order to force Schoen to give them up. The lists were important. Without them Drexel-Pace wouldn't have been able to communicate directly with Schoen's shareholders concerning the tender offer—or with the holdout shareholders at this time on matters concerning the upcoming annual shareholders' meeting. Notices had to be mailed containing the nominees for the slate of new directors and the proposal of Schoen's new auditors.

A soft knock sounded at the door, which immediately opened to the face of the blonde secretary Decker met in the anteroom minutes earlier. "Mr. Shaughnessy and Mr. Moran are here to see you, sir. Would you like me to show them in?" Her southern accent was mild. On the whole, very attractive, Decker thought again.

"Thank you. Hurry them on in. And Christie?"

"Yes, sir?"

"You can take the rest of the afternoon off. Have a nice weekend."

"Well, thank you very much, sir."

Decker saw the old southern tradition was still very much in operation. Attractive servile women with deferential addresses. Maybe someday he could relocate.

Shaughnessy and Moran plowed into the office in a wave. Actually the wave was made by Joe Moran, though Decker noticed he seemed to have shed some pounds since their last meeting. Moss greeted each with a firm handshake.

"Welcome to Atlanta," hailed Shaughnessy. Seeing Decker's glass he supplemented: "I see Larry's greeted you properly."

"Very fine Scotch," agreed Moss.

"Any beer?" asked Moran of Carpenter.

"Should be a few longnecks in the fridge there, Joe. Help yourself."

Joe Moran was fast to the sideboard. There was some clanking of bottles in the miniature fridge and he came out with three. Prying open the tops and handing one to Kent, he stood looking around the counter. Larry caught his eye. "There aren't any chips and dip if that's what you're looking for, Joe."

"Honestly, Larry. You know I'm on a diet. You just don't give this office the class it needs. You should at least have some salted Georgian peanuts to offer your out-of-state guests."

"Shut up, Joe."

Decker surmised the two had a strange, yet close, relationship. Kent came around and sat on the couch beside him. Joe Moran followed and took the other facing armchair with his two long-necks. The chair absorbed his body like a bowling ball stuffed in a rubber bucket.

"You look different," said Moss to Moran, "somehow a bit smaller—?"

"Dieting and jogging." Joe hefted his longneck. "Works wonders, my friend."

Decker laughed inwardly to himself. Beginning a regimen of dieting and jogging for a man such as Joe Moran was a bit like getting a car's first oil change when the odometer hits the 100,000 mark.

"Sorry we couldn't be here earlier," Kent said. Switching his look toward Larry, he asked: "Have we missed much?"

"I was just getting a bit of Decker's take on the reaction up in New Hampshire to our buyout. Maybe you could discuss with him the first order of business."

"Of course." Kent Shaughnessy sank back against the arm of the couch and looked over at Moss. "I hope there hasn't been too much aftershock in your quarters. From my experience it's sometimes tough for a management team to adjust to the idea of having a new owner."

"They should be able to get over it," replied Moss. "Not Schoen, of course. In addition to him, several directors were quite angry with me about that environmental loss announcement. Everett Royce thought it was a 'dumb-ass move,' in his words."

"Your corporate counsel? What, because he's afraid you might be giving the EPA a closed case?"

"Exactly. That and for the fact it gave you a nice price to ride in on."

Kent shook his head. "What are they going to do, fire you for breaching your fiduciary duty to your shareholders? Won't happen. You made a call that was yours to make as CEO. And with regard to the EPA issue, from my dealings with them they'll treat you fairly. They and the SEC are now collaborating, sharing information, and we all know the SEC wants their registrants to come front and center with their environmental exposure. For the EPA to come down now suggesting you've admitted culpability in your quarterly financial statements would set the SEC's efforts to encourage voluntary disclosure back years." Kent took a swig from his beer and shook his head again. "No, Decker, you did a good job with that press release. Not too little, not too much. It was just right."

"Thanks. The price tumbled a bit more than even I expected. Far more than suggested by a fifty-million-dollar write-off."

"It's all the halo effect your firm has enjoyed," interjected Carpenter. "Happens sometimes. Glamour stocks are often overpriced, which is probably what Schoen's green reputation gave to it."

"So a fair value buy-out?" asked Moss, looking at Carpenter. He in turn cocked his head toward Moran.

"*Eminently* fair value," assured Joe. "Your shareholders made out very nicely. We took in forty-seven percent of the shares right away. The rest of the tenders trickled in over a four-week period. But I have to say, it was probably your environmental announcement that spooked most of them to ditch their shares so quickly."

Moran was going a bit farther in his delivery than Carpenter felt comfortable with. He cleared his throat. "Regardless of the reason, we have every cause for celebration." The Drexel-Pace CEO lifted his glass again, which they all returned.

Larry caught Kent's eye. The latter took the cue and set his beer bottle on the glass table in front of him. "We want to get moving as fast as we can on your Threonatrix deliveries," said Kent to Decker. "We also want to come in and size up your new peptide manufacturing operation. Any problems with that as far as you can see?"

"No, I wouldn't think so. After all, we're married now."

"Super. I'll assemble a team to get up there as soon as possible. But you're in charge, Deck. If we overstep any bounds, you just let us know."

"I don't see why there'd be any problem." Decker held a moment, wondering. "Why the new peptide process? I wouldn't think you'd even be aware of it."

"Of course we're aware of it," said Kent. "You hold patents on it. We've been doing research on some of your amino acid work and find it to be novel technology we just may find quite valuable. Protein engineering is complicated science." Kent Shaughnessy pulled out a thick, creased packet of papers from his suit coat pocket. Laying them down unfolded on the glass coffee table before him, he explained: "While we now own a majority stake we obviously don't control you yet. We've gotten the DOJ approvals, but until we vote in our new board at your April shareholders' meeting, legal red tape comes in the way of our free use of your technology."

Decker was taken off guard. "What're these, Kent?"

"Licensing and purchase option contracts. For your patents and peptide production trade secrets."

"Contracts? I wasn't aware of the need to sign my name on anything at this point."

"Only a legal formality, Decker," Carpenter mollified. "As we mentioned to you early on we want Threonatrix. We wouldn't want your board to go off and sell their crown jewels before we take control." The comment referred to another popular takeover defense. If a bride couldn't prevent a marriage she could certainly make herself look less appealing by ridding herself of her most attractive assets. "Your directors know we have an eye to own Threonatrix since we mentioned it in our written proposal and also at your board meeting. These purchase options only give us the right of first refusal should your board try to sell off certain targeted intellectual property. And the licensing agreements permit our free use of them now."

Moss sat forward and did his best to glean understanding of the first page of the creased documents. Failing to make any quick sense of all the legal jargon he pulled his head up. "I'm sorry, guys, but I can't sign anything at this point. I don't have any legal counsel with me."

The three Drexel-Pace officers presented each other lighted looks of surprise. "Decker," said Carpenter, "you're acting a bit like you question our motivations. That's not a very comforting start. We simply want to protect our interests and to ensure our work on Threonatrix and those peptides holds the stitches of legal propriety from this point forward."

"I understand that. But certainly you can continue your experimentation—"

"Decker, please," said Carpenter, annoyed, "just sign the documents. Let's not do anything to ruin the honeymoon." The elder man's deep facial lines constricted and his eyes revealed a brusqueness Decker hadn't witnessed before. Then, to his colleagues, Carpenter requested politely: "Would you gentlemen please excuse us for a moment?"

Moran grabbed his reserve bottle of beer and the two quietly shuffled from the room. When the door was closed Larry fastened a look onto Decker. "I asked them to exit so as not to embarrass you in any way. This is nothing out of the ordinary. You're green on these things and that's understandable since you've never been through this sort of deal before." Then with iron in his voice: "But if I'm ever going to put you on my board—ever—you'll not do that to me again. Do you understand?"

Moss riposted, meeting Carpenter with a matching look of hardness. "Larry, I admit I'm new at this. But signing something without legal representation? I'm not a foolish man, and if you ever want me to serve on your board I hope you wouldn't suffer fools." It took him back to the days he faced the defensive line in high school football games. The eye's strength was magnitudes its weight in muscle.

Carpenter was impressed. That was for sure. But he wasn't going to give up this hill, this measly hill that just minutes before he was certain was already his. "In your words you've proven your salt, Mr. Moss. There are no threats here. Only reason. And a reasoning man would surely see he had no choice at this point."

"But a reasoning man could walk out of here, Larry."

"A man could, yes, but not a reasoning man." Carpenter sat back in his chair and took a long sip from his cocktail, holding the stem of his martini glass with firmed fingers. His face turned crimson. "Don't forget there are four slots of directors whose terms come up this April, and your name's among them. Now, if you want the name 'Moss' to receive the backing of sixty-seven percent of the voting shares at your next shareholders' meeting, you'll act like the reasoning man you are and you'll sign those agreements."

Check.

"And, further, Mr. Moss, if you want Mr. Moran to come back into this room with his two longnecks to discuss with you our already typed out agreement offering you options with an in-the-money value of over eleven million bucks, you'll sign those damned documents before I finish my drink. And believe me, I'm very close to being in need of another."

Mate.

C. Decker Moss, if anything else, was no fool. There wasn't the processing time in his cerebral lobe to sort out the issues. Instead, in a simple disconnected response he removed the pen from his coat pocket and looked for the places that called for his autograph as Schoen's chief executive officer. Apparently there were more than a dozen patents they were interested in.

In less than a minute he affixed his signature to each.

"Thank you very much, Decker." Carpenter's kindly smile returned. "Now, unless you're the one to bring it up, no one will hear of this aberrant moment again." He stood from his seat and asked in a calm conversational tone: "May I freshen your drink?"

"Thank you, Larry. That would be just about what I need right now. Make it a tall one."

Carpenter smiled back at him. "That's my man."

* * *

Two hours later the drinks continued flowing as the four reclined aboard the Drexel-Pace Gulfstream jet enroute to Savannah. Larry Carpenter called an end to any further discussion of business that evening. There would be plenty of time to do so the next day. The forecast for Hilton Head and vicinity was for clear skies and calm seas, perfect for their planned Saturday excursion around the island aboard Carpenter's yacht. Their discussions would resume on parallel tracks at that time, he informed the men.

Decker interpreted the deferral of further business discussion, particularly about his stock options, as punishment for his misbehavior. Like a disobedient child he would have to wait until tomorrow for his goodies. Following the afternoon's touchy episode, there was an uneasy lassitude in his mood. He was angered at himself for being overcautious. The men had made clear to him from the beginning their desire to keep him on as head of Schoen. And the contracts he signed merely ensured that Drexel-Pace got what it had paid for. After all, what could go wrong?

What could go wrong, Moss, is if you made a perfect ass of yourself and changed these men's attitudes about you.

Carpenter had the only hand. With up to four new directors they could vote in at April's shareholder meeting, added to their certain loyalists—Riley and Richfield—Drexel-Pace was ensured a clear majority. They would carry the day however they wanted it.

Shareholders elected the board of directors who in turn hired corporate officers. Without the board's support, however, an executive such as Moss could be out the next morning on the streets looking for a job. It was all something he hadn't remotely considered in the whole ordeal. He felt like he had suddenly been shoved out on a tightrope without even being aware of it. The safety net of nepotism, which had always been there in one form or another, was no longer beneath him to catch a fall. Cyrus Schoen was no longer the chief shareholder. Even if he were, Decker knew the relationship with his grandfather was severely compromised. If not yet, then it certainly would be soon enough.

C. Decker Moss was going home from the dance with a very different date from the one he arrived with … unfortunately, a date that was not yet ready to put out.

* * *

Saturday, November 28, 1992
Hilton Head, South Carolina

The weather cooperated with the forecast. The morning sky was bright blue, and the air, redolent of a salty breeze, glistened prismatically in the spray of waves sliced by the bow. It was a yacht worth millions, thought Decker: a twin diesel, 68-foot Hatteras, customized with a Eurostyle sport deck and VIP staterooms. Looking out over the stern was a large, open-air aft deck, shaded under the cabin roof's overhang and comfortably furnished in cushioned white rattan. Along its bulkhead, in true Drexel-Pace tradition, was a well-stocked mini bar.

Moss, Moran and Shaughnessy stood in the open breeze on the fly bridge. Carpenter occupied the captain's chair in their midst, piloting the boat from the upper-deck cockpit controls. Decker's mood returned early on as Carpenter conveyed again his promise to keep him on as "captain" of Schoen—a term no doubt inspired by their environs—and to place him on Drexel-Pace's board. All subject, of course, to shareholder approval. Carpenter assured him the latter was a non-issue.

The compensation package was outlined by Moran in detail and documented with signed legal papers, post-dated to become effective upon Decker's reelection to Schoen's board in April. Joe Moran finished with his explanation of the terms of the option piece of the agreement.

"The vesting period is one-fourth over each of the three years of your board term, the first allotment exercisable immediately upon retaking office in April. Of course, the options aren't transferable. But if you have any problem coming up with the cash, Deck, you can just sign us a note and we'll spot you the strike price." Exercising stock options required cash. For stock valued in the millions the availability of cash obviously posed a problem. "At yesterday's closing price that first installment alone is worth close to four million."

Moss brightened. His dance date had just put out.

Some dolphins broke the surface off to the port side and briefly diverted Joe Moran's attention. "Man, those are beautiful fish. Don't hit them, Larry."

"I'm not going to hit them. What do you think, that they're incapable of steering out of my way?" Carpenter's voice evidenced irritation. "Besides, they're not fish. My God, sometimes you really disappoint me, Joe."

Amused at Larry's annoyance, Moran smiled and strolled to the side of the bridge to observe the dolphins more closely. He was wearing neon-pink swimming trunks and a tropical colored shirt that reminded Decker of a large tent, the type that might be pitched by a creative hippy on LSD. Decker's momentary concern about the vessel's shift in center of gravity was quickly averted—as it had been several times that morning—on seeing no discernible list with Moran's movement. It was a sturdy ship, thought Decker.

Carpenter turned to Moss. "So, you're agreeable to our compensation package?"

"Very, as long as there remains an active market for the residual shares."

"Well, if we're eventually able to acquire the minority shares as well, you can just cash in your options. Those that remain unvested could simply be converted at fair value into options for Drexel-Pace shares. Nothing difficult about that."

Decker concurred with a smile and an approving nod. "Thank you, Larry. The arrangement is very generous. You, also, will be quite pleased with the value I bring to your firm."

Carpenter offered his long boney fingers to Moss in a conciliatory handshake. "I'm quite confident of that, my friend." Any animosity that may have existed between them the day before had clearly dissipated.

"Gentlemen," said Carpenter, "I say we shut this bathtub down and drift the rest of the afternoon."

"I'll drink to that," said Moran. They had been out on the water since nine that morning and it was now going on noon. "I'll also eat to that."

The bar and refrigerator were stocked in the predawn hours by a hired shore hand. Decker noticed a similar amount of pre-preparation went into the previous evening's dinner on the plane. The ribeye steaks tasted as if they had just come off the grill. So satiated were they from the evening meal, the group opted against having breakfast that morning.

Kent Shaughnessy addressed Decker over his Heineken bottle. "You mentioned yesterday that Everett Royce was disappointed with your handling of the environmental disclosure. I take it he's also the one on your side spearheading the EPA mess?"

Decker nodded, downing a swig of beer.

"Is he the type of guy who would give us any trouble?" asked Shaughnessy.

Moss contemplated the question a moment, sinking back into his thick-cushioned oval chair. He swiveled around to catch the view of the horizon off the yacht's stern. "That depends on what you might mean by trouble. He's a pretty passive type, but then again, very astute … although I've never seen him in a situation where he might feel cornered."

"Cornered? How, for example?" asked Moran, cradling a beer between his knees and working his sandwich plate on his lap.

"For example, when I bring home those contracts I signed yesterday. I don't think he'll like that one bit."

"Then again, don't forget his director term expires this April as well," said Carpenter dryly, his eye catching Decker's in a fish-hooked way. "Besides, there's absolutely no need for him to even know about them. If I were you, I'd just file them in your office and forget about them until we formally gain director control. At that time they'll become moot anyway."

Now Decker understood why he had been asked to sign purchase option and short-term licensing agreements rather than simple contracts for sale. Selling the patents and trade secrets outright would have had to go through formal steps of recordkeeping, not to mention a potential challenge of his delegated authority, matters that would have certainly tipped off his other directors that he was engaged in a bit of treason.

"I may have to be the one to make that point clear to him," said Moss in reference to Everett Royce's term expiration. "We haven't discussed what becomes of his position next April."

There was a stint in their conversation. Moran threw a piece of crusty bun from his sandwich out to the stern. Some gulls immediately swarmed down on it.

"Dammit, Moran! What'd you do that for?" Carpenter quickly got up from his chair and entered the bulkhead door. Joe Moran made a look like he wasn't sure what he had done wrong. Seconds later Carpenter was out cradling a two-barreled shotgun. In what appeared to be a single movement he hefted the barrel, cocked, and fired a quick succession of shots at the birds. Gray and white plumage filled the stern area like blowout from a pillow fight. Some of the birds floated dead in the water while the others dispersed in a fuss.

"Sorry to disturb the peace, men, but the damned things are a nuisance. 'Keow-keow,' he screeched in a throated cackle, mimicking their call. "I'm not going to listen to that infernal noise all afternoon!"

"But Larry, those are federally protected birds," said Moran.

"Federally protected, my ass. They're filthy sea rats that'd do nothing but hound us all throughout this restful excursion."

"Well, that's one way to take care of the problem," chuckled Decker. "Say, guys, I wonder if they taste like egret."

The quip drew a laugh from the others. Carpenter went to return his rifle, then came back out and reclaimed his seat. "Now, where were we?" he reflected thoughtfully. "Oh, yes, Mr. Royce." Slugging down a generous gulp of beer he directed his eyes at

Moss. "One thing I'd like you to do is to take him off that EPA matter."

Decker's face lighted surprise. "Why's that?" he asked.

"Because it won't be necessary. It's not going to be Schoen's problem anymore."

More befuddled, Decker surveyed Carpenter's expression, which was deadpan. Then he turned to the others.

Larry clarified: "Drexel-Pace has decided to assume that environmental liability of yours. Entirely. It'll be our way of mending the fence. We want to infuse some needed trust in our new marriage."

Moss moved forward in his chair. "I have to say, Larry, that's an incredibly generous offer. When did you come up with this?"

"I brought the idea up at our last board meeting. We all agreed some goodwill gesture was needed, and the Superfund thing just seemed to make sense. After all, what's fifty million compared to a one-point-two billion-dollar investment? I think we can handle that kind of pocket change, don't you?"

At which Joe Moran interjected: "And with our assumption of the liability you'll be able to reverse your environmental provision. We have to formalize things, of course, but perhaps the second or third quarter of next year ..." Joe lifted his empty bottle with a grin and got up to get another. "Your stock options should float quite a bit higher, my man."

"Nice," acknowledged Moss. The day was turning into a very good one indeed.

Moran laughed from the refrigerator. "Schoen's bottom line is going to have more bounce to it than a rubber ball." Then he called out: "Hey, Larry, last time I was on this boat you had some smoked oysters. I don't see any."

"Well, unless some gremlin opened a can they wouldn't be in that fridge, Joe. Check out the galley cabinet. And it's not a boat. Ships carry boats, but boats can't carry ships."

The CFO uttered a snort and exited their company through the bulkhead to the below deck.

"What a horse," Carpenter blurted, refocusing his diverted attention back Decker's way. "So, has Royce met with the PRP group yet?" He knew he hadn't.

"No, not yet. He's been too distracted with the takeover mess. But the more he says he studies the matter, the more he's convinced we can get a *de minimis* settlement. He's got some meetings in the next couple of weeks with the PRP group and the EPA."

"Is that so?" remarked Kent. "Well, we'll send a couple of our legal staff along with him. Not to help, but to take over the baton. We want Royce off of it."

Decker was confused. But before he could get a question out about the matter, Carpenter said: "I hate to say it, Deck, but we don't see a fit for Royce. We only want people on Schoen's board we know are with us one hundred percent. Especially in that kind of position. Royce leaves far too much uncertainty for my liking."

"Well, as I said, I honestly haven't spoken to him about his status down the road. I have to tell you, though, I was more than a little annoyed by the way he challenged my media release in front of my fellow directors."

"Definitely unacceptable for a subordinate to do that sort of thing," agreed Carpenter. He brushed his chin with his long-tapered forefinger and then folded his hands in his lap. "He's a queer, you know."

Decker's brow curled at the senior man's comment. He didn't know if it was a joke but he laughed anyway. "I know he's flamboyant and more than a bit eccentric, Larry, but it *is* the nineties."

"No, Moss, *screw* the nineties. The man is a closet queen and I'm an old-fashioned genteel southerner." Larry Carpenter shifted his gaze, staring in Kent's direction. The two men shared imperceptible nods.

Shaughnessy lifted a manila envelope from the attaché case sitting at his side and unclasped its fold. "Decker, these were taken at a 'bike and dyke' joint just south of Manchester." Handing the 8x10 glossy photos to him, Shaughnessy supplemented: "We have more explicit photographs, but I think you'll get the picture."

Decker obliged a scan of the grainy photos, studying them at first with disbelief and then acceding to the truth they depicted. He couldn't help breaking into a smile. Royce was on a stage dancing with another man, both wearing leather G-strings. Decker tried hard to suppress a laugh. "Oh, Everett, Everett. What would your wife and kids think?"

"Precisely," responded Larry with emphasis, "what *would* his wife and kids think? What does it say about a man who presents one life to the ones he loves and works with, and then quite another on the reprobate outings he's in the habit taking on the weekends? Leather jockstraps in dicey perverted hangouts? I'll tell you what it says. It says something about the man's character, his integrity. To say nothing of his wholesale lack of judgment and the vulnerability he leaves himself open to."

Joe Moran returned to the deck clutching an opened tin of morsels and party crackers. He sat down and lifted the tin. "These are great, guys. Want some?"

Ignoring him, Carpenter said: "Anyway, Decker, Royce's name won't be appearing on our slate of director nominees. I hope you understand."

Moss was surprised such surveillance measures would be taken. These men were serious in a form and plane he had never experienced before. Nonetheless, Carpenter's intentions about the matter were clear. It would be an all-out "proxy fight," one in which Drexel-Pace would nominate directors that would oust those nominated by Schoen's board. Ultimately, Decker shrugged at the conclusion without objection and handed the photos back to Shaughnessy. He in turn placed them back into the envelope, which he handed to Decker. "You keep those. You never know if you may need them."

And then Larry Carpenter changed subjects again. "The final issue of business is Schoen's auditing firm. Not a big deal, really, but it is a proxy matter that merits discussion." He reached for a smoked oyster from Joe's tin. "I want to use MM&P's Boston group. Your regional firm up there wouldn't be as efficient if we had to paste their subsidiary work alongside ours. Far too impractical." Carpenter paused, grabbing a cracker from Moran's fingers and placing the oyster on top. "At our meeting with your board in Manchester I recall you talking to Alan Pelleman. You mentioned you knew an MM&P auditing partner in Boston."

"You have a good memory, Larry. Yes, his name's Jonathan Sands. An old college buddy."

"Still close now?" Larry asked, chomping down the hors d'oeuvre.

"Well, after college we exchanged some Christmas cards, but you know how it is. We kind of just parted ways." Decker didn't know what else to say.

"Regrettable," said Carpenter. "Bankers and auditors are the best kinds of friends to keep. But you'd probably have no trouble stoking old fires, right? It's important to have a good close working relationship with your auditor."

Decker caught Carpenter's streamlined thinking. "You mean a green eyeshade who wears rose-colored lenses once in awhile?"

Carpenter nodded. "Not that we'll need it in this case, but you never know. I already took the liberty to speak to Allen Pelleman about it. He apparently loves Sands's ass ... says he'd like to get him down to the Atlanta office someday. Anyway, Pelleman contacted the managing partner up at the Boston office yesterday and they both think Sands would fit the engagement perfectly."

Decker was again surprised Carpenter would initiate such a maneuver, obviously under the premise that their old friendship was opportune. It had been years since he talked to Sands, but recycling older conclusions about him now on the fly, Decker comforted. "Jonathan Sands will work out fine. Like I said, we were old buddies. He actually owes me ..." Decker wondered if the drinks might be bending more soberly-taut lines, so he chose not to say more.

"Excellent," said Carpenter. He stood up and patted Moss on the shoulder. "It's funny how nicely things work out sometimes."

Carpenter walked over to his CFO. Extracting another oyster from the tin, he said to the red-haired fat man: "I'm glad you found these in a can, Joe. Otherwise you'd have to go diving for some. And as much as I like you, I'd hate like hell to see what you might look like wearing a skinsuit."

* * *

Following lunch, the men proceeded to down a couple pitchers of margaritas, spiritedly enjoying the lazy afternoon. Shaughnessy opted for a short nap below deck while Moran had another sandwich and went for a swim. The surf didn't really comport with peaceful body flotation, but he did so anyway. Decker looked out at him bobbing in the water. The ebb and flow of his white belly drifting in the waves was comically Melvillian.

"Ready for some fun?" asked Carpenter, exiting from the cabin, holding two drivers and a basket of golf balls. A Churchill cigar was lodged and unlit in his teeth.

"I'll take one of those if you have another," Decker said, pointing.

"Sure do, straight from Cuba."

Larry noted Decker's confused expression as he extracted another stogie from a leather pouch he carried in his shirt pocket. Clarifying, he said: "Via Switzerland, which is about as straight from Cuba as I can get." Carpenter clipped and lit the Havana with a combination gold lighter made for the purpose.

Decker drew in a long puff and grabbed the club Larry handed him. "So what's our target?" He grabbed a ball from the metal basket.

"Do I really have to tell you?"

Carpenter fingered his stogie, lighted it and looked out in Moran's direction, floating perhaps 50 yards off from the stern. "We should wake him up anyway. I'm certain Jaws would find that fluorescent pink bathing suit he's wearing an irresistible temptation to bite him in the ass."

Decker bent over in laughter.

"Tell you what, Deck," said the skipper. "If you end up hitting Moby Dick out there I'll give you this lighter. Cost me two hundred bucks. If you even get it close enough so he knows you're shooting at him, I'll give you my pack of cigars, case included."

"You've got yourself a deal." Decker was pretty tight. Taking on the old-time college-boy challenge he set his ball down on the carpet and sighted his target. Although the boat was listing in the waves, he knew he could do it. Then, drawing back his club, he let go a full swing.

A whiffle.

Carpenter howled loud and long enough to bring Kent Shaughnessy out from below deck.

"What's going on out here! Is a little peace and quiet too hard for you guys?"

"Decker's got wussy legs."

"Bet you can't do it," challenged Decker.

"Oh yeah?" Carpenter wobbled over to the stern plate. "You just watch how the old sea dog handles this. You'll be eating some of that gull yet."

The CEO kissed his ball and set it down. He looked out at Moran who had drifted another ten or so yards away. "He's a moving target but I'll get it close, of that you can be sure, my friend."

Decker stood smugly with his palm perched atop the handle of his club. "Tell you what, old man. If you get it out there so he even knows you're firing at him, I'll give you this." He undid the band of his gold wristwatch.

"What's this piece of crap?" Carpenter grabbed the timepiece, turning it over in his unsteady hand and studied it. "No, I take that back. It's a Rolex. But it's engraved. Now I know you're drunk, Moss." He threw it back at Decker.

"It was a gift from an old girlfriend."

"Yeah? Well, that's no wonder. A man who would give up an engraved gift like that on a drunken wager doesn't deserve to have a girlfriend!" Carpenter laughed, collected careful aim, and fired away. The club slammed the carpet hard beneath the ball and the two objects sailed out together a good thirty feet into the water.

Now Moss and Shaughnessy bellowed over with laughter.

"So that's how it's done," Decker cackled. "You didn't tell me that!"

Carpenter harrumphed and reached for the bridge ladder. "Draw in men! Time to rescue our whale out there before the sharks get him."

* * *

After hauling Moran aboard, the quartet sat around the sundeck again and serviced another couple pitchers of drinks, this time gin and tonic. The afternoon sun was slumbering in the sky and Moran was now slumbering it off in a cushioned sofa along the gunwale. Carpenter knew they only had another hour or so before they had to head back to shore.

"You in any shape to pilot us back, Captain?" Decker asked, motioning his glass clumsily at the CEO, causing some of his drink to spill.

"I think so. No cops, kids or jerks to worry about. You guys can help when it comes time to find ourselves into port."

"Wonderful," murmured Moss. "I can just see us ramming into a cruise liner."

"He's pretty good at it," comforted Shaughnessy. "I've seen him pull it off in worse shape than he's in now, and that was a night landing." Kent looked over at his superior. "Remember that, Larry?"

"Can't say I remember much about that night, Kent. Luck was all." He turned in Decker's direction. "So, did you have a good time today, my friend?"

"The day's not over, Larry. You get us to back to shore without getting us shipwrecked and I'll put the day right up there with the best of my others."

"Glad to hear it," declared Carpenter. Then, clearing his throat: "You know what, Deck? It's actually much better than you're even

222

aware of. With Drexel-Pace now owning Schoen we're gonna turn the whole world upside down."

"Yep." Decker bobbed in agreement with a sloppy expression on his face.

"No. It's much more than you know. *Far* more."

Larry's emphasis got Decker's attention. "What's that? You got more options to give me?" he asked with a chuckle.

"Your options will be worth twenty-X what we led you to believe this morning. Hell, all of us are going to be richer than the filthy oil sheiks. You got any comprehension of that, Moss? Yachts three times this big docked at your own island off Belize. You know what I'm saying?"

The man was drunk, Decker knew, yet he also knew Larry Carpenter wasn't one given to exaggeration. The elder man hunkered forward in his chair and slurred: "To give it to you straight up, Moss—your firm, our firm, the four of us here," he gestured a circling vortex with his glass, "the four of us here ... we now own the cure for AIDS."

The men watched Decker's face slowly turn color. The drink he was holding slid a bit in his hand. In a maladroit move he tried grabbing a firmer hold, but it spilled entirely onto the deck.

"Get the man another drink," ordered Carpenter with a laugh. "He needs it."

Shaughnessy dutifully got up and tended to the task.

"Another joke on me, right?" asked Moss.

Kent brought a fresh drink and towel over to Decker, proceeding to ruffle his sweaty scalp. "You going to be all right, Deck?"

Moss didn't say anything. He downed a huge gulp.

"We couldn't tell you earlier for obvious reasons," Carpenter explained. "A bench scientist of ours happened onto the discovery a while back using some modified Schoen compounds. Threonatrix is an important part of it, but more important is one of those synthetic peptides you assigned over to us yesterday. That's why I got so serious about it. They and your patented methods are all necessary, as are your production processes. But your firm couldn't duplicate it because it has to be processed in a very particular way, as our scientist discovered."

Decker's incredulous expression went floundering, and then went over to Moran, who was now lounging on the rattan couch with a giant smile on his face.

"So, telling me about it wouldn't have done Schoen any good," asked Decker.

"That's right," replied Shaughnessy. "In fact, we still don't know exactly how it works ourselves. But the fact is, the stuff *does* work. I've seen the results firsthand."

"And you trust me with this information?" Decker asked, still uncertain.

"Of course we trust you," Larry said straightly. "You've proven your loyalty to us, and what man would just throw away hundreds of millions of dollars?"

Decker Moss nodded with pivoting eyes. There was nothing like a shock of the sort to sober one up. He held a moment and asked: "Who else knows about this?"

Shaughnessy, who was marginally less inebriated than the rest of them, took the next several minutes to fill Decker in on the details, including the Harare operation and the progress they had been making with their cohort of southern African governments.

"And all of this can take place without FDA approval?" asked Moss.

Kent leaned back into his chair and smirked at the question. "Deck, it's pretty easy to sit here without appreciating the complete devastation this disease is bringing to the third world. We have our expensive little symptomatic cocktail drugs and our token educational programs, our pat relegation of the problem to the homosexual community. But I'll tell you what, until you've seen for yourself—not from the media—really seen for yourself the Gehenna that's out there, you'll know these countries don't give a damn about the FDA. Or patents, or country boundaries. They'll do anything, pay anything, even break international laws if they have to."

"So the whole thing's illegal? How could we ever get away with it?"

Shaughnessy glanced at Carpenter for permission to explain, who in turn nodded.

"What we're doing now, our pilot operation, is *technically* illegal," Shaughnessy said, "but not in spirit. Would you run a red light if doing so meant saving someone's life? Even the FDA permits patients to receive experimental drugs in terminal situations. We're seeing hundreds of people cured, at their request and permission, and we're documenting our findings."

Shaughnessy sipped from his drink. "You're now one of a very select number of people who even know about it."

"I would think your scientists would want to scream it out to the world," exclaimed Moss.

"Only two scientists even know about it. The bench scientist here who made the discovery—who, by the way, we've also rewarded generously to keep him shut up—and a chap in Harare who has HIV himself and wouldn't dare do anything to compromise the program's success. He's now clean as a whistle."

"Amazing." Decker slumped back in his chair, musing over what had been said. "But what about your board?"

"They have no inkling of this," answered Carpenter. "Not one iota. Nor do our lawyers or accountants, or even our wives for that matter. And we have to keep it that way until we get final approvals from our cohort African governments. If you're wondering about my board's agreement to the buyout, it's all because of Threonatrix and the other reasons I shared with your board. Those reasons remain very legitimate all on their own."

Still, Decker couldn't see how it could possibly work. "Wouldn't we be breaking our own laws by selling it to them? Down the road, I mean, if we were to take this full scale?"

"Yes, if we exported the drug we would," said Shaughnessy. "But there are ways around that. You can't prohibit the export of *knowledge*."

Decker stared at the man. Comprehension slowly registered on his face. "Sell the recipe for the drug?"

"Not sell it," answered Shaughnessy. "*License* it. The Zimbabwean government goes into the drug manufacturing business ... a state run laboratory."

Decker's fixed expression then broke into a laugh as he conjured up an image of African witchdoctors dancing around flaming cauldrons, chanting incantations to the beat of tribal drums. When the others didn't join with him in his laughter, he realized they were serious. "You're not joking. I don't get it. How would that make us rich? Any licensing arrangement other than a set fee would require a method of monitoring their production output. Otherwise, nothing would stop them from playing with the numbers."

Kent threw the towel at Decker, noting the perspiration still running down his face. "That depends on which numbers you're talking about."

225

Moss set his glass down and wiped his forehead.

Carpenter stood up with difficulty and wobbled over to pee off the stern. "Well, gentlemen, it's time to head back. Kent, why don't you explain your little business model to Decker while I drive? I'm sure he'd be impressed with that clever idea of yours."

As the Hatteras sailed westward, Kent outlined the most masterful twist of commerce Decker Moss had ever heard. Drunk or otherwise.

In the time left to set into port, Moss took a place at the bow's front railing by himself, staring out at the coral-colored sunset in front of him. Contemplating as much as he could through the cracks left by an afternoon of strong sun and strong drink, he thought it all too unbelievable to be true.

Was it really possible?

But it *had* to be true. Why would they make up such a story otherwise? The takeover all made perfect sense now. Their adamant contrivances and back deal workings for Schoen's intellectual property rights and production trade secrets all made sense now.

As he smiled about the implications of their revelation, even his unwitting part in it all, his thoughts drifted to Jonathan Sands. Although the cutoff was unmistakable, Decker surmised long ago he probably would have reacted the same way. As far as Sands was concerned, the possibility Decker might at some point lever their secret would always remain a lingering doubt. Indeed, Moss had planned for various outcomes years earlier. Contingency plans that could be set in motion at any time, perchance the need.

Watching the sun sink fully below the horizon, he let his mind drift with the waves. With them, the waves of any residual doubts scattered, and like the diamond-like reflections shimmering atop their crests, his reflections, too, lit up for the brighter.

No. Sands was a non-issue.

And the smile that had degenerated moments earlier returned resplendent upon his face.

Chapter Twenty-One

Monday, November 30, 1992
Boston, Massachusetts

JONATHAN Sands was just reaching for the mug of coffee on his desk when the phone rang. Diverting his hand, he answered. "Yes, Dianne?"

"There's a Decker Moss on the line. Would you like to take the call?"

"Moss—?" he said, clearing his throat. "Yes, sure, I'll take the call." Jonathan depressed the button for the outside line. "*The* Decker Moss?"

"The one and only. How are you doing, old buddy?"

Sands shifted in his chair. "After all these years, it's amazing to hear your voice again."

"And it's good to hear yours, too. I hope I'm catching you at a good time."

"Well ... sure." Jonathan felt an arid sensation creep along the back of his throat and completed his reach for the coffee mug. "How've you been?"

"Enjoying the good life as usual—that is, as much as Manchester, New Hampshire, has to offer." Decker sounded to Jonathan as gregarious as ever. "I'm heading up Schoen now."

"I gathered that. Congratulations. You've been making for some pretty pasty newsprint lately."

"You've read about it?" Decker asked.

"You know me."

Moss laughed. "Still a machine, huh?"

"And I see you haven't changed either," returned Jonathan with matching sarcasm. "Married?"

"Are you kidding? I said I was enjoying the good life. But what about you? Certainly you've gotten yourself tied down."

"Yeah, I'm tied down," said Sands. "Tied to the firm and my house ... and my car." He felt like adding 'and my past,' but didn't want to get into that.

"That's too bad. I was hoping to hear you had a beautiful wife with five kids."

Ignoring the comment, Sands took the pause to take another sip of coffee and changed the subject. "So, are you going to survive that hostile takeover?"

"Yeah, personally I should do fine. Drexel-Pace was successful in their buyout, but they've assured me I'll be staying on at the helm ... actually with a nice raise to boot."

"Well, good for you. I hope you realize you've beaten the odds. Takeovers like that usually go in the way of an entire sweep of top management. How were you able to pull that off?"

"Keeping my job?" asked Moss. "I suppose they just recognize irreplaceable talent when they see it."

"Either that or they haven't gotten to know you yet," Jonathan quipped. He felt some of his tension subside.

"I suppose you must be quite the star up there at MM&P," Decker said. "I hear they even wanted to make you head partner of the office."

"How on earth did you ever hear that?"

"It's a small planet. Actually, that's the reason I'm calling."

Jonathan knew it wasn't a personal call. Friday afternoon he received word from his boss that MM&P's Atlanta office wanted the Boston office to take on the Schoen audit, and they specifically requested Sands to head up the engagement. Something Sands found puzzling. But he also understood the pressure his boss faced to accommodate the request. Its source, Alan Pelleman, was Drexel-Pace's in-charge auditor in Atlanta, and also happened to be the firm's East coast managing director for assurance services.

Jonathan waited for Decker to explain his side of things, which he did directly. "Drexel-Pace, our new parent company, uses MM&P as their audit firm down in Atlanta, and they'd like to put Schoen on the same bill up here. I guess they prefer to keep all their subsidiaries under the same watchdog umbrella."

"It's not that so much," explained Sands, "it's just more efficient that way, especially if there are significant inter-company transactions."

"And from what I hear every CPA firm has their own geeky way of doing things."

"Gee, that one never gets old, Deck. You're right though. We do have our own way of doing things."

"So are you interested?"

"You mean me speaking for MM&P, or me speaking as the potential in-charge partner."

"Both."

Sands paused. "Well, personally I'm very busy. You're a 12/31 audit and I'm already swamped with a full docket of calendar year cutoffs." The excuse was the same one he gave his boss. "I'll have to pass on this one, but we have others who—"

"No, Jon," Moss abruptly interrupted, "they'd really like you to do it." Decker checked himself and corrected for the lighter. "Larry Carpenter, Drexel-Pace's CEO, spoke to his auditor who came up with your name. He had only glowing things to say about you. Imagine something as crazy as that. Anyway, his name's Alan Pelleman, out of your Atlanta office. Ever heard of him?"

"Of course I've heard of him."

"Would you be willing to call him about it? I got the sense from Carpenter that Pelleman would love to work with you on it."

Jonathan stopped again, contemplating the request. As they had over the weekend, over the hanging balance of silence, his thoughts traveled a labyrinth of conflicted feelings: the supposed closeness he and Decker once shared; the nagging questions about Decker's actions that night; his confession about the medal. Even now the sound of Moss's voice made Jonathan's stomach muscles tighten. He couldn't help but wonder if there might be some other motive ...

"What do you say, Jon?" Decker pressed.

You were always there for me, weren't you, Decker?

"Jon?"

Preferring more time to consider the matter, Jonathan quickly gave a conditioned reply: "Tell you what, I'll think about it. But I can't promise anything."

"Sure, Jon, no promises. I miss our friendship. I'm sorry we let it lapse like we did." Then Moss's voice turned jovial. "You never responded to any of my Christmas cards, so I crossed your name off my list. Hell, we were as tight as can be at one time."

Jonathan remained silent, knowing the truth of the statement.

"I guess it can never be the same after I told you what I did," resumed Decker lowly. "I'm very sorry about that, Jon. I always have been."

There was a foreign-sounding veracity in Decker's words, and although Jonathan supposed his old friend was still very much the same person, he had no doubt matured a great deal. "You were drunk, Deck. We both were." Then, believing such matters best left unspoken over the phone, Jonathan suggested: "Listen, I'll call Alan Pelleman and see what we might be able to work out."

"Great," said Moss, followed by a pause. "Let's make it work out, Jon. I'd really like it to, for old times' sake. I'd like a chance to right the rail."

Not knowing what more to say, Jonathan simply said: "Good to talk to you again, Deck. I'll get back to you."

"Good to talk to you as well, my old friend."

* * *

Jonathan sat in his office ruminating over the conversation. It wasn't that a client's request for a specific partner to head up an audit engagement was unusual. That could be done for good enough reasons. Yet Jonathan suspected Decker's contact implied something else.

The Pelleman connection was one thing. Sands had distinguished himself in the firm as being one of the most knowledgeable auditors in the technology and industrial manufacturing sectors.

But the Moss connection was quite another.

Jonathan's thoughts carried him back to the article he read about the hostile takeover … and then to the earlier press release about the environmental write-off.

He wondered again if they could somehow be related.

* * *

Later in the day, Sands poked his head in the door of Jensyn Chandler's office. "How are you with mixtures and potions?"

"Huh?" Jensyn had become accustomed to him opening conversations with odd segues. "Actually, I'm pretty good with orange juice and tomato soup, as long as they're out of a can and all you do is add water."

"Tomato soup's better with milk, Chandler, you should know that." He stepped in and took one of the seats facing her desk. "How would you like another 12/31?"

"Jonathan!"

"No, hold on. We can give next year's Crenfield-Shores engagement to Baker. I think you'd be perfect for this and you'd find it far more interesting. It's a chemical company in Manchester, which is a shorter trip for you than to Maine. And you know you

OPTIONS

love the technical stuff. You've demonstrated your mastery over and again." He smiled.

Jensyn gathered he was referring to the recent Freon issue. "I used a consultant for that."

"Still, it was your idea, and you knew enough to call in an expert in the first place. Besides, Baker enjoys retail and you don't."

He was right, of course. Retail was boring and she was hoping to forge her career in technology. "What kind of chemical company?"

"You'll like this. They're a relatively new listing on the Big Board," he said, referring to the New York Stock Exchange. "Bioengineering, pharmaceutical intermediates, that sort of thing. Not much in the way of everyday smokestack stuff. Anyway, they were just bought out by Drexel-Pace Pharmaceuticals. I got the prospect this morning. Interested?"

"Sounds interesting," she admitted, but held a moment, rolling her pencil in her fingers. She looked up at him. "Would you be working with me on it?"

"I doubt I'll be the one to head up the job. But you were the first one I thought of to manage it. It would be perfect for your portfolio." As a relatively new audit manager, Jensyn Chandler hadn't yet managed a first-time audit from scratch.

He watched her as she seemed to mull the idea over. Eventually she hinted a nod.

"Is that a yes?" he asked.

"It's a provisional yes. I'd like to hear more about it, just so I feel more comfortable about it."

Jonathan glanced at his watch: *4:15.* "Well, I have quite a bit yet to find out myself. I have a telecon at 4:30 with Drexel-Pace and their audit partner in the Atlanta office. I should be done at about five, maybe five-thirty." He thought a moment. "I'm flying out for New York tomorrow. Are you planning a late workday, or should I call you tonight at home?"

"I was going to take my run before dinner down at the gym." The basement level of their office building housed a large workout facility.

"Gym? I thought you said you liked to run the streets of Boston."

"Maybe you haven't noticed it's snowing outside?" She gestured to the window behind her desk. The snow was falling heavily.

231

"Never stopped *me* before," said Sands.

"Well, maybe I'm not a masochist like you."

Jonathan had a locker in the basement facility for his workouts. "Tell you what, I'll meet you down there at five-thirty."

"Sounds good. I'm getting tired of watching CNN."

* * *

Other than for Jensyn and a couple of bodybuilders who were grinding away on the weight machines across the room, the gym was deserted, which was uncommon at the end of the day. Most who used the facility couldn't fit in a decent workout during their lunch break, choosing to do so instead after hours. Tonight, however, the first heavy snowstorm of the season had no doubt prompted the commuters in the building to scoot home as early as they could.

Jonathan found her jogging on the end treadmill in a row of six when he strode in. She was wearing free-fitting red nylon shorts and a black t-shirt that read: HAVE YOU HUGGED YOUR ACCOUNTANT TODAY?

"I hope that's not an open invitation" he said on approach.

"What?"

He furtively pointed to the guys across the room and then at her shirt. "Because if it is, I bet the Brutus Brothers over there would love to take you up on it."

Jensyn stared at him confused, then, catching his gaze, looked down at her front. "Very funny."

Climbing the treadmill next to hers, Jonathan asked: "How do you work this thing?"

"You've got to be kidding."

"Nope. Never been on one."

She cornered her eye dubiously at him. "First you take that stringy-thing there, attach it to your shorts, and insert the key." Pointing, she spoke between pants.

He stared down at the console, surrendering a shrug. "Stringy-thing?"

"Dangling from the bar there." She pointed again.

"Oh, this stringy-thing."

"There's no other one. That's the only one."

"Got it." Jonathan clipped the safety cord to his shorts and scrutinized the flat piece of plastic on the other end, holding it up. "Is this thing the key?"

232

"Yes, slide it into that slot just beneath the panel."

He studied the console without success. "Sorry, but there's no keyhole in this—"

"Look at mine."

"Ah."

Jensyn chuckled. "Is one of the masterminds in this building mechanically challenged, Mr. Sands?"

As he inserted the key, the tramp of his machine caught him by surprise. He calibrated his stride to catch up with it. "Sorry I'm a bit late."

"That's okay. I was too. How'd your teleconference go?"

"Well, Schoen looks like it's a go. The change won't be formalized until their annual meeting, which should be early April. Of course, we'll have to do our communication thing before we can accept the engagement." The auditing profession required successor auditors to communicate with predecessor auditors prior to accepting a new client. The move was necessary to ensure accounting disagreements didn't provoke the change.

"So, have you decided whether you're going to take on the account?"

Jonathan tried to speed up his machine, but it was screaming away at its highest setting. He had to speak loudly over his strides. "Not yet. But either way you should be able to begin your preliminary work in March, per diem billing. In the meantime, I'll work up an engagement proposal and fee schedule, which shouldn't be a problem. Hopefully their auditors will let us review their working papers." It was difficult to hear each other over their stomping and the whining of the treadmills. "You really like these things?" he asked.

"You get used to it. So, who's their current auditor?"

"Wilcox & Kline ... their Manchester office."

"I'm sure they're going to love us for taking their client away from them." She shifted her eyes briefly at his. "I love friction-filled meetings, you know."

"I know. You have a personality quirk."

Jensyn frowned at him.

After a while he asked: "How long have you been at this?"

"About ten minutes."

"Well, I've been on this contraption less than two and already I'm bored."

"Thanks a lot," she said.

"No, not you, the machine. I feel like a gerbil." He turned to her. "You know, it's a well-known fact gerbils go insane."

"Really?"

"Absolutely. They've done a million studies on it. Throw in a babe gerbil of the opposite sex or put them on Prozac and they don't want to have a thing to do with treadmills anymore."

"I can see your sense of humor hits new heights in the evening, Jonathan. Well, it's better than nothing when the weather's bad."

"The weather's beautiful. I looked out the window before I came down."

"Snow's bad as far as I'm concerned," she said. "Until somebody comes out with jogging snowshoes, I think I'll do my winter running indoors, thank you very much."

"Jogging snowshoes? Now there's a great idea." Mimicking the fast-talking Ronco announcer's voice he parlayed: "Sled'n Peds, the amazing new product from Slip-Shod Company. Only nineteen-ninety-nine, plus twice that for shipping and handling—but wait, there's more! We'll throw in a third shoe for free"

Jensyn smirked at him. "You're pitiful."

After a minute more of romping he pulled the key out of his machine and hopped off. It stopped. "That does it. I can't take this anymore."

Stupefied, Jensyn watched as he pulled the safety key from her machine as well. "What do you think you're doing?" she asked.

"Time to do some real running. We're going outside."

"But it's *snowing* outside."

"You got a sweat suit in your locker?"

"I—"

"Go get it." He pointed in the direction of the women's locker room. "It's time a lady from old England finds out how things are done here in New England."

She interleaved her arms and pursed her lips at him in defiance. A strand of wet temple hair fell from behind her ear. Meeting her challenge, he folded his arms as well.

"Is this an order from my boss?" she asked.

"No, it's a request from a friend."

"Can you be both at the same time?"

"Well, if the friend thing ever interferes with the boss thing, I'll just fire you."

Chapter Twenty-Two

LARGE snowflakes drifted to the ground in a blanket of crystalline down. The evening air was serene and cool, and although the sun had long since set, the snowfall lit up the sky in a zillion dots of refracted light.

From State Street heading north, they jogged to Quincy market, picked up the Freedom Trail at Faneuil Hall, and then headed west in the direction of the Boston Common. The Trail consisted of two and a half miles of interconnected sidewalks and pathways that circuited many of the city's historic buildings and revolutionary landmarks. They had it essentially to themselves, which consoled Jensyn since she doubted her footing in the shadows of the street lamps.

"The air smells so fresh and clean," she remarked.

"Sure beats getting nowhere in a smelly old gym."

She spied the firm features of his profile and the way the snowflakes lit on his thick lashes. "Thanks."

"Thanks?"

"For being insistent."

"Just a gentle prod," he said turning. "I knew you'd like it. Sometimes doing something new … you know, the idea of the thing is harder than the thing itself. And then you find you actually enjoy it once you're into it."

"Like managing an entirely new audit from scratch?" she asked.

"Right." He smiled at her.

Jensyn hoped he hadn't misread her hesitancy about managing the new engagement as a show of insecurity. It was just that recently promoted audit managers typically supervised clients they already had considerable experience with. Yet she appreciated the faith Jonathan placed in her abilities, and she appreciated also his efforts to consign her to a fast track of sorts.

They passed the cobblestone rings marking the site of the Boston Massacre and headed in the direction of the Old State House.

"So, tell me about this company," Jensyn asked.

"Schoen? Actually, the CEO's my old college roommate."

"Really?"

"His name's Decker Moss. We shared an apartment together our junior and senior years at Middlebury. Not long after graduating we lost touch and I haven't spoken to him since. I guess that's some of my hesitation about whether to take it on as the partner in charge."

"Nothing in our Code of Ethics about old friendships," she said.

"Right, but ..."

He knew it wouldn't be prudent to get into the fact they hadn't parted as friends. Or even much of anything else about their relationship, for that matter. On the other hand, while for years he had determined to cut Moss completely out of his life, this sudden new contact with him was something of a tempting opportunity to pursue. Sands was more than skeptical about the man—who he was back then, who he was now. With Jensyn managing the audit, if any new suspicions arose ... The question he debated, literally on the run, was whether this could be a fortuitous reconnection with Moss. Was it only a fanciful notion it might somehow lead to answers he yearned for nearly half his life?

"Anyway," he continued, "Schoen's his grandfather's name, so it's a family affair. The company went public a few years back. They used to be heavy into generic chemicals, but then moved increasingly into specialty chemicals ... biopharmaceuticals in particular, with impressive growth."

Jensyn had a comfortable knowledge of industrial manufacturing, and indeed had experience with a couple of Boston-based pharmaceuticals. But there would necessarily be some background study of the chemical industry. "Is there much different about them I should prep for?"

"I wouldn't think so. Not much. Their plants are FDA approved, so nothing new for you there. Environmental compliance will be important, of course. You'll have to review some of the more significant state and federal regulations just so you're aware of them when designing your compliance study. We have plenty of materials at the office." Jonathan wiped some melted snow from his forehead with his sleeve as they cornered a turn. "Actually, they were recently named in connection with a Superfund site ... just booked a loss for it."

"Recently named and they booked a loss already?" she asked, surprised. "That's unusual."

OPTIONS

"I had the same reaction when I first read about it. But more power to them. We can ask their auditors about it, but I suspect it had to do with the recent buyout. You know, full disclosure before the tender offer?"

"That wouldn't make sense if it was a friendly offer."

"It wasn't. It was hostile." He caught her eye. "And if you wanted to scare off an undesired suitor wouldn't you want to make yourself look less attractive?"

Jensyn hadn't thought of that before. "Warts and all, I guess." Then she reflected on the matter further. "But obviously it didn't work," she said, folding her hair behind her back. "They were bought out anyway."

"Yeah, but anti-takeover tactics often aren't successful, Jen. When a firm wants another firm badly enough, things can get pretty ugly, fast. Heck, that's what the eighties were all about."

"And a lot of men went to jail for their schemes."

"You studied that at Harvard, too?" he asked.

"Just some of the more interesting cases. Business ethics."

"Never had any of that when I went to school."

She laughed. "Which is probably why we had the problems we did in the eighties."

The footpath led them to the Old South Meeting House, a brick and steeple building that looked like a church. He turned in his gait and asked: "Do you know your history?"

"Huh?" Jensyn glanced at him with a puzzled look. "Who would know my history any better?"

"No," he laughed, "I mean American history. Of the Revolution."

"Oh ... well, yes, believe it or not, we did get an education in London. The British were a bit involved in that war, too, you know."

He gestured to the building they were passing. "That's where the whole thing started. Thousands of irate Colonists came here in December, 1773, to protest the tea tax. It began the revolt that came to be known as the Boston Tea Party."

"What are you, some kind of encyclopedia?"

He enjoyed her teasing expression. "I happen to enjoy history," he replied. "When I first moved here, there was nothing else to do on the weekends, so I'd often walk this Trail, eventually just soaking it all in." He caught her eye again. "So did they give it

237

to you straight, or did they just fill you with a bunch of propaganda?"

"Propaganda?" she asked. "What are you talking about?"

"How we kicked your British butt."

"*Jonathan!*" Jensyn stopped. "How dare you!" She stretched down to scoop up some snow and made like she was going to throw it at him when he sprinted away like a kid. She took off after him with her snowball, sculpting it firm as she ran. "You just better not stop because I've packed this thing tight as a cricket ball!"

Jonathan checked his back periodically, keeping just more than an arm's throw distance in front of her. They ran for several blocks like that until their route eventually took them into the Boston Common. It was a 50-acre open field park, replete with history. Once used by the Boston townspeople for grazing cattle, it later became the site of the British Army camp during their occupation of the city.

At a nexus of walkways on the southern side, Jonathan abruptly skidded and turned around. "Halt!"

She did, sliding a bit in the slurry.

"I'll give you one shot, Chandler. But make it good!"

"Only one?"

"Only one. And I tell you what. I'll stand here like your nation's venerable army used to do, without cover. Or should I say 'vulnerable' army? Either way, you have less than thirty feet. You should be able to nail me good from there."

She gathered her footing and took aim, drawing her arm close behind her ear. "I can't. You look too defenseless standing there like that."

"That's right. Defenseless, like your forebears in arms. Now shoot me!"

With her draw still up behind her ear she said sheepishly: "But I can't."

"Then put it down!"

"No way!" she laughed. "I worked too hard on it."

"If that's the way you want it." He bent to his knees for a clump of snow of his own.

At that she went ahead and threw her round anyway, but it arced several feet above him and to the left. Then she turned, running into the field to escape the path of his impending fire. He lobbed a loose-packed ball, catching her square in the back with a splat.

"*No!*" she cried.

"Surrender!"

"You've got to be kidding. That didn't even hurt!" She crunched down in the snow again and quickly fashioned two more snowballs. He already had a new one and began charging in her direction.

"No!" she yelled, looking up at him as he ran towards her with coiled arm. She took off, darting left and right in a zigzag sprint. Then, in a single sliding moment, she abruptly turned to go left but caught the edge of her foot and toppled to the ground.

Jonathan studied her downed form in the snow from a distance. "I suppose this is some kind of redcoat trick!"

"I surrender," she yelled, holding her ankle.

He jogged over to her and knelt down at her side. "Are you alright?"

"I don't think so. Did you hear the crack?"

"Oh, Jen, I'm so sorry."

He reached for her right foot and carefully raised the cloth of her sweat pants. Jensyn winced as he gently examined the bruised ankle from both sides. "Well, thank goodness it's not broken. But you do have a nice sprain here." He gathered a handful of snow and slid it beneath the elastic of her sock, kneading it to form a pack.

"That hurts worse than the sprain!"

"Don't forget pain and reward."

She set the back of her head down in the snow and stared up at him. "Now what?"

Sands looked around the field and at his situation. No phones or help in sight. The road was a good distance away. Then he eyed her. The falling snowflakes melted on her perspiring red cheeks and forehead but remained crystallized a moment longer on her lashes and brows.

"I guess I have to take you prisoner."

"Prisoner. Then what?"

"Are you going to be a good prisoner or bad?"

"Oh, Jon, I'm cold and this is killing me."

"In that case, Chandler, I guess there's no need for torture." He bent over for her to place her arm around his neck. "Ready to stand up?"

"No," she said, and then, "yes. Yeah. I guess so. Be gentle."

"Trust me."

He hefted her to her good leg. "I *did* trust you. That's my problem," she said.

He steadied her balance, holding her around the waist. "Can you walk on it?"

She cautiously placed her foot into the powder and slowly tried her weight by degrees. "Ouch!"

"That answers that. Here, put your arms around me and climb on."

"Climb on?"

"My back."

"You've got to be kidding."

"Either that or you freeze to death out here."

"I …" Jensyn tried to think of the alternatives but they weren't good. It could take a long while for him to get help, and even if he found a taxi outside the park, she would still have to travel a good distance on foot to get there. "Are you sure you can carry me?"

"You don't look more than what—one-seventy, one-eighty, right?"

"Very funny." Then, grabbing him from behind with both arms, she jumped up with her good leg and cradled his back.

Jonathan firmed his hands beneath her thighs and teasingly dipped up and down with bent knees. "I underestimated."

"Oh, shut up."

Rather than their originating easterly direction, Sands headed north across the shadowed length of the field, whistling Yankee Doodle.

"Where are you going, may I ask?"

"My house. It's right over here in Beacon Hill."

"What?"

"It's not far that from here. The office building's more than a mile away, and who knows if we'd ever find a taxi in this weather. I'll call for one from the house."

"No, Jon, I really think we should head back to the building. My things are there."

He sighed. "Suit yourself, Chandler. Just don't blame me if I have a heart attack and die on the way." Jonathan obligingly changed directions.

After a period listening to his perceptibly deeper breaths as he trudged through the wet snow, she said: "Beacon Hill, huh? You must be rich."

He laughed. Pacing for a period across the field, he said almost below his voice: "Rich would be having memories and someone to share them with."

She was surprised by the comment. Then again, the whole evening had developed into something of a surprise. And she found herself enjoying it, privately amused. "I think it's time I heard about that, Jon." She was close to his ear. "After all, I think I should know something about the man on whose back I'm riding."

Her words and the warmth of her breath against his ear were sensuously disarming.

There was a barricade Jonathan Sands had placed about himself, erected by years of resolve to shut in and to shut out. He distinctly remembered—regretted—the last time he shared his childhood story. It was with Decker Moss, when they were forming a close friendship at school, before they were housemates. *Was it an abused trust?* He doubted he would ever know the answer.

"It's not very pleasant," he said after a while.

"I'll be gentle. And this time, give me the dinner version. Your lunch version was pitiful."

He turned his head back to her and smiled, his cold cheeks touching hers.

So, with her on his back, trudging through the snow, Jonathan told her what came to be surprisingly easy to him: his father's alcoholism; the abuse of his mother; his father's eventual suicide; and his own charge for misdemeanor battery when he was a teenager. He paused every so often to catch his breath, and now his breathing was very heavy. "Are you handling my sordid history okay?"

"It's fascinatingly honest. It must have been terrible for you."

"How's your foot?" he asked.

"It fell off a ways back. Go on."

Jonathan arched forward in an attempt to stretch his back muscles. "Do you want to stop and rest?" he asked.

"Me? No. What about you?"

"I'm fine," he lied.

"Then get on with your story." Jensyn squeezed her legs against his sides.

"What do you think I am, a horse?"

"No, I'm fascinated. Go on!"

"You really want to hear more?"

"Of course I do."

"What if that's all there is?" he asked.

"Right. That takes you to age sixteen. Maybe there's twenty-plus years more?"

Sands remained quiet, from which Jensyn considered he had finished all he wanted to say. She took the time to look around at the old section of Boston. The streets were literally deserted. The snow continued falling, reflecting an ambient glow from the street lamps.

"It all kind of reminds me of north London, back home."

"You still consider London your home?"

"Home is where your memories are, I guess."

"I thought you said you had to get away."

Jensyn tried to grab a firmer hold around his shoulders and neck. Her back and stomach muscles ached from the strain. "I haven't shared anything with you yet about my better memories." She paused. "So, are you just going to leave me hanging on like this or are you going to finish your story?"

Jonathan didn't say anything. The snow now literally covered them and he was cold and exhausted. They turned the final corner for the office building.

"Are you finished?"

"Sorry," he said, "I'm finished. My arms and back are killing me."

Although the doors were locked to the gym, he fortunately had a master key and they gained access to the shower rooms. Thirty minutes later, as he waited in the lobby to drive her to her apartment, she eventually hobbled out the door.

"Are you going to be alright?" he asked.

"You may be hearing from my lawyer."

"Can you make it to my car, or do you want to hop on my back again?"

She smiled. "What if I were to say both?"

Chapter Twenty-Three

Tuesday, December 1, 1992
Manchester, New Hampshire

CYRUS P. Schoen and Everett Royce played proper office etiquette in their request of Decker Moss's secretary to meet with him. The unlikely pair approached her desk first thing in the morning. Fortunately, Decker's calendar was free of scheduled appointments for the next hour.

"Mr. Schoen and Mr. Royce are here to see you."

Surprised at his secretary's announcement at the door, Decker replied: "A ... yes, of course, Jean, send them on in."

The two men charged into Moss's office with agenda faces. "What's going on, Decker?" Schoen barked.

"I'm sorry, Cyrus, but this is quite unexpected. I haven't even finished my first cup of coffee yet. What are you asking?"

"The shareholder records. How did Drexel-Pace get hold of them?"

"Shareholder records? Gee, I must have missed that memo."

"Yes, the ones you gave Drexel-Pace so they could make their bid directly by mail." The usual antique pallor of the old man's face was now fully flushed with life.

"Sorry, but I still don't know what you're talking about."

"Oh I think you do," challenged Everett Royce.

Decker turned to his sudden adversary. "Don't forget who you're talking to, Everett. I'd weigh my words pretty carefully before I spoke them."

"Well, I won't weigh my words with you, young man." Schoen slammed his palm down loudly on the desk. "You've sold my company out from under me."

Decker pulled back in his chair. "Cyrus, you can think what you will, but I didn't sell anything out to anybody."

"You're not being truthful with me. You gave those pimps my shareholder records they could whore me off!"

Decker reeled fast forward in his chair, pointing his finger. "*You're* the one who shunned this offer! *You're* the one who couldn't see a bag of gold if it were thrown in your face. I've turned this damned company of yours into more than you could ever dream of. You and your pitiful generic chemical business that would go bankrupt in another year. You should be happy I've given you some means to retire on."

"Go to hell, Decker."

"Mom wouldn't like to hear you speak to me like that."

"Your mother would regret the day you were born if she knew what I know about you. You got those records from our registrar and you sold me off!" C.P. Schoen hit the desk with his fist again. Then he sunk into the facing chair and turned sideways, moistness in his eyes.

"I know you did it, Decker," said Royce, flittering his eyeballs. "I spoke to our registrar and he said you asked for them. You obtained the shareholder records ... not once, but twice. How could you *do* this?"

"Gentlemen, if we're going to continue with this conversation, then I ask you for a little decorum." Decker nodded alternately at the two of them seeking their cooperation. Royce joined Schoen's side by taking a seat.

Schoen, in turn, pulled a handkerchief from his suit coat pocket and wiped at his eyes. "Did you honor me with decorum, Decker? Did you seek my counsel or even hint to me what you had in mind? My God, man, I'm the founder of this company and the Chairman of your board. And your blood!"

"Look, I'm not going to sit here and admit I gave anybody those records. Because I didn't. I wanted them for myself to determine the extent of our institutional holdings. In fact, my reason for getting them was quite contrary to what you're accusing me of. But I'll tell you this: I'm not the least bit sorry about the way things turned out. Drexel-Pace is the right place for this company. You're the one who's breached your fiduciary responsibility to our shareholders. Not me. I wanted to take the offer to them to let *them* decide." Decker gestured towards Royce. "And so did *he!*"

"Yeah, but not like this," objected the corporate counselor.

Decker fleered at the egghead who wore leather strappings on the weekends. "Everett, just shut up. You may be a lawyer, but you're not a man."

"How dare you!"

Decker stood up. "Look, unless you gentlemen have anything substantive to say, or can point to facts that impugn my obligations to this company in any way, then I suggest you leave. I will not sit here as a target for your baseless suppositions and mischaracterizations."

Schoen stared down at his age-spotted hands. The bushy eyebrows overhanging his ageless eyes quivered with silent fury. "Decker, you may have done everything you thought was right for yourself. Even for this company, for that matter. But I want you to remember something when it all falls down on you. It would have all been yours anyway. Every one of my shares would have been yours. You didn't have to do any of this. And even all that doesn't amount to anything. A man arrives here with nothing and he takes away nothing. Nothing but his integrity. That's my question to you. Will you leave here one day, maybe sooner than you know, and still be in possession of that?"

The question didn't deserve a response as far as Decker Moss was concerned. Still, he wouldn't leave such a remark go unanswered. He got up and walked thoughtfully to the window. "I came here with nothing, Cyrus, and maybe I will leave here with nothing. But I'll tell you one thing. What I finish here will be far greater than you ever dreamed." He turned around to face his grandfather. "I heard your little speech in that meeting about chemicals for livelihoods and wars, and things that make this country great. Well, what about chemicals that make lives even possible? What about chemicals that make what you've had the privilege of living seventy-five-plus years living even a dream? You, who thinks knows so much, yet knows so little. In the end you'll see. In the end you'll know it was *I* who made the difference."

Schoen eased out of his chair, drawing on Royce's arm for support. "Oh, you may make a difference, all right, young man, but it won't be a good one."

Moss stood with his eyes fixed on his grandfather. "The difference I make will be meaningful."

"Mark my words, Decker, the difference you make will be very regrettable." Schoen turned his back abruptly on his lamentable progeny. "Good-bye." And with that, the company's founder lumbered out of the office.

Royce was just about to exit as well when Decker called after him. "Royce, get back in here!"

The lawyer twisted at the doorway, wearing a mousy expression.

"Close the door and sit down." He did so and Decker nailed him in the eyes. "That's the last time you'll act insubordinate with me again. I've taken enough crap from you and I won't stand for it, do you understand?"

"Crap? What crap have I given you?"

"In front of my directors in that teleconference? Saying you thought my announcement was, quote, 'a dumb-ass move'?"

"Well, I happen to think it was. That's all the EPA needs now to support their case against us, to say nothing about the other PRPs. You can't play the game that way."

"You seem to forget our board endorsed the idea in the first place, to scare away other bidders. Anyway, Royce, you're off the EPA matter."

"*What!*"

"Don't raise your voice with me."

"But I have meetings with them next week. I know I can prevail against these people."

Decker took his seat again and grabbed his mug, taking a sip. "Everett, I'm going to share something with you that is strictly confidential. Can you just hear it and shut up about it?" Moss set his cup down, leaned back and folded his arms across his chest. "I've been in negotiations with Drexel-Pace and I've been able to convince them to assume that liability."

"I *knew* it! You *have* been working with those people."

"No, not like you're accusing me. But, yes, I was able to persuade them of the need to make a goodwill gesture. They own us now, or most of us, and it's time to extend a branch of peace. You should be pleased with my accomplishments."

"It's a withering branch, Decker. There's not going to be any exposure anyway. The case law is too shaky on successor liability. I've been doing my research."

"Good, I'm glad to hear it. Drexel-Pace's legal team will be very interested in what you've come up with. But you're off the case, Royce. I need you to devote your time to more critical matters concerning the acquisition."

"I'll do that, too, but I'm not getting off this case. Not when I know I can prevail."

Decker glared at the lawyer. "You'll do what I tell you."

Royce returned the hard look. "I'll take it to the board."

"Is that a threat?" Decker asked.

"I think they'd be very interested to hear of your behind-the-scenes talks with our hostile buyer. And I know I'll find proof you were the only possible source of our shareholder records. It could very well get you fired."

Decker stood. "That does it, Royce! Dirty men like you apparently only know how to play dirty." He reached down into his desk drawer, grabbed a manila envelope and flung it atop the desk. "There! Take those home for your family photo album."

Everett Royce reached for the envelope with nervous fingers. He looked up at his superior, then at the envelope. Unclasping it, he pulled out the photographs, staring at them one by one, disbelieving. "You lousy—"

"I have more if you'd like to frame some to hang around the house, Everett. Your wife and kids would enjoy those even more."

Royce stood up, ripped the photos into pieces and threw them at the man facing him. Then his shoulders hunched as he pulled his face into his hands. "How could you do this? We were friends."

"No, Royce, I was your boss and you were my demented corporate counsel. You dropped your fig leaf in a most inappropriate way. That's now over. If you wish to keep your job, there will be no more of that stuff. I'm giving you another chance. Do you understand?"

The defeated lawyer eventually managed a feeble nod.

Decker went on: "Now, here's what you're going to do: you're going to write a report, appropriately documented with full legal justification and cost analyses, supporting that fifty-million-dollar write-off. I want it for our auditors. By this time next week. You're going to conclude the amount of the write-off is probable and reasonably estimable, given the facts known to you. Those are to be your words: 'probable' and 'reasonably estimable.' Do you understand?"

Again Royce surrendered a nod.

"That's good, Everett. If you prove yourself faithful, I'll prove myself faithful. Nobody will ever be aware of this little situation. However, if you screw with me again you're finished."

Unable to look up, Royce turned and exited the door.

Chapter Twenty-Four

Wednesday, December 2, 1992
Boston, Massachusetts

JONATHAN poked his head into Jensyn's office and knocked on the opened door.

She looked up from the work on her desk, pursing a smile. The blue cashmere overcoat he was wearing was damp from the morning snowfall. He entered and pulled out what he held hidden behind his back.

"What the—?" Jensyn stood from her chair and took hold of the gift: a stuffed toy gorilla. Its leg was in a cast and in its hands was a pair of miniature wooden crutches. "Where on earth did you ever find him?"

"FAO Schwarz. It's a huge toy store in Manhattan."

She knew Jonathan was in New York the previous day on business. "You're unbelievable." She turned the stuffed animal around in her hands and felt its black rubber lips. "You didn't have to do that." Setting it down, she retook her seat, smiling.

"His name's Gimpo." Jonathan removed his overcoat and draped it over his arm. "I was just hoping to make amends for what I did to you the other night. I'm very sorry, Jen. Do you forgive me?"

Jensyn rested her elbows on her desk and folded her hands beneath her chin. "I spoke to my lawyer yesterday."

"Oh, did you? How do things look?"

"Good for me, bad for you. A boss forcing his subordinate to go running in inclement weather against her will? From which she suffers injury? I don't think you'll be living in Beacon Hill much longer."

"Well, then, what if I bought the plaintiff a nice lunch? Just to talk over an agreeable settlement, of course, nothing else. Would she be open to that?"

"Possibly, but no promises. What time and what terms?"

"Noontime and favorable terms. Maybe some laughs. Then back to work."

Jensyn tried to suppress a smile.

248

"I really am sorry, Jen" he said. "You must be pretty upset with me."

"I don't know. Not really an overly bad time, all in all."

"So, is that a 'yes' for lunch?"

"If it is a 'yes,' would I get part two of your story?"

"Part two?"

"What you've been up to the last twenty years?"

"It might put you to sleep."

"Those are my terms," Jensyn said steadfastly.

"Then, in that case, I suppose I have no choice."

She eyed him a moment. "This wouldn't happen to be getting serious, would it, Mr. Sands? Because, if it is—"

"Dinner would be serious, Jen. This is lunch. Nothing serious about lunch."

Looking down at her work and then up again, Jensyn said: "Okay, boss, I'll see you at noon."

* * *

When Jonathan entered his own office suite that morning he grabbed the previous day's stack of phone messages handed him by his secretary. Sitting at his desk he leafed through them one by one, rearranging them by importance.

Then one pulled the air out of his lungs.

Caller: *Edward Fitch, FBI*

Time: *12/1, 8:15*

Message: *Will call back tomorrow.*

Nothing else but a return number. His mind shrouded over as he tried to think what it could mean.

Why is all this coming back into my life now?

With a sense of foreboding he stared at the phone, trying to muster strength before eventually picking up the handset. Jonathan immediately recognized the black man's voice in his greeting.

"Hello, Mr. Fitch. This is Jonathan Sands, returning your call."

"Ah, yes, Mr. Sands. Thank you for getting back to me. Your secretary told me you were in New York yesterday?"

"Yes, how may I help you?" Jonathan's impersonal tone belied his more cordial attempt. He didn't feel inclined to fabricate meaningless niceties.

"You remember who I am?" asked the agent.

"Yes, of course I do. Not one of my fondest memories, but nothing personal."

"No, of course not." Fitch paused. "I was wondering if we might be able to arrange a time to get together. I know you're a busy man."

"Yes, who's not busy? How may I help you?"

"It would be better if we were to talk in person."

"I'm sorry, but I'm far too busy for that. You must have something we can discuss over the phone."

"I don't think the phone is the proper format."

"It is the proper format because that's what I'm choosing. I'm sorry, Mr. Fitch, but whatever you might have to ask me I can deal with right now."

Ed Fitch forced equanimity. "In that case, would you mind if I recorded our conversation?"

Sands recoiled in his chair. *What the hell could this mean?*

"As long as you send me a copy of the tape, Mr. Fitch. I don't have spy devices on my phone."

"Okay, then that's the way we'll deal with it," answered the FBI agent. "When I begin recording I'll ask you some standard questions for you to acknowledge your identity and also your understanding that I'm recording our conversation. Is that okay with you?"

"Yes, yes, just get on with it."

"I'm beginning my recording right now." Jonathan didn't hear anything, but suspected a tape recorder had been activated. "My name is Edward Fitch, Senior Special Agent of the FBI, Albany office. It is December second, 1992." He then spewed a litany of questions.

"Is your name Jonathan Thomas Sands?"

"Yes."

"Do you grant me permission to record our conversation after declining a personal meeting?"

"Yes, I do."

"And are you aware that I am recording our conversation at this time?"

"Yes I am."

"Is your employer Marsh, Mason & Pratt, located in Boston, Massachusetts?"

"Yes it is." Jonathan was beginning to tire of the nonsense.

"And were you formerly a full time student at Middlebury College, Vermont, during the years 1974 to 1978?"

"Yes, yes. Is all of this really necessary?"

OPTIONS

"I just have to establish for the recording that your identity is not in question and that you are fully cognizant that your statements are being recorded. I apologize for the redundancy."

"Mr. Fitch, I fully concur that I am who I say I am, that this is the date it is, and that this is all being recorded. Now please take this forward."

"Mr. Sands, in the matter of the Karen Wyman disappearance, was it your previous statement to me on November sixth, 1977, that you did not see her the day or night of Friday, November fourth, 1977, the day of her disappearance?

"I can't be sure of the date I spoke to you, but I made such a statement, yes, that I did not see her the night she disappeared." Jonathan's voice quivered.

"And was it your statement that that was also the night you went drinking at Smitty's and got drunk?"

"Yes."

"And did you say drinking was out of character for you? That you did not usually do that sort of thing?"

Jonathan couldn't imagine where this was going. "Yes, that was my statement. At least I think I told you that."

"I'm sorry, Mr. Sands, that was a bit ambiguous. Could you clarify?"

"I think I told you I didn't usually drink much. That's correct. I didn't usually drink much. Hardly at all. But the night I went to Smitty's I got so drunk I don't know how I managed to walk home."

"Thank you, Mr. Sands. Now, for the recording, will you tell me if you have any memory of ever being drunk before that night?"

"I have no memory of getting drunk after high school. That's what I told you."

"So you weren't a drinker at Middlebury College before that night, is that correct?"

"No, I didn't say that. I said I wasn't a partier. There's a difference. My roommate, Decker, was. I had an occasional beer or two, but never like I did that night at Smitty's."

"But, before that night at Smitty's you may have had a beer or two while at Middlebury, and that was it, correct?"

"Yes, to my recollection, that is correct."

251

"Mr. Sands, was it also your statement to me on November sixth, 1977, that you walked home from the bar and didn't get a ride in Karen Wyman's car?"

Jonathan was now very alarmed. "Why are you asking me all this again? I already told you I walked home and didn't see Karen that day."

"I feel the need at this time to inform you of your right to request a lawyer before answering any more questions. Are you aware of that right?"

"My God, Fitch. What is it you think you have on me?"

"Do you now choose to go on with this recorded conversation without legal representation?"

"I want to know what the hell you're getting at!"

"Is that a 'yes' or a 'no'?"

"Yes," Jonathan stammered. "I mean no. I don't need a lawyer. Not yet I hope."

"You may wish to reconsider that. I would advise you to do so."

Sands squirmed in his chair. "Then, in that case, will you answer a question for me, Mr. Fitch?"

"Possibly, though I'm under no obligation. What's your question?"

"Why are you asking me things I already told you fifteen years ago? Why now?"

The FBI agent thought it was a fair question. He wished to be a fair man. "I have new evidence you were in Karen Wyman's car the night you were at Smitty's."

"*You what!* What new evidence could you possibly have?"

"Are you aware of DNA evidence, Mr. Sands?"

It felt like a blast of cold against Jonathan's spine. He went silent.

"There was some congealed saliva found on the passenger door when her car was found. It matches your DNA."

"DNA? How on earth do you know that?"

"From your hair."

"Hair?"

"Yes, your hair. I can always order a new sample of your DNA, but it's your hair. When I was in your apartment the night I interviewed you, I took the liberty of extracting some strands of hair from your hairbrush in the bathroom. Along with Decker

Moss's. Fortunately, some of them had enough follicle material to provide your genetic blueprint."

There was a long pause. "And what makes you think it was from that night?"

"Were you ever in her car before that night?"

"I ... I don't know. Maybe I was. So, what? You can't pin me in her car *that* night."

"Oh, I think I can, Mr. Sands. Based on the testimony I just recorded."

"But I told you I wasn't in her car that night."

"You also told me something very unique about that night. That it was only on that night you drank heavily enough for my other evidence to have legitimacy."

"Other evidence? What are you talking about?"

The FBI agent took a moment before responding. "When we first extracted the saliva back in 1977, we did some tests on it. It had traces of alcohol in it. Such traces wouldn't have been detected had you not been drinking—indeed, had you not been rather inebriated."

Dead silence.

"I'm turning off the recorder now."

Jonathan remained quiet.

"I suggest you get a lawyer, Mr. Sands."

"Are you going to arrest me?"

"I'm reopening the case," answered the agent.

"So you don't have enough to charge me."

"I believe you know much more about that night than you've shared with me thus far. A bit more investigation might or might not lead to a warrant."

"Good-bye, Mr. Fitch." Jonathan slammed the phone down into its cradle.

* * *

He didn't return any of his other phone messages; nor did he turn over a single work file on his desk. He just sat motionless, staring into space.

At long length he rang his secretary. "I'm not feeling well, Dianne. I'll be going home for the rest of the day. Any urgent messages for me you can patch over to my home number."

"I've never known you to be sick before, Jonathan."

"Cancel my meetings this afternoon with my regrets. See if you can reschedule them. Better make them for Friday morning. I have a late afternoon flight to San Francisco.

"It sounds serious."

"Thanks, Dianne, I'll be fine."

* * *

Later that morning Jensyn hobbled on her crutches into the anteroom of Jonathan's office.

"Dianne, Jonathan just called me from home. He's not feeling well."

"Yes, I know. It was very odd. He seemed fine when he arrived and then an hour later he looked awful." Dianne, Jonathan's secretary, was a handsome woman, a kind personality in her mid-fifties. "What happened to you?"

"Oh, just a twist of my ankle in the snow. Nothing serious. Anyway, there's a memo in his office that I need. Would it be okay if I looked for it?"

"Of course. Do you need my help?"

"No thanks, I think I know where it is."

Jensyn entered Jonathan's office. She needed a memo relating to an audit she was working on, but it could have waited till the next day. What she really wanted was something to provide some hint of his mood change, as much as she tried to tell herself otherwise. He sounded like a completely different person on the phone ... canceling their lunch date as impersonally as one would change a dentist appointment. Something was responsible, and it must have been serious enough for him to leave the office.

She left the door slightly ajar and turned on the light. The pad of paper on his blotter was blank. His desk was stacked with papers and folders, neatly arranged, and she quickly leafed through some of the files.

Nothing she needed. And no hint there.

His computer was off. Her eye caught the pile of pink phone messages next to his phone.

Feeling guilty, yet wanting to know, she flicked through the slips of paper. Some of the callers she recognized, most she didn't. But nothing looked unusual, no apparent personal messages.

Across the room was a meeting table that also had stacks of folders on it. She went over and fished through the papers as quickly as she could. She eventually found the lengthy memo she was looking for.

Dianne, Jonathan's secretary, would begin to wonder what was taking her so long. About to turn off the light and exit the door, she panned across the room a final time. She looked down.

The trashcan?

Crutching over to it she peered inside. There lay a single piece of crumpled pink paper. She unknotted it and read.

From: Edward Fitch, FBI

"Oh, Jonathan," she whispered to herself in alarm.

Chapter Twenty-Five

Wednesday, December 23, 1992
Atlanta, Georgia

DR. Dieu-Donne Milongo scrutinized once more the microphotographic images depicted of the chromosomes he was studying, wondering if it was just a mistake. He referred again to his scribbled notes, pulling back on his stool, perplexed.

There was one other possibility that came to mind, and the young scientist breathed in with hope as he extracted another sample and treated it with a special stain. He carefully prepared his specimen and placed it on a blank slide. Then he looked back through the viewfinder.

There was no mistake. The evidence of chromosomal translocation was irrefutable.

Sliding over to the computer at the adjoining table he transcribed his hastily scratched findings.

But why? he asked himself.

That was the next question to be explored. And it could take a long time to find out. *Days ... months ... years ... a lifetime?* He didn't know.

Still, there were other results he was anxious to check out before heading home.

'DeDe' Milongo, originally from the Republic of Congo, had a seven-year old Ph.D. in molecular biology from Virginia Tech. Following a thumbs-down tenure evaluation at the University of Georgia, he was picked up by Drexel-Pace for immunological research. A little more than a year earlier, his failed academic career turned winning in private industry with two fantastic discoveries. Both occurring in this lab, the first was entirely serendipitous. He had incubated Schoen's peptide, HX413, with glycoprotein 41 and ran it onto gel without denaturing it. They bound together. Spectacularly. His second discovery was driven by the first. Subsequent animal testing on a Threonatrix-based metabolizing agent indicated a hopeful delivery mechanism. Subcutaneous injection of the peptide looked to be possible without immune system rejection. Human testing was all that was lacking.

OPTIONS

Milongo glanced at his watch. She'll understand, he thought. He picked up the phone to call his bride of six months to explain that he'd be late getting home again.

* * *

The music was turned on. The oven for their late dinner was turned on. Now all he wanted was for his wife to be turned on. She was readying herself in the bathroom for him when the phone rang.

"Milongo's at it again," said the raspy voice on the other end.

"You're sure?" asked Kent Shaughnessy.

"Do you think I'd bother you at home if I wasn't?"

"That's five nights in a row, Slade."

"I know. And two weeks after your ultimatum." Slade's voice was belligerent.

Shaughnessy sat up in his bed. "And you're sure he's researching the product?"

"Of course I'm sure. I cracked his computer files early this morning. File updates in his lab journal last night after midnight, along with the four nights previous. They're definitely related to the product. I'm no scientist but what else could he be referring to by 'HX413'? It's plastered all over his journal."

Kent remained silent.

"There's also another document he's working on," continued Slade. "Looks like a research paper."

"A research paper?" Shaughnessy was now even more alarmed. "Does it reference the product?"

"Not exactly. But it's definitely related. Same jargon, same abbreviations—transcription factors, molecular translocation, 'HOXA' clusters—that kind of shit."

Scientists, Kent thought to himself disdainfully. *Notoriety always seemed to be more important to them than a paycheck.* Considering the problem in silent contemplation, he came to an undeterred conclusion. "You know what to do, Slade," he said, his hand cupped over the receiver.

"Yes, I know what to do, Mr. Shaughnessy. And it will be a pleasure."

"I want those files, Slade. Everything he's updated in the past two weeks."

"You've got it," the gravelly voice assured. "Don't worry about it."

Kent hung up the phone.

* * *

DeDe Milongo felt a presence behind him. He turned around. "Oh, it's you."

The burly visitor leaned against the counter. The lab area was huge, an entire open floor of the Drexel-Pace headquarters building. A few other scientists were working far across the room, oblivious of them.

"Hi, DeDe. What's that you're working on there?"

Milongo fidgeted. "I had to get some readings on an experiment I'm running that couldn't wait till tomorrow. You know how it is. Timed chemical reactions don't always fit an eight-to-five schedule."

"I see." Slade picked up a flask and looked at it as if studying its contents. "It wouldn't be the product, would it?"

"Oh, no, nossir. Mr. Shaughnessy was clear about that. It's just some work I'm doing on our Lixipell upgrade."

"That's good, DeDe. Because he would be pretty upset if you were working on the product, wouldn't he? He's paid you handsomely not to do that, right?"

Milongo nodded. He didn't like the chief of Drexel-Pace security one bit. The scruffy-cropped beard the man wore was an ineffectual attempt to cover a heavily pockmarked face and double chin. It was a spooky face to begin with, housing lifeless eyes and a menacing tone.

"It's time for you to leave now, Doctor. It's getting late and it's Christmastime. You have an Amazon woman at home? Waiting for her warm Neanderthal man to cuddle up with?"

Milongo did everything he could to keep from slugging him. He swiveled on his stool back to the computer screen.

"No, I'll shut it down. Mr. Shaughnessy told me to tell you you're to get home pronto. He's not happy with the late hours you've been keeping."

Now very concerned, Milongo turned around to the security officer. "I want to get some things on a diskette, in case their lost."

"Mr. Shaughnessy was insistent you're to leave right away."

"Okay, okay." Milongo hit the on/off-switch to his computer, knowing that anything that had not been saved was now lost. Fortunately, he still had his hardcopy notes.

OPTIONS

He grabbed his loose-leaf notebook and placed it in his briefcase.

"No, I want you to leave that all as well," ordered the security officer.

"But this is *my* stuff," the scientist protested.

Slade grabbed the briefcase from Milongo's hand, extracted the notebook and turned to the last pages. He couldn't make out all of the scratchy writing, but he did make out a reference to HX413. "I thought you said you weren't working on the product."

DeDe knew he was caught. "You don't know what this is all about, do you, Slade? You have absolutely no idea that these discoveries of mine could turn out to be the biggest medical breakthrough of the century. They put a clamp on my research, hoping some money could buy me off. Well, I have a right to follow through with my work. The company can't just gag me like that. They can't gag the world like that."

Geoffrey Slade stared at the scientist with his dark lifeless eyes. "Just go home, Doctor. You'll feel better in the morning after you give your jungle cock a dip."

This time Milongo didn't hold back and threw his fist at the man. But Slade artfully deflected it. Milongo gathered his briefcase and jacket and stormed out of the lab.

The parking garage took up three sublevels of the Drexel-Pace Atlanta headquarters building. Milongo's car was parked on the lowest. The resonance of the lone firing ignition filled the vacated area. Just about to reverse out of his spot, he flinched at the sight of the security man standing at his side window.

"You going to climb in and follow me home too, Slade?" asked the scientist as he rolled his window down.

The representative casually looked around. "No, you're going to a different home." He lifted a silenced Glock semi-automatic from his shadowed side and shot Milongo squarely in the forehead. He then opened the car door with his gloved hand and threw in a few 'street packets' of Drexel-Pace opiates.

Leaving the engine running and the car door open, he thought some unfortunate passerby would happen upon the scene in the morning.

259

PART III
THE AUDIT
(1993)

Chapter Twenty-Six

"MR. Schoen, wonderful to see you again."

Jonathan directed the elderly gentleman to the chair fronting his desk.

"Would you like a cup of coffee?" Sands asked.

"No, gave the stuff up long ago," Cyrus Schoen replied. He removed his camel-hair overcoat and set his walking cane against the desk. "Eats holes in your gut and wears out the piping. And being a chemical man, I know the importance of good piping."

Jonathan chuckled at the comment and took his chair. "Still, you look good, sir. We met way back, at Middlebury's commencement, remember? You look very much the same."

It was a white lie. Schoen now looked to be edging the grave.

"You're looking well yourself," said Schoen. Then, abruptly, he fixed an out-of-place glare at his host. "But let's dispense with the niceties, shall we, Mr. Sands? I'm running out of time, and time's my most valuable commodity at this point. Not pipes."

Jonathan angled back in his executive chair with a querying look. "I was curious about the message you left. My secretary said you had some concerns about the audit?"

"I hear you're going to be the one to do it."

"Well, yes, our firm is in line for it, though it's still a matter for vote at your shareholders' meeting."

"No, I'm not talking about your *firm*. I'm talking about *you*. As in you, personally. You're the partner who's going to head up the engagement." The assertion hinted of aggression.

"No, not necessarily. But I wonder how you heard that."

"It's wasn't that difficult to find out. I still own fifteen percent of my company's stock after all."

Jonathan grabbed a pencil atop his desk and fidgeted with it. "I was asked by my boss to be the in-charge partner, but I haven't made up my mind whether to take it on."

"I bet. By whom?"

"By whom?"

"Come on, Mr. Sands. Who was it that asked you to head up the audit?"

"Drexel-Pace's audit partner in Atlanta approached my boss, who asked me if I would be interested in taking them on as a new client. I told him I wasn't sure … that I was already stretched thin. But it's natural I'd be asked since I head up the technical manufacturing sector for our office." Jonathan paused. "Look, Mr. Schoen, it's obvious you have issues with this. Why not just share what's on your mind?"

"I should have known Decker would try to pull something like this. First, ripping my company out from under me, and then hiring his old buddy to do the post-takeover audit. All very convenient. And all too acceptable, isn't it, Mr. Sands? Because 'good old boys' aren't mentioned in your code of ethics are they?"

Jonathan now knew where this was going. "No, nothing's mentioned about 'friends' in our professional conduct standards, if that's what you mean. But while I grant you we were friends in college, we—"

"The conniving bastard stole my company from me. Sold me out. Decker … now you," he pointed, "you're all in this together, aren't you?"

"We're not in *anything* together. Your grandson and I—"

"He's no grandson of mine," Schoen shouted. He grabbed his coat and cane and stood up. "Damn the whole lot of you!"

As Schoen paced the reverse distance to the office door Jonathan stood and said in a firm voice: "I said we *were* friends, Mr. Schoen. *Were*, as in past tense. We could hardly be considered friends now. Now sit down and give me the cordiality this meeting is due." The emphasis of Sands's command stopped the old man.

"Whatever ideas you may have about duplicity on my part are completely unfounded," said Jonathan. Hoping to draw composure to the irregular confrontation, he came around from behind his desk and reached for Schoen's arm. "Please, sir, if you'll just have a seat you can help my understanding. However you see it."

Schoen slowly followed Jonathan's leading and resettled in the chair. He took a few moments to collect himself before resuming. "I told you, my time is short. I have no one else to turn to. I was robbed of what I worked for all me life. I just don't know how he— how *they*—pulled it off." He tilted his head, trying to discern the meaning of Sands's previous statement. "What do you mean you could hardly be considered friends now?"

OPTIONS

"We're estranged. After graduation we had a falling out ... Look, the details aren't important now anyway, but I'm being completely truthful with you about being asked by my boss to take on the engagement. I'd prefer not to, and in my position, I don't have to. But if Decker's involved in something that merits closer investigation on this audit then it's our firm's professional obligation to pursue it."

At that, Schoen came forward in his chair, weaving his hands together over the handle of his cane, as if in supplication. "I've been sick about this for months now. I've obviously become very frustrated, and I apologize for my rude behavior. You see, there was no way Drexel-Pace could have communicated their bid by mail without those lists—Schoen's stockholder lists. Oh they could have announced their tender offer in the media, the newspapers, but how many of my shareholders could they have reached? No, Mr. Sands, Decker gave Drexel-Pace the shareholder records. I just can't prove it."

"So, you think Decker was working with Drexel-Pace to make the takeover happen?"

"I *know* he was. He requested the shareholder lists from our registrar, which even he admits. He just denies any wrongdoing with them, and I can't prove otherwise."

Jonathan hesitated, digesting the point. "So, if I understand you correctly you'd like us, our firm, to find the proof?"

Schoen answered straightly: "I'd like nothing more. And I'll pay you nicely for it."

"Mr. Schoen, we're not exactly in the business of taking contingency payments for forensic auditing." Jonathan got up and paced over to the window across the room, looking out beyond. "But if what you say is true, it would mean a serious breach of his fiduciary duty. To say nothing of the Federal securities laws." He turned back around, shaking his head. "It's almost inconceivable. Complicity on his part as CEO of the target firm in a corporate takeover?"

"Inconceivable, my withering ass. They stole my company from me. I'm just asking you to help me prove it."

Sands shoved his hands in his pockets and just stared at the feeble figure before him. Fate or otherwise, Jonathan knew his decision had been made for him. "I'll do what I can, sir."

Chapter Twenty-Seven

Wednesday, February 17, 1993
Manchester, New Hampshire

"I can't believe how good you look. How do you do it?"

Decker Moss envied the fact that Jonathan had aged so regally. His hair remained as full as it used to be, though now of course it was cut much shorter and styled differently than it was in the 70s. And unlike his own ashen row along the sides there wasn't a single gray hair Decker could see. Not a single wrinkle along his eyes. "What do you do, bathe in formaldehyde?"

"A heavy dose of exercise and a meager existence can work miracles in a person."

"That's a crock. Partner of an international CPA firm? No kids? You must have women climbing all over you. It can't be as bad as all that."

Jonathan deflected the compliment by reciprocating: "You look good, too, Deck. More distinguished. Seems like life has a funny way of drawing circles around its dancers."

"Circles, squares, who knows? It's a dance, though, I grant you that."

The two were sitting at a table at Jesse's, Decker's favorite local restaurant. It wasn't a posh place, but it had excellent beef and a great salad bar. Jonathan drove that afternoon from Boston. The men had pushed away their emptied salad plates and were waiting for their entrees to arrive.

"How's your mom?" Decker asked, changing topics.

"She's doing well. Her name's Greenfield now. Remarried pretty soon after we graduated."

"No kidding. That's wonderful," said Decker. "Greenfield, huh? You can't get more Vermonty than that."

Jonathan obliged a smile. "Yeah, I suppose you're right."

"And still living in Montpelier?"

"Not far from there. In Stowe. Her husband's a lawyer who does lobbying work at the Statehouse. She's happy."

Their meals arrived. Jonathan picked at his trout with pensive absence. He wasn't really in the mood for fish and wondered why he had ordered the thing. His contribution to their conversation was superficial, little more than token responses to Decker's questions.

"This mood of yours," Decker said finally, knifing his filet mignon, "it all has to do with Fitch, doesn't it?"

Jonathan set down his fork and looked around. Soft jazz was playing in the background. "It just came out of nowhere, Deck. It was insane. I was finally beginning to feel I might be able to get on with things. I even found someone ..."

"You did?" Decker asked with a raised eye. "Tell me about her."

"It doesn't matter. It wasn't going to work out anyway."

It had now been more than two months since his ephemeral 'romance' with Jensyn—if it could be called that. He doused the fish with a squeeze of lemon and forced a bite. "So, Fitch calls me out of the blue. And now I wake up every morning just waiting for another call, or for the feds to show up at my door with handcuffs."

Moss leaned in over the table with a quietly assuring voice. "Jon, without a body there is no crime—*corpus delicti*. And without a crime there is no suspect. My God, man, when are you going to realize that?"

"*Presumptive evidence*, Decker. A body isn't required." Jonathan picked some more at his fish. A moment later he laid down his fork and said: "Maybe I just want it to happen."

Decker went backwards in his chair. "I'm not even going to dignify that with a response, Sands." He carved a piece of his steak and dipped it in béarnaise sauce. "As I told you on the phone, I took care of all that for you when I talked to him. He's got nothing now." Moss downed a generous gulp of Merlot.

Fitch had called Decker Moss following his threatening call to Jonathan, and Moss was quick on the fly with the contrived explanation. The fact that Moss had handled the FBI agent's questions so smoothly gave Decker even more private assurance of Jonathan's allegiance to him. *Funny how nicely things work out sometimes*, he remembered Carpenter saying.

"But Fitch couldn't have fallen for it," Jonathan said. "Not after we told him I was basically a teetotaler."

Decker's patchwork story to the agent—which Jonathan had no choice now but to corroborate following Decker's warning call—was that a few days before Karen disappeared they had too many beers at a pizzeria in town and phoned her to pick them up.

"Besides, why wouldn't you have had Susan pick us up?" Jonathan asked, referring to Decker's girlfriend at the time.

"I tried to, but she was at the library, don't you remember? Karen was the only one home." Moss recited his fabricated lines as if from a script. "Testimony of two witnesses. Hell, you were simply too embarrassed to let Fitch know you got plastered twice in three days."

Jonathan shook his head. Was it really possible for a friend to possess such loyalty? To continue spinning stories at the risk of incriminating himself, even after all these years?

"I'm here for you, Jon. I've always been there for you. And I'll be here in the future. Now get off the crapper and start living your life, you ass."

Sands tacitly studied his one-time best friend—possible betrayals of the eyes or body movements– anything? Jonathan wished he could just ask a few questions and get some honest answers.

"So he sounded like he believed you?" asked Sands again.

"I told you. What's he going to do, call me a liar?"

Jonathan reached for a dinner roll from the basket.

"I think you could at least thank me for that," Decker stated.

Buttering the roll, Jonathan said: "You just keep taking this thing deeper. Eventually we're both going to get caught."

"Appreciation accepted."

Jonathan mouthed a bite. "I got a lawyer."

"A lawyer? Why would you go and do that?"

"He told me DNA evidence is getting better all the time, but right now the mapping technology's still too sketchy—that it's like trying to take a sentence out of *The Grapes of Wrath* and conclude it was written by John Steinbeck. They can't nail the odds down better than one in a hundred."

"See? There you go. Now stop worrying. Either way, that's how I remember it. And that's the way I told it to Fitch. So you better stay with the story."

Sands felt it was only a matter of time before technology went the needed distance. He looked down at his trout. Preferring not to know what the thing might look like rotting and washed up on the shore, he wondered why on earth restaurants presented them on the plate like that: exaltedly with shriveled heads and skin and fins still attached. How was that supposed to be appetizing?

Decker changed the subject. "I'm glad you've finally decided to be partner in charge of the engagement. Meeting with my old CPA firm tomorrow, huh?"

"I hope you've been good."

"Right, with what I've been paying them over the years, what else could they say?" Moss presented his familiar roguish grin. "Just think of the blast you'll have poring over my books, Jon."

"I can only imagine. I bet you're quite the cook." Sands watched Moss continue to work his plate. "Tell me the truth," Jonathan asked Decker, "that write-off of yours … is there any more to it that I should know about?"

"That's for me to know and for you to find out."

"No, seriously."

Scraping out the insides of his baked potato like a kid scooping out a jack-o-lantern, Decker took a last mouthful and looked up at his old friend.

"Seriously?" he repeated. "Of course not. My firm had only two choices of dealing with that environmental thing: either sweep it under the rug like everyone else seems to do, or to come out fully in the open with it. Cyrus Schoen has this idea about accountability to our stakeholders. It's a trait the old man insists upon, and which, quite honestly, I've come to admire and agree with. Usually, that is. Anyway, our green reputation would have suffered far more if I didn't do what I did. So I put it full out there." His hands stretched outward, like a politician's evincing plea of transparency.

"Warts and all," mumbled Sands.

"Huh?"

Jonathan pushed his barely-touched plate forward.

"What's wrong, not hungry?" asked Moss.

Jonathan ignored the question. "And you really think you'll be held liable for fully half of the ROD estimate?"

"Jon, you and I both know how these things go. The EPA's cleanup estimates are purposely understated until the perps fess up to the blame."

"I don't know about that."

"Oh, I do," countered Moss. "They know that if they put those estimated remediation costs too high, nobody would sign a consent decree … not unless forced to following a bitter legal fight.

I didn't want to play that game. Besides, it all came to us at what we thought was a very propitious moment."

"The takeover bid?" Jonathan asked.

Moss nodded. "So what? My board agreed that coming out with the Superfund citation as we did was probably the best defense we had at the time to thwart a takeover. We're a young firm. Young in a public sense. We didn't have time to implement some of the shark-repellant charter amendments other battle-scarred firms have adopted."

"I suspected something like that." Jonathan was also aware New Hampshire hadn't adopted liberal anti-takeover laws like most other New England states. "My only concern is that you didn't purposely *overstate* your exposure."

"Overstate it? Why would I do that?" Moss asked frowning. He folded his arms. "Look, I'm not a lawyer, but I have a damn good one on my team. He's the one who put together the legal backing for our estimate. My auditors have his report. You'll certainly have complete access to it all tomorrow."

"Don't misunderstand me," Jonathan said, leaning back in his chair. "It's just that when questions like this come up in my mind, you can be certain they will arise in investors' minds—and those at the SEC. You don't want them hounding you. You'd never win."

Decker shucked the comment aside, tending to the last juices on his plate. The potato beneath his fork looked like a deflated football.

"So everything's kosher on your side?" asked Jonathan. "About the takeover, I mean?"

Moss looked up at him, wiping his mouth with the linen napkin from his lap. "Kosher? How couldn't it be? It was a fair market bid that drove up our share price."

"Your grandfather doesn't think so."

The words caught Decker by surprise. "You talked with Cyrus?"

"We had a meeting, yes."

"And I suppose he told you I somehow stole his company from him, right?"

"That's what he said."

Moss's expression turned dour. "Well, it's nothing but a bunch crap. Senile nonsense. It was the right thing at the right time. And it still is. I can't do anything about his paranoid provincial attachment to the firm aside from giving my shareholders their best return possible. All of them, including *him*."

"So, I'm not going to find out there's more to the story?" Sands pressed. "You didn't misuse the shareholder records ... manipulate anything?"

The question obviously struck a nerve. Moss stared hard at Sands. "Look, Jon, let's cut the crap, shall we? There was no manipulation. And I'm not using our past to manipulate you, if that's what's playing around in your mind. It wasn't me who wanted you on this engagement. Carpenter's ass-loving partner did."

Jonathan didn't respond, which angered Decker even more. "You probably think I was hoping for some opportunistic loyalty on your part. Leveraging something from you like I have something to hide in my books? Well, I *don't*. The transaction was legit." Decker glanced to his side and then back again, trying to regain composure. Then more quietly: "You've always acted like it was somehow my fault what happened that night. But you know what? If I weren't so drunk that night and had the chance to do it all over again, I never would have done what I did to rescue you. I should have just let you hang. Instead, you ditch my friendship fifteen years ago and come back now shooting me with this shit. Do you have any idea how much that hurts?"

Sands wasn't expecting it. He looked around at their surroundings, wondering if anyone could hear them. But the lateness of the evening left the restaurant sparse of diners, and those few who remained were out of earshot.

"Just tell me one thing, Decker. With years of little else to think about, I have several questions. Will you answer just one of them for me?"

Moss's face flashed back and forth. "Yes, I'll answer a question, Sands. I'll answer any damned question you have."

"Why did you knock on my bedroom door that night?"

"*That's* your question?" Decker asked, laughing. "Because it was locked."

"Yes, that's right. It was locked. But I never knocked on your door when I knew you were with Susan."

Moss rolled his eyes. "What are you talking about?"

"You didn't know I was with Karen?"

"Of course I didn't know you were with Karen? How could I have known?"

"Because her car was in our driveway."

"I told you, I didn't notice her car when I came in."

Jonathan raised an eyebrow. "You told me that? I don't think you ever said that. You told me the other guys didn't see her car because they dropped you off out in front of the house. You never told me you didn't see it when you came in the back way."

"Well, that's ridiculous. Of course I didn't see it. It was covered with snow and it was dark and I was wasted. You know there wasn't any light on back there." Moss shoved his plate forward. "Look, can we please knock off this bullshit? You're tilting at windmills."

Over the trailing silence Jonathan's eyes remained fixed on his old roommate. "The snow, Decker. There was fresh snow and tracks around her car when we brought her down to your car."

"Of course there were tracks. She carried you in."

"No, Deck. There was only slurry then. Yes, she carried me in, but there was no snow when we drove into our driveway. Only slush."

"There was, too, snow. Come on, Jon, you were wiped out. You don't remember. It was snowing the whole time."

Sands held his look steady. "I was wasted, yes, but I remember when I came out of the bar there was only heavy slush on the ground. No white stuff. I noted it because I knew Karen was driving. The tracks I saw alongside her car when we dragged her down from the apartment were in fresh snow. *White* snow. Lots of tracks. For the longest time I thought I was just making it up in my mind, that it was only a distorted memory due to the booze. But much later something came to my thinking that's very important. And this is very clear in my memory. You asked me where her keys were right after we put her in your trunk. You said they weren't on her, or in in my room. That you searched for them. But why would you ask me that without even checking her car first? You must have been the one to make the tracks in the fresh snow, to see whose car it was. You *knew* she was with me."

Decker slumped.

First sign? Jonathan wondered.

Moss stared at him incredulously. "Man, I can't *believe* what you've been conjuring up in your imagination all these years. You were shit-faced. Whatever tracks you saw were *yours*, which just got covered up afterward. The stuff was falling like crazy when I got home. I didn't see her car. I didn't know she was with you. Don't forget I was drunk, too, Jon. I didn't think of looking in her car before asking you about the keys. And as much as I might find your dreams entertaining, I can't imagine how any of it could make a difference anyway. Your door was locked. You were naked. She was naked with your belt around her neck."

"Yes, the belt …" continued Sands softly. "Why would I use my belt? Not exactly my *modus operandi*, is it Decker?"

"Huh?"

"You know I use my hands when I try to strangle someone."

Decker laughed derisively. "You've got to be kidding. Please tell me you're kidding."

"Not really, but let's forget that. My bedroom door was locked, but you could have locked it."

"Me? How the hell could I have locked it? It was a chain. Do you really think I could have slipped through the door opening, like some kind of Gumby-doll after locking it? My God!"

"No, but there were windows in my bedroom."

The air went electric.

"*Fuck you, Sands!*" His expression screamed, but he forced his voice low and jabbed the table with his index finger. "What window do you have in mind? The window over your bed? *Right!* I would have had to crawl over you to get to it. So what if it was just above the front porch roof? Do you really think I could have done that without waking you? And the other window went straight down to the driveway. A hard asphalt driveway two stories below. Does that insane imagination of yours really make you believe I could possibly jump down two flights and not break my neck? Or maybe you think I rigged up some kind of rope contraption and closed the window on the way down with my fall. And replaced the screen too!" Livid, Decker got up, threw his napkin down on the table and veered off in the direction of the men's room.

The round was played. Jonathan knew it was all too incredible, but this was his only chance to get some answers to questions that had haunted him for years.

On one occasion he had even taken the time to install a chain lock on one of his own bedroom doors. Experimenting with a coat hanger he found he could unlock it after several tries, but to *re-lock* it was quite another matter. Half an hour was his best time and that required a carefully twisted loop at the end, a steady hand, and a lot of luck. Together with the fiddling noise it made while bending and re-bending the thin metal rod around the door made it very unlikely. Still, if he were drunk enough not to hear …

The door to the attic located in his bedroom was the only other exit, yet he had dismissed that early on since there were no operative windows in the attic, only two fixed stained-glass decorative octagons positioned high in the cornered eaves. Even if they could be opened they were far too small for a person to fit through.

Although he had other questions, they were trivial in comparison to the ones he risked in this meeting with Moss. And there was nothing remotely approaching leverage to pursue them anyway.

Once Decker returned to the table, the lingering tension held throughout an ensuing long period of silence. Decker's face remained taught and flushed. Ultimately, Sands's expression evolved to display what he could of an apologetic eye. "I'm sorry, Deck. I hope you understand. With years of no one to talk to, and then with what you did with my medal … well, my mind takes me places. Maybe only places of hope on my part."

At that, Decker's expression also showed indications of loosening. "Look, Jon, *of course* I understand," he answered with whispered strength. "I can't imagine where you've been … the hell you must have gone through all these years. But don't place your wishful blame on me. You're looking in the wrong place. Your fanciful imaginings, whatever they are, simply aren't justified. I gave our friendship my best back then, and I'm still willing to do so now. As much as you're about to shred it. I've always regretted what I did with your talisman. It was just a stupid, drunken act."

"You said I would get over it," Jonathan said, "but it's not true. This place called hell, what's said of it … the worm never dies. It eats you and it keeps eating, and you wish for a point when there's nothing left for it to feed on."

"But like I also said way back then, we have to move on," mollified Decker. "I'd prefer to do so together." He grabbed his friend's wrist and held it firmly. "I just can't have you making me the target of any more baseless accusations. I don't deserve it. I've given you everything. You have to *believe* me, Jon. I had nothing to do with Karen's death."

Jonathan left his arm on the table under Decker's hold for a moment. Then he turned it over and gripped Decker's hand in a firm, conciliatory handshake.

After a while, for a change of topics, Jonathan asked: "You still get together with your old frat brothers? Peter Roy?"

"You mean the guy you nearly strangled to death in the bar?" Decker asked with a disingenuous chuckle. "Yeah, we get together every so often. We happen to be the only two remaining bachelors left in the bunch."

Jonathan didn't say anything. Instead, he only seethed inwardly at the memory of the person who was probably much of the reason for the ruinous change in his life.

Eventually, Decker smiled, this time genuinely, and with his free hand he hefted his glass of wine. "Too bad you don't drink, Jon. Otherwise, we could have a good time right about now. There's a place down the road where the women just about plop themselves in your lap."

"No thanks," Jonathan answered, staring off to the side at nothing in particular.

"You haven't changed, Jon."

A pause. "Nor have you, Decker." Jonathan turned back to face his old roommate. "Nor have you."

Chapter Twenty-Eight

Thursday, February 18, 1993
Manchester, New Hampshire

THE next morning, at five to ten, Jonathan pulled his car into the parking lot for the offices of Wilcox & Kline. Jensyn was standing at the doorway. She was wearing a full-length navy wool overcoat with her briefcase slung from a shoulder strap. It was snowing.

As he walked towards her he greeted apprehensively: "Did you have a nice trip?"

"The blacktop's beautiful when it's white," she answered. "How about you?"

"Not bad." Jonathan opened the glass door entry for her.

"Spend the evening reminiscing about old college times?" Jensyn knew he made the trip the previous afternoon to meet with Decker Moss.

"In a manner of speaking."

The receptionist greeted the couple and promptly escorted them to Leonard Pane's office. He was an agreeably-aged man—in his mid-fifties, Jonathan guessed—wearing an expensive charcoal gray suit and a salon-purchased tan. With prefatory courtesies out of the way their conversation came to focus on the transition of the audit engagement. Leonard Pane, partner in charge, assured the couple there were no unresolved differences between Schoen and his audit firm, and that the 1992 fiscal year audit was concluding smoothly.

Predictably, the issue of the Superfund site came up.

"We were as surprised as anyone about Schoen's third quarter loss provision," said Pane. "But it holds water. We have to rely on expert opinion, of course, and that came from their corporate counsel. Man named Royce. It looks to be a very complete analysis."

"Was there any external counsel?" Jonathan asked.

"Some on pending lawsuits and unasserted claims, but no, not on the environmental matter. Nor could we make them. Given the circumstances of the case, however, I feel comfortable with what they gave us."

Jensyn was busy scribbling notes. She directed a question at Pane: "The news release said there were six other PRPs associated with the site. Why would Schoen find it necessary to book a loss for fully half of it? On top of that, half of the high estimate?"

"Fair question. I had it as well." Pane looked at her appreciatively, which Jonathan gathered was more than just business. "Royce's analysis took a representative sampling of past EPA cases and found that initial ROD estimates were understated relative to experience by ten to twenty percent. Not that those are intentional understatements, necessarily. It's just that the nature of chemical cleanups makes their cost very difficult to estimate up front with much precision. You see only the tip of the iceberg at first, and most cases drag on for years, suggesting still further cost overruns and forecast adjustments. From there Royce added the likely litigation costs and legal fees."

"And the six other PRPs?" Jensyn probed further.

"Again, Royce's approach seemed sensible to me. He based the proportion of responsibility on the number of containers that are Schoen's. It's admittedly crude, but better than anything else at this point. Furthermore, his work confirms a strong bias against deep pocket firms. The other PRPs on the list are small time players—private firms, individuals without financial means, recalcitrants and the like. So, taking it all together, Schoen's write-off may actually hover on the low side."

"Did you speak with any of them? The other PRPs, I mean?" Jensyn asked.

"No," Pane replied defensively. "That wouldn't be our job. But again, this is a loss we're talking about, not a gain. I might seek more assurance if it were the other way around."

Jensyn pursued still further: "Did Royce mention any PRP correspondence in his report? Any meetings with them?"

"No, I don't believe he had met with them at the time of his report." Pane raised an eyebrow at his two visitors. "Look, because of the concerns both of you are raising, I'll have my secretary quickly run off a copy of his report. Let me go dig it out for her."

The man got up and exited his office door.

Sitting quietly for a moment, Jensyn looked over at Jonathan. "Hi, there," she said.

"Hi, there, back."

"Do you think he's getting bothered?"

"You have a way of doing that to men in business meetings."

"Thanks a lot."

Jonathan smiled. His gaze went to the vanity wall behind Pane's desk.

Jensyn's eyes fixed on him. "I don't suppose you'd like to have lunch with me after our meeting's over. Dutch, of course."

"No, I don't think that would be wise."

She contrived a sigh. "Okay, Mr. Sands, I'll just ask Mr. Pane to lunch. One partner's as good as another to me."

Jonathan laughed. It was the first time she had seen him laugh—indeed, come to life—since the morning she discovered his phone message from the FBI. For two-and-a-half months he had been nothing but starch-suited business, which she found intensely frustrating.

Pane returned. "Carol will have it ready for you by the time you leave."

"Thank you very much," Jonathan said. He cleared his throat. "Leonard, we were hoping you also might be willing to share your audit working papers with us."

The man had been expecting the request. He preferred not to but it was the professional thing to do, and when it came to a regional firm dealing with an international firm, it was also the politically wise move as well. "Yes, given the circumstances of this transition I'd be agreeable to that. We're hoping for an early March field date. Schoen's set a stockholders' meeting date for April twelfth, I believe." Pane swiveled in his chair and pulled a calendar up on his computer screen. "Yes, that's correct. That should give you plenty of time to tighten up your engagement proposal. I'll have copies shipped to you."

"Very courteous of you," said Sands. "I won't forget it."

The conference lasted another forty-five minutes, dealing mostly with Drexel-Pace related-party transactions and other minor matters concerning the buyout. When it was over, Jonathan escorted Jensyn to her car in the parking lot. "See, that didn't go badly, did it?" Jonathan asked.

"No, he's actually a very nice guy." Jensyn tilted her head up at him. "So are you going to make me go back and ask him out to lunch?"

"Jensyn."

"Jonathan," she teased back.

They stood staring at each other.

"You're miserable," she said. "You have been for months. Whatever it is you're going through and holding from me may just be something I can help you with."

"No, it isn't." Jonathan veered his gaze down the road. The snow had stopped.

"Are you in trouble?"

He didn't answer.

"Jon?"

"I can't, Jen. I want to tell you … but I can't."

"Are you in trouble with the police?"

He turned to her. Her eyes were imploring.

"How did you know that was my problem?"

"At Oxford. They had a course on dysfunctional men."

"Oh, I see."

Noting the golden arches of a McDonalds across the street, he said: "I am a bit hungry …"

* * *

After pulling their orders from the counter the pair found a corner booth at the back of the restaurant, next to a window. Jonathan devoured half his cheeseburger before either spoke. "Aren't you hungry?" he asked.

Jensyn lifted the bun to her McSomething-Or-Other and wrinkled her nose. "I don't know what you Americans love about this outfit, but I find it a bit revolting."

"Ah, but you Brits have no class when it comes to food. Everybody knows that. Compare the success of this outfit to the fish and chips establishments of your ilk."

She tossed a French-fry at him.

"You look nice today," he said, grabbing the fry off his lap and chomping it down.

"You always look nice. Too bad your personality doesn't match."

"My personality?"

"Yes. You're a cad."

"A what?"

"You heard me."

"I'm sorry, Jensyn."

"I am, too. That I ever met you." She lobbed another French-fry at him.

"Would you stop doing that? People will see you."

279

"So what, Mr. Beacon Hill man? Mister hot-shot partner who wounds his employees in the snow. So what?"

"*Jensyn!*" he cackled. "Now stop it. Can't you see I'm trying to eat?"

"I hope you choke to death." Then, reacting to his chagrinned look: "I'm sorry. I was just playing. I don't really want you to choke to death. I just want you to choke enough to get some sense in your head."

He set his burger down. "Jen, I don't want to do any more damage than I already have."

"Damage? My God, Jonathan, you're a blooming Jekyll and Hyde."

Sands surveyed her expression, appreciating the tension it depicted, wondering if he could ever communicate to her his own … wondering now, also, if agreeing to lunch was mistake. "If I were to give you the McDonald's version, would that be all right?"

"That would put it a big notch below the lunch version, and you already gave me that."

"No, I mean part two of my story. The part you haven't heard about. But only a fast-food piece of it and only on condition that you don't push me for more than I can tell you. Would you be okay with that?"

"That's a bit like asking a starving bloke if he'd like a few kernels of unbuttered popcorn."

Jonathan smiled at the analogy and took the last bite of his burger. Crumpling the sandwich paper in his hands and catching her eye, he asked: "Promise you won't push?"

She nodded.

He turned toward the window, roving his eyes out at the bland scenery outside. "It's all about a girl I knew in college. Her name was Karen. She was the roommate of Decker Moss's girlfriend. We were together only a short time during my senior year."

"Short time?"

"One day in fact."

"You're able to do a lot of damage in a single day, Mr. Sands." She smirked at him but he didn't see it. His stare remained fixed out the window.

"It happened to be a very important day," Jonathan resumed. "It was early in November, a Friday. I got my offer from MM&P that morning in the mail. Decker said I had to get out and celebrate. As you know, I wasn't a drinker. I'd have a beer or two every so often, but that was all, and he used to rib me about it. Anyway, I agreed to meet Decker and his friends out at a bar that night after my run to celebrate."

Jensyn listened without interruption. Her sandwich sat untouched.

"I felt like things were really coming together for me. I liked her for months and I kept hearing how she liked me. Decker and Susan—his girlfriend—were always trying to set us up. But I didn't do anything about it. I thought there was no way for it to work out because we were both going to be graduating and heading off our separate ways. A lot of it had to do with my parents, what I told you about ... I just never wanted to make the same mistakes they made. I wanted to be settled first."

Jonathan lifted a napkin from the table and wiped his lips. "That is, until I got the job offer from Boston. Karen had been accepted into Harvard's law school, and I thought maybe this thing could really work out. When I went running that afternoon I happened to see her in the parking lot of her apartment. It was raining and she invited me in, and we talked until it was time for me to get to Smitty's."

"Smitty's?"

"The bar where I was going to meet Decker. Anyway, I didn't have a car in college and I had to walk there. It wasn't far from the apartment, but I had to get home and shower first. I didn't have time for dinner, which is why I got so drunk that night. The guys just kept ordering more. Pitchers, shots, it's only a blur. I don't blame anybody but myself, but I felt pressured to stay up with them. I didn't tell Decker that Karen was going to pick me up, and when it came time for me to meet her out front, I just got up, staggered out of the place and ended up getting sick and passing out by the shrubs. She found me there, unconscious and soaked. She drove me home and helped me into bed and I passed out again."

Jensyn waited for him to continue. He played a bit with his napkin and gazed off above her, searching for the right words. Then he turned back down and spoke plaintively, framing what he had to say as briefly as he could yet with the care she could hear: "Jen, what you've seen of me is who I am and who I've been for the last fifteen years. Before that, I'm not sure. Time won't heal it."

Her expression had gone serious and his voice turned lower. "If I tell you any more, you will either want to have nothing more to do with me or you will always wonder, as I do, whether I am who I think I am. Because I'm not sure myself. I was too drunk. So before I tell you, I just want you to know that."

"I know who you are, Jon."

"That's a nice thing to say, but it's not true."

"I know who you are *now*."

"Jen, that night you and I talked meant more to me than you may realize. It was cathartic for me. I felt I could tell you anything. And I could tell you some story now that would keep you in the dark about all of this, and I'd get away with it. But you deserve more than that. I don't want to cause any more damage than I already have."

"You haven't caused any damage. Whatever you did back then, you're not that person now."

"But it could be me. Remember what I told you about my father and his drunken blackouts? My conviction for assault and battery? It really *could* be me. All these years I've wrestled with those facts, and I've researched the subject to death in the time I've had."

He paused as if deep in thought, and then continued. "Blackout is the blockade of information from short-term memory into long-term memory, despite the presence of short-term awareness. During an amnesic episode a person can be quite aware, passably conversant, even engage in complex behaviors, such as sex and violence. Fragmentary memory loss is known as brownouts, but the rarer and more serious 'en bloc' blackout variety is the complete inability to recall any details whatsoever from events that occur while you're drunk. The memory loss can span several hours of time. Alcoholism isn't necessary because en bloc blackouts are widely reported in studies of college binge-drinkers. And the factors believed to significantly increase their likelihood were very present in my case: the rapid increase in blood-alcohol concentration due to my empty stomach at the time, and, most important, my father's history—his genes."

The silence lasted seemingly long minutes. It was an implied decision for her to make, and she did what she could to weigh it through.

Finally, she said: "I want to know."

"Are you sure?"

She rubbed her temples. "Look, Jon, if you're asking me what I think you are, it's this: Do I really want to risk knowing the truth about you if the downside would mean me getting in over my head, legally or otherwise, or me being repulsed by you? Is that right?"

He thought it was a funny way to put it. "Very good, Chandler." Then he grabbed the saltshaker and stared blankly at it for a period.

"Just tell me," she said impatiently.

Jonathan set the shaker down and looked at her steadfastly. "Jen, Karen was never heard from again after that night."

She slowly pulled back against the bench. "She what?"

"Just that. For fifteen years I've been the key suspect in her disappearance."

"But you said you were bloody bladdered ... that you liked her. I, I don't understand—"

"And I don't understand what happened that night either, not all of it, and that's the God's honest truth. But the fact is, and what nobody else other than Decker knows, is that I was the last one to see her. We covered up the fact that I was with her that night."

"Covered it up?"

"So I wouldn't be a suspect in her disappearance." Jonathan answered, exhaling deeply. "Look, there's more to it than that, Jen, more than I can say now, but my life has been hell because of it ever since."

Jensyn felt gnarled. The drain on him to share even that much was obvious, yet ironically, the fact he did so made her feel closer to him. At least now the phone call from the FBI agent made some sense.

Sands went on: "I was drunk and I did something very stupid and very wrong that night, what I know about it ... but not what I don't. I've long suspected Decker Moss does. This contact with him and this audit may very well be my last chance to find out."

It was as if she had to decode each word. All abstruse and lacking interpretation. She sat forward, seeking what she could of a clarification: "I don't get it. How could any of this have to do with an audit?"

"Because of Decker," he said straightly.

"In what way? Because he helped you?"

"Yes, because he helped me, and because I've never really understood why. Look," he said, shaking his head, "why would he do what he did for me? For my friendship? That's what he said, and back then I believed it. But I've doubted it ever since. I've had years to think about little else and it doesn't add up. We were both very drunk that night, yet I have good reasons to believe he knows far more about this thing than he's ever admitted to me."

The thought struck her. "You think Decker might have been responsible for what happened to her?"

Jonathan looked at her deep-green eyes intently. "What I think is that after fifteen years of having no contact with him, and with the same amount of time with only questions and blurred memories to look back upon, I now have a chance. A final last chance, hope, to find out."

She remained confused. "And you think you'll somehow find out now during an audit? How could you?"

Jonathan shook his head again. "It's only a sense, Jen. Wouldn't you take the opportunity if you had it? Sometimes the truth about a person, or what he may have done, can be as simple as finding out who that person is now and what he does now. If someone shows you who they are, believe them. People don't change. I don't want to go more into it than that, but things I can't share would just make far more sense to me if that were the case."

Playing hard with the paper napkin he had twisted into a cane he looked out the window again. The snowfall had resumed. Heavily. He stared at it … its quilted accumulation layering all that could be seen, the bleach white purity of it, blanketing all outside that was dark and gray and dirty, as if bestowing on those who braved its offering a comforting expiation … a cleansing hope. And he breathed it all in deeply.

Then he turned to Jensyn, taking in the warmth of her eyes. "One thing I know about him is that he's always been an opportunist, and he's always been clever. He grew up rich, but his parents said he was on his own after he graduated. There was always this guise of friendship I now see was one-sided. From the very beginning. He wanted me to room with him, though I know now it was only because he wanted me to help him with his grades. We had very different personalities. He was an extrovert, a big partier, and I wasn't. His parents paid most of the rent in order to get him off campus, which also helped me out at the time. But it didn't take me long to find out he was into cheating on exams and plagiarizing papers. He wanted to involve me in his stuff."

"Stuff?"

"He used to offer me money to write his papers, take his exams—you know, those big classes your first couple years at college where the professor doesn't know the difference."

"Did you?"

"Of course not," Jonathan said turning back to her. "But he'd be furious at me about it for weeks. And then as I got to know him more there were always these little hints of jealousy, these little jabs, like he not only didn't really like me much, but that he actually kind of hated me. As I've matured I see now what I didn't see back then."

"And that's what you mean by having a sense?"

Sands nodded.

Question lingered in her eyes. "But you must have some reason for thinking he isn't clean now. Why?"

Jonathan shared with her about the meeting with Cyrus Schoen. When he concluded, he said: "That's when I decided to accept the engagement."

Now it was Jensyn's turn to pause in her thoughts. She looked around the restaurant and eventually looked down at her cold sandwich. She crumpled it up in its wrapper. "So you think Decker Moss is involved with fraud?"

Spoken aloud it sounded less plausible than it did in his thinking. He nodded anyway. "I'd say with a high probability. As you know it's very difficult to detect, especially at Decker's level. But I want to try to do my best."

There was a stint in their exchange, blanketed by the motion and chatter of the restaurant. She looked around again, seeking to digest it all. "You really can't share the rest?" she asked finally.

"No, Jen, I can't."

With a languishing expression she eventually asked: "Should I be scared about you?"

Myriad possibilities vied in his mind for a simple answer to that question. It was a fair question, he thought, one he would have as well. He was looking out the window again. "Would I wonder if I were you? Yes. Should you be scared about me? I honestly don't know. One thing I do know is this: I'll never lie to you." He looked down at his watch and then up to her. "Look, in little more than half an hour you've heard more from me than anyone else has ever heard in my life. That says a lot about my feelings for you. It also tells you why I ran away two months ago."

She struggled with the mix of emotions she felt. His wounded expression didn't help, and she reached for his hand. "I can help you, Jonathan."

He stared at her.

"I can help you," she said again. "As partner you won't be there to do the on-site work, not the day-to-day stuff, the digging in the records I'll be able to do. And you know I'm damned good with the details. I always have been. I'll tear the prig's books apart."

He chuckled. "You'd do that anyway, Chandler. That's just the way you are."

Then he regarded her squarely. "Look, Jen, I'm a poor risk. Either way, however, I have to come clean. I can't go on with this anymore. One way or the other I have to put it right."

She gathered the weight of his remark and the possible finality of it.

"Jail?" she asked.

Jonathan got up and grabbed their table litter to take to the trash bin.

Returning and reaching for her hand, he nodded.

Chapter Twenty-Nine

SCHOEN Chemicals Corporation concluded its annual shareholders' meeting late in the afternoon at Manhattan's Grand Hyatt Hotel. Decker Moss and the three Drexel-Pace chief officers presently footed their way down 42nd Street, heading west towards the Times Square district.

It was a crisp clear day and their moods matched chipper. Except for some pesky questions about the environmental matter from a few irate shareholders—one obnoxious heckler in particular who had to be escorted out of the place—the meeting went without a hitch. The voting outcome, both for the new directors and the new auditing firm, had gone predictably in their favor. Cyrus P. Schoen and Everett Royce were now officially off the director board. Helen Anderson was also removed, payback for her negative vote on the merger. The three of them were replaced with high profile men whose gold star credentials stood up in the proxy fight.

Larry Carpenter beamed vindicated joy. It was a golden nail in old man Schoen's coffin, to be voted off his own company's board.

"There're some great international restaurants down here," Carpenter said to his mates, mouthing an unlit stogie the size of a utility pole.

"Larry, I was hoping we could get pizza," said Moran. "New York pizza is like nowhere else in the world."

Carpenter pulled his CFO off to the side by the sleeve. "Joe, if you think for one fat man's moment I'm going to have pizza for dinner my night in New York, then you're even more gauche than I thought."

"But you can't get it like this in Atlanta, Larry. The crust is so chewy you have to work at it with your teeth, and the cheese just oozes down your face."

"Shut up, Joe."

Larry Carpenter wanted international fare, which is what it would be, he unilaterally informed the gentlemen. Not any Americanized junk, as he put it.

He eventually chose a posh French restaurant off Third Avenue. The menu was written entirely in French and, as Moran was soon sad to discover, the waiter knew about as much English as a Parisian street child. He ended up with a plate of crepes and a few colorful sauces.

"I had to wait an hour for *this*?"

"It's all in the presentation, Joe," said Larry.

"Presentation of what?" retorted the CFO. "I'm not eating pancakes for dinner!" He looked at his boss's full plate of rare beef with envy.

"A little less food and a little more culture is what you need, Moran." Carpenter carved a piece of his chateaubriand. "Now pipe down and enjoy it."

Decker wanted more bread but Joe Moran had gobbled it all down during their wait. Hefting the basket Decker beckoned to the waiter, who acknowledged his request.

"Make that three loaves," added Moran with command. "And don't forget the butter, garçon! *Butteure grandé, mon Franky, s'il vous plait!*"

Carpenter rolled his eyes and then turned in Shaughnessy's direction. "Kent, why don't you update Decker on our African connection?"

Moss was getting accustomed to potent updates from these men. He wondered what surprise they had in store for him next.

"Ah, yes, our African connection ..." Shaughnessy looked to be genuinely enjoying his *canard a l'orange*. "The last time I spoke to you on the phone, Deck, I think there was some concern about that. Well, time seems to work wonders in the affairs of the desperate. We now have four countries on board: Zimbabwe, Zambia, Botswana and Mozambique. I'm still working on Namibia and Angola. Zimbabwe's Health Minister, James Tsumbia, has been running something of a silent campaign for us. He and his heads of state agree our findings are as convincing as they could hope for."

Decker downed a piece of his filet mignon, following it with a generous amount of cabernet. "What I don't get is how you've been able to convince them the efficacy results we present to them are legitimate."

OPTIONS

"What would we gain by playing with our results?" said Shaughnessy immediately. "The stuff works. Don't forget our business model."

Moss acknowledged the point with a nod, marveling again at the cleverness of the plan Kent shared with him on the yacht about recovery statistics. "What does the timeframe look like from here on?" he asked.

"Another twelve to fifteen months, I would say," replied Shaughnessy. "By then Zimbabwe should have a production plant tooled with the technical people to staff it. They'll likely recruit their scientific talent out of the toppled Soviet Bloc. They come cheap now, you know."

"And product supply for the other countries?" asked Decker.

"Initially they'll be taking their supply out of Harare. But I've been informed by Tsumbia that their governments will likely gain regulatory approvals straightaway. That would buttress our case and a speedy review here by the FDA." Shaughnessy set down his glass of white burgundy. "Now wouldn't that be a twist?" He strung his hands wide in the air in a simulated banner: 'Third world beats U.S. to AIDS cure.'"

The men laughed.

"And there's really no evidence of any side effects or other safety concerns?" asked Moss.

"Like I said before," Kent answered, "it's got the magic of Pasteur's rabies vaccine. A one-hundred-percent survival rate. That's about as good as you can get, wouldn't you say, my friend?"

Carpenter raised his wine glass in toast to the men. "To our new bride, Schoen Chemicals. Salute."

For three of them it was a fully satisfying meal. But when the men exited the restaurant Joe Moran headed directly to a corner pizzeria and ordered a large pepperoni pie to take to his hotel room.

"Can't enculturate a pig," said Carpenter to the others.

They left Moran to his own and walked on.

Chapter Thirty

IT was the phase in the audit sequence known as compliance testing. CPA firms didn't track every nickel and dime that ran through a company's books. Instead they relied on a sampling of records from various transactions to ensure proper protocols had been followed. Clients whose tested accounting records showed tight correspondence with appropriate safeguards against errors, manipulation, or other irregularities provided their auditors needed assurance for certifying the firm's financial statements.

Jensyn Chandler had been on site at Schoen Chemicals for six weeks now, returning home only on the weekends. After her Monday morning meetings with Sands to update him on her findings, she would travel back to Manchester.

It had been five months since their lunch at the McDonalds' restaurant, the wake of which had reduced to nothing. Inured to Jonathan's reticence over the months, she recently accepted a date with another office worker. He was also a manager by rank and quite attractive. And although not really looking for it, she genuinely enjoyed his company.

Presently Jensyn was reviewing a set of working papers submitted by one of the senior auditors on the engagement. It was an analysis of Schoen's sales and receivables cycle. One of the schedules, prepared by a first-year hire, caught her attention. It provided a listing of year-to-date sales volumes to Drexel-Pace from Schoen's biochemical division. Her interest in transactions with Drexel-Pace arose not only because of Jonathan, but also because related-party transactions required special scrutiny under the standards of the profession.

The sharp upward spike in sales of two products by Schoen to Drexel-Pace surprised her. She flicked through the records of the file, then searched for an analysis she had perused earlier—a sampling of various shipments to Drexel-Pace, tied to the related receivables/payables postings and payments. Several of them showed large dollar volumes of Threonatrix shipments.

Threonatrix, she repeated to herself, drawing on a faint memory.

Then she recalled the name of the product from her preliminary study of the client, specifically in the transcribed minutes of Schoen's board meeting with the Drexel-Pace executive team regarding the merger. It was a drug currently under review by the FDA.

Why was Drexel-Pace buying so much of it?

Certainly not for resale since it hadn't yet received regulatory approval.

For experimental study, perhaps? Would there really be a need for such large amounts, and at regular bi-weekly intervals?

She looked at the other product whose sales volumes likewise shot off the charts. It carried a non-commercial label: HX413. Apparently it was very expensive stuff ... over six thousand dollars per gram.

She made a note to herself to look into the two products more fully.

* * *

Monday, August 2, 1993
Boston, Massachusetts

A few minutes past eight, Jensyn entered Jonathan's office for their weekly Monday morning meeting. It was when the two regularly got together to discuss the progress on the Schoen audit and to make any needed revisions to the upcoming week's schedule.

She was clutching an armful of files, wearing a red skirt and white blouse.

"Soon you're going to need a file cabinet on a dolly," he said as he helped her with the stack of folders to the conference table at the far side of his office.

"I just didn't want to forget anything you might want to look at," she said, taking a seat.

"I'd say you brought everything I want to look at," he said, getting up. She smirked at his back as he walked to the door. "Want some coffee?" he asked.

"Thanks. That would be nice."

After giving his secretary the request, Jonathan rejoined Jensyn at the table.

"I think you're going to be interested in some things I found," she said. "I certainly can't figure them out."

"Really? What's that?"

"Well, before I get to that, let me fill you in on what I've been doing."

Jensyn took twenty minutes to outline her team's progress on the internal control study, leafing through the folders as she did so for his approval. He initialed each working paper at the bottom as the in-charge partner of the engagement, holding a few out for a more careful reading later.

"And that's when I came across this." She handed a paper-clipped set of sheets to him, taking a sip from her coffee.

Leafing through them a moment Jonathan handed them back to her. "Schoen's product sales to Drexel-Pace for the first two quarters," he said matter-of-factly.

"No. Look at them closely. What pops out at you?"

He scanned the numbers down the columns again, wondering what she was referring to as he flicked through the pages.

"Come on, Jon. Look at the sales growth percentages relative to last year."

"Oh ... well, I see one ... no two, products here that have done very nicely. That's good."

"Now look at this." She handed him another detailed schedule, this one showing the chronology of sales for those two particular products. The dollar volumes and shipment quantities were both significant and uniformly increasing.

"Looks like they're real winners."

"Jonathan, neither of those has FDA approval. Why would Drexel-Pace be buying so much of the stuff when they can't market it?"

His answer came without the benefit of much thinking. "To do research on it. They do a lot of that."

"Research? Those aren't the kind of volumes you'd see if they're just doing laboratory research. Not commercial quantities maybe, but still far more than you could fill a lab with. And it's very expensive stuff."

He studied the numbers more dutifully, agreeing with her latter point. "I don't know, Jen, but I'm sure it's probably legit." He looked up. "Did you look further into it?"

"I wouldn't have brought it up to you if I hadn't."

Jonathan watched her appreciatively as she dug out another file. Irrespective of his personal feelings for her she was unequaled on the job.

"These are faxes of Drexel-Pace's receiving reports for those products surrounding the dates indicated on Schoen's sales invoices for the recent quarter. I had Doug Benton send them to me."

"Benton?"

"He's one of the MM&P managers on the Drexel-Pace audit team working down in Atlanta."

Jonathan scanned the faxes a few minutes, comparing the dates of Schoen's bi-weekly shipments to the dates of Drexel-Pace's receipts. Every one of them matched up within a few days— acceptable lag time for transport, he thought. "I'm sorry, Jen, but you're losing me," he said finally. "All those shipments are accounted for as far as I can see."

"So you would agree they received them, right?"

"Of course I do. Why not?"

"Because they're not there, Jon. They never were. Doug Benton's the audit manager in charge of inventory, and he says there's absolutely no record of those shipments ever being entered into their stock."

"Doesn't D-P have production and warehouse facilities in the area?" he asked.

"Yes, they do. But again, Benton assures me they're not listed in their computer system as ever having been entered into stock. Certainly nothing like those quantities."

"How about other R&D labs or subsidiaries or offices they might have immediately shipped them to?"

"Doesn't look like it," Jensyn answered, taking another sip from her coffee. "D-P's research facilities consist of three floors of their headquarters building, and any turnaround shipments would have been entered in and recorded with appropriate shipping documents. You know pharmaceuticals have to follow especially stringent tracking requirements."

Sands stood and paced the few steps to his window, musing it over. "So what do you think happened to them?"

"I have no idea. But I'd like your permission to find out."

He turned back to her. "Permission?"

"To head down to Atlanta."

"Oh, Jen, I don't know about that," he said tentatively. "We don't want to go stepping on any toes down there."

"But we're part of the same audit firm working on a parent-subsidiary audit. And you and I both know we can't just rely on them to do it." She cupped a hand to her ear simulating a phone call: "Hello, would you please do me a favor and find out how Drexel-Pace snookered us and hid those drugs? We smell fish."

Jonathan smiled at her. Then, resting his chin between cleft fingers, he reflected on the matter some more. "It *is* a related party transaction," he conceded. "When could you do it?"

"I leave Wednesday afternoon from Manchester." She looked up apprehensively at him. "I already booked the tickets."

"Jen!"

Lifting from her seat she gathered the files in her arms. "Sorry, Mr. Sands, but I want to check out every possibility."

"But this isn't even about Decker. It's about Drexel-Pace."

"What if they're in bed together?"

"I can't imagine how that might be," he replied. "But I have to say I love your drive."

Jensyn tilted her head at him, thinking better of what she wanted to say about his 'drive' comment, and walked to the door. "I'll be back late Friday afternoon." With her hand on the knob she turned back around, a strand of orphaned hair falling down her face. "Maybe if you wanted to pick me up at the airport we could catch a bite to eat. Business, of course."

Jonathan smiled at her.

She smiled back.

"I wish I could, Jen ... you understand."

"No, Jonathan, I don't understand." She exited and shut the door a bit harder than necessary with her passing.

Chapter Thirty-One

DOUG Benton met Jensyn Chandler at the airport just before five in the afternoon. He was a smarmy guy with a workout build, the cutesy vanilla sort that a lot of women seemed to fall for. Jensyn suspected it came from hours of primping in front of a mirror. Probably the type who would actually shave his body hair.

Dropping her off at the entrance of the Marquis Marriott, he asked her if she wanted to have dinner with him. She politely declined. He told her he'd pick her up at 7:40 in the morning.

The hotel's spacious atrium core was fully open from lobby floor to multi-story roof, with center column elevator banks serving fast glass-cased cars. After checking in and unpacking her things, Jensyn ran the treadmill in the workout facility and then showered for an early dinner in the garden floor restaurant. It was lonely. When she returned to her room, she noticed the red light flashing on her bedside phone. She hit the dial sequence for the recorded message and listened. It was Jonathan.

> *Jen, I just had to call to see if you got there all right. You've been putting up with a lot these past several months and I'm sorry. I want you to know that if our circumstances were only different ... well, you know. Good night.*

It was all he said.

"Yeah, I know. Good night, Mr. Hyde," she said to the phone.

After undressing and climbing into bed, she stared across the dark space of the room. Then in the direction of the telephone.

She activated the message button and listened to it again.

Then another time.

Eventually the comforting tiredness of sleep came.

* * *

Stephen J. Dempsey

Thursday, August 5, 1993

After picking her up at the hotel and driving the few blocks to the Drexel-Pace headquarters building, Doug Benton showed Jensyn the rooms on the eleventh floor where he and his audit team worked, introducing her to a few of his staff. He acted like the kind of supervisor she was glad she never had, at one point grabbing a sheet of paper from one of his charges to see what she was working on. "File this by ten o'clock, Jackie; you've spent enough time on it."

Benton poured himself and Jensyn a cup of coffee and led her to his cubicle. Corporations the size of Drexel-Pace underwent a virtually continuous audit throughout the year. The auditors and on-site facilities they occupied were thus more or less as permanent as that of the regular Drexel-Pace personnel.

"I did some more investigation of those product codes last night after I dropped you off," Benton said. "Once they're entered into accounts payable they're charged entirely to the R&D expense accounts. That explains why nothing shows up as inventory. All R&D has to be expensed, you know."

"Yes, of course, I know that. But what about for internal recordkeeping?"

"Right." He pulled out a computer printout. "So I checked into that. Internally they keep perpetual records of the supplies and raw materials employed by the R&D department. There was a relatively small amount of HX413 on hand last December, but it was all requisitioned for experimentation. As for Threonatrix they currently have some of the stuff on site, but nothing like the quantities we're looking for." He sipped from his styrofoam cup and leaned back in his chair. "If you hadn't detected it up there in Manchester, I surely wouldn't have. It's not big enough here to bother with. Way off the radar screen."

Jensyn thought he said it condescendingly, like his role was somehow superior to hers. CPAs employed a materiality threshold for the dollar amount of error that could be tolerated in the accounts. Accuracy was always a cost-benefit issue, and for a multi-billion dollar firm like Drexel-Pace, a few million here or there was nothing to worry about for financial reporting purposes.

"Doug, it doesn't make sense. There's far too much of the stuff for simple R&D experiments. Repeated shipments of significant volumes and dollar volumes don't just disappear in expense accounts. With no record of stock on hand?"

"I agree. At least on the face of it." He grabbed a pad from his desktop. "We have a meeting down in Shipping & Receiving in twenty minutes. Did you have any other ideas we might pursue?"

"Well, I was hoping you might know more about this operation."

His fingers drew tight around his pencil. "It's a big operation, Ms. Chandler," he said with a bit of annoyance, "much bigger than Schoen's. I handle the purchasing cycle and the fixed asset group of accounts. We've got three other senior managers on this audit, and a partner who devotes nearly full time to it."

"I didn't mean anything by that, Doug. Don't take me wrong. I was just hoping you might know what such chemicals might be used for."

"Unfortunately, I have no idea. I'm not a scientist. As I said, R&D has requisitioned both products, but for the HX stuff that was a long ways back. We could talk with some of the folks down in R&D." He looked at his watch. "Somebody might be in, but you know how scientists are." He winked at her and dialed the company operator. It took a few patches to finally get someone in the R&D lab who was able to speak with him.

"Brad Fray," answered the connection.

"Yes, Mr. Fray, this is Douglas Benton, with the MM&P audit team. I was wondering if you—or maybe somebody you could put me in touch with—might have information on some particular Schoen Chemicals products."

"Schoen Chemicals?"

"Yes, a while back there was some work being done on a couple of products down there. Biochemical compounds supplied by Schoen." Benton leaned back in his chair and put his feet up on the desk.

"Sorry, Mr. Benton, but we have a large staff here. Several hundred scientists working with thousands of chemicals every day. Could you give me any more information about what they're used for?"

"Just a second." Benton covered the mouthpiece of the phone and whispered to Jensyn: "What would the products have been used for?"

She couldn't believe the question, but tried not to show her irritation. "I told you, I have no idea. Just give him the names."

Benton looked at the notepad sitting in his lap. "One's called HX413 and the other is called Threonatrix."

"Threonatrix?" repeated the scientist. "That one sounds familiar. Hold on."

A few minutes went by. Benton looked at his watch again. "I think we're going to be late for our meeting down in Shipping & Receiving."

"They'll wait," Jensyn said.

"Yeah, they'll wait." He spent the time drumming his pencil against his thick leg.

Dr. Fray eventually came back on the line. "Yes, Threonatrix is being worked on by several teams down here. I had to do a computer search on my inter-office memo updates. The HX product sounds like a peptide compound, but I have no record of it on my side. We have some people in molecular biology that might be able to help you, but they won't get in until nine or so."

"That'll be fine," answered Benton. "We have a meeting we're late for now, but we could be there by ..." He looked at his watch. "Nine-thirty? Would you be able to put us in touch with them?"

"Sure." Fray then told Benton where to meet him.

* * *

The Shipping & Receiving Department was a spacious concrete dock with four bays. The daytime manager, Griffith Taylor, greeted them. They made their introductions.

"You're a very pretty young lady," the gray-haired man said in a friendly southern drawl.

"Well, thank you very much, Mr. Taylor," Jensyn said.

"And a beautiful voice as well. Hope you don't mind me saying so. British?"

Jensyn nodded. Benton cut it off immediately to business. He explained the matter to the man in very general terms, hoping he'd be able to give them some insight about how certain products received might not have gone into inventory or to R&D stores.

"Been working here near twenty-five years. Coca-Cola before that. Can't say much about recordkeeping, but I can tell you what we do if that's what you'd like to know."

Before getting a reply Taylor went over to the desk against the wall where two computer terminals were located. "One or two guys takes the stuff off the trucks, another marks off the receiving report for the product and quantities received, and then me or another manager—there's three of us—logs them into this computer. One copy of the receiving report goes to accounts payable. Another goes with the goods. After that, I can't say what happens."

Benton knew where the documents went from there. At least he thought he did. "But the goods are carted right off to inventory, right?" asked Benton.

"Yep."

"Are there any exceptions?" Jensyn asked. "Does anything ever arrive here at the dock and not go directly into the building?"

"Oh, sure, we get some stuff like that. Some redirects, damaged goods, some that goes to the other warehouses or to our main plant in Macon."

"But they always go once you enter them into your computer here?" she asked.

"Yeah, but for those I got a special place I put them in. Called 'Trans-Out.'"

"Can you show me on your screen?"

"Sure." The man happily punched some keys at his terminal. "We have several choices for 'Trans-Out.'" Up came a menu on his monitor. Jensyn quickly perused the long list of site names on the screen.

"How many of these are in the Atlanta area?" she asked.

"These two warehouses here, and this is our Macon plant." He pointed at the screen, scrolling down the list with his finger. The others, he explained, were for other states and international warehouses. "Ain't much to go international from here though."

She noted the names of several foreign cities. "Does any stuff get transferred out that's received from Schoen Chemicals Company?"

"Schoen Chemicals?" He turned around to her, surprised. "No, not by me, but funny you should ask. Schoen's deliveries are handled by someone else."

"Someone else?" Jensyn asked.

"Yes, ma'am. Security. We get a shipment from Schoen and we call Security right away. They're the ones who deal with it."

Jensyn caught Doug Benton's eye with guarded excitement. Benton probed the man further: "What do they do with it?" he asked.

"Well, some stays here and some goes to our Macon plant. But the other stuff they repack and guard until the truck for international shipments arrives. I don't ask questions, but I suppose it must be very important stuff if it requires such special treatment."

"Do they enter the international shipments into this computer?" asked Jensyn.

"They enter it, but I have no idea what it is or where it goes."

Chandler and Benton traded looks again.

"Can you call up international shipments?" Jensyn asked, gesturing at the terminal.

"Sure, we can call up the last three shipments from here. It takes a bit more work to go farther back than that."

The man tapped a few keys on his keyboard, demonstrating an example for the first international site on his screen: Düsseldorf, Germany. The three most recent bills of lading were displayed. The auditors perused the product codes as Taylor scrolled down the list, but they didn't see the items they were looking for. Nor did they see Schoen as an originating shipper. Jensyn knew it would take far more time to run through all the international sites before they had to get to their next meeting.

"Thank you, Mr. Taylor, you've been very helpful." She glimpsed at her watch and then looked up at Benton. "We have another appointment?"

"Very glad to meet you young folks. Come and visit anytime."

* * *

Dr. Bradley Fray was a short, portly gentleman, with wire-rim glasses and hair tied back in a ponytail. After clearing his visitors through security, he showed them into a massive open-room lab area. It was quietly bustling with white-coated scientists engaged in the secretive craft of their occupation.

"I located some people over here that will be happy to discuss Threonatrix with you," said Fray. "Not any details, of course, but they might have the information you're looking for." He walked them over to the lab station where the two scientists—a man and a woman—greeted them.

Doug Benton took the lead to introduce the nature of their inquiry. "We're looking for anyone who might be working with, or has worked with, fairly large quantities of Schoen Chemical's products. In particular, Threonatrix and a compound called HX413."

"Several of us are doing work on Threonatrix," said the male scientist. "But none of us require much of it, maybe a few grams a day. I don't think I've ever heard of the other one you mentioned." He glanced at his female colleague.

"HX—?" She asked, looking at Jensyn.

"413 ... HX413" Jensyn repeated.

"No, can't say it sounds familiar to me either. Do you know the dates when it was requisitioned?"

Benton referred to his yellow pad of notes. "We know ... yeah, I can get that information."

"Well, if you know the dates you can check the materials requisition forms. We have to sign out for everything we take from stores. You can find out which scientists work on it that way. It's down on the next floor. They keep the forms filed by date."

Of course, Benton thought. He felt foolish for not thinking of it earlier. "Thank you very much."

Jensyn, too, felt embarrassed. She relied on the manager of Drexel-Pace's inventory audit to know his systems well enough that if such records existed he would have mentioned them. She silently fumed in her resolve not to trust him for much further beyond the basics. This was too important.

Once out of security and alone on the elevator she eyed him hard. "How could you not know they have requisition forms for R&D? I just figured they didn't or we wouldn't have to go through all this nonsense."

"Sorry about that, Ms. Chandler."

"Sorry? My God, Benton, that's Accounting 101."

"Look, you're the one who called me about this idiocy. Do you know how trivial the amounts you're wasting my time to find really are to this company? R&D requisitions? Hell, they don't amount to a fart in a shit field."

Back in his office Benton rummaged through some printouts of the R&D supplies inventory—output from a computer query he made to extract the dates of HX413 requisitions. He handed her the stack of paper. "Here, go back downstairs and sort out your own mess. I've got more important things to work on."

"Gladly." Jensyn glared at him and exited his cubicle.

* * *

She gained entry to the lab area on her own after having the security officer on duty phone Brad Fray for authorization. The

R&D storeroom was on the fourth floor. The stores clerk gave her access to the materials requisition forms and she sat at a side table looking through them.

Leafing through the documents chronologically she compared their line-item entries to the computer printouts Benton provided, which amounted to hundreds of sign-outs each day. It was tedious work. What made it worse was that Schoen's products weren't listed by name; Drexel-Pace apparently assigned each of its raw materials a unique, in-house, six-digit alphanumeric identification. Fortunately, however, the computer printout Benton gave her listed both. The transport records she observed earlier on the computer screen had similar six-digit codes. Now she knew what to look for when she trekked back down to the shipping dock later in the afternoon.

Fifteen minutes into her search Jensyn frowned. The numerical sequence of several requisition forms was interrupted. She checked the other dates surrounding those on her printout but their sequences were unbroken, as they should be.

"Do you have any idea why some forms would be missing?" she asked, peering up at the stores clerk who was working at the other side of the room.

"Missing? No, nothing should be missing." The man came over to her. "Show me."

Jensyn did so.

The clerk scratched his chin. "I have no idea. Even the voided ones should be there." He wrote down the missing form numbers on a sheet of paper. "I'll have to ask my supervisor. Let me know if you find any others." Hovering awkwardly about her a few more minutes, not knowing how else to help, he eventually went on to his other business.

Jensyn spent nearly two hours going through the rest of the dates indicated on her list, but she didn't come across a single requisition containing the Drexel-Pace ID code for HX413. There were now thirty-two missing forms, all of which just happened to coincide with the dates listed on her computer printouts. None were missing on any other dates that she could find. But there were at least two more weeks' worth of listings she had to go through, and she pressed on.

Her vision began to blur as she scrolled through all the numbers. It was mind-numbing work and a struggle to maintain focus. But then something alighted her consciousness. She pulled back the card she had just passed.

There among a list of several other materials on the same form was the ID number for HX413. She noted the signed name on the bottom: *D.D. Milongo.* His signature was scratched over his printed name.

"May I get a copy of this one?" she asked the stores clerk.

"Of course," he answered. He was nervous about the missing forms and wanted to comply with any request the auditor made.

With the copy in hand she excitedly jogged the stairs back up a flight, bypassing the need for hallway security clearance. In a few minutes she was able to locate the two scientists she and Benton had met earlier in the day.

"Would you know a scientist named Milongo?" she asked.

Their faces went taught. Jensyn handed the photocopy of the requisition form to them, pointing to the name at the bottom. "D. D. Milongo," she asked again.

"Jensyn, right?" inquired the woman scientist, wanting to be sure of her name.

Jensyn nodded.

"I'm sorry, Jensyn, but DeDe's no longer with us. He … was killed."

"Killed?"

"Yes," said the man. "DeDe was apparently involved in some thefts from our inventory. Narcotics. The police said it was a drug sale that went bad. He was shot in our underground parking garage, just before Christmas."

Stunned, Jensyn dropped her hands to her side, clutching the photocopy, and gazed away.

"We all thought a great deal of him," said the woman. "It was a real shock. Nobody suspected a thing. He had a new wife, a bright new career, some research he was very excited about. But he kept to himself mostly, and it's always hard to read people like that."

Jensyn looked emptily at the two scientists, not knowing what to say.

"But your questions don't have anything to do with that, do they?" asked the woman.

Jensyn shook her head. Then with an unspoken "thanks anyway" expression, she walked for the exit.

* * *

Following a bland lunch in the building's cafeteria Jensyn Chandler returned to the shipping dock area. She found Griffith Taylor sitting at his desk eating a home-packed sandwich from a paper bag.

"I was wondering if you could give me access to your computer again," she asked, "those screens you showed us earlier for your redirected shipments?"

"Of course. No traffic down here at the moment." Taylor lifted from his chair and offered it to her. "Have at it yourself."

"How do you get to those screens?"

"Oh, here, sorry." He hit a sequence of buttons and brought up the incandescent green menu. "Which site do you want to look at?"

"You said Schoen's redirects went to Macon and some were repackaged for the international truck. I want to look through those if I may."

"Down here." He brought up the sub-menu. "Hit any one of these sites with the enter key. It gives you the three most recent shipments. You hit the enter key to get to the next one and the escape key to come back."

"Thanks."

She noted the Macon site contained hundreds of product entries. Yet, unfortunately, they weren't in alpha-numeric sequence. Apparently the shipments were in the order of their physical placement on the delivery trucks, since that would have been the sequence in which they were entered into the computerized manifest.

She found a number of records where Schoen Chemicals was listed as the originating supplier, but none with the product IDs for HX413 or Threonatrix.

Two hours later she came to the international site for Harare, Zimbabwe. The name of the city was unfamiliar to her. When she hit the return button a message appeared on the upper left-hand corner of her screen: ACCESS DENIED.

She tried again. Same thing.

"Mr. Taylor?"

"Yeah?" He was across the room.

"I get a message here that I don't know what to do with."

Taylor came over to her and looked where she was pointing. "Access denied, huh? Don't know what that means."

He tried it himself. "Harare, you say?"

"Yes. I did the same thing as the others, but that's all it gives me."

He looped back to the main menu and tried going directly to the Harare selection, but with the same result. "Can't imagine why. Works for all the others."

"Seems to," she agreed. "Has this ever happened to you before?"

"No." The man took his hand to his jaw. "But to tell you the truth, I can't say as I've ever tried Harare before. Never had to redirect any shipments there."

She looked at him inquisitively.

Returning her gaze, he said: "I wonder if that isn't where Schoen's repackaged redirects go that're handled by security."

* * *

Following her work at Drexel-Pace headquarters, Jensyn returned by foot to the Marriott. Not feeling in the mood for a workout she took a shower and put on her bathrobe. Then she ordered room service for dinner.

Now, with the curtains drawn and the lights turned off, she lay on the bed in the shadows trying to sort out the puzzling findings of the day.

She had completed her review of the other international sites that followed Harare on the screen, but she didn't find Threonatrix or HX413 for any of those either. Yet Schoen's records and Benton's faxed copies of the receiving reports clearly showed that a Schoen shipment of the two products had been received as early as last week. For all the sites she examined, the three most recent bills of lading records would certainly have captured a 'trans-out' if it occurred. Each of them had dates straddling the most recent Schoen delivery date.

They had to be going to Harare.

But why? And why were all the requisition forms she looked for missing except for that single one?

Was it just missed by someone trying to hide them, perhaps? Milongo himself? Could he have been selling the stuff on the street?

Thinking about that possibility some more she concluded it didn't make sense. A great deal of the two products had been shipped by Schoen to Drexel-Pace since Milongo's death in December—and just recently—yet those supplies were missing as well. And any police investigation into Milongo's thefts of

305

inventory would certainly have turned up missing requisition forms. It would have been the focus of their investigation, the very first place they'd look.

No, she concluded, the forms had to have been removed since that time. If someone had sought to purge evidence that those products were being used in R&D experiments, they must have simply missed that single form. Which was reasonable since it contained HX413 buried in a list of other materials simultaneously signed out.

But if someone had tried to hide the evidence of experimentation on the products altogether, why wouldn't the perpetual inventory records likewise have been manipulated? The computer printout given her by Benton clearly showed R&D requisitions for HX413.

Then a thought hit her: What if they weren't trying to hide the fact that the product was used in experiments? What if they were really trying to hide the identity of the person who was working on it? *Milongo himself.*

Jensyn felt a chill.

She looked at the clock: *6:35.* She dialed Jonathan's office number. No answer. Grabbing her purse for her address book she found Jonathan's home phone number.

"Hello," he greeted.

"Oh, Jonathan, thank God you're there." Her breathing was fast.

Picking up the distress in her voice, he asked: "What is it, Jen?"

"I have to talk to you."

"Why? What's going on?"

"They're hiding records, Jonathan. They're hiding those shipments. They're going to Harare!"

"What are you talking about? Calm down and give it to me slowly. Where are you?"

"I'm at the hotel. I just finished searching for those product shipments and they're going to Harare. And a man is dead. He was working on the stuff. They must have killed him! They said he was caught stealing narcotics, and he was killed in a bad drug deal."

"Jensyn, come on! What man? Where's Harare?"

"Harare, Jon. It's in Zimbabwe. The man who was doing experiments on the drugs is dead and they tried to hide the fact he was working on them. They killed him!"

"Jen, this isn't making sense." He paused and steadied his voice. "Can you get a flight back tonight?"

"I don't know. I don't know the number. I—"

"Give me your hotel number and I'll call the airlines."

She read the number off the telephone to him.

"I'll call you as soon as I can. In the meantime, try to calm down. It can't be what you say."

"I just put it all together, Jon! He must have found out something about those drugs. Please call soon."

"I'll call back as soon as I can. Hold tight."

Jensyn replaced the handset and got up from the bed. Nervously she looked around the room and began to gather her things. Getting dressed again she turned on the TV, hoping it would help settle her nerves. It didn't.

The phone rang.

"Jonathan?" she quickly answered.

"No, sorry. Is this Ms. Chandler?"

She didn't recognize the raspy male voice. "Yes," she said hesitantly.

"My name's Geoff Slade, head of Drexel-Pace security. I understand you were looking for some missing requisition forms today?"

"Yes?"

"We don't know how that happened, Ms. Chandler, but we suspect it was due to an incident that took place with one of our scientists a while back. He was caught stealing drugs from our inventory. A very unfortunate affair. I'll look into it further and will be back in touch with you."

"I … well, thank you." The stores clerk must have reported the missing forms to security. Jensyn knew the man had to be lying and she tried to conceal her nervous tone. "That's very kind of you."

"Certainly. Again, I'm very sorry about the inconvenience to your audit. Will you be back in the building tomorrow?"

"Yes, thank you, Mr. Slade. Doug Benton will know where to find me."

Jensyn cradled the phone and sat in silence for a moment.

How odd. For corporate security to call me at the hotel?

Something about that bothered her, and her eyes slowly drew large.

Security! Griffith Taylor said they're the ones overseeing Schoen's international shipments!

307

She shivered.

The phone rang again. Guardedly, Jensyn answered it: "Hello?"

"Are you okay?" Jonathan asked.

"Were you able to get me a flight?"

He told her the airline and gate information. "The ticket will be at the counter but you'll have to hurry. It departs at 8:05. Can you make it to the airport in time?"

She looked at the bedside clock: *7:03.* "I … yes, I think so."

"I'll meet you here at Logan. Hurry."

* * *

"We've got problems."

"What is it now, Slade?" Kent Shaughnessy took the phone call in his home office.

"Two auditors were down in R&D and at the receiving dock today asking about the products. I think I've covered for the lab but it looks like they might have a tag on Harare."

"That's great, Slade, just great." Kent pinched his eyes. "How the hell did that happen?"

The head of Drexel-Pace security shared what he had learned about the two auditors' movements during the day. "I have no idea how the woman picked up on the Schoen goods, but that was definitely her interest. And she discovered the blocked access screen for Harare. She knows something's up."

Jensyn Chandler. Shaughnessy remembered the name—a woman that beautiful would be hard to forget—he had met her at Schoen's stockholders' meeting.

"Can't you get a programmer to doctor the Harare records?" he asked, continuing to rub his face.

"No, not tonight. It would take too long. Besides, that would involve another person."

Shaughnessy nodded concurrence.

"But I have another idea," said Slade. "The dock manager told them he thought the Schoen goods she was looking for go international."

"He *what?* She'll know those goods aren't FDA approved!"

"Hold on. That could work in our favor. I told him they don't really go international; that they actually go to a secret lab here in the city for security reasons, and that he should just shut up about it. If the auditors press us, we just fill some commercial space with equipment and store some product over there. We're testing shelf-life or something … the old stuff is just thrown out."

"I don't know," said Shaughnessy, "but it might be the best we can do."

There was a pause.

"Of course, there's always the other alternative," said the security man obdurately.

"No, Slade, enough of that. Get some commercial space and fill it with the product. When's the next shipment due?"

"Tomorrow."

"Well, at least that's one good piece of news." Kent held the phone a moment. He was thinking of the aberrant data Graham Woods was sending him recently. "It will mean an interruption in the Harare operation. But that may also work in our favor."

It was about time they brought their scientist stateside anyway. The executive team was long overdue for a full debriefing from Woods on the concerns hinted in his faxed reports.

Chapter Thirty-Two

Thursday, August 5, 1993
Boston, Massachusetts

JONATHAN greeted Jensyn outside the terminal security gate. She was spent. Slinging the strap of her overnight bag over his shoulder, he walked her to his car in the lot.

"Security called me at the hotel right after I first talked to you," she said. "They're the ones responsible for shipping the drugs to Harare."

"Jen, you have to give it to me slowly and in order. I won't be able to follow otherwise."

As they drove into the city she gave a much more composed version of what took place in Atlanta.

"So the security officer said you were the first to discover the missing forms?"

"That's what he implied, but I don't believe it. He sounded creepy. I just know something terrible is going on. Why would a criminal investigation not have picked up the missing forms? If Milongo was stealing drugs from stock I would think that would have been the first place the police would look."

"It's a good point. I agree."

"They must have pulled the forms *after* the investigation. They weren't for narcotics, and the police wouldn't have any interest in those requisitions from stock. They simply didn't want anyone else to connect Milongo to them at a later time. Like now. And why would Harare be the only site blocked from computer access?"

"I trust your judgment, Jen. We'll find out what's going on." He leaned forward to slide a cassette into the tape deck.

The two listened for a while in silence as they rode.

"That's lovely. I've heard it before … Samuel Barber, right?" she asked.

"Yes, very good. *Adagio for Strings.*"

The music was somber, and with Jonathan at her side, Jensyn began to feel some of the day's tension begin to subside. She turned to study his profile in the dim interior lighting. "It meant a lot to me that you called and said what you did. Did you mean it?"

"What's that?"

"That if our circumstances were only different?"

He smiled. "Yes, Jen, I meant it."

After driving twenty minutes in silence, they pulled up in front of her apartment building on the west side of the city. He helped her out and walked her up the steps from the sidewalk, carrying her suit bag.

"Are you going to be okay," he asked.

"As long as there isn't a hit man waiting for me behind my door." Jensyn turned her key in the foyer lock and came around. "You're welcome to come inside if you like."

Sands didn't answer.

"Things *can* be different, Jon." The street lights reflected in her eyes.

"No, Jen, they can't. Not now. I'm sorry."

She held his look for a moment. Then in a low voice she said: "Good night."

He tried to rescue himself. "Jen, I'm sorry. It's just that—"

"No, please. It's okay." She placed her finger on his lips. She grabbed her bag and entered the door, looking back at him before closing it. "I'll see you tomorrow."

It was an enigmatic expression, he thought, one that seemed to have a hint of finality to it.

* * *

Friday, August 6, 1993

"You can reverse that environmental write-off, old buddy."

The weighty statement stopped him. He switched the phone to his other ear. "What're you talking about, Decker?"

"I just got formal word, which you'll receive shortly," Moss answered. "Drexel-Pace is completely assuming the liability. They're going to fax their board minutes to you, with a letter from Larry Carpenter stating that whatever exposure may exist from the Mullins plant is completely theirs. *Carte Blanche.*"

"I don't believe it," responded Sands.

"It's a fact, my friend."

"Why would they be willing to do that?"

"Well, actually, I've been trying to talk them into it," Decker lied, "to mend fences after the takeover fallout. I guess they just heard what I had to say."

"This just better be clean, Decker," Jonathan said pointedly.

"Look, Sands, knock it off," rattled Moss, "it's perfectly clean. I told you, Carpenter's going to send you his board minutes. Do you really think his entire board would be involved in some kind of corporate coup d'état? Get reasonable. Cyrus Schoen's got you hunting for ghosts."

After an uncomfortable period of silence, Jonathan offered: "Well, then, good for you. I always knew you were quite the politician." He thought some more between words, concluding there'd be time for a fuller assessment later. "I'll have my tax people work on the deferred tax issue. You'll also have to submit an 8-K filing." Jonathan looked at his watch. It was getting late. "You're sure it's a complete assumption?" he asked.

"Every dime," assured Moss.

"Okay., then, I'll look for the fax and should be back in touch with you on Monday. Is afternoon okay?"

"Sure. Oh, and Jon, one other thing. Larry Carpenter mentioned that one of your staff was down in Atlanta looking for records on some of our product shipments. That she couldn't find them? Well, I assure you, they were bona fide sales. They received every one of those shipments. I would never fabricate our revenues."

"I never implied—"

"I guess they're doing special shelf-life research on some of our peptides, which they took off-site for experimentation. Some kind of secret lab work they're dong that they didn't want to have leaked out. Anyway, you'll certainly have access to all of it. They just weren't expecting your people down there."

"Of course," Jonathan said, disguising his doubt. "Okay, look, I'll talk to you Monday."

* * *

After hanging up, Moss meditated long and hard about Sands. He had thought their conversation at the restaurant nearly six months ago, as disturbing as it was, had put an end to Sands's suspicions. But Larry Carpenter's call the previous evening about Jensyn Chandler nosing around in Atlanta, particularly about her possible discovery of the Harare shipments, was more than alarming. And now on the phone Sands sounded doubtful again. Aggressive even.

What the hell is his problem?

Decker went over it all again, eventually concluding, as he had many times over the years, that he ultimately held the upper hand.

* * *

The flower arrangement had arrived and was sitting at the corner of Jensyn's desk, next to Gimpo. Also sitting at her desk, unfortunately, was Edward J. Mockridge, IV, the tax manager with whom Jensyn was now getting somewhat involved. At least that was the rumor that carried along the flowing currents of the office gossip stream.

"I'm sorry. I'll come back later," said Sands, apologetically.

"No, that's alright," Jensyn said, standing. "We were just finishing."

"Please, sir, have my seat." The young man stood and gestured to his desk-facing chair. He was a dark, mousse-haired, good-looking sort, though with a deeper facial shadow than that suggested by the sundial. Jonathan doubted he was really Jensyn's type … too smooth a character.

With Mockridge's departure Sands closed the door on the trail of his cologne and pointed out the window behind her desk. "It's not snowing. Would you like to go for a run?"

"Huh?" She turned around to catch his angle of sight at the bright summer day.

"I'm sorry, Jen," he said.

Still standing, she hovered above her desk, looking somewhat uncomfortable. Then she sat down. "I guess you just caught me at a weak moment last night after all I went through yesterday. I suppose I'm the one who should apologize." She smiled diffidently. "Thank you for the flowers."

"You're very welcome." Jonathan took the seat and gestured at the arrangement. "You should probably just freeze-dry those for the next time I have to make amends."

Jensyn pursed a smile and spun around to her computer screen. "Give me a second. When Ed stopped by I was just finishing a memo I have to get off before I leave."

Sands knew she was leaving town for a week of professional development training in Nashville. Several minutes passed as she plucked away at the keyboard.

"Do you run with him?"

Jensyn didn't answer.

"With Iv?" Jonathan asked. "Do you?"

The upturn in his voice registered, but not the question. She looked back at him.

"I asked if you run with Iv?" he asked again.

Confusion crossed her face. "Do I what? What are you talking about?"

"'I-V,'" Jonathan said, "you know, as in 'the fourth.' That's how his first name shows up in our computer system. Someone must have keyed it in the wrong field in the database."

Jensyn shook her head, sighing frustration. "No, Jon, I happen to play racquetball with him. 'Iv' lets me beat him. There, are you satisfied?"

This time Sands didn't answer.

Jensyn continued frowning over her shoulder at him, but he just stared inscrutably out the window behind.

"What is it you want from me?" she asked, turning fully to him. "My God, Mr. Sands, you're the most frustrating person … I don't even know how to react around you anymore."

"I don't mean to be frustrating. I just want you to go running with me." Taking his gaze back to her, he said: "I happen to enjoy your company."

"Oh, yeah? Why's that?"

"Do such things really require an explanation?"

"Well, *you* require explanation, Mr. Sands," Jensyn snapped. "After all, if it's only company you want, go buy yourself a blooming houseplant."

Jonathan stood, and Jensyn immediately regretted her words.

But it was Jonathan who mollified. "I enjoy being with you, and I happen to enjoy you being with me back."

"What? What on earth does that mean?"

"I enjoy your liking my company in return." He walked over to the wall carrying her diplomas, CPA license and other honors. Below them was a framed, stitched wall hanging: *All things work together for good.* "Did you make this?" he asked, pointing.

"Yes."

He noted the Bible verse reference below it. "Do you believe it?"

"When the thing actually came out so nicely after all the hours I spent working on it, yes, I believe it."

"Do you believe in God?" he asked, still with his back to her.

"What kind of question is that?"

He didn't answer.

"Yes, I do. I happen to. Do you?"

After a moment he nodded. "I just can't figure him out, is all."

"Well, I think it's obvious, if he happened to want us to figure him out, he could have made that much clearer. So, I guess I just accept him on his own terms. He does have the upper hand, after all."

Jonathan pivoted and faced her, shoving his hands uncomfortably into his pockets. "I'm sorry, Jen. I really haven't been playing games with you; not intentionally."

She regarded him with a furrowed brow. "Seriously, Jon, I don't know what you want from me. That crazy night you carried me half across the city you said something that meant more to me than you may realize. You said being rich meant having memories and someone to share them with. Well, memories are too precious not to be made, and life's too dear not to have someone to make them with. I thought if you want to go on wallowing in your junk without me, or talking to me about it, then that's your choice. But I'm done with wallowing. I've had my share of wallowing. I didn't go looking for it, but I happen to like Ed. And to be honest, you were the one who made it possible for me even to move on."

"Move on? Good for you. Ed's a fine guy. You look nice together."

"I didn't say that I have. I just said you made it possible for me to."

Jonathan glanced at his watch. It was after six. "So, Iv lets you beat him at racquetball, huh?"

"I've suspected so."

"That's a pretty sexist thing. I wouldn't do that. I'd cream your butt every time."

"Jonathan!"

"Come on, Jen, let's go for a run. I have some news on Schoen I want to talk to you about."

She patterned a glare at him. "It's always got to be business with you, doesn't it, Mr. Sands?"

Chapter Thirty-Three

THE pair followed the same route they took in the snow more than six months earlier, running along the pathways of Boston's Freedom Trail. The pedestrian traffic was much heavier this time of year, despite the late time of day. But the summer evening sun gave clear light to their footing, which Jensyn appreciated.

"Doug Benton called this afternoon," Jensyn said as she wiped some sweat from her brow. "He told me he was, quote, 'pissed off' I wasn't there when he showed up at the hotel to pick me up this morning. Serves him right."

"I'd say you snookered him," Jonathan said.

She smiled at him. "Anyway," Jensyn resumed, "I told him about the missing requisition forms. Now it's his responsibility."

"We'll get to the bottom of it, Jen."

They entered the Boston Common. She had jogged it many times on her own since her ankle injury, but it was especially good to share it with him again.

"That's just about where I downed you," Jonathan said, pointing to the field off to the right, at the nexus of walkways.

"You didn't down me. I downed myself. You just got lucky."

"No, you were a clod. Do you realize you didn't even come close to hitting me that night? What is it about women and throwing? Their arms go into this contorted mess that lacks any sense of coordination. No fluidity whatsoever."

Jensyn turned in her gait and stuck her tongue at out him. Just then a saucer flew in their direction, from a man playing with his golden retriever. Jonathan romped around a bit with the dog and flung the plastic toy back with a perfect backhand shot.

"You looked like a dog man just there," she said when he rejoined her.

"I suppose I am."

"Do you have one?"

"No, I'm away too much. I'd kill it. Just like my houseplants."

They ran for a while and Jonathan changed subjects. "So, about Schoen ... you're not going to believe this, but Decker called and said Drexel-Pace is going to assume that environmental liability."

OPTIONS

"What!" She turned towards him, incredulous. "Assume it?"

"The whole thing," Jonathan affirmed. "That's what he said, anyway. Some sort of goodwill gesture. We'll have to back out the liability in this quarter's financials."

"And that doesn't strike you as a bit odd?" she asked.

"Of course it strikes me as odd. Still, stranger things have happened. Maybe Moss just got lucky."

Jensyn cackled disbelief: "No way, it's too far-fetched for me."

"Okay, give me your take on it."

Contemplating, Jensyn took the opportunity to jog over to a park water fountain. Jonathan followed. Lifting from her drink, she said panting: "I think that write-off was probably the thing that made the whole buyout possible. A so-called green company announcing a huge environmental loss right before it becomes a target in a hostile bid? Freaked out shareholders wanting to sell off, and then after they do the whole thing is fully reversed? Like I say, it's too fishy, far too convenient." She took another sip of water.

In just a few sentences Jensyn had articulated his concerns precisely. "I'm with you, Jen, and I would be fast onto it if not for one thing."

"What's that?"

"The EPA," Jonathan answered. "The citation came from them. An independent, very official, very stiff-armed agency of the government." He took his own draw from the faucet. "What's convenient is that it happened at just the right time."

"I'm not arguing that point," Jensyn acknowledged. "I just think it smacks of something. And I'm not sure what it is … or how."

Sands shook his head. "So that's what your intuition tells you, Jen? Okay, we'll write that up in our working papers. Client committed fraud, with a supporting tick-mark: 'based on Jensyn Chandler's British sterling intuition.'"

She folded her arms and squinted sourly at him. "If I weren't happening to enjoy this run so much, I'd have a bit of a spat with you right now. And then I'd get directly to it. And I'd find it, too."

"So the EPA is in on it with Decker? Come on, Jen. Mullins was Schoen's plant."

"I'm not saying the EPA was in on it. There are other possibilities."

He studied her with curiosity. "I'd be interested in hearing what they might be."

Jensyn took off jogging down the path again and Jonathan followed. "Well, for one," she continued, "maybe Schoen somehow made it look like they were a party at that Superfund site when they really weren't involved at all."

Jonathan considered her statement, wondering if she were joking. Her come-back look told him, however, she wasn't.

"If you weren't the brilliant person I know you are, I'd say that's idiotic."

"Wait a minute. Take one step at a time, not three in a row. What's so crazy? What if the EPA had been presented evidence of Schoen's involvement at the site that wasn't really genuine? Just appearing genuine enough that they were brought in?"

"Okay, for argument's sake, let's suppose that's the case. By doing so, Schoen obviously takes on a phantom liability that becomes very genuine. Some fifty million dollars genuine by the looks of Royce's report."

"Right, so they take on a liability that really wasn't theirs to take on. Then ask yourself why a firm would willingly assume such a liability?"

The question wasn't difficult to answer, not in theory, and Sands did so directly: "Only if they expected to get a benefit that exceeded that cost."

"There you have it. And what benefit did they get?" asked Chandler.

Jonathan evaluated her thoughts in the order she presented them, thinking they were sensible on their own, yet lacking any sensible conclusion. "I give up. What benefit did Schoen get?"

"I have no idea."

This time it was he who stuck out his tongue at her.

Trotting for a while in silence, Sands shifted to his other item of news. "Decker also told me those Schoen shipments weren't going overseas, that they were really transfers to a makeshift lab right there in Atlanta. For shelf-life research. Carpenter wanted us to know."

"Shelf-life research? That's ridiculous. Not with those quantities."

"It may or may not be. Either way, it won't be difficult to verify. I'll ask Alan Pelleman to check into it. An easy matter."

As they traveled the northern portion of the park that flanked the Beacon Hill area, Jonathan's mind ran back through Jensyn's steps of logic again, thinking of the benefit issue. And then, like a slap in the face, it struck him almost immediately. "Jen, of course! Schoen wasn't the one to benefit. You already said it. *Drexel-Pace* benefited! Their buyout may not have been successful without it."

She glanced sidelong at him. "So, Drexel-Pace presented evidence to the EPA that implicated Schoen?"

"If we go along with that wacky theory of yours, then, yeah."

"You really think it's wacky?"

"I just can't imagine how they could possibly dupe the EPA about such a thing. Bury drums and make it look like a twenty year-old dumping? No way."

She agreed. It sounded implausible. "You're probably right."

"No. Keep pushing me. Let's not give up on your idea yet. Drexel-Pace benefited. They got the shares."

"But did they get a bargain?"

"A bargain?" Thinking more to himself, his panting became heavier. "That would only happen if the market overreacted to Schoen's environmental announcement."

"What did the news articles say?" she asked.

Jonathan tried to recall. "I don't remember any mention of the stock price reaction to the news. Now I'm disappointed with myself for not thinking of it." They exited the east side entrance to the park, him now in front of her. "Come on, let's get to the office and find out!"

* * *

Jensyn had trouble keeping pace with Jonathan's fast clip. The evening was warm, and by the time they arrived back at the building they had soaked through their T-shirts. He didn't want to waste time to shower and change downstairs, and headed instead for the elevator banks.

"You're a genius, Chandler." On the eleventh floor the two of them jogged down the hallway to his office suite. Save for a few late workers, the place was deserted, most doors closed and locked for the evening.

"Looks like we have to go back down to the gym to get our keys," she said. "I want to shower anyway."

"Hold on." Jonathan reversed course down the hall to the sound of vacuuming. In a minute he was back with the night's janitor in tow, a kindly man with graying hair and a generous beer belly.

"What's that you're doing, Mr. Sands? Jogging in the hallways?"

"That's right, Chet. Great exercise."

"Left your keys inside?"

"Yeah, I thought they'd be safer in there." Chester opened the door to the anteroom. "And my office too, if you don't mind," requested Sands.

The man complied.

"Thanks, Chet, I'll remember this."

"No problem, Mr. Sands. You need anything else, you just holler. And keys ain't no good behind the lock, you should know that."

Jonathan turned on the lights and hurried over to his set of file cabinets.

Jensyn passed a frown at him. "You're so bad. He thought you were serious."

"Chester and I go way back. He thinks I'm funny."

"You're a bloody riot."

In a moment Jonathan was cradling Royce's report to his desk.

"What do you want me to do?" Jensyn asked.

"Do you know where they keep the back copies of *The Wall Street Journal* down in the library?"

"Yeah, but ..." She made a gesture of turning a key in a lock.

Jonathan handed her his keyring, indicating the master key and she took off. Returning to his chair and donning his reading glasses, he pored through a file he removed from a stack. His eyes came up and caught hers over his lenses: "The day Decker issued the press release was October nineteenth. Could you check their share prices a few days before and after that date? Schoen's ticker is SCHO and Drexel-Pace's is DXP."

She turned off towards the door. He noticed the sweat trail following the center of her gray T-shirt to the curves of her shorts. "Jen?" He got up and went to her. The reading glasses slid down his perspiring nose. "Thank you for the run today. Look, would you like to do it again tomorrow, before you leave for the week? Maybe we could head out to the Cape?"

She looked off uncomfortably. "I ... I can't."

"I thought you were leaving on Sunday."

"I am, but—"

"I understand."

"No, it's not that. It's just that I already have plans."

"Mockridge?"

She nodded. She held his eyes a moment and smiled uncomfortably. Then she took off for the library down the hall.

At his desk, Jonathan leafed through Royce's report, trying to re-familiarize himself with the legal issues involved. Emphasis was given to recent cases whose findings went against the defendant on the basis of successor liability. *U.S. v. Distler.* It was the theory upon which Schoen's legal exposure seemed to be entirely dependent ... almost as if Royce was intentionally supporting the EPA's position on a seemingly weak argument. Why? It was dry stuff, Jonathan thought, and like taxes, he found the law to be arcane at times. He concluded there must be more behind Royce's rationale than his non-legal mind could appreciate.

Fifteen minutes later Jensyn returned with the share price information. She pulled a chair up next to him. He pulled out a pad. "Okay," he said, "Schoen's stock price the day before Decker's announcement was thirty-four and a third. The day after, it closed at twenty-nine." He looked up at her. "That's a *huge* drop."

"I'll say."

Jonathan fingered through a stack of files on his desk and found the one he was looking for: *Schoen, 1992 10-Q's*. It took a moment to locate the item in the SEC filing he wanted. "There were approximately forty million shares outstanding at that time." Sands worked out the numbers on his calculator. "That's more than two hundred thirteen million dollars of lost market value!"

"For a fifty million dollar earnings charge? How can that be?"

Recalling an academic journal article he had read a while back, Jonathan came out with the only possibility that came to mind: "Overreaction to bad news, perhaps. It happens. Remember, Schoen's a relatively thinly traded stock, not held by institutions. Selling pressure probably came from socially-conscious investors who liked Schoen's environmental record. When that blew up in their faces, they jumped ship."

"From Drexel-Pace's standpoint don't you have to take two thirds of that since that's all they purchased?"

"You're right." He hit some more buttons on his calculator. With his calculation completed he turned to her. "That's still more than a hundred-forty-two million, nearly a hundred million more than their write-off."

"And the fifty-percent premium they paid over market for the stock?" she asked.

"Don't forget. That premium was based on the share price *after* Decker made his announcement. So what Drexel-Pace paid was actually much lower than what it would have been, a savings of an additional fifty percent." He did some more quick ciphering and looked up at her with an amazed look on his face. "Bottom line, after their assumption of the environmental liability, Drexel-Pace came out benefiting by more than a hundred-sixty-three million dollars."

Jensyn stood stunned. "This has more fish smell to it than even I thought. A new publicly-traded chemical company with a Greenpeace seal announces its first Superfund liability and gets slaughtered. Then it gets gobbled up. Who could have masterminded such a thing?"

Jonathan nodded and wiped the last bit of perspiration from his forehead. "Unfortunately, it's all only circumstantial at this point. We have no proof."

Sands then summarized where they stood, quickly jotting some items on his yellow notepad. After rearranging the list with arrows and scratching out others, he delineated his thoughts aloud: "It means three things as far as I can see. First, I think it's time to have a talk with Everett Royce. He, Schoen and Anderson were all canned in that proxy vote. I can understand Schoen, of course, since he was the key dissenter with power. Anderson I don't know about, but Royce wrote the report." He turned to her. "Have you had a chance to look over those internal board minutes? The ones for the meeting about the merger proposal?"

"Yes, I have, and you're right. Schoen's comments were quite negative."

"But what about Royce and Anderson? Why would they have been targeted as well? Was there anything in the detailed transcription of the minutes to suggest they were a problem?"

"I can't remember." Jensyn brushed a strand of hair from her face. "No, wait, Royce is the lawyer, right? He made some comment about patents on that product I came across. Threonatrix. That's why I wanted to learn what it was."

"Really? Do you have a copy of those minutes in your office, or are they up in Manchester?"

"I keep them here. Shall I get them?"

"Yeah, in a moment. But let me go through the rest of my thinking first." Jensyn came to stand next to him as he checked off the first numbered item on his list. "Second," he resumed, "how would Decker have made out personally? If he was involved in conspiring the write-off, then there's a reason. And if I know him, it was financially motivated." He looked up at her. "Were there any compensation changes since that meeting? Bonus agreements? Stock options or appreciation rights?"

"He had a fair number of stock options," she answered, but then she shook her head. "They were awarded long before his loss announcement. I also looked into the SEC notices of insider trades around the announcement date. I didn't find anything."

"You did that already?"

"I've been busy."

He smiled at her. "Okay, then we have to look elsewhere." Jonathan circled Decker's name on his yellow pad. Something still bothered Sands about the compensation issue. He would have noticed if Decker had been written new options since they would have been mentioned in Schoen's proxy materials, submitted well before the shareholder meeting in April. But there was nothing.

In the interest of making progress, Jonathan checked off the second item on his list. "Finally, and to me, most important, why would Drexel-Pace want Schoen so badly? If a scheme really existed, why would they have wanted to run such a risk? It all has to hinge on the answer to that question."

Jensyn's response was almost immediate: "I'd bet it's all about those products they've been hiding away in Harare. And that scientist who was killed."

Jonathan tossed his pencil down. "You know what, Jen? I think you may be right."

"I'll go get those board minutes." Jensyn grabbed his master key again and quickly headed off out the door.

Jonathan picked up Royce's report and leafed through it again. The lawyer wrote it in support of Schoen's liability estimate but then he was canned. *Why?* What was more troubling to Sands, however, was the fact that Royce estimated fully half the loss as being Schoen's. Was it really because of deep pockets?

Jonathan doubted that.

He flipped to one of the appendices of the report where the other PRPs were listed, studying the six names again. None was familiar. Had Royce even talked to them? Nothing was mentioned in his report about such a meeting if it occurred. Why wouldn't he have interviewed the other PRPs to see where their defenses stood?

A few minutes later Jensyn returned with the internal board meeting record. "Here's where Royce made a comment." She pointed out the section to him. "It was the only one noted for the whole meeting, as far as I can see," she said.

Jonathan set Royce's report down on the corner of his desk, folded at the appendix, and grabbed the meeting minutes from her, reading the section she indicated. He was glad the board secretary recorded the identities of the discussants at the meeting. It was actually more of a transcription than a set of minutes, most likely taken directly from a tape recording. By contrast, board minutes made available for public consumption followed Robert's Rules of order, without identification of discussion participants.

"It says Royce questioned why Drexel-Pace didn't seek usage patents for Threonatrix instead of seeking to buy out the whole firm." Reading on for the reply to Royce's question, Jonathan paraphrased out loud: "Because usage patents aren't effective for pharmaceutical applications." He paused in thought. "So, more credibility to your theory, Jen. They were definitely interested in getting control of Threonatrix. Yet why not license the stuff? Companies do that all the time." He looked up at Jensyn who was still standing.

Her eyes were opened wide. Having lifted Royce's report from the corner of the Jonathan's desk she was staring at it, as if mesmerized.

"What is it?" he asked.

"Jonathan," she said, "you're not going to believe this, but I recognize one of the names on this PRP list!"

"What do you mean? You've been through those names before."

"Yes, but not since I was down in Atlanta. *Columbia Chemicals!*" Jensyn set the report down in front of him, her finger pointing. "Columbia Chemicals was one of the suppliers on their receiving reports. I know it was."

"But that wouldn't necessarily mean anything. It *is* a southern chemical company after all."

Pacing away from his desk, she said with her back to him: "Jon, all this time we've been looking at this PRP list from the standpoint of Schoen. We never considered it with respect to Drexel-Pace. Maybe there's something to that."

He nodded in thought. Both knew her statement was possibly relevant, yet neither knew how. He took off his reading glasses and rubbed his eyes. Then slowly he focused on her as she turned around, his eyes now also widening.

"It's a chemical company!" he shouted.

Turning fast to his computer he flipped it on. MM&P subscribed to Lexis-Nexis, an information search service that made pre-internet online queries over a phone modem.

"What?" she asked to his back.

"I'm just wondering if Columbia Chemicals is affiliated with Drexel-Pace."

"Of course it is. It's a supplier."

"No, not that. What if it's *more* than that?"

Jensyn Chandler stared at him, fomenting realization. "*A subsidiary?*" She came around his desk to his side. "Surely someone would have thought of looking into that. Royce or somebody."

"Why would they? We didn't. Not until now, and you've seen that PRP list only because of Royce's report. He apparently never even met with them."

"Well somebody would have just noticed it, I would think."

"You don't just notice that sort of thing, Jen. Not for a firm like Drexel-Pace. It probably has dozens, maybe hundreds, of subsidiaries. You have to look for it."

The computer monitor finally resolved its display and he logged on. Following the prompts he queried for the SEC's required listing of subsidiaries for Drexel-Pace. They waited. When the record finally came up he scrolled down through the names.

"You're right," she said, "there's a gazillion of them."

"Yes, a gazillion." He looked up at her with a smirk.

"Oh, shut up, " she said, swatting his shoulder.

Most of the subsidiaries carried the Drexel-Pace name in their title in some form or another—many of which were foreign. But, unfortunately, Columbia Chemicals was not among them.

"Sorry," she said, deflated.

Jonathan continued staring at the fruitless green display before shutting it off. "Oh, well, it was a worthy idea."

She folded her arms. "What were you thinking? I mean, if Columbia happened to be a subsidiary?"

"It's a bit too cloak and dagger anyway. Never mind."

"Look, it's late and I'm hungry. And you're right, it's a bit too skulldaggery."

"Skull*duggery*," he corrected. "Cloak and *dagger*. Skullduggery. "

"Whatever."

Jonathan looked at his watch. "By the time we shower and get out of here it'll be late. But I've got an idea." He got up and walked her to the door. "There's this clever little place just down the street."

"Really?" she smiled. "What is it?"

"Irish, I think, or maybe it's Scottish—I can never keep them straight—anyway, it has a novel kind of efficiency to it. Great deals and we'll get our meals in no time."

"A Scottish restaurant? I've never heard of such a thing. What's it called?"

He turned off the light.

"McDonald's."

Chapter Thirty-Four

SHORTLY after one in the afternoon, Everett Royce welcomed Jonathan Sands into his office. Royce had landed on his feet following the Schoen buyout and now worked for a corporate law firm in Syracuse, New York, specializing in patent law and intellectual property licensing. It was a meeting Sands arranged the previous day. From experience he knew there was no substitute for a face-to-face meeting when the subject matter was sensitive. And Jensyn couldn't do it because she was in Memphis for a week of professional development training.

The pair sat at a round table in the corner of Royce's office. "I've read the report you wrote for Schoen's executive board quite thoroughly," said Sands. He reached for the bound volume from his briefcase. "I have to say, however, that it raises several questions for me."

Royce played with his bowtie. "Serious enough questions to justify making the four-hour drive from Boston, Mr. Sands?"

Jonathan garnered a look from the lawyer that depicted implicit understanding of a subtler meaning. "Yes, Mr. Royce, serious enough questions for that."

"I was wondering, even hoping, it might come to this. In that case, I think your drive here won't have been a waste of your time." Royce batted his eyes and gestured at the report Jonathan held with a dismissive hand. "But you can put that away."

Surprised, Sands squinted curiously at the man. "Would you be willing to elaborate on that?"

"Jon—may I call you that?" Sands nodded and Royce continued: "Jon, you strike me as a candid person. I prefer not to put on airs myself."

The comment was at humorous variance with the way Royce was dressed: a yellow blazer, pink shirt, and a bowtie patterned after a child's finger-painting. But Jonathan was glad diplomatic probing wouldn't be necessary. He dispensed with his mentally rehearsed points of questioning. "I appreciate that, Everett."

The dome-headed lawyer leaned against his chair back and folded his arms across his chest. "I'll begin by telling you that the report you hold is a complete crock. Right up front I'll tell you that, because that's what it is."

Jonathan stared at the man dumbfounded. "But why? What would make you write something that seemingly makes the EPA's case against Schoen a log roll?"

"Well, let me back up a bit," Royce said as he patted a bit of his frizzy hair. "The issue of successor liability was a viable possibility, and I mentioned it early on to Decker as my only theory for the EPA's case against us. But the more I studied it, the more I came to the conclusion that it was a very weak argument. Even if the Mullins plant were found to be culpable, we—Schoen, that is—had a better than excellent chance of prevailing."

"On what theory?"

"On the theory of just cause." Royce took a pencil to his lip and explained. "Look, judges occasionally fall to the politically correct three-step of our times. What else would you expect in the environmental arena? Some of the precedents were decided more on the basis of judicial crusading than on a strict reading of the law, and some of the successor liability cases I relied on in that report were only straw men. Legit, but weak, in my opinion."

"Did you ever have discussions with the EPA about it?"

"I was about to."

"What do you mean?"

"What I mean is that I had scheduled meeting with them, but then I was informed that the Drexel-Pace lawyers were taking over the case."

"Taking it over? Really. By whom were you informed?" asked Sands.

"By Decker Moss."

"When was that?"

"Early last December."

Jonathan tried to place the date in the timeframe of the takeover. "So, way before the April change of board control."

Royce laughed. "Jonathan, there was no change of control in April. Control changed immediately in December, probably even before that. Moss was a puppet of those people right off. In fact, I'm sure he was responsible for Drexel-Pace's ability to make the takeover even possible. He gave them our shareholder records."

Sands nodded. "Cyrus Schoen suggested that as well."

"Ah, so you've had a meeting with him? Well, take his wise counsel. I can't give you tangible proof, but Drexel-Pace took advantage of Decker's access to our shareholder lists. There would be no way for them to make their bid by mail without them. I looked into it with our securities registrar. Not once, but twice Decker requested them. And guess *when* he requested them?"

New territory not discussed with Cyrus Schoen, Jonathan pondered the strategic times such lists would be most advantageous. Ultimately, it wasn't difficult. "Just before the tender offer was announced and just after the tender period expired."

"Exactly, within a couple of days for both," said Royce.

"So, you're saying you think Moss sold Schoen out? Worked with Drexel-Pace to see that the takeover was successful?"

"I don't think. I *know*. I just can't prove it."

Jonathan mused over the weighty dose of corroborating information. If true it would lead to serious action against Decker Moss ... assuming hard evidence could be obtained.

"And you know what else?" Royce added. "He told me Drexel-Pace was going to assume that liability."

"Yes, I know. They did assume it. We just got word."

"Just got word? No, Jon, Decker told me about that assumption last December as well."

"*December?*" said Sands.

"That's right. He told me he had already worked it out with them. He played like it was some goodwill gesture he arranged overnight, though I don't believe that for a second. The media release about that liability made it possible for Drexel-Pace to get the control level of shares they needed. There's no way Schoen's loyal stockholder base would have come unraveled so quickly without it. And then Drexel-Pace just sweeps the liability under their big imperial rug? Tell me you don't think that's a little too coincidental, too convenient."

Jonathan had always thought that. He just wasn't sure how. If Decker Moss knew about the liability assumption back in December, then that made Schoen's 1992 financial statements fraudulent. The loss provision had been signed off by his auditors when Decker knew full well that the liability didn't exist from his firm's standpoint. And the shareholders were harmed in the process. Jonathan leaned back in his chair. "I'd like to hear all you think happened, Everett."

The lawyer gathered himself to the edge of the table again, drawing some doodles on the pad in front of him. "As I said, when we first received word of the citation, I had a meeting with Moss and our chief financial officer. I was more than a little surprised the EPA would put us on the PRP list when the alleged dumping took place long before we ever owned the plant. I was aware of some of the successor liability cases, and I shared with Decker that it was the only legal theory I could see them justifying such action."

"Did he seem surprised about the citation?" Jonathan asked, "at that time?"

"Oh, yes, I would say he was at that time. Quite. But that was right before our board meeting with Drexel-Pace's team. When the vote went against further merger negotiations with them we had a special teleconference the following day to discuss our response. Decker suggested we go public immediately with the EPA notice and go heavy with our write-off as a defensive strategy. Despite my best efforts to argue against it, the rest of the board apparently liked his idea. They weren't only concerned about Drexel-Pace going forward with a hostile bid, they also wanted to ward off any interest by other potential bidders."

"A takeover frenzy." Jonathan spoke it as a matter-of-fact statement as he penned notes. Then he looked up. "So, you were against the merger?"

"No, actually I was pretty much for it and voted in favor of further negotiation in our board meeting. What I was opposed to was the *de facto* admission of liability by making such a media announcement. Later, in a board conference call, I said I thought what Moss did was stupid." Royce paused. "He didn't appreciate that."

"I bet."

"He's a bastard, I don't care. He can go to hell."

Sands directed an inquiring look at the man. Royce picked up on it and continued, drawing concentric circles on his yellow pad. "It's a private matter, but I was … blackmailed. Decker Moss somehow obtained information about me that was very private and very personal. He used it against me. He coerced me to write that report."

Jonathan stared down at the bound report in his hands, regarding its author with some pity. "Please know that I will maintain any confidence you desire, Everett."

"Thank you. I appreciate that. You don't need to know the details."

Sands probed a bit further. "Would this private information Decker had … would it also possibly explain why you were voted off the board by Drexel-Pace?"

"I suspect it does."

"Can you tell me why Decker would want you to write such a report?"

"Oh that's very easy for me to answer. He needed it to support his write-off. It was necessary for our auditors, Wilcox & Kline. You have to know I feel no pride in doing what I did. But I really had no choice."

"Which also explains you being so candid with me now?"

Everett Royce drifted with his eyes a bit. Decker Moss couldn't hurt him now, he thought. He was on an entirely new career path in an entirely different city; he had even shut down that private part of his life. And the motivations underlying his report, or the "professional" judgments they contained, could never be proved to be made in anything but good faith at the time.

Eventually Royce nodded. "I will trust you in how you handle this, Jon. He's a very cunning man, and if you choose to respond to my private information you'll have to obtain your own independent proof. I mean that because I'd never testify about the blackmail issue. But that said, I would like nothing more than to see you nail Decker Moss to a tree."

* * *

Springfield, Massachusetts

Sitting in his car in an evening downpour, in the parking lot of a strip mall outside Springfield, Massachusetts, he took a few moments for himself. His decision had been made. The nondescript setting belied the enormity of what he was about to do. The risk was huge—more than huge, based on what he knew about his adversary—but the leverage to be gained hopefully justified it. Circumstances now made it necessary.

He pulled a pair of latex gloves from his attaché case and drew them on. Then he extracted a sealed manila envelope he had prepared some days beforehand in the face of this possibility, reviewing its typed address one more time.

331

With final resolve he got out of the car and paced the few steps in the rain to the outgoing mail drop box. The postmarked point of origination couldn't possibly be traced back to him.

And with less than a moment's more hesitation, he let it fall.

The end game was on.

Chapter Thirty-Five

Wednesday, August 11, 1993
Nashville, Tennessee

"I have some more news on Schoen," Jonathan said when Jensyn answered the phone.

"Such a warm greeting."

"Sorry. I've tried calling a few times but you weren't in. You haven't found another partner down there to go running with, have you?" he asked.

"No, Jon, not a running partner, but an audit partner. He's fat and ugly, but filthy rich, much richer than you."

"A fat sack of dough, huh?"

She laughed. A slight echo played off the cinderblock walls of her dorm room. Attendees of the Marsh, Mason & Pratt professional development training center in Nashville lightheartedly referred to the accommodations as a "bed and head." It was a converted campus from a bankrupt women's college. She lay in the bunk, wearing a bathrobe and a towel wrapped around her drying hair. Festive noise from a cocktail party that had formed after dinner on the lawn could be heard through her pried window.

"So is the news about Schoen good or bad?"

"It's confirming," answered Sands. "I want to talk to you about it. Can I pick you up at the airport Sunday?" He knew she had taken a taxi when she left, and was returning Sunday afternoon. Her entire week following would be spent in Manchester for Schoen's onsite audit work.

"I …"

The uncomfortable silence was enough for him to know. "Mockridge?"

"I'm sorry. He asked me out last week for dinner. I only have the weekends, you know."

"Exactly."

"Though, to be honest, I'd rather—"

"Ah-ha! Then break it off."

"I can't do that!"

"Sure you can," rallied Sands. "Tell Iv that your boss requires you to work Sunday night, which if we talk business, you'll be doing."

"No way. If I break off a perfectly fine dinner date to go out with the likes of you, then it won't be business. Dinner becomes serious—your words, not mine. And I want you to tell me more about yourself. Not the old Middlebury stuff, I want the last twenty years stuff."

"I'll have to spike your drink first."

"Dinner and details, Mr. Sands. No Mickey Finns. You have one option, take it or leave it. And you better act fast before I reconsider this silly discussion."

"One option, huh?"

"Yes, take it or leave it. You'll not get another. And it better be a restaurant where you have to leave a tip."

Jonathan thought for a moment. "Then, I guess you just forced me to take it."

"Ask me decently."

"What do you mean, ask you decently? I just did."

"You did not. Ask me decently or I'm hanging up." Jensyn smiled as she listened to a muffled scratching over the line, which she took to be him switching the phone to his other ear.

He cleared his throat. "Jen, seriously, I've been thinking that it is time for me to tell you more. I trust you. You've become a very special friend through all this … if that's the word for it. I'm not sure dinner is the best place since what I have to say is hardly romantic. It certainly won't endear you to me. But would you, Sunday night?"

"Where?" she asked.

"The best restaurant in town."

"And where's that?"

"I have no idea, but I'll find out."

Jensyn's tone turned brighter. "What should I wear?"

How should I know? "Whatever it is, I'm sure you'll look lovely," he answered.

Jensyn turned over on her side. "What are you going to wear?"

He thought a moment about his competition. "Well, for one thing, I'll be wearing a heavy dollop of mousse."

* * *

OPTIONS

Dr. Graham Woods never had the privilege of visiting the States. What little he saw of it following his flight into Kennedy Airport and then the connecting flight into Atlanta was only fleeting. And, quite honestly, unimpressive. Heavy traffic made for the whole way into the city. After living more than a year in Harare he felt a bit overstimulated by the bustle of the western world. That and his jet lag caused a spotty night's sleep.

First thing in the morning, the three men making up Drexel-Pace's executive team strolled into the conference room where Woods sat waiting. His briefcase and a glass of water rested on the table in front of him. The room was set up with a projector for the slides Woods wanted to share with the men.

"Great to finally meet you, Doctor Woods," hailed Carpenter with an outstretched hand.

"Likewise, sir, truly an honor." Woods then shook the hand of the one standing at Carpenter's side. "Mr. Shaughnessy, wonderful to see you again."

The latter gestured to the man behind him. "This, Doctor Woods, is Joe Moran, our chief financial officer."

"A pleasure to meet you as well."

"Wholly mine," said the red-haired CFO.

The four gathered in their seats around the table. Following some gratuitous small talk about travel conditions and the like, Carpenter pointed at Woods's briefcase with his long bony finger: "I sure hope what you've carried around the globe with you is good news."

Woods veered a look to the tabletop and loosened his tie a bit. "Well, sir, for the most part we have happy news to report."

Carpenter wondered whom the other person or persons in the 'we' might refer to.

"There's been no change in the T-cell count data," comforted Woods. "In fact, those results are as strong as ever."

"You imply some other results?"

"That's correct, Mr. Carpenter. I've been doing some auxiliary research into a potential problem that surfaced while I was conducting blood sample tests."

"Then I think it's time for you to present us with your findings."

"Gladly." The doctor extracted a box of slides from his briefcase. Joe Moran hoisted his bulk out of the chair and turned on the projector. The screen was already down. As the first slide dropped into position, a convoluted image of blobs, blots, and diagrams appeared on the screen.

"Bottom line it for me, Doctor Woods," said Carpenter. "You're not going to be able to educate me with this crap."

"But, Larry, it looks like he worked hard on it," objected Moran, gesturing towards the screen.

"Quiet, Joe. I can see what I'm in for, and it's not happening." Carpenter turned to the scientist with a pointed eye. "Please continue, Doctor."

"It's called chromosomal translocation. Chromosomes break apart and rejoin, causing new genes to form at the splice points. Something in Schoen's peptide causes chromosome 16 to form an inverted translocation."

"I'm sorry, Doctor, but can you bottom line this somewhat further?"

"Certainly," the scientist said apologetically, though wondering how to do so. "HX413 is a small chain of amino acid derivatives. A synthetic peptide. It binds to a critical protein called GP 41, which is required in the transmission of HIV into the cytoplasm of the T-cell. That's why the drug works, because it closes the door to infection. The problem, however, is that it also seems to bind to a similar receptor which causes translocation, or inverse splicing to occur."

"Thanks, Doctor, that makes it all very clear to me." Carpenter turned to Kent Shaughnessy with an annoyed look.

Moran interjected. "I think the bottom line, Larry, is that there are adverse side effects associated with the drug."

Carpenter grimaced. "Dammit, Joe, do you really think I failed to gather that?" The CEO drew his head up to the standing South African scientist one more time, and said slowly but stoutly: "Doctor Woods, what specifically, but in very practical terms, does this translocation mean?"

Woods's eyes circuited his onlookers. Then he fixed an eye on Carpenter. "Leukemia," he said simply.

"*What?*"

"That's what the evidence seems to suggest. I can't tell you for certain with my limited equipment, but I strongly suspect a translocation in chromosome 16, which alters the work of a certain protein that is necessary in cellular blood control. I have a lot more research to do with far more sophisticated equipment than I have available to me before I can give you a more precise description of how, and why, it takes place. You can't simply view the causal influences of chromosomal translocation in a microscope."

"Have your subjects in Harare exhibited signs of Leukemia?"

Once again the man measured their looks before speaking. "Yes, sir, I'm afraid so. In fact, the leukemic symptoms were what first caught my attention. I can't give statistical significance levels due to my small sample size, but the incidence of acute lymphocytic leukemia is roughly two hundred times higher than the normal base rate."

"My God!" uttered Carpenter, his head frozen in his hands.

Moran also cocked a look of bewilderment. "*Two hundred times?*"

"That's correct. I need better equipment and more data over a longer time period to nail the rate down better than that, but we've got a double-edged sword here, that much seems for sure."

"So the culprit can't be isolated? The good from the bad?" Shaughnessy asked the question.

"My guess is that they're one and the same. Again, I can't be certain, but since we're dealing with a foreign peptide here, there are unlikely to be exogenous factors at play."

"Dammit, Doctor! Can you please speak English?"

Woods proffered a frown. "Sorry, Mr. Carpenter, I meant that HX413 is probably the reason for the side effect. No systematic outside influences or interactive effects that I can determine or think of."

"Thank you, sir, that's much better." Larry Carpenter stood up and paced the back wall of the room. "How about yourself, Doctor. Do you show any symptoms of Leukemia?" Carpenter knew that the scientist was also a guinea pig of sorts.

"No, my blood results are normal, and no other symptoms."

"In terms of real numbers, then, what are we talking about?" Carpenter asked. "Mathematically, two hundred times may still not be large in terms of absolute cases if the base is small, correct?"

"Well, yes sir, that's correct. The base rate is about one in ten thousand per year, and despite popular belief, it's about ten times more likely among adults than children. I have nine cases out of four-hundred-sixty ... all adults."

"Nine out of four-hundred-sixty? That's *nothing*!"

"Well, I agree, it doesn't sound like many, Mr. Carpenter, but …"

"And you can't even detect a statistical relationship, right?"

"No, the sample size is too small for statistical power."

"Statistical power, my ass," countered the CEO. "Nine out of four-hundred-sixty is nothing. Nothing but noise. And yet all of your subjects are showing no signs of AIDS, correct?"

The scientist didn't appreciate the chastisement he was feeling. "I'm only here to share with you my concern, that's all, Mr. Carpenter. You wanted to know, and I've given it to you. I'd like to give you more information, but the operation is small and the sample size is necessarily lacking. Yes, there is a one hundred percent success rate rectifying the HIV problem. But there appears to be an unequivocal side effect for a disproportionate number of patients. Use the data as you like."

Shaughnessy spoke up: "Larry, if I may make a suggestion?"

"Yes, Kent?"

Shaughnessy folded his hands atop the table. "Given the doctor's concerns that this may be more than a chance relationship, and given the fact that we could use more data on the various other strains of HIV for which our sample is lacking, it might be appropriate to move the operation into another locale. Zambia, perhaps."

There was a period of silence.

"No," enjoined Carpenter finally, reclaiming his seat. "We don't have a warehouse in Zambia, and there would be far too much time involved, too much risk and money wasted setting up a new lab."

"Then what about expanding our existing operation in Harare?" pursued Joe Moran. He looked alternately at Carpenter and Woods.

"I'm maxed out already," replied the scientist. "I don't see how I could do that with the limited resources I have. I'm also nervous word may be getting out. My hospice social workers are starting to get enquiries."

"Inquiries?" Carpenter came forward in his seat.

"The townships around Harare are densely populated," Woods explained. "You have to expect folks to ask questions when their neighbors and friends are rising out of their deathbeds. I'm just waiting for a knock on the door from the press."

OPTIONS

The executive team sat quiet in their emergent concerns. Shaughnessy broke the silence: "And don't forget, Larry, we may still have an auditor problem. We got that decoy lab set up, and we're supposed to get some visitors this afternoon. But if they're not convinced by our ploy, and if they continue to have any inkling that illegal shipments are going to Harare, they may just be buying plane tickets to pay our warehouse down there for a visit."

Carpenter laughed. "They'd never do that, are you kidding? No, Kent, it's up to you to close the loop on that question for them." The Drexel-Pace Chairman stood to his feet again and stretched his morning muscles in conclusion. "We stay in Harare for the time being. That's my decision. But, Doctor, I want you to immediately phase out of this sample and identify a new one, in completely different locations outside Harare. Farther out. Is that a possibility?"

Graham Woods thought the question through. "It'll take some logistical details to work out and some new people. But, yes, we should be able to do that." The scientist paused. "If possible, however, I would like to keep my current leukemic subjects for longitudinal study. And some more equipment. That is, if you don't mind."

"A reasonable request," concurred Carpenter. "Just maintain complete discretion. Don't spare any expense on this, Doctor. If you need further funding for more lab equipment, or whatever, Joe can take care of that for you."

* * *

Friday, August 13, 1993
Boston, Massachusetts

Late in the afternoon the next day, Jonathan's desk phone rang.

"Mr. Alan Pelleman out of the Atlanta office is on the line for you."

"Thanks, Dianne." Jonathan quickly depressed the lighted line. "Yes, Alan, thanks for getting back to me so quickly."

"Sure thing." The partner in charge of the Drexel-Pace audit had a pronounced accent, which while unmistakably southern, carried the enculturated tenor of polished timber. "It took a small bit of work, but I got the information you wanted. On your first question, we looked into the issue of Schoen's shipments. It turns out they're not being shipped anywhere but right here in Atlanta. D-P's doing shelf-life experimentation on some of Schoen's new products and they didn't want to utilize their regular R&D lab space for it. Top secret stuff, they said. So they leased some offsite space. They've done it before. I had a couple of our people check it out yesterday afternoon, and there's a healthy supply of Schoen's product there. They end up throwing out the spoiled goods."

"So that explains why the quantities are so large and go missing?" asked Sands.

"I'd say so. I guess unless it's kept refrigerated the stuff has a short shelf-life. They want to increase its longevity, hence their off-site experiments."

"Both Threonatrix and the peptide?"

"That's what they told me."

"Well, then, if you're satisfied, Alan, so am I," said Sands. "What about the compensation issue?"

"On that I have more interesting news. It's quite unusual, at least from my experience. But your question was a very good one. It turns out that Drexel-Pace has indeed awarded Decker Moss with incentive compensation. They wrote him some fairly unusual stock options."

"Stock options?" Sands tried to hide his surprise, knowing there was no mention about them in the proxy statement. "Is that so? What's so unusual about them?"

"They're not for Drexel-Pace shares. If they were, I would have known about that and told you earlier."

"Not for Drexel-Pace shares?"

"That's right," answered Pelleman. "The options were written for Schoen's shares. Shares they took in on the buyout."

Executive stock options for a firm's own shares were commonplace, Jonathan knew, even for executives of a subsidiary. But for a parent company to write options in the *subsidiary's shares* was something he had never heard of being done before.

Alan Pelleman expounded: "As I said, I would have had to know about them if they were in Drexel-Pace stock, since that's a required SEC disclosure for my client. But these? I wouldn't have even been aware they existed unless you asked."

"Are they significant in amount?"

"Quite. Over eight hundred thousand shares."

Jonathan exhaled under the receiver. "Eight hundred thousand? You're kidding."

"No, so I'd say you'd have to report them in Schoen's SEC filings. It's not an express requirement, but I certainly think it would be considered material compensation under section 12b-20. I'd do it to cover myself."

"Absolutely." Sands fidgeted a bit with the phone cord. "What are the exercise prices?"

"Only one strike price: twenty-nine a share, exercisable pro-ratably over three years, the first installment already vested."

Sands suppressed a reaction, knowing the exercise price was no coincidence—it was the closing price of Schoen's stock after Decker's news release. "Thank you, Alan. That's very helpful of you."

"No problem. I'll fax you a copy of the option agreement for your files." Pelleman paused a moment. "Everything else going okay up there?"

"Fine ... yes, fine," Jonathan replied as he scrounged around the top of his desk for the sheet of paper he had scribbled notes upon following his run with Jensyn. "Thanks again. I'm looking forward to our meeting next month."

"You wouldn't have a heart for the South, would you, Jon?"

"Is there an offer in that question?"

"Could be a very nice one. We could use your talent down here. Atlanta's where high-tech is happening these days, you know."

"Tell you what, I'll give it some thought." Sands paused before bringing up the next issue. "If you could do me one last favor, Alan ... would you also fax me the address of Drexel-Pace's warehouse in Harare, Zimbabwe?"

The request came as a surprise to Pelleman. "Sure, but why would you want that?"

"Just doing some routine FDA tracking reports. Sampling, that's all."

"Oh ... well, sure, Jon. I'll get that to you as well. How do you spell it?"

Jonathan did so and the men broke line just as he placed his hands on the sheet of yellow tablet paper he was looking for. He did some quick ciphering from the data.

The number of shares represented by Decker Moss's stock options came to approximately three percent of the buyout total. At current market price that came to ... *more than eleven and a half million dollars.*

Sands studied his calculations again, first awestruck, then entrenched in thought, now knowing at least two things:

Moss not only conspired to make the marriage with Drexel-Pace happen.

He also received a bountiful enough dowry to make the marriage worthwhile.

The remaining questions were whether the EPA write-off was contrived. And, if so, why Drexel-Pace wanted Schoen so badly ... badly enough to offer Decker Moss that kind of generous payoff.

Chapter Thirty-Six

OWING to a mechanical problem, Jensyn's late afternoon connection out of Philadelphia to Boston was delayed three hours. Unable to contact Jonathan about her situation, she went ahead and ate in the Philadelphia concourse. Now seeing him at Logan's security gate, she was happy to find he had maintained good spirits despite the long wait.

She, in turn, looked to him none the worse for wear. "So, you've snookered me for dinner," he said. "We're even,"

"No, we're not even. You've snookered me for ages. You still owe me big time."

Jonathan picked up her carry-on suit bag, now the second time doing so in as many weeks, and concluded she was an over-packer. "You know what, Jen, most hotels have a workout facility. You don't have to pack your weights."

"Oh, shut up."

As they walked the length of the terminal he asked: "So, how was your dinner?"

"A six-buck day-old ham sandwich in a crowded airport ... delightful."

"God's judgment for what you did to Iv. You shouldn't have done that, you know."

Jensyn smirked at him. "Sometimes your sardonic humor is a bit too much, do you know that?"

"Still, I bet you find me funny."

"I find you borderline tolerable ... a victim of your own demented off-hours personality." Jensyn squeezed his arm. "Did you eat?"

"No, of course not. I'm loyal to my commitments."

"Do you want to come over to my place? I know you like fast food."

"Fast food?"

"Tomato soup out of a can? With milk?"

343

Pulling his car out of the airport parking booth, Jonathan asked: "So, how was your week of professional development? Are you feeling more developed?"

"Boring mostly. We had some decent sessions on earnings management—you know, when companies play with their numbers just enough to make them look the way they want. There was a guy from the SEC who gave a talk about materiality, which was pretty interesting. He was actually funny."

"A funny guy from the SEC?" Jonathan chuckled at the contradiction of terms. "You've got to be kidding."

"Not really. Get me home and I'll show you."

"Huh?"

"Just drive on," she said.

In the tunnel beneath Boston Harbor Jensyn peered over at the speedometer. "You're going a bit fast, Mr. Sands."

He glanced down at his speed. "I am not."

"It's a thirty-five and you're doing forty-four," she said, challenging. "Slow down."

"So what? They're not going to stop me."

"But you're breaking the law."

He squinted at her. "So, you're a nag on top of everything else, Chandler?"

"No, you clot," she laughed. "I'm teaching you a lesson."

"Lesson? What lesson?"

"Materiality. How fast do you think you can go before you'll get pulled over?"

"Oh … I get it. Very clever, Jen. You're a fabulous teacher." He rolled his eyes and pushed in the cassette tape that rested in the player. Pachebel's Cannon came over the car's speakers.

Jensyn hit the eject button. "No, Jon, answer me. How much over the limit do you think you can go before getting pulled over?"

"I don't know," he said, "maybe ten miles an hour. Who knows?"

"So there you have it. That's your definition of materiality. You think the bobbies use the same definition, so you push them to their limit, based on your experience."

"Yeah, I guess so. Why? What *is* their limit?"

"I have no idea. But you have to know they get together in some room every so often and decide what it is. Pull them over if they do this or that."

Jonathan gave her a sidelong look. "So, the lesson you learned after a full week of CPE is not to go ten miles an hour over the speed limit."

"No. What I came out with is that clients will take advantage of our audit materiality threshold. You can't ignore the little things because the little things can add up to a big thing."

He reinserted the cassette, and after a moment she drowsed in the darkness. In the western part of the city, on a side street just a block away from her apartment building, Jonathan abruptly slowed down. "*Jen, that's it!*"

Her sleep reflex caused her leg to hit the glove box. "What?"

"Of course!" he exclaimed. "*Columbia Chemicals.* It's not material! That's why it wasn't listed."

"What are you talking about?" she asked, rubbing her knee.

Jonathan quickly made a U-turn, heading in the opposite direction. "It's the SEC rules. Drexel-Pace doesn't have to list all of their subsidiaries. Man, why didn't I think of this before?"

"Where are you going?" She wiped a bit of dribble from her lip.

"To the office." The tires squealed as he negotiated jarring turns. "It's a ten percent materiality rule. Subsidiaries that account for less than ten percent of sales or assets don't have to be individually listed in the SEC filings. Columbia Chemicals is way too small to be shown for a firm the size of Drexel-Pace!"

"You're taking us to the office for that? You don't even know if they're owned by them."

"That's why we're going, to find out." Jonathan ejected the cassette. "But so much of this thing would make more sense to me if they were."

The pair made the trip to the State Street parking garage in a fast clip. Once on their office floor, she followed his quick pace to the library. He unlocked the door and raced to the shelves.

"What are we looking for?" she asked him from behind.

"It's a directory called *Who Owns Whom.* Columbia Chemicals isn't publicly traded. If they're owned by another corporation, they'll be listed in it." He searched through the stacked titles.

Jensyn had never heard of the publication before, but gathered from its existence that tracking down corporate ownership was a trickier matter than she would have thought. A moment later he came out with it. She was wide awake now and took a seat across from him at the library table as he flicked through the alphabetical listings. His index finger drew down sequentially on the pages.

"*AHA!*" Jonathan shouted, slamming his palm down hard on the volume. "There, Ms. Skeptical, have a look for yourself!" He slid the book across the table, turning it around and pointing.

Any wariness she may have felt was now gone. There, listed with Columbia Chemicals, was its ultimate parent company: Drexel-Pace Pharmaceuticals.

"I can't believe nobody's picked up on this!"

"You can't, Jen? Even after all we've gone through ourselves as auditors when we have every reason for searching in the first place?" Jonathan leaned backward in his chair, drawing his arms behind the nape of his neck. "Publicly available information? Yes, all of it. Going after it and putting it all together? That's very different."

"So, what do you think it means?"

He came down in his chair again. "I don't *think*. I *know*. Columbia Chemicals was cited by the EPA early on. When the new drums were discovered, Drexel-Pace somehow made them look like they were Schoen's. More specifically, Mullins Chemical's. It's ingenious. Drexel-Pace knew the loss was going to be theirs anyway by virtue of their ownership of Columbia, and by linking the new evidence to Schoen, they not only made the buyout possible, they may have gotten out of the new tag altogether. With that successor liability crap."

"Crap? Royce's report made it sound like successor liability was a very real possibility."

"No, Jen, while you were gone I had a meeting with Royce. When I spoke to you on the phone, that's what I said I wanted to talk with you about."

Jonathan recounted the facts he had gathered from Everett Royce on his trip to Syracuse, including Decker's blackmail and knowledge of Drexel-Pace's assumption of the liability back in December. "I suspect the reason Drexel-Pace wanted to assume the liability from Schoen was to avoid any further probing by Royce that might have eventually tipped him off. And that's why they wanted Royce canned."

Jensyn stood up, marveling at the cunningness of the plot. "My God, we've got cloaks and daggers here after all."

She went to the window and pulled open the Venetian blinds. Looking outward at the lit reflection of Boston Harbor, she said:

"But it's all only circumstantial. Only hypothetical. We don't have any proof."

"I'm very aware of that. And now we're going to get it."

"Get it?" she asked turning around. "How?"

"You and I are going to take a trip."

"What? I can't take a trip. I'm way behind in Manchester."

"No, Jen, you're way ahead. We're going to corner Decker."

"Decker? This has nothing to do with Decker."

"Oh, yes it does. I'd bet my life on it. Royce said Decker was surprised about the initial EPA notice, but then he quickly changed his stripes on the thing. Royce thought Moss was working behind the scenes with Drexel-Pace to make the buyout happen." Jonathan filled her in on Everett Royce's suspicions concerning the shareholder records.

"But why?" Jensyn asked. "What would Decker have gained?"

"He gained a great deal. Decker has options amounting to over eight hundred thousand shares in Schoen's stock."

"No he doesn't. He only has—"

He cut her off. "Jen, remember how we looked into the possibility of new stock options being written around the time of the buyout? Well, we didn't find any because they arranged a very clever way of disguising them."

"Disguising them? *Who* did?"

"Drexel-Pace."

Jensyn stared at him confused. For several moments she held her expression, then alighted with realization. "Drexel-Pace wrote Decker options in *Schoen's* stock? That they obtained in the buyout?"

"That's right. I had Alan Pelleman look into it for me. They awarded Decker claim to three percent of the shares they took in. A fax of the option agreement is in my office. And guess—just guess—what the strike price is?"

She looked out the window again. It didn't take her long to answer as she came around. "Twenty-nine."

"You got it. The exercise price was set at the closing price the day of Decker's news release. Which means that upon Drexel-Pace's tender offer announcement my old college buddy became a millionaire—eleven times over."

"Eleven million?"

Sands nodded. "And now with the reversal of the write-off and the certain increase in their stock price, who knows how much more it'll be."

"I just don't believe it." She returned to the table and sat down. "I just can't believe nobody's caught onto this." Jensyn studied him a moment, still awestruck.

He, in turn, closed the directory and went to replace it on the shelf. "Where there's a lot of money there's a lot of brains. Not always scrupulous ones."

He turned around to her. "Repack your bags, Jen. We're heading for South Carolina."

Chapter Thirty-Seven

Tuesday, August 17, 1993
Columbia, South Carolina

THEIR two o'clock appointment with W. Scott Wolcott, President of Columbia Chemicals, was arranged by Jonathan Sands the previous day. Wolcott's name and number were in the *Who Owns Whom* directory, along with the address of the firm. The corporate head sounded reticent on the phone, but when Jonathan informed him that it was only a meeting to gain some history about the Superfund site, and the relationships that existed among the other PRPs, Wolcott obliged.

"It sure gets hot down here in the summertime. How do you manage to stand it?" Jonathan asked. He was already sweating in his khaki suit despite the building's air conditioning. The temperature outside was approaching the century mark with shower room humidity.

"Oh, you get used to it." Wolcott spoke with a cotton-field twang. He was an oversized man in hard-worn sixties, with a bulbous red nose and tobacco-stained teeth. Lifting a bowl of mints from his desk, he said: "I'll take my summers over your winters anytime."

Jonathan declined but Jensyn fingered off a couple. "Yeah, but you can always add more layers in the winter," she said. "Once you hit skin down here there isn't any more to peel off."

The man appeared to unpeel her with lingering eyes and Jonathan quickly switched to point: "As I told you on the phone, Mr. Wolcott, we're doing the audit for Schoen. Although Drexel-Pace has assumed the Superfund liability for this year we have to review the previous years' numbers. I was hoping you might provide us information about the notifications you received, as well as any correspondence you exchanged with the other PRPs."

"Happy to." Wolcott grabbed a file that he had pulled out in preparation for the meeting, donned a pair of reading glasses, and took his visitors through the chronology of events surrounding the Camden site. It was a seamless version that held no surprises. When finished, Wolcott concluded by saying: "So, the dumping

349

preceded my time here by a good ten years. We didn't have the environmental requirements in the 60s and 70s we have now. Though, as you know, the EPA doesn't care a hoot about that."

"Have you had any meetings with the other PRPs?"

"Yes, of course we have, but they've been a fiasco. All Daisypatch folk. I can't imagine the feds ever getting anything out of them. Can't squeeze wine from collards."

Jonathan suspected the revenue base of Columbia Chemicals didn't exactly place it in the deep pockets region either, but he didn't press the point. "So, in your opinion, whatever the EPA is able to come out with, it will have to get from you? You and Drexel-Pace?"

"I reckon so. Not that it's fair."

"When did you become a subsidiary of Drexel-Pace?" asked Sands. He was interested in the man's reaction to the question.

But Wolcott returned nothing but a level response. "They bought us under one of their holding companies back in eighty-six. I came on in nineteen-ninety. We were, and continue to be, a supplier of some of their basic raw material needs. Nothing exotic."

Jonathan pushed for a reaction: "So does it surprise you that Schoen, one of the other seven members of the PRP group, just happened to be purchased recently by Drexel-Pace?"

Wolcott came forward to the edge of his desk. Jonathan glimpsed the man's interleaved fingers. But they showed only steadiness. "If it's one thing I've learned over the years, Mr. Sands, there ain't no surprises when it comes to surprises. The businessman who doesn't expect them gets caught with his pants down. As for the coincidence, I think it's unfortunate a fine company like Drexel-Pace has to clean up two other firms' messes that it had nothing to do with in the first place."

"So, you honestly don't think any of the remediation costs will be—or would have been, as of last year—covered by the other parties?"

"No, no way. Won't happen. My lawyers have done their work pretty thoroughly and there just isn't anything there. In fact, one of the trucking companies recently filed Chapter 11."

Jensyn, who had remained studiously silent thus far, came forward with a question of her own: "Mr. Wolcott, the barrels that were discovered subsequently—out away from the main site, and which bore the Mullins name—did you do any research into those yourself? Into their chemical contents, for example? Why they might have been in a different location from the rest?"

"No. I have no idea why their barrels would have turned up buried away from the others. The farmer's plot of land was a big one though. So why not?"

"How about their contents?" she probed further.

"Can't help you there. You'd have to ask the environmental folks about that."

Jensyn looked at Jonathan indicating she had no further questions. He in turn shook the man's hand. "Thank you very much for your time, Mr. Wolcott. We'll show ourselves out."

Exiting Wolcott's office into the anteroom, they passed his secretary, who was wearing the same warm smile she presented upon their arrival. "It was a pleasure to meet the two of you," she said. "I hope you can stop by again."

"Thank you, Mrs. Dahl," said Sands. "Perhaps we will." He opened the outer door for Jensyn to exit.

"If you see Mr. Carpenter please tell him I said hello."

Jonathan stopped at the doorway. He turned around. "Carpenter?" he asked the secretary.

"Yes," she said, slight confusion showing on her face. "Aren't you the auditors for Drexel-Pace?"

"No, we're working for another client."

"Oh, I'm sorry. When you told me you were auditors from Marsh, Mason & Pratt, I just figured ..."

"But you know Mr. Carpenter?"

"Well, yes, of course I do," she tilted, smiling. "He's Mr. Wolcott's brother-in-law."

Jonathan sensed Jensyn bristle at his side. "Is that so?" he asked, gesturing for Jensyn to reenter the office door. "I didn't know that. Does he come by here often?"

"Once or twice a year, I'd say. A wonderful man. Insists on taking all of us out to lunch whenever he comes to town."

"Now, I'd say that's a nice kind of guy to know." Jonathan came over to shake her hand. "Again, it's been wonderful to meet you."

The pair clamped shut the full distance to their rental car in the parking lot. When the doors were closed, before she could react, Jonathan said under his breath: "Just act completely natural, Jen. Don't say anything." He pulled out of the lot and headed out onto the highway. Peering into the rearview mirror and not seeing anything, he let out a heavy breath. "There was a guy in the lobby who looked interested in us."

Jensyn squeezed his forearm. "I noticed him, too. The guy with the scruffy beard?"

Jonathan nodded. He glanced up at the rearview mirror but didn't see a tail. "You have those directions?"

She pulled out a folded piece of paper from her purse.

"So do you see the significance of what we just discovered?" he asked.

"Of course I do. I'm not just a dull commoner you know. The collusion connection between Drexel-Pace and Columbia: Carpenter and Wolcott. Whoever discovered those additional drums would have contacted Columbia first, directly, instead of Drexel-Pace, or even the EPA." She paused. "I've always heard blood congeals tightly down here in the South."

"In that case, I want you to use that uncommon mind of yours and figure out how they managed to dupe the EPA."

"Okay, boss" she said with a smirk. "I'll get right to it."

* * *

The drive took slightly more than a half hour, which got them to the hazardous disposal facility outside Columbia a little before their two-thirty appointment with the EPA Remedial Project Manager. They sat out the excess minutes in their air-conditioned rental. A green-veiled security fence in front of them abutted a small white office building to their left. The fencing was capped with coiled razor wire. Jonathan gestured at it: "I'll bet you a thousand nice dinners our answer's just right in there." He squinted as he tapped the steering wheel with his fingers. "But it won't be obvious."

"Obvious? A thousand nice dinners with you would be a miracle." She paused. "Do you know what you're going to ask him?"

"Well, first I want to find out about the contents in those drums, whether they were the same for Mullins and Columbia. Second, I want to know how the Mullins drums were discovered in the first place. Third ... I have no idea."

"Great."

He glimpsed down at his watch. "Time."

They got out of the car and walked the few paces to the office. A clean-cut bespectacled man came out to greet them. "You must be Jonathan Sands."

"Yes, and this is Jensyn Chandler."

"Dan Lipsius," he said in introduction. "Nice to meet you." Extending a handshake to each, he then directed them to the doorway. "You said you were interested in the Camden site. The Mullins Chemical containers in particular?"

"That's right," Jonathan confirmed. "We're working on the Schoen Chemicals audit and wanted to see what we're dealing with." He had already stated the reason for his inquiry the day before over the phone.

"No problem." Lipsius led them through the building to the rear door, which provided access to the fenced-in yard. "The containers are right over this way." The man gestured weakly to their left.

The site stretched out across several acres that they could see, filled with thousands of stacked drums, barrels and tanks, all neatly arranged. Many were stored in large open concrete pits. "Are all these actually filled with chemicals?" asked Jensyn, wiping the humidity that was already beading on her face and forehead.

"Oh, no, not at all," said Lipsius. "Many have been packed. Their contents have either been reclaimed or incinerated."

Apparently the containers weren't "right over" anywhere, Jonathan was disappointed to find out. The three had already traveled a good hundred yards in the sweltering heat. "Just how does one prepare for your line of work, Dan? Do you have a science background?"

"No, nothing of the sort. I leave that to others. Actually, I was a Classics major at Clemson. A lot of good that's done me. But like most things, you learn from doing. I think of myself more as a ghostbuster than anything else."

"Ghostbuster?" Jensyn asked.

"You know, Bill Murray and Dan Akroyd?"

Jensyn's face returned a blank. Jonathan recovered for her: "She spent the eighties in London, Dan. It probably wasn't that big a thing over there."

The group finally came upon the area where the Camden drums were located. Lipsius pointed with his clipboard in hand: "Not much to look at, as you can see."

The two auditors looked out at the stacks of 55-gallon blue-colored drums. They stood two high and stretched down in long rows. All were dented and considerably rusted, some with gaping holes in their sides.

"Which of these are the Mullins drums?" asked Jonathan.

"Those two rows there." Lipsius directed to his left, referencing his clipboard notes. "There's just over a hundred of them."

"And these are Columbia's?" Jonathan asked, gesturing to the larger stack of identical-looking barrels nearby to their right.

"Yes, that's right. How'd you know?"

Sands didn't answer. He studied the sides of both, running his fingers along the rusted blue metal, noting their similarity. "They look very much alike."

"How were you able to determine which are Mullins's drums and which are Columbia's?" Jensyn inquired.

"I can see why you'd ask that, looking at them from the sides, but they were buried just about the same time. We identified their source from the markings on the lids."

"The lids? May I see?" asked Sands.

"Sure, there's a couple down here." The EPA man traveled the corridor separating the stacks of drums to the back and found two from either row that sat on their own. The auditors followed his leading and inspected the tops of the barrels he pointed to. "We kept these two out from the rest as samples."

Flakes of rust and patches of wear impaired a reading of the lids, but the names could still be made out, albeit with difficulty. The typeface of both was patterned in what reminded Jonathan of field military insignia, stenciled in inch-tall block letters. He drew his index finger over the names and compared the two.

MULL NS CH M. CO
C LUM IA   EM. CO.

"They look so much alike. Same abbreviations, same style." Jonathan surveyed the face of the drums and traced them with his fingers again. Then he walked the corridor back to its entryway, like one would travel the paths of a garden nursery. Chandler and Lipsius followed. "Would you mind showing us some from another site? Just for comparison?"

"Sure," the EPA manager accommodated. He walked them to several other specimens in the yard. The drums were red but also rusted, though not as severely.

Jonathan scrutinized the labeling on the lids. "These have numbers on them whereas the others don't. And these don't look to have removable lids." He turned back to Lipsius, question in his eyes.

"Some lids are removable, some aren't," answered the EPA manager. "Actually, at the time your drums were buried there was no requirement to even put the manufacturer's name on the barrels. But once they got serious about chemical wastes it became law to label the lids with company names and manifest document numbers, as well as an identification of the chemicals inside."

"When did that become law?" asked Sands.

"In South Carolina? Seventy-nine, I believe."

Jonathan turned around and gestured toward the rows of containers from the Camden site. "And their contents? Were you able to ascertain what they carried?"

"Well, from the groundwater tests there were over two hundred organic chemicals, many of which couldn't be identified."

"What about the drums themselves?" persisted Sands. "The nature of the chemicals contained in each?"

Lipsius referred to his clipboard. "The soil was contaminated with organic and phenolic compounds: chlorobenzene, creosote, dichloroethane, halides, naphthalene, toluene, vinyl chloride, and xylene. Soil concentrations were highest for naphthalene."

"No, Dan, I mean inside the drums themselves. Did you sample their contents?"

"Oh, no, I'm sorry, Jonathan, we couldn't. By the time of our excavation the chemicals had long earlier either seeped out or had solidified at their bottoms into the substance of tar. They'd been exposed to underground conditions for too many years."

"I see. So, there's no way to tell whether the contents of the two companies' drums were similar?"

"I don't have that information. But I would think that it would be on my report if the content analysis had been able to determine that." The man appeared apologetic. "I can look into your question further if you like."

"Thank you. I'd like to see if that's possible."

Jensyn wanted to know more about the financial issues surrounding the Camden site. "The EPA estimated the cleanup costs to run between seventy-five and a hundred million. Could you explain why it's so high?"

"Have you read the ROD?" the EPA man asked.

Jensyn shook her head. Jonathan also responded in the negative: "We haven't yet, but we will." They knew Lipsius spoke in reference to the EPA's Record of Decision, which was the summary of the remedial investigation study.

"Well, if you've seen all you want to out here, let's head back inside and I'll go over the findings with you."

Jonathan and Jensyn were glad to get back into the air conditioned office. The supervisor of the facility was sitting at a government-issue metal desk along the back wall, currently on the phone. Dan Lipsius stepped over to a Formica-topped utility table in the corner where his briefcase rested, and from which he extracted a copy of the ROD. The three of them took seats on hard metal folding chairs.

Finding the summary he was looking for, Lipsius explained that the majority of the estimated costs were associated with constructing and operating the groundwater extraction and treatment system. "Unfortunately, the wastes couldn't have been buried in a worse location. Camden's got sandy soil, which is just east of the Piedmont divide. Another twenty miles west and we'd be dealing with heavy clay and granite, a very different situation. The aquifer in the Camden area flows rapidly and in a southerly direction, posing a serious threat to the potability of residential wells. Several nearby creek beds and streams likewise showed evidence of toxic discharge. We estimate the operating and maintenance costs of the pumps and treatment system to be approximately three million per year. Discounting that to present value gives you more than sixty million in today's dollars, just by itself."

"Dan," Jonathan said, "are you aware that Schoen booked a loss in its financial statements for its share of those costs?"

"No, I wasn't aware of that. I haven't had any talks with Schoen in months. My dealings have been with a legal team hired by Drexel-Pace." Lipsius returned Jonathan's question with an intrigued eye. "It's rare for a corporation to book a loss before a deal has been struck with the Agency, isn't it? How much was it for?"

"Fifty million."

"*What!*" the man ejaculated. "*Why?*"

"Under the theory of deep-pockets," Jonathan answered.

"Folks, there's no way on earth they would be saddled with that sum. The state and federal governments typically assume a significant portion of the costs, to say nothing of the other PRPs …" He shook his head. "I agree that the other PRPs may not be as financially viable, but that's just an incredibly high amount."

"And to be honest with you, that was our feeling as well." Jonathan turned to his cohort. "That's why we're here."

"But I thought you were Schoen's auditors."

"*Current* auditors," Jensyn clarified. "Schoen reported the loss provision last year when a different audit firm was on board. No negative reflection on them, mind you. They did the best they could with the information they were given."

Jonathan decided to push it further. "The other major PRP—Columbia Chemicals—have you dealt directly with them or with Drexel-Pace?"

"Why would I deal with Drexel-Pace for them? They own Schoen. Columbia's not their problem."

Jonathan caught Jensyn's eye with a lift of his brow.

"Mr. Lipsius," Jensyn continued warily, "how many years has Columbia been a PRP?"

"I believe the general notice letters went out early in nineteen-ninety. Why?"

She felt she had to gamble on her next question, and she did so measuredly: "Are you aware of whom it is that owns Columbia?"

Lipsius slid a bit uncomfortably in his chair, knowing there was more behind the question than the obvious. "The EPA takes the corporate boundaries of liability very seriously, Jensyn. We don't like to push financial responsibility upward unless the circumstances force us to. But, to answer your question truthfully, all I know is that Columbia is a private firm, held by a holding company … DP Holding something or other. I don't know who owns it."

Jonathan asked: "So, as a matter of principle the EPA doesn't like to pierce the corporate veil?" By law, corporations were regarded as distinct legal entities whose liabilities weren't passed onto their owners unless unusually dictated to do so by the courts.

"Not as a matter of practice. But it's always open for adjudication if it comes to that."

Then Jensyn straight-arrowed the EPA man: "Mr. Lipsius, the 'DP' in DP Holding stands for 'Drexel-Pace.'" She waited for the statement to have effect. "Drexel-Pace owns Columbia Chemicals. One hundred percent of it. They own both Columbia and Schoen."

Lipsius's expression alighted shock. "You're kidding."

"No, it's a fact," Jonathan affirmed. "It would have come to your attention in time no doubt, but the association of Drexel-Pace with two PRPs out of seven on the site is a significant one we felt should be brought to your attention, if you weren't aware of it."

"I appreciate that," was all the man said. He was stymied. He looked to be thinking about the matter for another several moments, and speculated finally: "And you think there may be a link between the drums found bearing the Columbia Chemicals name and those bearing the Mullins name?"

Jonathan nodded. "You can understand our interest in determining the answer to that question."

"Yes, I certainly can." Dan Lipsius stood up and paced a few steps across the tiled floor. Then he turned to the two auditors. "What's your thinking?"

"Well, I wouldn't phrase it so strongly as to say it's our thinking, but it does beg some questions for us. I'd like to know more about how the Mullins drums were discovered, who discovered them, and why they were found so far off from the main site."

"They were uncovered by an excavator, the one who did the site work for us. Apparently, he was digging for fill dirt when he came across them. We hadn't gotten that far out with our metal detection equipment, but in retrospect we should have. We have now. He called me up about a year ago to tell me of his discovery and I headed immediately out to the site."

"So, the excavator is an EPA employee?" asked Jensyn.

"Oh, no, not at all. Customarily, local contractors are hired to do the excavations. Actually, the PRPs are responsible for that phase of remediation pretty much entirely. We only supervise."

Jonathan took in the information with interest. "Are you saying the PRPs hire the excavation work themselves?"

"That's correct. It's standard practice."

"Which of the PRPs hired him?"

Lipsius now didn't want to answer, but knew he had to. "Columbia," he said reservedly.

Jonathan leaned back in his chair, simultaneously sighing and giving one of his furtive glances at Jensyn. "Really?" He couldn't believe a police force as powerful and significant as the EPA would have such a lapse in internal control as that. The dirty one hiring the digger to dig up the dirt? Then it occurred to him with blunt irony: *didn't the auditing profession do the same thing?*

"Would we be able to speak with the excavator about this?" Jensyn asked.

"A … no, unfortunately, you can't," replied the governmental man. He cleared his throat. "He's no longer with us."

Jonathan's expression was blank. Jensyn, however, had heard those words before.

Lipsius clarified: "The week he made his discovery he committed suicide."

* * *

"This has more skull and crossbones to it every minute," Jensyn said when they got back to their car.

Jonathan peered at her over the roof.

"Okay, what did I say wrong this time?" she asked.

"Right phrase, wrong context. 'Skull and crossbones' is for poison. 'Cloak and dagger' is for mystery, and 'skullduggery' is for cunning crimes. I think 'cloak and dagger' fits the bill for the drums, and 'skullduggery' probably holds for the excavator's death. 'Skull and crossbones' is the stuff in the ground." He looked over at the white office building. "But, you know what, Jen? Things do smell like fish."

She lip-rolled annoyance at him and got into the passenger side.

They drove northeast out of Columbia on I-20 toward Camden. It was a town Jensyn felt somewhat negative about even before visiting. Camden Town, north of London, was the location of her fiancé's fatal auto accident.

Before leaving the disposal facility they obtained the name of the excavator, Elwood Darby, and planned to find out what they could about him.

Fifteen minutes onto the interstate, Jonathan said: "Jen, don't be alarmed, but pull your visor down and check out your mirror."

She started to turn around and he grabbed her arm. "No, Jen, just look in your mirror."

She did.

"That gray Honda a few lengths back. It's the same one I thought might have been following us to the waste facility."

"You didn't say anything about us being followed."

"I wasn't certain. Now I think I am."

She perused the mirror. "How do you know? The one behind the lorry? It looks like an Accord. There's millions of them."

"Georgia plates puts that number down a little."

Jensyn studied the mirror again, trying to make out the driver as the car gained on them, but was unable to do so. "See what he does if you speed up," she said.

Jonathan accelerated and put some distance between them. By the time they took the exit for Camden the gray car was no longer in sight.

Chapter Thirty-Eight

Camden, South Carolina

APPARENTLY Camden, South Carolina, was a popular destination for summer tourists, featuring Revolutionary War landmarks and an equestrian museum. The town's motels were all full, save for only one they could find. At a little past five in the afternoon, Jonathan and Jensyn checked into the Camden Motor Inn, signing for the last two juxtaposed rooms available. "They're modest, but clean," said the proprietor.

To say that the rooms were "modest" was to put it charitably. Both had a lone double bed, hard as plywood, flanked by chipped Formica end tables that wore the char of careless cigarette smokers. The 70s-era orange shag carpets were matted like barn straw, sprayed hard to obliterate years of abusive odors.

"I guess this explains the vacancy," said Jonathan, attempting to turn the broken knob on Jensyn's air conditioner. He turned around. "Am I seeing right or does that TV actually have a coat hanger for an antenna?"

"You're seeing right." Jensyn threw her suit bag down on the bed as Jonathan eventually succeeded turning the knob.

"I don't like TV anyway do you?" she asked.

"No, except maybe for the Lotto pick and perhaps some good mud wrestling."

"I'm going to take a shower," she declared. "See you shortly."

In his own room, sitting at the foot of his bed, Jonathan removed his shoes and socks. He stared at a Chinese umbrella light that dangled from the ceiling. It was strafed with a polka-dot pattern of holes from a cigarette. Momentarily struggling to imagine why someone would want to do that, he panned the room, wondering how many other things had taken place in the space he didn't wish to think about.

He located the local telephone book in one of the bedside table drawers and leafed through its war-torn pages. *Darby*, he spoke to himself, loosening his tie. *Dabner, Danforth, ... Darby. There.* Three Darbys were listed, one of which was *E. Darby*.

He dialed it. As expected it was out of service.

Ringing the second, he listened until an answering machine eventually clicked on. The recorded greeting was in a Dixie drawl that reminded him of a *Hee Haw* character.

"Hello, my name is Jonathan Sands," he spoke into the recording, "from the CPA firm Marsh, Mason & Pratt in Boston. I'm in town doing some work that concerns Elwood Darby's affairs prior to his passing. If you know him, or could help me find any of his kin, I would be very grateful." Jonathan looked down at the phone for the number and recited it.

He hated answering machines, always second-guessing his performance. But then he thought of the likely audience and comforted.

The third number also rang to a recording device, and he repeated his message, hoping to hear back from one or both. If not, he would visit the town's police station in the morning.

Several minutes later there was a knock on the door. Jensyn's hair wasn't quite dried but she looked sporty, wearing an untucked dark blue sleeveless blouse and white cotton pants.

"I want to wait a bit before heading out to dinner," Jonathan said, "just in case any of my calls are returned."

Jensyn took a seat on the bed while he walked off to clean up. The bathroom door was warped and didn't seat properly. When he eventually exited after a bit of a struggle with the door, he spied the room again, focusing on a large gaudy mirror hanging on the wall. Walking over to it he peered behind.

"What are you doing?" she asked.

"You can't be too careful about these places. They have peep holes."

"Oh stop it. Whoever might be looking would be mighty disappointed anyway."

The phone rang.

Jonathan looked at his watch. It was a few minutes past six.

"Hello?" he answered.

"Yas'r. Name's Murray Darby. You the one who called?"

"Yes, thank you for returning my call." Jonathan sat down on the side of the bed. "Are you any relation to Elwood Darby?"

"Yas'r, his brother. How can I halp you with?"

Jonathan placed his hand over the mouthpiece and smiled over at Jensyn. "Thank you, Murray. I was hoping I might be able to ask if you could help me piece together some things about Elwood's business just before he … passed away."

"Wazzat? Ain't know nothin' 'bout it."

"Would he have any records of what he was doing at the time before he died?"

There was a moment's pause. "Don't know of none. He got a place out on 97 ain't sold yet. Town keeps pestern' me 'bout taxes. Damned if'n I'm gonna' pay El's tax bill. Think they'd leave me alone 'bout a dead man's tax bill."

"Sorry to hear that, Mr. Darby. You say Route 97?"

"Yas'm. Near the railroad."

"Would it be an inconvenience for you to show me?"

The man spewed a string of curses. Jonathan pulled the phone from his ear and back again. "I could make it worth your while, Mr. Darby."

"Wazzat? You think there's anythin' out Elwood's place ya wanna look at?"

"Not necessarily, sir. I was just hoping to see if maybe I could figure out what your brother was doing before he died."

"Workin' some Sup'fund site. Hated the place. Said he's gonna die a cancer breathin' it. Don't know why, though. Elwood smoke cat shit if he had to."

Jonathan felt a culture chasm in the exchange. "Tell you what, Mr. Darby. I'll pay you fifty bucks if you show me the place."

There was another string of epithets. "Wazzat your name was?"

"Jonathan Sands."

"Soun' like a Yankee."

"I'm from the North, but I'm no Yankee. I'm actually an Atlanta Braves fan." Jonathan looked down at Jensyn, who had lain down on the bed and was beginning to look a bit impatient with the exchange.

The comment drew the first hopeful response from the Southerner. "Tell you what. You come by here'n pick up the keys."

"Thank you very much."

"But it'll cost you seventy-five."

Jonathan rolled his eyes. "Okay, Mr. Darby. Seventy-five."

* * *

A little past seven, with keys and directions in hand, Jonathan pulled into the gravel driveway of what had once been Elwood Darby's home.

"This is so sad," Jensyn remarked, staring at the place. "How could anybody have lived here?"

They sat in the car for a moment, looking at the tall overgrowth of weeds, the junk in the front yard, the decrepit trailer. "I doubt the man actually lived like this," Jonathan said. "It was probably a very beautiful place when he was alive."

Jensyn frowned at him and exited the car.

On entering the mobile home Jonathan's best guess was that there was probably a large animal that had somehow gotten inside, trashed it, and then died. Jensyn held her nose as she followed Jonathan through the rooms, thinking of the better uses of his seventy-five bucks. "What are we looking for?" she asked.

"I have no idea. Search around in the drawers and things. Receipts, journals … whatever might have a date on it."

"Was he killed in here? Because if he was, I'm going back outside."

"Jen, how should I know? We don't even know if he was killed. And I have no idea how or where it happened. We didn't ask."

"Hmph." Jensyn headed down the hallway.

The summer evening sun was still high enough to cast dim light through the torn curtained windows. She looked through the bedroom and bathroom areas while Jonathan focused on the living room and kitchen. Darby's brother told him there wasn't anything left of value in the place, the truth of which Jonathan gathered in just a few minutes of roaming. He understood now why Murray didn't want to join them. He also understood why he wasn't able to sell the property, probably hoping the town would snatch the problem out from his hands for the taxes in arrears.

"I can't stand the smell anymore; it's getting on my clothes. I'm going outside."

Jonathan followed Jensyn to the door, locked it, and then exited himself.

The heat of the day was finally dissipating. She wiped her brow and quickly headed to the car. "I *was* starved, and now I'm hoping to get my appetite back. Let's go."

He appraised her from behind, not helping to notice the callipygian curves of her snug-fitting white slacks. "Jen, we have to check the shed out back first. Come on." Jonathan turned the corner of the trailer before she had chance to object. Frustrated, she slammed the car door shut and followed him.

OPTIONS

The Quonset shed in back measured about twenty by forty, with an entranceway of large bi-fold wooden doors that was secured by a rusted padlock. After opening it with one of the keys given him, Jonathan wished he had a flashlight. He hit the light switch along the side doorjamb, but of course the electricity had been shut off. Thankfully, the rusted corrugated metal roof allowed a few holes of daylight, and a single soiled window along the back wall presented pale visibility along the rear half of the building.

The pair adjusted their vision to the shadows as they walked across the slab floor. The air smelled heavy of petroleum. Pieces of automotive junk and liquor bottles lined the perimeter of the shed; chains, ropes and pulleys hung from beams above. Any valuable tools and heavier equipment must have been removed and carted away long ago. In the back of the shed were a workbench and some old filing cabinets, toward which they headed.

Jonathan set about searching the file cabinets while Jensyn sauntered through the space, looking at the odds and ends about. She was conscious of her white slacks in the dank surroundings. She periodically checked the soles of her dockside shoes.

Each folder Jonathan extracted had to be taken over to the light of the back window to read. Darby apparently kept a file for everything and nothing. They started out more or less in alphabetical order, but as Jonathan leafed through them he soon concluded they were the work of a confused mind:

Anvil.

Anmals (sic). Wondering what on earth that could be, Jonathan found a receipt for a pig and a 1988 record of payment to a pound for the ransom of a dog.

Bank. It was a thick file of account statements and overdraft notices; Jonathan set it aside.

Camden. A number of files beginning with the Camden name, mostly businesses, but no records of the EPA site he was able to find.

Following the Cs, any semblance of alphabetical order disappeared altogether. *Tools-Car; Tools-Truck; Tools-Auto, Tools-House,* where "House" had been scratched out; *Armchair, Gravel, Fishing lisense* (sic); *Excavation Jobs.* The latter records were three files thick, and Jonathan leafed through the names of each of the customers, not finding the EPA site. *Gartner* (a welding job from the 70s).

And on it went. Nothing of relevance.

365

Jensyn sighed several times in boredom as he leafed through the mess. She headed to the back wall of the building where there was more junk … sheets of metal and plywood, vertically stacked. She began exploring the area.

Continuing at the file cabinet Jonathan found a file labeled simply 'P.' In it were some centerfold pictures, which Jonathan quickly stuffed back into the folder. 'P' might have also stood for something else. Then, in the bottom drawer he eventually found a file that caught his attention. Labeled *Sup Fund* in smudgy letters was a thick file that he took to the light of the back window. He fingered through the contents, copies of invoices marked "Paid." The last was dated June 30, 1992, for $1,957. Grabbing the *Bank* file he had set aside earlier Jonathan found the last bank statement. The deposit was made on July 3rd. His eye caught the final deposit on the statement. It was for $5,000, on July 5, the largest deposit he could find in any of the recent statements. Unlike the others there was no matching invoice for it, which he thought curious.

Although there were some other sundry items kept in the folder, nothing caught his eye, and he grabbed the next file folder behind it. Unlabeled and stiff, he opened it.

"Jonathan—"

"*No, Jen! Come here!*" he shouted, taking the manila file's contents to the window.

Jensyn wavered, holding up the stacked sheets of plywood where she stood.

He turned in her direction: "Jen, come and look at this!"

She ran over to him, letting the stack she held fall to the floor with a thud.

He pulled the two sheets of plastic from the file folder, which from their painted sides ripped a bit of paper along with them. He held them up to the window for light. The auditors stared in shocked wonder at the black paint-stained stencils.

There, held together in his hands, the two stenciled cutouts formed the words:

MULLINS CHEM. CO.

"My God, Jen. This is our proof right here!"

Jensyn pointed to the stack of plywood she had just let drop. "And I—"

Just then a sound came from their behind.

OPTIONS

Jonathan turned.

"You can hand those over to me, Mr. Sands."

* * *

The raspy voice carried ominously over the concrete floor of the garage. At the front entranceway was the silhouette of a large man. His arm was raised.

"Who are you?"

"Never mind who I am," came the acerbic voice. The backlight made the shadowed form appear spectral, and as he moved forward it became clear that he held a gun. With a silencer. Gesturing with a wave of his pistol, the man ordered: "Just hand those over to me and get outside."

Jensyn knew who he was. She recognized his unforgettable raspy voice.

Jonathan and Jensyn moved cautiously forward, and now with the better lighting both also recognized the scruffy bearded face—the one who was watching them as they left the Columbia Chemicals building. Seeing no alternative Jonathan surrendered the plastic stencils to the man, who immediately shot a blow to Jonathan's jaw with the flat side of his revolver. Grabbing Jensyn's arm he flung her toward the front of the shed and out the door. Sands went livid and charged him, drawing just short of the business end of the Glock as it met his eyes. "Unless you wish to die before you have to, Mr. Sands, I wouldn't do that. Now get outside."

Jonathan did as commanded, meeting Jensyn in front of their Caprice rental. She reached up to the blood that ran from Jonathan's lip.

"What a cute couple," the stranger snarled. "Now, give me your wallets."

Hesitantly, Jonathan lifted his from his hip pocket, veering his eyes side-to-side before surrendering it to the man. Other than for their rental, Jonathan saw no parked car in sight. Then he turned to Jensyn, who in turn gestured to the car. "Her purse is inside," said Sands.

The man opened the car door and fumbled around in Jensyn's purse while he held the gun on them. Extracting it he said to Sands: "Now, get in. You're going to drive this car. Your girlfriend here is going to ride with me in mine. You follow me, and if you try anything, believe me, I'll have a lot of fun with her before she dies. Do you understand?"

Jonathan held the bruiser's cold look. "If you touch her, I'll kill you."

The man pistol-whipped Jonathan again.

* * *

The abductor's gray Honda Accord was parked just down the gravel road, along the shoulder in a stand of pine trees. When he and Jensyn got in and drove off, Jonathan followed.

The car led for miles along a series of country roads, making seemingly random turns for remoter places. The horse farms and open fields surrounding Camden gave way increasingly to forested pine. The sun now sat low in the sky, casting oblique shadows on the road.

Jonathan fought his adrenaline, trying hard to think through his situation. He was certain of the man's intentions, in a location far from Darby's in order to hide a connection. Without wallets it would be made to look like a robbery. Jonathan knew he had precious little time, and his only advantage at the moment was that he was alone.

A weapon.

He glanced at the seats, front and back, but there was nothing but Jensyn's purse. His mind momentarily went to the trunk where he knew there would be a tire iron. But there was no way. He opened the glove box, seeing only the rental documents and registration materials.

Then he looked down at Jensyn's pocketbook again, feeling through it. Nothing felt remotely usable.

After fifteen minutes the Accord slowed. There was a long stretch of woods on either side with no houses in sight. The stranger nosed his car into a patch of clearing that abutted the shoulder, just enough space to get the two cars off the road. With one prepared hope, Jonathan pulled his car tight against the Honda's driver's side and turned off the engine. He looked over at the bearded man, who was mouthing obscenities at him, motioning for him to move his car over. Jonathan fumbled at the steering column. The man drew up his pistol.

"*No!*" Sands screamed, working fast at the ignition. His hand jerked and he came up with a frantic expression, holding half of a broken key from its yellow rental tag.

OPTIONS

The man rolled down his window, aiming the pistol directly at Jonathan's face.

"*I can't! It broke in my hand!*"

Frantically, Sands leaped out of the car and ran around to the Honda's passenger door, opening it. "*It just broke in my hand! I was nervous!*"

The bearded man clawed Jensyn's arm, pointing the gun at her head.

"*No! Please!*" Jonathan yelled again into the car.

"Get out! I can't wait to blow your boyfriend's head off."

Shuddering, Jensyn peered up at Jonathan through the doorway with tears streaming down her face. He stood sideways to her as he reached for her arm with his left hand. His other was in his coat pocket. Helping her to her feet he mouthed the words: "*Run as fast as you can into the woods.*"

She hesitated.

The man was now sliding over the transmission console with his gun pointed at the couple. "Move back," he growled with a curse.

Jonathan, wide-eyed, urgently repeated his pantomimed command to Jensyn: "*GO!*"

In a blur several things happened at once. Jensyn tore off around the rear of the two cars and the man was fast out the door. He pulled his pistol over the roof to aim at her sprinting figure, but Jonathan came down hard with a crashing blow to his arm against the rooftop. A wayward shot spit off. Simultaneously, Jonathan yanked the small aerosol can he was holding in his coat pocket and sprayed it into the man's eyes. Then he threw himself to the ground and rolled behind the protection of the open door and to the front end of the car. Screaming in pain, the man got off two rounds in his blindness, in the direction of the scuffling he heard. The shots blew out the passenger window and strafed the ground, missing Jonathan by just inches.

Without looking up or back, Sands rolled and scrambled to his feet, managing to scrape off in Jensyn's direction in a wild sprint into the trees.

She was a good distance in front of him and craned her head around.

"*No! Keep running!*" he screamed.

More spits of shots went off to their rear into the trees without mark. Seconds later they heard the car rev up and peel into reverse.

They plowed through the woods, trying to maintain their clip despite the dim light of the canopy. Fortunately, the pine stand was mature, with first row branches mostly at or above shoulder height.

The braking squeal of tires erupted loudly through the trees. Sands knew their frantic movement was probably still discernable from the road, though he couldn't know of the man's condition. Then there were more spits; the bullets whizzed just above them into the overhead branches.

The pair charged relentlessly forward, bending low, fueled by fear, cutting through what branches lay in their path. With little undergrowth, the fir needles lining the wooded floor cushioned their feet and muffled the sounds of their strides. But their lungs pumped strenuously, aching to draw in oxygen from the thick, humid air.

Twenty minutes later with little drop in pace they came to a break in the trees. It was lighter again. A creek bed stood before them, and on the other side was a tobacco field. They panted heavily.

"I've got to rest," Jensyn said hoarsely, bending at the waist to clutch her knees.

"No, we've got to keep going." Jonathan took off his blazer, wiped his face with it, and handed it to her.

"But where?"

"I don't know." He turned in both directions, then looked across the brook to the field. There had to be a farmhouse nearby. "How long does mace last?" he asked.

"I have no idea," she said, handing his blazer back to him. "I bought it years ago."

Jonathan thought on their situation some more. "Even if we were able to get to a phone and call the police, then what? We'd be stuck filling out reports all night and he'd probably pick up our trail again."

"Well we can't *walk* back to the motel."

"No we can't." Pondering further, he said: "We can't go back to the motel at all. He'll be looking for us to return."

"But our plane tickets are there!"

"I know, Jen." Jonathan stared down at the stream, knowing also that the man would probably be expecting them to show up at the airport. The blackish water was a good six feet across and probably just as deep. He thought of the presence of water moccasins. With little more evaluation, he concluded: "We're not flying home."

"What!"

"We have to get back to the car. He'll be on the roads looking for us, but he'd never expect us to go back there."

"With good reason. You broke the key in the ignition."

He looked at her. Her face was scratched and dirtied from the branches they had plowed through. "No I didn't." He reached into his pants pocket and pulled out a key with an impish grin.

Her eyes went wide. "But I saw you! The key was broken—"

"Caprice's have a separate trunk key. I worked at it while I was driving and threw the other half out the window." Gripping the key and then pocketing it again, he said: "It would be impossible to break a key in the ignition. But I've heard of it happening with GM trunk keys, which gave me the idea."

"You're amazing! And he won't think of that?"

"I'm gambling he won't, at least not until it's too late. Come on."

They turned back into the woods, progressing cautiously toward the road in the dim dusk shadows. Every few moments they stopped to listen for hints of their pursuer, but heard nothing. The shadows thickened as the evening's sky matured.

It took more than twice their ingress time before they finally came upon the road again. The night was now country black.

"Which way?" she whispered.

Jonathan looked off in both directions, clueless. He remembered the forested trees started about a half mile down the road before they pulled off. "Let's head this way first," he said, pointing right. "When you're right handed, you tend to lead with the right foot and head to the left. We probably did that in the woods without knowing it; more so on the way back walking out than when we ran in."

Jensyn submitted to his judgment, holding his hand nervously as he led the way along the country road. They monitored careful ears and eyes for approaching cars in either direction. Twice it happened and twice they jumped out of sight into the brush.

"There!" he said, pointing down the road.

Once at the car, they quickly turned back in the direction of town.

"I was sure it was all over for us," Jensyn said, nerves still overwhelming her voice.

"I did too." He grabbed hold of her hand. "You've got to admit, Chandler, hanging out with me isn't dull. With Iv you'd probably live a whole lifetime and not face real bullets."

"Very funny. Where are we headed?"

"To get some money."

She was glad to find her purse still sitting on the seat. Fishing through it she found the ten spot she kept tucked in a side pocket and handed it to him.

"Thanks, but we're going to need a lot more than that to get us back to Boston."

"What're you planning to do? Rob a petrol station?"

"I'm getting my money back." Jonathan turned to her with a devious squint. "Murray Darby sold me an unsatisfactory bill of goods."

He took comfort in the fact that the gas gauge on their rental still read three quarters full. Doing some quick mental calculations—assuming he was successful getting a refund from Darby—with Jensyn's ten, seventy-five bucks should be plenty for gas to make the trip. It might even leave a bit for food.

Then he soured at a thought: *I had the proof right in my hands.*

A moment later Jensyn said darkly: "I know who he is."

"Yeah, the guy who was staring at us back at the Columbia Chemical's building."

"No, I mean I know who he is. I recognized his voice." She turned to him. "His name's Slade. The security man from Drexel-Pace, the guy who called my hotel room in Atlanta. I'll never forget his creepy voice."

"Then that completely closes the loop. This is all Drexel-Pace's doing." In Jonathan's thinking there was still the off-chance that Columbia had been responsible.

"But how? How could they have exhumed and reburied drums to make them look like they had been there all those years?"

Jonathan looked askance at her. "Jen, really? I thought you knew."

"Knew what?"

"They didn't re-bury those drums. They left the drums right there where they were. They were Columbia Chemicals drums. The stencils—Darby just switched the lids."

She peered up at him. "Of course!"

As they got closer to town, Jensyn calmed down some and came out with a curious statement. "Before you head for Darby's place you first have to head for Darby's place."

"Huh?"

"You have to head back to Elwood Darby's place. There's something there you're going to want to take back home with you."

"What are you talking about?"

"Just drive, you'll see."

* * *

It was eerie on return, yet Jensyn strode brazenly back to the shed in the rear with Jonathan trailing behind. He had pulled the car around to the side of the trailer, leaving its headlights on in front of the building for lighting. The doors were still open.

"Wait out here," she said, "I want to surprise you."

He couldn't imagine what she was talking about. He stood watchful, staring back at the gravel road, listening for traffic. Moments later she exited clutching a large piece of plywood, roughly four-feet square.

"Check this out." When she turned it around in the headlights, what displayed was the most spectacular sight he could imagine— Elwood Darby's thousand stenciled attempts to get it right:

MULLINS CHEM. CO.

Chapter Thirty-Nine

JONATHAN drove through the night, stopping only once for gas and a large cup of coffee. He had the radio tuned to an all-night talk radio station to try to stay awake. Jensyn slept, alternating her position every so often between his shoulder and the passenger door, using his sports coat as a pillow.

He smiled to himself as the episode at Murray Darby's place replayed in his mind. They had secreted their car off the road a way from his bungalow, and upon returning the keys to the man, were invited inside. Murray—who lived alone far out from town, and had been deep into the bottle by the time they arrived—seemed to undergo a liquefied personality change. Jensyn cleaned herself up while Darby put ice in a towel for Jonathan's bruised face, with no question of its making, and then challenged Jonathan to a game of checkers.

"Tell you what," Sands had suggested, "let's make this interesting. If I win you give me back my seventy-five bucks, but I'll buy you two tickets to a Red Sox game and pay for your airfare and lodging for three nights in downtown Boston. If you win you still have to give me back my seventy-five bucks, but I'll buy you two tickets to a Red Sox game and pay for your airfare and lodging for three nights in downtown Boston."

"Wazzat?" The liquored man was understandably confused.

"Dead serious. You've never been up north, have you, Mr. Darby?"

"Ain't never had no thought ever gettin' up there. Why for?"

"Good looking women up there, that's why."

Darby seemed to study Jensyn a moment and Jonathan said, "They all look as nice as Jensyn in Boston, Mr. Darby. And you'd love their accents, too. Nice city. Nice people. Bostoners are such friendly and easygoing folk. You'd have a lot of fun." Jonathan felt a pang of guilt about having to lie about New England cordiality.

The ruddy Southerner stared at Jonathan a moment as if he was screwy. "You got yourself a bet, mister."

Presently Jonathan's eyes were getting heavy, and he caught himself swerving a couple times on the interstate. The dash clock read *7:21*. He reached over to pinch Jensyn's leg. "Hey, can you spell me for a while or do you want to die?"

She pulled herself out of a fog and wiped her lip. "I wish we could stop. I just want to crash."

"Oh we can do that. Unless you pull your weight around here we're going to have a doozie."

She grabbed his tepid cup of coffee from the holder and slurped a swig. "Okay, Mister Feebly-Weebly, pull aside and let me take over." She smiled at him. "Thanks for letting me sleep."

They got off at the next exit, which was just north of Baltimore. He refilled the tank and counted his money. Forty-three bucks. Not that it mattered but he let Darby win the checker game.

"We should probably eat before we hit the New Jersey Turnpike. Are you hungry?"

"Starved," she answered. "I have been since last night."

It occurred to him she had once again been let down on a promised dinner date. "I'm sorry, Jen."

"It's okay. I'm used to either no or third-rate fare with you."

* * *

Inevitably, McDonalds was the only open restaurant at the exit. Jensyn carped some about it but consented out of necessity. They sat at a table in the back.

She gently touched the bruises on his lip and jaw. "It doesn't look good. Does it hurt?"

"Some. Do I look like a thug?"

"Yep, and kinda sexy."

"You're a sick woman, Jen."

She attended to her Egg McMuffin. Which she actually seemed to enjoy. "What are we going to do now?" she asked.

"About what specifically?"

"About all our evidence."

Sands drifted in silence a moment between bites of his sandwich. The salt of the bacon stung his lip. "I think it's time for me to have a talk with Decker."

"Blackmail?"

"No, graymail. Strong-armed negotiation with maybe a little intimidation thrown in." He chomped from his side-order of hash browns.

"And what do you hope for?" Jensyn asked skeptically.

That was the multi-million-dollar question. "He has a fortune at stake, Jen. I could turn over all my evidence right now to the Justice Department and all of that would be wiped out. They'd undo the takeover in a second if they knew what we know." Jonathan carefully wiped his bruised mouth with a napkin.

"But even if Decker does know more about that night—even if he was responsible for Karen's disappearance—I can't understand what makes you think you could get it out of him. From your standpoint, isn't the truth whatever he says it is?"

Jonathan regarded her a moment. Eventually, he said: "Have you ever heard of 'game theory,' Jen?"

"Game theory?" She asked, shaking her head. "No."

"How about the 'prisoner's dilemma'?"

"I've heard of it, but I couldn't tell you what it is."

"When two accomplices to a crime are kept in separate cells, both of which know the truth, but neither knowing what the other might share with their interrogator ... in order to get a reduced charge, can you see how the interrogator can use that as leverage to get to a fuller picture of what actually happened?"

Jensyn nodded. "But you said you don't know the truth."

"Well, no, I don't. But that's what makes it a game. Suppose I know some things Decker is unaware I know, key things, and I'm also the interrogator. Suppose further that my leverage is eleven million bucks, which he only gets to keep if his story completely fits with certain details I know. What would you do if you were him?"

"Jon, you can't let him keep that money!"

"Did I say that? He only has to think there's no other way I'd let him keep it."

Jensyn shook her head in frustration. "This is too much. Why would he think you would let him keep it? No way."

"Jensyn, I'm going to ask you something very important. I'm going to ask for you to trust me ... trust that I know what I'm doing." He drank down the last of his orange juice.

She eventually nodded and he continued. "Gaming is all about probabilities. I've got a lot more of those on my side now than I've ever had before. Unfortunately, I'm only going to get one throw of the dice, and if it doesn't go my way you could be an accessory-after-the-fact. That is, if I tell you anything more."

OPTIONS

The sleepless headache she was feeling caused her to take her fingers to her temples. "My God, how can I possibly know what to think? If it weren't for the fact you've been right about so many things up to this point, I'd just tell you to blow off."

"Thanks a lot."

Jensyn studied him a moment. "So, where do you place your odds?"

He turned and looked out the window. "At best?"

"Yeah, at best."

He turned back to her. "Fifty-fifty."

"Great."

Reacting to his defeated look she reached for his hand, staring him fully in the eyes. "You don't have to tell me anything more, Jon. I trust you. I always have. Probably more than you trust yourself."

It was a quixotic statement, yet also welcomed at the moment. Little else could make him feel as secure about what he had already decided to do.

* * *

Having unloaded his drowsiness at the exit, Jonathan declined Jensyn's offer to drive. He knew she didn't really want to anyway.

They covered a small piece of Delaware before crossing into New Jersey and then headed north on the NJ Turnpike. "I'm sure you're aware their hunt isn't going to just stop now that we're out of South Carolina," Jonathan said. "They're serious."

"Oh, really?"

Ignoring her sarcasm, he said: "Slade will surely be coming after us."

As they drove, her face froze in realization: "We can't go home!"

"No, we can't. At least not for long."

"Then where? We don't have any money!"

"I'm sure I have a credit card or two at my house. How about you?"

"No, I don't," she said, "every one I get in the mail I scissor up. The only card I have is in my wallet, and Slade now has that."

He glanced at her. "But your passport's at your apartment I hope."

"Yeah, why?"

"You have to get it. And you have to pack again for another trip." He paused. "After my little talk with Decker, we're heading for the dark continent."

"Are you crazy! We can't go there!"

"We have no choice, Jen. I've been thinking it through and we have no alternative. We have to know what's going on in Harare."

"So, we just get others to look into it for us," she exclaimed.

"We don't have people down there. MM&Ps closest office is in Johannesburg, maybe 700 miles away. Even so, what do we say, 'Please send an audit team to Zimbabwe to snoop around for us? We smell fish.'"

Jensyn turned toward the window. "What about the FBI? CIA? I don't know. Interpol? There's got to be someone!"

"No way. Not Africa. Not based on what we have. And even if we could involve others in an official capacity somehow, in the time it would take us to do that, Drexel-Pace will be long gone. You know what the governments are probably like down there." Then, with soft finality: "No, Jen, I really see no option."

The inchoate thought travelled a logical path in her thinking. Given their situation, the urgency and timing, she eventually concluded he was right.

* * *

Columbia, South Carolina

Geoffrey Slade, head of Drexel-Pace security—a.k.a. 'representative,' a.k.a. 'street cleaner'—was a Vietnam vet who, in 1970, was court-marshaled and dishonorably discharged for striking his platoon leader in an argument over the handling of some civilian 'gooks.' His officially-documented breakdown painted a psyche as incendiary as the napalm dropped on the forested enemy. Subsequently declared rehabilitated, and following a failed stint in the Georgia state police academy, he was hired by Drexel-Pace for a security position. He rose through the thin ranks of the force, proving himself as faithful to his tasks and paycheck as a man could be. Although his superiors always suspected a blade or two remained loose on his fan, he was quite good at the darker crafts his position occasionally called for.

Presently his gravelly voice carried wrath over a pay phone as he recounted recent events to Kent Shaughnessy. With little trouble breaking into the auditors' motel rooms at the Camden Motor Inn, he spent a long night waiting for the pair to return.

"This is a major setback," said Shaughnessy.

"You think I don't know that?" Slade took a heavy draw on his filterless cigarette. "I'm going to kill them. Just give me one more chance and I'll gut out their entrails."

Shaughnessy grimaced at Slade's word picture. "What could they know at this point?"

"Serious suspicions, that's for sure. Especially now. I don't think they have any physical evidence, but they certainly have a strong story they can tell."

"And they left everything at the motel, their airline tickets and everything?"

"That's what I said. They must be hunkering down here someplace or found a car somehow."

"There's no way they could have gotten out on that flight?" pursued Shaughnessy.

"No way. Without those tickets and their wallets they wouldn't have been able to board the plane."

"What about other flights? Last night, perhaps?"

"You're not listening," Slade shouted. "They don't have their fucking wallets. Besides, there were no flights out to Boston last night. I checked."

"Could they have gotten their car back?"

"No fuckin' way. The asshole broke his key in the ignition." Slade butted his cigarette against the metal phone booth counter and then ground it between his fingers.

During which Shaughnessy pondered his last statement. "That would be pretty tough to do, Slade. Breaking a key in the ignition? Are you sure?"

The representative squirmed in his shoes as he looked down at the thickness of his own car key. "Of course, I'm sure. I saw it broken in his hand. What do you think I am, some dumb ass?" He covered the mouthpiece and uttered some obscenities at himself, angered for not checking the car's ignition socket.

"Okay, but you know they'll be heading back up to Boston, one way or another."

"Of course I know that." The street cleaner hated being told the obvious. What he hated worse was being made a fool. And Sands had done just that.

"Then get to Boston, Slade," Shaughnessy commanded. "And, this time you better not screw up. Do you hear me? You screw up once again and it's over for you. And it better be clean as ice."

"Oh, it'll be ice, all right," Slade replied. But it was a reply dead to an already disconnected line.

* * *

Boston, Massachusetts

A little after one in the afternoon, they pulled into the driveway of his Beacon Hill townhouse. Jonathan's "flat," as Jensyn referred to it, was a three-story, two-bedroom brick townhouse northeast of Louisburg Square. Fortunately, his keypad security system didn't require keys, something she didn't even think about until they arrived. The residential area was peppered with moderate traffic. Just to be sure, they had circled the block a couple times in search of any sign of surveillance. None obvious.

"I'll be right out." Jonathan jumped out of the car and entered the front doorway.

In his absence, Jensyn's nerves rose to the surface of her arms like needle pricks. She climbed into the driver's seat of their rental and kept peering to her back for passersby. The tree-lined street was quiet. Jonathan assured her it would have been extremely unlikely for Slade to beat them into town since he would have had to catch an evening flight out. The fact Jonathan hadn't been able to find such a flight in the first place was the reason he originally booked their return travel for that morning.

Clutching his suit bag and briefcase, Jonathan exited the townhouse and ran along the fencing to the garage in back, a relative luxury for those living in the Beacon Hill area. After dumping his things into his car, he returned to the rental for the sheet of plywood in the backseat.

"Are you sure it will be safe here?" she asked.

"I'll put it up above the rafters in the garage."

Through the windshield she watched him do so. When he was done she reversed out of the driveway. He pulled his Mercedes out and followed her.

Jensyn's time inside her apartment was significantly longer. When she finally emerged from her apartment building she was carrying a suit bag and sizeable suitcase.

OPTIONS

"What are you doing?" he yelled. "You look like you've packed for a missionary tour."

"I didn't know how long we'd be gone." She threw her things into the back of Jonathan's car and trotted to the Caprice.

Following the return of their rental car to the airport depot—with due apologies for the lost trunk key—they headed north on I-93 toward Manchester.

Jonathan called Decker's office on his car cell phone to set up an appointment for the following morning. Although Moss wasn't in the office at the moment, his secretary was able to pencil Sands in for a half-hour block at 9:30.

Then he dialed his own secretary. Not wishing to risk using either of the two spare personal credit cards he retrieved from his house, he asked her to arrange purchasing two tickets in the firm's name to Harare, Zimbabwe, for departure the following day, if possible, with pickup at Logan airport. Obviously, she had to ask the question, to which he replied: "It's a business emergency Jensyn and I have to take care of, Dianne. Just tell anyone who has to know that we'll be out of town the next few days. Don't let anyone know where we are. I'll call in for my recorded messages. Reschedule my appointments. Can you do all that?"

"Of course, but—"

"I'll fill you in when I get back," he said, cutting her off. Fortunately, his personal secretary was a trusted hand, assigned to him six years earlier when he first made partner.

An hour later she called back to inform him their flight would leave Logan Airport at 6:00 a.m., the next morning, for Atlanta. From there they would catch a South African Airlines flight to Johannesburg, with a connection on to Harare. The tickets would be ready for pickup at the airline counter.

He had hoped to finally take Jensyn out to a decent dinner that night, but this time it was her turn: she declined due to fatigue. In the end, they took juxtaposed rooms at an economy motel and had Chinese takeout for dinner.

Chapter Forty

Thursday, August 19, 1993
Manchester, New Hampshire

MOSS greeted Sands in his customary convivial manner. "If I'd known you were in town I would've treated you out to breakfast. Why such a surprise visit, Jon?"

"Surprises don't come planned, Decker. Hope you don't mind."

"No, of course not. Have a seat." Moss studied Jonathan with curiosity and motioned for him to take one of the two cushioned chairs angled in front of his reception area's sofa. Before sitting down himself, Decker asked: "Like a cup of coffee?"

"No thanks. I've already had two this morning."

"Well, if you don't mind, I'd like another." Decker cracked open his office door to give his secretary the request. Returning, he slumped down in the opposing chair and exhaled a sigh. "It's been a crazy week. Starting Saturday, though, I'm finally on vacation." Decker narrowed his eyes. "What happened to your lip? A woman get you?"

Jonathan ignored the question. "Where are you headed for vacation?" he asked.

"Same place as always. Lake George."

"You still have your place in Lake George?" Jonathan knew he did.

"Of course. You don't let go of family treasures like that."

Sands surveyed the office and then looked hard at Moss. His stare held longer than was comfortable for his friend.

"What's the matter?"

"We have to talk, Decker."

"What is it?"

"I want you to tell me what's going on."

"Sorry, Jon, but I'm not following."

"Royce. Drexel-Pace. Columbia Chemicals. Threonatrix. I want to hear about all of it."

Decker tried with failure to gather the meaning of his sudden challenger, wondering how much he knew. "Royce? Columbia

Chemicals?" He threw his head to the side, taking in the question again. "What are you talking about?"

"Royce told me his report was a bunch of crap, a sham, that there was no real liability exposure to your firm."

Decker discomfited. "Sour grapes, Jon. He didn't make the vote. The guy has an axe to grind, what else can I say?"

"He told me you coerced him into writing that report."

"Coerced?" Decker laughed. "Sorry, but if there's any crap surrounding his report, that's it. His analysis is as tight as can be. The legal precedents he cited are very legit, and very warranted."

"You didn't blackmail him?" asked Sands.

"*Blackmail?* What on earth are you talking about? What could I possibly blackmail him with?"

"He didn't tell me."

"And I suppose he wouldn't testify about me blackmailing him either."

"No. It must have been some pretty sordid stuff you dug up on him."

"That's enough, Jon! I'll suffer a certain amount of abuse from you, as I have before, but no more outlandish accusations. I'm going to forget you said that."

Jonathan pushed forward. "I wouldn't forget it, Decker. I'll come back to that and tie it all together for you if you'd like."

"Yes, my friend," Moss replied with matching aggression. "I'd like that. Why don't you tie everything together for me right now?"

A knock parted the chill. Decker's secretary poked her head into the doorway.

"Come on in, Jean," said Moss.

She handed Decker his cup of coffee on a saucer. "You sure you don't want some coffee, Mr. Sands."

"No, that's fine, Jean. Thanks anyway."

She nodded politely. "Just let me know if you change your mind."

Jonathan acknowledged the offer with a nod. When she exited he rejoined with purpose: "I can see you're not going to liberate me with your version of events, so I'll give you mine. You just interrupt me if my description doesn't square with your version of the facts."

Decker took a brief sip, squinting, indicating acceptance with a lift of his cup, and a barely detectable nod of agreement.

"Drexel-Pace was able to buy Schoen on the heels of your Superfund loss announcement quite cheaply. In fact, as a result of your press release, they saved more than two hundred million dollars on that purchase. The numbers are of record."

"I don't challenge the numbers. They benefited from some good luck and fortuitous timing, that's all."

"Just listen to what I have to say and stop me if you disagree." Jonathan said, holding assertively. "The stock options you received on the success of that buyout are worth more than eleven million bucks."

Decker raised an appreciative eyebrow, yet remained silent.

"Yes, Decker, I know about your stock options. It took a little work, but I found out. Very clever. And before you think this is all only circumstantial let me continue with my story."

Decker set his cup down on the table and looked at his friend, waiting for him to resume.

"I just returned from South Carolina. I've got evidence of everything I'm about to tell you. And I think you know very well what happened." Jonathan explored Decker's eyes for a hint of betrayal. None showed. He knew Moss was always very good at the eye game.

Sands parlayed and bore home: "Camden was all a hoax. Schoen was never liable because Mullins never dumped those drums. The evidence was planted. The drums were actually Columbia Chemicals' from the beginning. And guess what, Decker? Columbia Chemicals just happens to be a wholly-owned subsidiary of Drexel-Pace, through one of its holding companies. When the excavator discovered the drums and told them of his find, he was bought off and switched the lids for some he fabricated with the Mullins's name. After the deed was done the excavator was murdered, made to look like a suicide."

Decker's expression intensified throughout as Jonathan's spoke. In the end, his look was completely wide-eyed. "I can't believe what you're saying."

"Oh, I think you can, Moss. I think you know all about it."

Decker shifted his gaze, peering off to the side.

"You *do* know, don't you, Decker?"

"No, Jon." He drew his head back, displaying disbelief. "I honestly don't. I had no idea. It's too incredible."

"And the brilliant part of your plan with Drexel-Pace is that the switch not only made it possible for them to purchase Schoen at a steal, it also very likely negates a large part of their own liability at the site."

"How's that?"

Is it really possible you don't know? "Come on, Moss."

"Jon, if you say you have proof, I believe you. But believe me, I had no knowledge of any of this."

The clueless expression on the face of his adversary presented Sands with far less than he had hoped for.

Moss repeated: "I swear, Jon. I had no idea about any of this Columbia stuff. I swear to you." He rubbed his face. "How did they negate the liability?"

"With the straw man of successor liability. Drexel-Pace was both very clever and very lucky in their choice of the Mullins plant. It happens to be in South Carolina, and they knew you purchased it back in the eighties, long after the dumping took place. They also know the EPA throws a wide net when naming PRPs. Of course Schoen would be listed. It was brilliant."

Sands let his points sink before continuing. "But Mullins's responsibility, even if it existed at all—which it didn't—wouldn't have likely been extended to Schoen. Royce backed his report only with case law that sides with the successor theory. But a far greater number of cases, more recent cases, have found against such a claim. Decisions that aren't inflamed with politically motivated findings of judges bent on turning the screws on corporations for fault that isn't theirs."

Moss lifted himself from his chair and sauntered over to his office window that looked off over the Merrimac River, stupefied. He appeared to stare out as one who had been duped. "So, by switching the drum lids, they took a real liability and framed my company, with the very likely outcome that I wouldn't be found liable at all in the end." Decker's words trailed in contemplation. He turned around. "I didn't know, Jon. I believe what you're telling me, but I honestly didn't know. How on earth did you find out all of this?"

"You happened to have hired the wrong man if you were hoping to play games with your numbers."

Moss laughed. "I'll admit to a little earnings management, Sands, but nothing like this."

"What *will* you admit to, Decker?" The question carried ominously across the room.

Decker Moss took his gaze back out his office window. "No, Jon, as your friend, I'll admit to you the amount and timing of my press release. But as your client I'll deny it publicly if you ever try to pin me on it."

"Nice." Jonathan looked down at his hands as if watching water slip through his fingers.

"Someone was actually murdered as a result of this?" asked Moss somberly.

"At least one person. Probably two ... almost four."

Moss whipped back. "Four? Who are you talking about?"

"Before I get to that part of the story, I want you to tell me about something else."

"What?"

Sands steadfastly held Moss's eye. After patience-straining long length he said simply: "Harare."

This time Jonathan noticed a very discernable twitch in Moss's expression, a clear reaction.

But Moss simply feigned ignorance. "Harare?"

"Yes, Decker. I know all about Harare," Jonathan bluffed. "I want to hear your side of it."

"My God, Sands. How the hell—?" Decker caught himself. "Why would you think I have anything to do with Africa?"

In that statement Jonathan was convinced of Decker's involvement. "So you know Harare is in Africa?"

"Well, of course it's in Africa, isn't it a ... Zambian city?"

"Your knowledge is suddenly much richer than your education, Decker. Isn't that a stretch?"

Moss sallied back to the sitting area, though still standing. "Look, Sands, enough of this fucking game you're playing. I don't know what the hell you're talking about."

"Suddenly Decker Moss knows things he never had the time to study in college. After all the hours I wasted trying to tutor that thick skull of yours, you actually remember a bit of geographic trivia?"

"Screw you, Sands."

"Harare is the capital of Zimbabwe, and you know damn well it is." Jonathan paused, meshing his fingers. He gazed up at the man standing before him. "Decker, I'm going to lay all my cards out on the table. Does that sound fair enough to you?"

Decker Moss didn't respond. Instead, he reclaimed his chair in agitated silence.

Then Jonathan cut through his adversary with surgical intensity in his eyes. "I can sink you, you know. All of you. Do you realize that? If I were to take what I know to the Justice Department, they'd undo your little merger in an afternoon. And a lot of people would go down. But I know you. You, who had me believe I was your friend all those years in college, I know you. You couldn't part with eleven million bucks. No way. You'd do just about anything before giving that up, wouldn't you, Moss?"

"What is it you want, Sands?"

"It will cost you nothing."

"What the hell are you talking about?"

Jonathan leaned back in his chair and crossed his legs. His voice was calm. "I'll play completely dumb about all I have if you just give me one thing. And I promise it won't cost you a dime. A very simple thing."

Decker struggled uncomfortably with the uncertainty of what he was about to be asked. He nervously grabbed the coffee cup from the table and gulped down the last bit with quivering fingers. "What do you want?"

"The truth. You give me the truth, and I know nothing about any of this. I play completely dumb. Does that sound like a deal to you?"

"You said you already know the truth."

"I'm not talking about any of this, Decker." Jonathan came forward in his chair again. "I know the truth about this. What I want is the truth about *Middlebury*! Sixteen years ago … in our apartment. If you just tell me what really happened that night, I'll let you keep your newfound bloody fortunes here free and clear."

"You know very well what happened that night, Sands! You were there!"

"No, Decker, I was too drunk to be there. Either you tell me now, or I'm walking out of here and things will never be the same for you again. You'll be wiped out."

"*Fuck you, Sands!*"

Jonathan stood. "So be it."

"*Sit down!*"

Jonathan remained standing defiantly.

"You act like you have me, but I can destroy you. Or have you somehow forgotten that little fact? The great Jonathan Sands, who I've been protecting all these years … do you somehow think I'd just continue to be loyal to our little secret and let you try to ruin me?"

"Oh, no, of course not." Sands threw his arms out in a masquerading buyback of his words. "How could I have been so stupid? Please forgive me."

"What the hell game are you playing now?"

"The game you want me to play. But I'm not going to play by your terms, Moss." He turned toward the door. "Don't forget, Karen's body just happens to be out in front of your vacation spot. That should be a fun one to explain."

"Not hard to do," Moss replied with a supercilious smirk. "You visited me the summer before, remember? An ideal place to dump her."

Jonathan held himself back, fighting to let the air settle before continuing. "Let me know if you want to negotiate, Decker," he said more calmly. "You've got my cell phone number. My silence for your truth." With his hand on the doorknob, he added: "The feds will be very interested to find out about Camden, and your stock options so conveniently priced, to say nothing of what I uncover about Harare."

Then Moss lifted abruptly to his feet. "You leave Harare alone! You mess with it and I'll kill you, do you hear me, Sands?" The nerve had been exposed. It was raw and effused prominently in the veins of his neck and corpuscles of his face. "A nice long sit-down chat with Fitch? The guilt I've felt covering for you all these years? The 'plans' you said you had that night, as Matt Schulman told him you mentioned at the bar before you left? The truth about your locked door not really being typical for you? It should take his investigation all the paces needed in your direction."

Jonathan Sands studied his one-time college roommate with a cold look of finality. "Then it looks like the truth is going to come out one way or another, *Cyrus*." He turned the doorknob without opening it. "My sixteen years of hell will be over and yours will just be beginning."

Before Jonathan could exit, Decker said with a smeared smile: "You've seriously miscalculated, Sands, as you'll be certain to find if you just do a little research of the 1977 Lake George police records. Do you remember that trip I made for a pre-winter check-up of my place after that night? Do you remember? You'll find there was a reported break-in of our boathouse. The lock was broken off."

OPTIONS

Sands stared at him, frozen.

"You sonofabitch." He opened the door and then slammed it hard with his exit.

Chapter Forty-One

WHEN Decker Moss answered his phone the first thing the next morning, Larry Carpenter was on the line. "Sorry to have missed your call yesterday, Decker. Your voicemail sounded urgent."

"Damn right, it's urgent, Larry." Moss quickly came forward in his chair, taking the handset to his other ear. "And more than just a bit. You can begin by telling me what Camden is all about. And you better give it to me straight!"

The loud decibels crackled in Carpenter's ear. "Whoa, hold on there, friend. No need to lose control."

"Well, I don't particularly like getting surprises from my auditor. Not when I've been taking it sideways without even knowing it."

"What are you talking about?"

"No, you tell me what it's about," yelled Decker. "And I'll give you a hint. It involves your undisclosed little subsidiary, Columbia Chemicals, and a bit of midnight musical drums."

The Southern patrician went silent. When he finally spoke he did so lacking his customary jaunty manner: "Okay, but not over the phone. It probably sounds much worse to you than it actually is."

"Yeah, right," Decker flashed, his breathing loud.

"Can you possibly make a weekend trip to Hilton Head?"

"No, I'm going on vacation tomorrow. And up until yesterday I was looking forward to it. You can tell me now."

"No," said Carpenter, "I'm not doing so over the phone."

"Well, you better do something soon because things are about to blow up."

"Why do you say that?"

"Sands. He was here yesterday and he gave me an earful. And not just about Camden. He knows about Harare as well."

"*Harare?*" Larry Carpenter had been getting timely briefings from Kent Shaughnessy about developments with the two auditors, including the Drexel-Pace security chief's trip to Boston the day before. Slade had come up completely empty on the matter of their whereabouts. "He mentioned Harare? Where is he now?"

"How should I know?" Decker vociferated. "Probably back in Boston preparing his report for the Justice Department."

"That's enough, Moss. Stop. What did he say about Harare?"

"Nothing. Other than he knew what was going on."

"Do you think it's possible he's heading there now?"

"I don't know where the hell he is or what he has." Decker probed his memory. "He might have said something about uncovering things in Harare, as in future tense. But I'll tell you one thing, Larry, I know Sands. He's no fool and he possesses the drive of a madman. If he wants something, he'll get it."

Carpenter digested the news. Finally, he concluded somberly: "We have to talk, Decker. Put off your vacation a couple of days. This is too important."

"I'll say it's important." Moss tried to hold calm as he fingered the calendar pages on his desk. He had cleared it for two weeks.

"Decker?"

There was a guarded jealousy Moss felt about his time at the lake that could only be understood by those facing another New England winter. A long pause ensued before he eventually spoke again. "Okay, Larry. But you better be straight with me. No bullshit."

"I'll be straight. I wanted to tell you earlier, but the others thought it might lead to your defection. They were wrong, though, weren't they?"

"Partners don't defect, Larry. Not as long as they're treated like partners."

* * *

Saturday, August 21, 1993
Harare, Zimbabwe

With only five hours of sleep, Jonathan awoke to an African evening at 7:15 local time, which was a quarter past noon Eastern biological time. Rest on the fifteen-hour flight from Atlanta to Johannesburg had been fitful. Disembarking the short connection to Harare International, the pair finally logged through customs dead tired.

Sands used his credit card at the airport's currency exchange to purchase three thousand Zimbabwean dollars—slightly less than

$500 U.S.—which made for a nice wad in his pocket. They rented an Audi. Under the recommendation of the car rental agent they registered at the Meikles, a luxury hotel in downtown Harare. He charged the two rooms to his card.

Jonathan showered and dressed while Jensyn slept next door. He then headed out to locate some coffee and a paper down in the hotel lobby. When he returned he gently knocked on her door. It took a while for her to answer. Peering through the crack, holding her robe lapels tight, she smiled with sleep still in her eyes.

"Time to get up," Jonathan said, handing her a Styrofoam cup of coffee. "It's getting late."

"Late?"

"Yeah. We slept through the day. Time to get up and enjoy the night."

"I want to sleep through the night, too."

"Are you hungry?" he asked.

"Famished."

"I doubt we'll be able to find any breakfast around. How would you like that nice dinner I've been promising you?"

"What?"

"Dinner."

"I can't eat dinner *now*. Are you crazy? I just woke up."

"But that's all we'll find."

"Forget it, Sands. I want a crumpet and some coffee." She closed the door on him.

Jonathan withered a frown as he went back to his own room. This dinner issue was becoming a real thing, he thought to himself. The night before it was Kentucky Fried Chicken. Neither was feeling festive at the time, not that there was a surfeit of dining alternatives in or around the Boston airport. He picked up the phone to dial the front desk for the location of the nearest "crumpet shop." There wasn't one.

* * *

Following a sampling of their rooms' complimentary fruit baskets, the pair got some directions with the help of the hotel concierge and headed to the Drexel-Pace warehouse. Alan Pelleman had faxed the street address to Jonathan a week earlier. As from the Harare airport, Jensyn drove since she was more accustomed to left-lane driving.

OPTIONS

The sun had long since set, causing a sub-equatorial winter's darkness. Fortunately, the warehouse turned out not difficult to find. It was located in a new industrial park about ten kilometers outside of the city, not far from the airport. They parked alongside the road that curved in front, with a line of sight of the building.

"Now what do we do?" Jensyn asked.

"I don't know. I guess we just scope out the joint for a while." He stared out into the darkness.

"Such a clever snoop."

It was an unremarkable bit of architecture, a steel structure that sat amidst a row of likewise nondescript warehouses on either side. An overhead lamp lit up the street side façade. There were no formal markings other than a street number above the side entranceway. A lone car was parked next to the building, which was something Jonathan found curious given that it was nighttime on the weekend. He opened the glove compartment for light and peered at his watch: *9:15.* He had reset it for local time.

"I don't see the slightest bit of activity," Jensyn said.

"What did you expect? It's after nine on a Saturday night."

"Then why did we come out here?"

"I just wanted to see what we're dealing with. Maybe spot something. That car sitting out there in the parking lot has me wondering."

"What," she asked, "guerillas down from the hills for a drug shipment?"

He cornered his eye at her. "Narcotics? Is that what you think, Jen?"

"Well, it *is* Africa."

He turned his view back to the building. "I think it's much bigger than that. What comes to your mind when you think of Africa?" he primed. "Think disease. Think pharmaceuticals." He continued gazing at the shadowed building, wondering if she might arrive at the same conclusion.

"I don't know. Malaria? Tuberculosis? Snake bites?"

"Yes, snake bites are a regular epidemic down here."

She chuckled.

They sat quiet for several more minutes.

"My guess is AIDS," he said finally. "It's rampant here. There was a series in the *Boston Globe* about it. It's completely devastated these countries. As much as a quarter of their population."

They spoke sporadically with their eyes glued to the building. Jonathan looked at his watch again. They had been sitting in the car nearly an hour. "Okay, let's come back first thing in the morning."

She started the engine and was just about to pull out from the shoulder when a dim flicker of headlights presented in their rear window.

"No, Jen, turn it off. Duck down."

They listened to the sound of a car slowly pass them by. Then they lifted to watch it pull into the warehouse parking lot, next to the doorway. A woman emerged and opened the trunk of her car. She pulled out a large plastic tub and carried it up the ramp to the door. At the stoop she depressed a button and spoke into an intercom. A moment later, in response to what Jonathan presumed to be a remote lock, she pulled open the door, lifted the tub and took it inside. The steel door bunted against the jamb.

"Now, tell me you don't think that's a bit odd," said Jonathan. "A woman with a full container visiting a remote warehouse late on a Saturday night?"

"I agree."

He ran over their situation, fidgeting with his watch as they waited. The woman didn't exit.

"I have to find out what's going on. Stay here."

Before Jensyn could react Jonathan was out the door, jogging across the street into the shadows of the building. At the ramp, he angled up to the steel door. It wasn't closed fully. He parted it slightly from the jamb to listen for any sound inside. Jensyn watched nervously from a distance. He motioned for her to stay where she was.

"No way, Sands, you're crazy," she muttered to herself. Grabbing the key she exited the car, crouching low, and traversed quickly to the building.

"What are you doing?" he protested in a whisper. "I told you to stay there."

"Forget it," Jensyn maffled back. She buried the car key in her pants pocket.

He carefully pried the door open a slice and looked inside. Holding his finger to his lips, he whispered: "Stay close." She followed his lead as they moved through the opening and into the warehouse. He was careful to let the door rest against the jamb without closing.

There was no sign of anyone.

OPTIONS

Along the main aisle that ran to the back of the building were rows upon rows of steel shelves, filled with boxes, all neatly stacked. There was an acrid smell to the air. He grabbed her hand and the pair moved behind a row of shelving units, out of the light of the main aisle.

Sands took to studying the dockets on the shelved boxes. They were computer printout labels, nondescript numeric product codes, but no company names appeared on any he could see. In his tracking of the aisles he also noted there weren't any plastic containers of the type the woman brought in with her. As he went on scanning the warehouse stock for clues of their contents, a low hum sounded at the back of the building. Seconds later there were voices. Jonathan pulled Jensyn down and away into the shadows. They found an empty space in a corner to the side of the front wall, behind a stand of cartons.

The voices grew louder. "It's not that easy to determine," said a male voice with a British accent. "I've sent samples to an old colleague in Cape Town. He has the lab equipment down there I don't. We should know for certain shortly."

"They aren't getting better, Graham. In fact, they're getting worse. The poor Zimba fellow may not make it through the night."

"I'm sorry, Millicent, we tried. You and I have both given it our best."

The pair was now at the front doorway, no more than twenty feet away from where Jonathan and Jensyn crouched low.

"Look here! You did it again, Millicent! By God, pull it shut behind you." The man pulled the door closed with force, as if in demonstration.

"Sorry. But it's tough to do when I'm carrying that tub."

Sands peered from around the boxes and watched the mid-thirties gentleman punch some buttons in a wall case. Then he hit the light switches and the two were out the door.

The warehouse went completely dark. After a while they heard the faint sound of two cars driving out of the parking lot. Several moments passed before either spoke.

"Okay, Sands. Get us out of here."

"Sure thing. I'll get right to it."

He felt his way out into the aisle, holding her hand. The absolute darkness reminded her of a high school trip she had taken to a cavern, a few hours west of London. The tour guide shut off a breaker to demonstrate, in his words, the true absence of light.

395

Jonathan eventually found the front door. "Don't touch the handle," he said.

"Why?"

"Because I have to deactivate the security system."

He felt along the wall for the box. Eventually locating it, he pulled open its lid, which revealed an illuminated numeric pad. "Here we go."

"Good."

Sands scrutinized it. "Not good. I don't see an override switch."

"Huh?"

"On mine I have a 'quick exit' key so you don't have to disarm and rearm the system. With this one you need to punch in an access code to exit, or the thing will go off." He reached for the doorknob. Reconsidering, he let it go, not willing to take the risk.

"I'm going to kill you."

"It's okay, Jen. What's the worst that can happen to us?"

She groaned at him. "I have to pee."

He found the light switch for the back of the warehouse. They walked together along the aisle to the rear. "There's got to be a bathroom in here someplace," he said.

The office in the back of the building was unlocked. Next to it was an open door. "Here we go." He gestured inside. "Wonderfully modern lavatory facilities."

In her absence Jonathan surveyed the office. He went to the desk, whose top was bare except for a blotter and phone. The drawers were locked. Then he checked the file cabinet against the wall. It was locked as well. There was a computer in the corner, which he switched on. While it was booting up he opened the door to what turned out to be a wide walk-in closet. Other than for a brass coat rack standing to the left it was completely empty.

Jensyn met up with him.

"Everything okay?" he asked.

"Fetching. Locked in a smelly warehouse in Zimbabwe, no food, and dead tired. How could it get any better?"

"I was afraid you might be a little disappointed." The computer chimed. Finding that the screen prompted for a password, he switched the thing off, and the two of them went out to the storage area again. After searching through the stacks a few minutes, he asked: "Do you recognize any of these numbers?"

"Not in the least. Why don't you continue here and I'll go to the front of the building. We'll meet in the middle. Look for SCH something or other. Both of Schoen's products start like that, but I can't remember the rest."

He followed her suggestion. There were two large walk-in refrigeration units in the rear corner of the building, one a cooler and the other a freezer, neither of which was locked. He proceeded to investigate each. Both were filled with inventory, but again, neither showed any presence of the container he was looking for. A half-hour later they met more or less in the center of the warehouse. "Nothing," he reported. Jensyn also shook her head. "What I can't understand is why we haven't seen that plastic tub she was carrying."

"I've been wondering the same thing," she said.

Jonathan climbed the end of a shelving unit and peered above it, then across the room. Not seeing anything, he climbed back down. "It's got to be in here someplace. We're missing something,"

They returned to the back office area. Being as clean as it was it wasn't difficult to comb through; no space was large enough for the container to be hidden. He sat on the desk corner with arms folded, holding his chin. She lay down on the carpeted floor and stretched out. "I'm beat," she said.

"Me too."

"If we have to sleep in this place, I'll never forgive you."

"It might be more than one night, Jen."

"What?"

"Tomorrow's Sunday. They take the Sabbath pretty seriously down here. Most everything closes. We might be in here all day."

"Then to hell with the alarm system. Let the bloody thing go off. I'm breaking out."

As he watched her get to her feet he noticed some shadows on the carpet next to her side. They went into the closet. He entered it and studied the footprint impressions inside. "Well, I'll be."

"What?"

"Come look at these carpet impressions."

She followed him into the closet area.

"So? It looks like a new carpet."

"Exactly. Look at those footprints." He pointed along the floor to the back wall. "I happen to know something about carpet footprints and they don't look like that." What he was referring to was the fact that they didn't break as they should away from the

397

baseboard, but appeared to continue right on into the wall. He crunched down, feeling with his fingers along the edge. "I don't believe it."

She squatted and met him on her knees.

"Jen …?" He looked at the corners where the perpendicular surfaces met. A very thin margin separated them. Then he looked up at the ceiling where it came against the wall. But it didn't really. At the point where the ceiling met the back partition of the closeted space there was a thin gap—no more than a centimeter wide, but still a gap—hidden by a phantom piece of crown molding.

"Jen, this is a fake wall!"

He lifted from his haunches and exited the office door into the warehouse, turning around to study the office wall exterior. She followed. The sheetrock finish climbed the full distance to the roof, another twenty feet up.

"The wall must move up into there," he exclaimed.

Catching his eye, she said: "But from the outside, the building didn't look much longer than this."

"And I bet it isn't. I bet what's behind that wall goes directly down to the basement."

"What could be down there?"

Jonathan stared at her. "Think. What did he say? When they were leaving?"

"Something about sending a sample to a friend."

"Right, because he didn't have the equipment here. Isn't that what he said?"

"I think so, something like that."

"Jen, I think we have a little research operation going on here. They're experimenting. It's a lab. They were talking about subjects … people. Someone was about to die."

She bristled. "Let's get out of here."

"No. I've got to get behind that wall somehow."

"*Jon!*"

"We're safe. Nobody would come here this time of night. I have to find out."

"How? Cutting a hole in the wall? Then they'd know for sure and we'll be hunted down and they won't give up."

"I think we're already there, Jen."

"No, Jon," she said adamantly. "It's time to get out of here. Do you hear me?"

OPTIONS

The defiant look in her eye told him it was one of those non-negotiable statements from a woman. "Okay," he swayed. Reaching for her hand he walked her to the front door. Then he turned off the light switch. "You got the car key?"

"Yeah." She withdrew it from her pocket.

He threw open the door and they ran beneath the outside alarm's cacophonous shrill.

Chapter Forty-Two

UNLIKE previous meetings among the gang of four, there was no backdrop of entertainment—no golf or boating or poker games. The Drexel-Pace executive team was all business, dirty business, and Decker Moss was all ears, turning dirtier as well. Lounging in Carpenter's villa in the afternoon the men diplomatically owned up to the Camden charade. Which in the end, after a few Scotches in him, Decker had to admit was superbly clever. Hearing it elaborated by them in detail, he also fully understood why they had kept it a secret from him. They vehemently denied any involvement in the excavator's death, however, stating their acceptance of the police finding of suicide. Decker didn't really believe that. The patsy committing suicide right after completing his fine handiwork and looking forward to his payoff? Doubtful. But, then again, he didn't really care. The excavator was a low-life.

Inevitably, the more troubling issue of the auditors came up. Short of revealing to Decker the failed attempt to eliminate the pair in South Carolina, Shaughnessy summarized Sands and Chandler's known activities and movements to date, stating merely that they had slipped away. And almost immediately after Shaughnessy was finished, Carpenter was near the screaming point. "What the hell is it that's driving them so determinedly on this thing? Auditors don't act like this!"

Decker knew what was motivating them, and he knew he had to share some of it with the men. "Cyrus Schoen met with Sands. He told him all of his suspicions about the takeover and my involvement with the shareholder records. After that, Sands met with Royce as well, corroborating Schoen's hypothesis and providing even more fuel for Sands's witch-hunt."

"Why didn't you tell us this earlier?" asked Shaughnessy.

"No need to alarm you about matters I thought completely capable of handling myself. I didn't think it would amount to anything. They had no proof then, and they have no proof now."

Carpenter stood up with his drink and strolled over to the unlit fireplace, staring at it. "Well, clearly you were wrong in your assessment, Decker. Their behavior is uncannily aggressive."

"That's what I don't get," offered Moran. "For them to take it this far so quickly, on the basis of some hearsay? It doesn't make sense."

"I agree," said Shaughnessy. "The depth of their probing suggests there's far more to it." He turned to Decker. "I thought you and Sands were college buddies."

"We were. And like I told you, he owes me some big favors. It's just that—"

"It's just what, Moss?" Carpenter interrupted as he turned around with a glare. "Tell us what the hell's going on!"

The command was delivered with unsettling volume, and once more Decker felt like an errant child who had to do what he could to regain his parents' favor. "At the end we had a falling out based on some notions he had—still has—about something I may have done way back. Let's just leave it at that. The details aren't important. But he seems to be playing a game with me now, trying to get me to confess to something I didn't do. And he's using this newly established connection to dig up whatever leverage he can to make that happen. I just don't understand why he would take the risks he's taking with all I have on him … It makes absolutely no sense to me."

Decker took the break to finish off the second half of his drink, which he sought dearly to settle his nerves.

"This thing you're talking about, it must be sordid," prompted Moran. "Did you cheat his girlfriend at strip poker? Guys don't like that."

"Shut up, Joe," bridled Carpenter.

"It is sordid," Decker said in response to the more substantive question. "But I'll beat him at his own game."

"This is all just too much." Carpenter said eventually, eyeing Decker for a long, uncomfortable time. "So it's the exact opposite kind of relationship we had hoped for, that you led us to believe, is that right?"

"It's different from what I thought when we initially talked about it, yes. I'll say that in my defense. But I'm still confident I can turn him around."

Shaughnessy looked up at Carpenter, whose hand was now clutching the mantle firmly. "What if he pursues Harare with the same kind of vengeance?" asked Shaughnessy. "Would auditors actually travel halfway around the globe to Harare? They don't have those kinds of resources, do they?"

"Not going to happen," responded the CEO. "I'm not going to let them screw this up! The problem has to be eliminated."

"What are you proposing to do, Larry, bump them off?" Decker asked sarcastically.

"What are *you* proposing to do, Moss?" Carpenter returned pointedly. "To somehow just bump them *out*?"

· The air suddenly became heavy and disturbing. Decker debated whether he had to confide with them his full arsenal—just to convince them of his ability to scare Sands away for good. The problem now, however, is that with Jensyn Chandler added to the problem mix, the cogs didn't quite mesh as well. Still, with some luck ...

"Look, guys, I have to hit the john," Decker said as he rose from the couch. "Just give me a bit more time. As I've been saying, he owes me big and he's a rational man, despite his recent behavior. I'll figure it out."

When Decker left their company, well out of earshot, Carpenter sat down in his chair again and spoke lowly. "Men, this isn't some sophomoric thing between two old college boys that's going to work itself out. We know it's damned serious, made immeasurably worse by Slade's screw-up. Those auditors know too much. They *have* to be dealt with now, and permanently. Kent, whatever it takes, I want you to find them and finish this off. Slade's shown his obvious limitations, and if we have to go external with it then that's what we have to do."

Upon Moss's return to the living room he was surprised to find Carpenter was now smiling. "Decker, we've talked it over. We've decided to give you the chance you've asked for to deal with this problem on your own. Just don't disappoint us."

"I'm glad to hear that, Larry." He held a fresh drink in his hand. "You can count on me."

* * *

Harare, Zimbabwe

This time Jensyn was the first to wake. Jonathan answered the knock on his hotel room door, rubbing his forehead.

"I'm starved. Let's go out to dinner," she said.

OPTIONS

"Dinner? Are you kidding? I want a crumpet."

Jensyn pushed the door against him. "No, it's dinnertime and you're not going to get out of it."

Jonathan quickly scrambled into the bathroom and shut the door. In front of the mirror he snapped the elastic of his boxer shorts. He felt flabby, though not for too much food. It had been days since he had a run.

"Let's go running first," he yelled out.

"No way," she countered. "Now take a shower and fluff up your wallet."

"You forget I don't have a wallet, Chandler. Slade has it."

"Then fluff up your plastic."

Thirty minutes later the couple emerged from the elevator to the hotel's lobby, wearing fashionable dress and overcoats. Jonathan asked the concierge for a nice restaurant within a reasonable driving distance. The man provided the names of a few, but pointed out that the hotel's own restaurant, the *La Fontaine*, was a five-star establishment. A study of the menu at its entrance certainly looked agreeable enough to both. They checked their coats and took a table. Located just off from the lobby area, the restaurant's huge exterior windows overlooked the grand fountains of Africa Unity Square.

"I never would have thought this would be such a beautiful city," Jensyn said. "Thanks for bringing me."

"We're not exactly here for a good time, Jen."

"Still, I'm having fun … a luxurious hotel, at a wonderful restaurant with a rich partner?" Then, tilting her head and dispensing with her teasing expression: "You know I'm just kidding about the partner thing."

"Just as long as I'm rich, huh?"

She laughed. "Thank you."

"Thank you?"

"For finally taking me out to dinner … even though you'll probably just put it on a travel expense voucher."

He lifted his bottled water. "To MM&P." He had no idea yet how he was going to explain to his boss his reasons for flying off to Africa. He realized he may have to suck up the cost himself. "And cheers to you, Jen … cheers and hope."

She chimed her bottle against his.

Their appetizers arrived: a Mocambique lobster tail salad. They sampled from it slowly, savoring it, along with the atmosphere and their mutual company.

"So, what's next on our agenda?" she asked.

"Well, first thing tomorrow morning I want to head back to the warehouse."

She lifted from her salad. "What for? We'll never get back inside."

"Somehow or another we have to find out what's going on in there. We'll just have to see how it plays out."

Jensyn's face soured. "I can't wait."

"Sorry, but we have no choice. I want to have all the evidence I can get before taking this to the Justice Department." Unspoken, he also wanted the noose as tight as possible around Decker Moss's neck before he sought his endplay.

"Do you think we're almost there?" Jensyn asked.

Jonathan thought on the question over his chewing. He gazed up at her. "It's hard to say. I certainly hope so. Once we return to the States we'll—"

His statement was cut off by a sight he caught over her shoulder, in the lobby. His eyes grew wide. Looking quickly around and then in the direction of the restrooms, he commanded quietly: "Get up and go to the ladies room."

"Jon—?" She started to peer over her shoulder.

"No, Jen, don't look back. Go to the restroom. It's behind you to your left. Stay there until I knock on the door."

The two of them lifted from their chairs, splitting, Jensyn moving to the other side of the restaurant outside the line of sight of the lobby and Jonathan moving forward behind the protection of the wall at the restaurant's entrance. He retrieved their coats and Jensyn's purse from the cloak room.

"Is everything okay, sir?" It was their waiter, footing toward him.

"No, I'm sorry, my lady friend is suddenly feeling ill. Nothing about the food. Please put the charges on my room bill."

"Certainly, sir. My apologies."

Jonathan gave the waiter his room number and risked a look out the glass panel into the lobby area. The identity of the man standing at the registration desk was unmistakable. The receptionist he spoke to picked up the handset to her phone. A few moments later Jonathan read her lips: "Sorry, no answer."

Of course Slade would try the major hotels. But how could he possibly know we're in Harare?

And then he thought of Dianne, his secretary.

Slade turned away from the reception desk and headed in the direction of the elevator banks, just out of sight from where Jonathan was standing.

Sands took off briskly to the ladies room and rapped on the door. Jensyn emerged. "What's going on?" she asked.

"Slade's here. Hurry, follow me." He handed Jensyn her purse and overcoat.

The waiter caught them mid-stride to the door. "Here you go, sir. No charge for the entrees."

Jonathan scratched his signature on the chit. Then he grabbed Jensyn's hand and exited the restaurant into the lobby area. In their trot he turned on his feet but didn't see Slade anywhere. "Hurry, Jen, go get the car."

Sands went over to the receptionist at the registration desk. "That man ... did you give him my room number?"

She stared at Jonathan clueless.

"My name's Sands. Did you give him my room number?"

"Oh, no, Mr. Sands, of course not. It's against hotel policy. He just asked me to ring your room."

Jonathan looked down at the phone sitting on the counter. The touch tone keys were clearly visible over the partition. If Slade hadn't made out the entire room number from her punched entry, he may have been able to ascertain the floor.

"Ring my room."

She hesitated. "But you're—"

"I said ring my room!"

She did as he commanded, noting she hit a prefix button followed by his room number."

"He's a dangerous man. I want you to have my room packed and put in storage. And my colleague, Jensyn Chandler's as well. Say nothing to him. Do you understand?"

The receptionist faltered.

"Dammit, woman, do you understand me?"

"Yessir, of course ..."

"I'll tip you handsomely when we come back for our things."

Before waiting for her reply, Jonathan heeled fast for the hotel's exit.

* * *

"How on earth does he know we're here?" Jensyn asked as she drove the Audi, her voice tense.

"I have no idea. Maybe he just deduced it when he couldn't find us in Boston. Or," he added with more concern, "he was somehow able to get it out of Dianne."

Jensyn shot him a desperate look. "Let's hope not!"

Staring out at the busy night-lighted thoroughfare, Jonathan said: "Take us out of town. We have to find someplace he'd never look for us."

"Can't we just stay in the city and register under a different name?"

"It's too big a risk, Jen. Besides, my name's on my credit card." Just for assurance, he reached for the plastic in his suit coat pocket. Then he felt the wad of bills in his pants pocket. He never left cash sitting around in a hotel room.

What he knew wasn't on his person, however, was his passport.

* * *

Accommodations that night couldn't have been more obscure: a thatched roof cottage in a place called Mbizi Lodges, a thousand-acre safari game park located just a few kilometers south of the airport, yet worlds away. Being the off-season, remodeling work was underway at the cottages. Fortunately, there happened to be a vacancy available, one with two bedrooms and running—albeit unheated—water. Jonathan paid cash and registered them under the names of Wayford and Kitty Schwarzkopf. The proprietor rolled his eyes at the names, but happily took his cash.

The first thing Jonathan did was to head out and find a pay phone to call Dianne, his secretary. To his relief she sounded fine, other than for her concern about the workload piling up on his desk. She was still at the office, seven hours earlier Boston time, and she shared the basic messages Jonathan had received during his days out. But no to his questions: there had been no message from Decker Moss, and she hadn't told anyone where they were.

Sands briefly explained that he and Jensyn were pursuing a critically important special investigation and that he would call again the following afternoon. He reiterated the importance to her not to share their whereabouts.

Back at the cottage the lights were out and Jensyn was asleep— at least he thought so since there wasn't a sound when he entered and her bedroom door was closed. Stepping quietly as he could across the squeaky wood-plank floor, he went to her door and listened. The doors were primitive, with slotted latches and gaps between the slats. "Jen?" he said softly.

"Mmhh?"

"Are you all right?"

"I'm cold, but I'm all right. Is everything okay at home?"

"Dianne's fine."

"Thank goodness. Good night, Jon."

"Good night, Jen." He stood at the door a moment longer. "I'm sorry about dinner."

She chuckled. "It's not your fault. You'll make it right someday."

He turned to his adjoining bedroom and found the paraffin lamp and matches on the dresser. Lighting it, he turned the flame down and rubbed his hands over the small flame. Completely unheated, the cottage was nearly as cold inside as out—in the fifties, Jonathan guessed—and a breeze whistled through the cracks of the uninsulated wall planking.

He undressed to his T-shirt and boxers and climbed into bed. The wool blanket and sheets had an earthy odor, a combination of wood, paraffin and thatch. Crossing his arms beneath his head, he stared above at the shadowed rafter beams, taking the moment in his drowsiness to think through the events of the past couple days. It was all a whirlwind ... yet, ironically, he felt a strange peace about it. Regardless of what happened from this point forward, he knew it was all coming to an end.

And then he dozed off.

* * *

It was a faint sound. A small squeak.

His eyes shot open.

A door hinge?

Then a creak along the outer room's floor planks, dry wood complaining beneath weight.

Jonathan froze.

How could he have possibly found us?

He quietly got out of bed and grabbed the only thing he could think of. He tiptoed behind the door jamb, listening intently. The fast beating of his heart pounded in his ears. The steps in the main room grew closer now, and then the latch release to his door lifted. The door squeaked open with a slow pry.

He raised his weapon.

"Jon?"

"*Jen!*" he exclaimed as he lowered his shoe and came around. "My God, what are you doing? You scared me to death!"

She stood in the doorway, clutching a Hudson Bay blanket about her. "I'm sorry. I'm cold and I can't sleep."

"I thought you were Slade. You shouldn't go around doing that!"

Looking at him and then at the shoe he held, her hand came to her mouth with a muffled laugh. "You were going to hit him with your wingtip?"

He tossed it across the floor and frowned at her. "Yeah, well, what else was I supposed to do?"

Jensyn reached for him. The blanket slipped from her hold and she tried to grab it, but it was too late. He caught her at the waist. Other than for her dinner-date chiffon blouse, she was wearing nothing but satin bikini briefs.

"Cold, huh? You might have thought of wearing your overcoat, you know."

Jensyn looked up at him in the wan light and took her hands to his shoulders, then to his neck. She stroked his cheek.

"I love you, you know," she said.

"Jen ..."

"No, Jon. Don't tell me you don't love me."

He ran his fingers through her hair and pulled her to himself. "I—"

"I what?"

"I *do* love you. That's why I can't ... this isn't a good idea, that's all. Not now, not yet."

"Not every idea has to be good. It only has to be right."

He wondered about that a moment. "Is there a difference?"

She looked up at him in the flickering light cast by the wick lamp and touched his face. "You're right for me, Jon. You may not be good for me, but you're right for me." She reached down for the fallen blanket and wrapped the two of them in it. Then she placed her face against his chest.

He finger-combed her hair again. In the moments of quiet as he held her he felt his pulse race. He felt her heart beating heavily as well. She shivered, and he firmly ran his hands up and down the full length of her back.

Looking up at him, she drew to his lips. His were receiving. Slow and tender at first, their kiss soon became impassioned. She reached for his free hand and brought it to her breast. He cupped its fullness atop her blouse.

Her head now upon his shoulder, she turned to his neck, and he felt the warmth of tears against his skin.

She reached beneath his T-shirt and placed her hand over his chest. "You're an amazingly special person, Jonathan," she said softly. She looked up at him with glistening eyes. "I know that about you. Even if you don't know it about yourself. You can have me if you want to. I know that I want you. And I'll be yours … for keeps. But if you really mean you can't now, I understand." She then tightened her hold around him. "I won't happen to like it, but I'll understand."

Pulling from her, he cradled her face in his hands, looking intently into her sea-green eyes, searching them, wishing for an answer.

"I want you, too, Jen," he whispered finally. "More than anyone I've ever wanted my whole miserable life." His palms caressed the swell of her hips and came to rest a moment at the elastic of her panty line. As he struggled for more words, hoping on the one hand to suppress himself, failing completely any such hope on the other, he took his arms around her to her backside, his fingers traveling firmly along the trough at the small of her back, coming eventually to rest at the sloping rise of her tailbone. Then, breaching the elastic band of her panties, he stretched his hands over the soft flesh of her cheeks, filling his hold … firm, yet supple in his grip. Crouching down to his knees, he kissed her there, there through the diaphanous fabric of her panties. There where he always wished he could kiss a woman he loved.

She moaned with her head craned backwards. He came up and unbuttoned her blouse, coursing his mouth over her breasts. Her nipples rose in response to the warmth of his tongue. Then he squatted and slid her panties off her feet, slowly licking the fine-haired vellus trail downward from her stomach as he did so …

The lamp flame flickered. The breeze outside wafted through the rickety walls of the cottage, splashing amber ripples of light across the room. Beneath the warmth of the blankets, very much

Stephen J. Dempsey

secreted from the rest of the world, they sought and shared an intimacy both had craved for so long.

For her, years. For him, a lifetime.

Now, awash in the aftermath and his back to her, she wrapped her arms around him in a spooning hold.

"Jen," he said quietly, in a near state of sleep, "did you happen to drop your blanket on purpose?"

"Not really," she whispered back in his ear … then, knavishly, "maybe." She squeezed him. "You'll never know."

He dozed off a moment, stirred awake again by his own broken breathing. "What about that wall-hanging in your office? About everything working out for good?"

"Hmm?"

"You said I was right for you, but that I may not be *good* for you." He turned over in the bed to face her and brushed a tendril at her temple. "What did you mean by that?"

"Well, what's right may only become good in time," she answered, touching his nose. "We may just have to wait for it."

"Oh, I see." Another few minutes of silence passed. "I have to fire you now, you realize, Chandler."

She was running her fingernails along his side and back. Then she pinched his bottom. "So, go ahead and fire me, Sands. Fire me all you want."

She reached around to find him again. "Just don't stop."

Chapter Forty-Three

Monday, August 23, 1993
Harare, Zimbabwe

PARKING their rental in an empty lot a few buildings down from the warehouse, Jonathan and Jensyn footed in the pre-dawn darkness to a copse of fir trees that provided a safe view of the front. The industrial park was interspersed with trees and landscaped shrubs, which helped conceal their movements. Suspicious behavior aside, however, a casual observer wouldn't have reacted casually to their non-casual dress. They had no choice but to wear the same attire they wore to dinner the previous evening. Both felt groggy from their sleepless night, despite their cold morning shower together.

A winter sunrise was just beginning to crease the sky. At the sound of an approaching car, Jonathan reached for Jensyn to crouch down low. Moments later it pulled into the parking lot. The occupant—Graham, as they now knew to be his name—got out with his briefcase and entered the building.

Half an hour later, and lumens of daylight brighter, another car arrived. Again, car and driver were familiar. Millicent, as her name was also now known, carried nothing into the building this time, and also unlike before, once she was buzzed in, she pulled the door fully shut behind her.

"We'd have been too lucky for her to do it again. Come on, Mrs. Schwarzkopf, let's get closer to the building." Jonathan crouched up from his camouflaged position beneath the branches.

"You're crazy if you think I'm going over there."

"Okay, then you stay here. I'll hide between that transformer box and air conditioner at the side of the building to see if I can hear anything." Jonathan made vertical and darted for the warehouse.

Jensyn turned over on her back in frustration. Then she got up and dashed after him.

The pair ducked down between the units and waited some time before some muffled voices could be heard inside. The front door opened.

"—which is why I had to change the password," said the unseen voice, barely audible above the hum of the air conditioning compressor.

"I'm sorry, Graham," the woman's voice replied. "It won't happen again."

Squeaking wheels of a dolly crossing the door's threshold stopped on the landing. "I received a fax from my friend in Cape Town. He confirmed the protein reactions I suspected with his crystallography equipment."

"Chromosomal translocation?" asked Millicent.

"I'm afraid so," answered Graham. "We'll just have to see whether they'll want to continue with the project or not. Given this news I'll have to object to it, but my voice is small."

Then, hearing them taking the ramp down to the gravel lot, Jonathan carefully peered around from his concealed position. Graham, wearing a white lab coat, helped Millicent carry some tubs to her car. He re-entered the building with the dolly and firmly shut the door behind him.

When Millicent pulled out of the driveway onto the access road, Jonathan and Jensyn quickly ran the distance to their rental. He called for her to throw him the car key.

"You can't drive on the left!"

"Oh, yeah? Watch me!"

The fast bends of the industrial parkway careened the Audi to its limits. Coming to the main intersection, Jonathan asked: "Which way did she go?"

"I don't know!"

"Come on, Chandler, use that British sterling intuition of yours!"

Jensyn pointed right, then left, and then looked at him flummoxed with a shake of her head. "I don't know! Go right!"

He took her suggestion, accelerating on a near two-wheeled pitch. The tires squealed as the car veered into the right lane.

"No! Stay to the left!" she screamed.

After passing two cars on the narrow road they eventually spotted the blue Peugeot station wagon about a quarter mile in front. "You're a genius, Jen, just keep it up."

"Slow down!"

He did so and grabbed her hand. "Sorry."

The remainder of the drive was too slow for his charged nerves. It was an easy tag into the township of Mbare, a suburb just south of Harare.

Jensyn stared out at the surroundings. Between each decrepit mortared structure were at least a dozen dispirited shacks, slapped together from plastic and other junk, relegated real-estate permanence. "I don't know how they live like this."

"I suppose they have no choice," Jonathan replied somberly.

Eventually, the Peugeot in front of them took an empty spot on a side street in the heart of town. The Harare bus station and a large marketplace were just around the corner. Growing morning crowds were milling on the streets.

Sands pulled to the curb several cars in front of the parked Peugeot. They watched as Millicent entered a building across the street.

"We can use some different clothes," Jonathan suggested. "What size are you?"

"Size eight slacks, medium top, size six shoes."

"Okay, I'll be right back." He jumped out of the car. "Beep the horn if you see anything."

"Right, like you'd ever hear it."

As he entered the loud Musika marketplace, Jonathan was immediately confronted by the fact that Zimbabwean commerce didn't follow the pattern of orderly western economics. Buyers and sellers were yelling at each other. The produce looked fresh enough, but the goods didn't. Aside from the African artifacts on sale everything appeared quite secondhand. And apparently the prices of everything were subject to heavy negotiation. Fortunately, English was the primary language of the country, though spotty in the outlying areas. He asked a merchant at a table he was tending about some hiking clothes he was peddling. All from Europe, the man informed him. At 6:30 A.M., and in need of a change of clothes fast, Jonathan wasn't about to be picky. He exited the stall with two pairs of khaki slacks and two black sweaters, the package dickered quickly down to $130 Zim, or $20 U.S.

"What am I going to do for shoes?" she asked upon his return. "I can't wear these."

Looking down at her pumps he said: "What's wrong with those? They have low heels."

"But they don't work with the slacks."

He gave her a look. "Put your clothes on, Jen."

413

She pulled off her pantyhose, drew the slacks on beneath her black skirt, buttoned and zipped them, and then removed her blouse. Turning her back to him she said: "Unzip me."

He did, wondering what women do when nobody else is around.

She removed her bra, and in a fluid move pulled the black sweater on. The bundle of discarded clothing she placed on the back seat. He smiled at her. "Something special occurred to me last night about you," he said. "Do you realize that when you moan you actually do so in a British accent?"

She smirked at him. "Is now the time for me to come up with some kind of witty double-entendre about your Yankee Doodle Dandy?"

He laughed. Then he caught a movement in the rearview mirror. "Don't look back, but she's behind us. She's taking the tubs out and putting them into a van across the street."

Jonathan studied Millicent's movements in the rear- and side-view mirrors. After removing four tubs, the woman spent some time with the fifth. It was difficult to make out clearly, but she appeared to be packing some things into a satchel. Then she carried the last container to the van, set it alongside the four others inside, and closed the rear door. She waived off the driver, who pulled out and was gone.

"Should I follow the van?" Jonathan asked.

"I don't know."

"Come on. Follow the van or stay with her?"

"You keep doing this to me."

"Jen, hurry!"

"I … I guess you should stay with her. She seems to be the leader."

"Right."

They got out of the car and followed stealthily on foot behind as Millicent walked toward the main thoroughfare with her satchel in hand.

* * *

Dr. Graham Woods was just about to get up from his work at the lab counter to relieve himself of his two cups of morning coffee when he heard the outside door buzzer.

"Yes?" he answered into the intercom.

"It's Slade. Open up."

OPTIONS

The gravelly voice sounded even more ominous over the tinny speaker than on the phone. "Sure, Mr. Slade, come on in." Woods hit the switch to deactivate the remote door lock, and then headed up the stairs to the warehouse. He greeted the security man in the main aisle.

"Did you find who you were looking for?" asked the scientist. Slade had made a phone call to Woods the day before about the couple he was hunting down.

"I had them at the Meikles last night but they slipped away." Slade glared at the smaller man with murder in his eyes, grinding his cigarette butt beneath his boot sole.

The men walked to the rear of the building. "I haven't found evidence that anybody got in," offered Woods. "Everything looks fine to me."

"Maybe to you, but *something* set off the alarm Saturday night."

"The only thing I can think of is that someone tried to pry open the front door. As I told you on the phone, everything looked tight as a drum when I got here after the report. There were no marks along the door I could see."

Slade concurred with Woods's observation, having just inspected the front door of the warehouse himself. "What about the access panel?"

"Again, it looks fine to me. Take a look for yourself." Woods gestured to the closet, which Slade entered. As the security man busied himself with his inspection, Woods said: "Excuse me. I was just about to visit the water closet when you buzzed."

Ignoring the scientist, Slade scrutinized the wall but found no signs of tampering. Nor could he make out anything from the matted footprints along the carpet. He doubted an intruder would be able to breach the panel access anyway, not without visible force. He roamed the back office a moment and then exited for the warehouse aisles.

Woods eventually rejoined him with a contemplative stroke of his chin. "I thought I left the seat up Saturday night, but it might have been Millicent."

"Millicent?"

"My courier. She may have used the lavatory, though I can't see how she had time after I buzzed her in. Anyway, she sometimes doesn't fully shut the door behind her. It sticks."

"Sticks?"

415

"It doesn't close by itself. She often forgets to pull it shut. If they got in here, it had to be after she came in."

"When?"

"Well, it's been happening lately. I think it needs oiling or something."

"No, Doctor Shit-Brains. I mean when, as in since they've been here? This weekend!"

Woods recoiled. "It happened Saturday night."

"Saturday night," the pit-faced security man repeated with scorn. He walked a few steps and turned back around on his heels. "That's just wonderful, Woods. So, Saturday night they must have gotten in here, and then without having any way to get out but to set off the security alarm, that's what they did."

"Come to think of it, I did see a car parked out along the front road Saturday night. I didn't think much of it at the time, but …"

Slade tried to predict what Sands would do next. There was nothing in the warehouse to suggest anything out of the ordinary. But he knew the auditor wouldn't leave it at that. "If Sands followed her this morning, could he have learned anything?" Slade asked.

"No, I don't see how," replied Woods. "She met me downstairs to pick up today's dosages."

"But he could've followed her to her destination."

"Well, yes, theoretically."

"Theoretically, my ass! That's what he did. Sands followed her!"

Graham Woods answered Geoff Slade's next question in the form of careful directions written out on a piece of paper.

* * *

The pair followed Millicent past the bus terminus, the Musika Market, and beyond, where vendors unwilling or unable to pay marketplace rents were busily arranging their wares on the street corners. The thoroughfare was loud and crowded. Locals shouted bids and offers for everything from beans to used tires to other recycled refuse. The hostels were crowded; gangs of seedy characters and solicitous women loitered their fronts, probably up all night, Jonathan thought. Children walked the streets in small groups to school, wearing ragged uniforms and torn shoes—some wearing no shoes at all.

He occupied nervous hands in his pockets, holding the wad of Zimbabwean currency in his right grip. Jensyn, who had wrapped her arm around his in a firm hold, mumbled comments about the bleak ghetto.

The female courier paced quickly a good distance ahead of them, following the pocked roads into a residential area. Trash was strewn everywhere. Homemakers of ramshackle huts swept their yards, dust mixing with the sordid odors of the neighborhood and filling the air. With no money for school, many of the children recreated early on the streets.

Fifteen minutes into their pursuit the woman cornered off to a wooden shack and knocked on the door. It pried open for her entry.

"We can't just keep following her like this," Jonathan said, looking around the area. "She's going to notice us."

"I say we just talk to whoever it is that lives in that hut after she leaves and then head back home. Then we'll have enough."

They backtracked a bit and crossed the corner to the other side. Several teenagers were playing a hack cricket game there in a sandy field. Jonathan watched them reflectively. He had read about AIDS orphans, children whose parents were both lost to the disease. *Who cared for them?*

Across and just down the street, Millicent exited the shack with a young black girl, who led her to another hut, a smaller one, to the rear of the main shack.

Wanting a diversion of sorts, Sands strolled over to the kids playing in the field. Without really intending to, he interrupted their game with his walk-on presence. They eyed him.

"I was just watching you guys. Looks like fun."

"What you want?" came the broken-English voice from one of the players. The pitcher, Jonathan thought.

"Oh nothing, just watching," he answered.

"We're playing. Stand away."

Jonathan shuffled back a step. "Say, would you mind if I tried hitting one of those balls?" He smiled at the boys. "Just one try? I've never played cricket before."

The group stared at him like he was a crazy person. Then the young black teen holding the ball came up to him. "You sound American."

"I am. Is that all right?"

"Americans play baseball. You a baseball player?"

"Nope. I played a little in high school but I wasn't very good at it. Would you pitch me a ball?"

"What you give me?"

Sands chuckled. "Give you?"

"Yeah, you a rich man. Americans all rich."

Jonathan held a moment and then pulled out a bill. It was a $5 Zim.

"No, ten. I'll bowl for you for ten."

Though the teen had a strong build, he had big brown eyes and a youthful-looking face. "Okay, young man. But then I want five pitches, and I'm not paying you until after you throw them."

Jensyn stood off a way with her arms folded, marveling at the transaction. Jonathan was handed the cricket bat and took his stand before the wicket. He held the bat completely wrong. When another player came up to show him the possible vertical and horizontal shot grips, he was ready.

The 'pitcher' wound arced, straight-armed throws overhead, which looked funny to Sands. The first two balls bounced in the ground and zinged by him. The kids laughed as he shucked aside. "What are you laughing at? The pitcher threw them into the dirt!"

"He's allowed to do that, Jonathan!" Jensyn shouted. "And he's not a pitcher, he's called a bowler."

"Oh."

The third ball he clipped, which escaped a laugh. Then the boy bowled a full toss—one that didn't do a ground bounce—and Jonathan nailed it. "*Ha!* See?" Jonathan caught Jensyn's eye with a proud look on his face "When he throws the thing right, I can hit it." He turned back to the bowler: "Okay, give me one more just like that."

The young man did, and Jonathan nailed it even farther. He completed the transaction by handing the teenager two bills, double what was bargained.

"Thanks, Mister!"

"You're very welcome. Thanks for the fun."

"Jonathan, it's time to go." Jensyn said it like a question, furtively gesturing to the other side of the street. Millicent was already on her way up the road.

The pair of them walked to the shack and knocked on the door. When it opened they were greeted by an adorable young black girl with tile-white teeth. Jonathan guessed her to be twelve or thirteen. Several younger children poked their heads out from behind her.

"Hello, young lady. My name's Jonathan and this is Jensyn. What's your name?"

"Nomsa," she replied warily. "Nomsa Zimba."

Jonathan and Jensyn exchanged looks, both recognizing the surname as being the same as that mentioned by Millicent in the warehouse. "Is your dad feeling any better?" Jonathan risked the question, uncertain if the "Zimba fellow" Millicent had referred to was her father or some other relative.

"No, he's going home to God."

"Can we see him?"

"Who are you?"

"We're Americans. We want to help if we can. We hope to learn about your father's illness. Would that be okay?"

The girl studied their faces a moment, speculating for risk, and then turned to tell her younger siblings to stay inside. Then she gestured for her unexpected guests to follow her to the hut out back.

The putrefactive odors were the first thing that hit them. The second was the blanketed skeleton lying on the thin mattress. Jensyn recoiled at the sight.

"How long has he been sick?" Jonathan asked, kneeling down alongside the emaciated man. He held his hand, which remained motionless and cold in his grip.

"Long time. AIDS. Momma died of it, and then Poppa got sick of it. He was to die and she came to help."

"Millicent you mean?"

Nomsa nodded. "She got him better. He got good for a while and then started to get bad again. It's lukema."

"How long did it take for him to get better?" Jonathan asked.

The young girl thought a moment. "I think … a couple weeks. He was good many months." Nomsa told them about the nurse's visits every few days throughout her father's sickness, how she gave him medications, took blood samples, and then recently gave her the news about "lukema."

"Did she think the leukemia had anything to do with the medications he was receiving?" It was Jensyn's first question.

"No." She walked over to her father and looked down at him. "But I think so."

"Why's that?" asked Jonathan.

419

"She told me some her patients used to have AIDS now have lukema."

"Really?" Jonathan and Jensyn exchanged looks again.

"Do you have help for lukema?" Nomsa asked hopefully. "Is that why you here?"

"No, honey, unfortunately, we don't. I'm sorry." Jonathan squeezed the man's hand again and stood. Even the treatments at home, he knew, required expensive chemotherapy or bone marrow transplants. "Is she still giving him the medications?"

"Yes, but she doesn't think they do no good."

Jonathan turned to Jensyn, impliedly asking if she had any more questions. She shook her head.

"Thank you, Nomsa. We wish you and your family Godspeed." Jonathan peeled off two twenties from the roll in his pocket and handed them to her. "I know this doesn't help much, but please accept it. For you and your family."

Her face lit up with a broad toothy smile. "Thank you."

The girl kissed her father's forehead and then led the Americans out the creaky door. After they said their good-byes the American couple turned toward the street.

"I'm going to cry," Jensyn said.

"Me too."

A moment later Jonathan turned around to shuffling he heard behind him.

"Well, if it isn't my favorite couple," said the gravelly voice.

Slade was wearing a cheap polyester gray suit. His right hand was stuffed in his side coat pocket, which bulged with more than just that.

"I see you packed your gun for the trip, Slade," said Jonathan, "seeing how you're not a complete man without one."

"Shut up, Sands. We'll see who's a man after I string you up and show this little bitch how it's done." He nodded to their front. "Now turn around, both of you, and head on to that car down the road."

They made their way down the street with Slade walking to their rear. Jonathan sneered back at the man. "You're going to die a miserable death today, Slade."

"Yeah, you wish, fucker. I should have shot you full of holes when I had the chance. Now keep walking."

Paces down, Jonathan veered his eyes to the cricket players across the street. They were oblivious of them. "Hey, boys! Want to play some more ball?" The teens' attention was immediately diverted toward Jonathan's direction.

Slade slammed Jonathan hard in the back. "Shut up or I'll put you down right here, you prick!"

Righting himself from the blow, Sands reached for the cash in his pocket and hefted the roll of bills in his hand. "Come on, guys!" He turned back around to Slade. "They're my friends." Then Sands flung the wad into the air, showering the area with paper magic. The dozen or so teenagers came running in their direction. Slade did a double take at the scene and Sands came down with a crashing blow against his arm. A shot went off through Slade's coat pocket, just grazing Jonathan's left leg. He didn't feel it then, but blood spilled from the wound.

The thunderous report stopped the boys in their tracks. Paper bills floated in the air and littered in the breeze to the ground. Slade stared at them furious as he tried to pull the Glock from the tangled fabric of his coat pocket. Then Jonathan charged him. Wrapping his arms around the Drexel-Pace security man in a vice-like hold, he took him down to the pavement. They writhed and struggled wildly upon the street, back and forth in frantic effort to gain positions for themselves, during which Jonathan was able to get a blow of his knee into Slade's groin. But Slade, the larger of the two, grabbed Sands by the hair and came out on top. With his grip still wrenching Sands's hair, he struck the back of Jonathan's skull against the pavement.

Just as he pulled his hand away to access his gun, several of the teenagers fell upon him. A couple of them clawed at his gun hand, trying to free the weapon from his pocket, while others held down his arms.

"*Get off me, you filthy niggers!*"

The words were like throwing gas on a fire. The boys who remained standing off to the side now came down upon Slade in a maelstrom, swarming over him like killer bees. Arms and fists went flying, most connecting some not. All were thrown hard. In the frenzy that followed the Glock finally came free from Slade's coat pocket and was thrown across the broken pavement. With his arms now pinioned behind him, the security man fell vulnerable to what followed. Sands got up and gripped his hands around Slade's neck and squeezed, throwing his head violently from side to side. Audibly, the gullet cartilage of his neck cracked, yet Jonathan held his death grip firm and forced more strength into his fingers.

421

Slade's face engorged and his eyes bulged in their sockets. A crimson flow dribbled from his mouth.

"Jonathan, stop!"

He didn't hear her.

"Jonathan!"

Sands kept squeezing. The skin at Slade's throat tore beneath Jonathan's thumbnails. He jarred his grip and ripped tighter and deeper, throwing the now flaccid neck he held until the meat of Slade's throat opened and his vertebrae snapped.

"Jonathan! Stop it! He's gone!"

The boys got off the men and stood off at the edge of the road, spellbound as the American continued on with his savage slaughter.

* * *

Jensyn knelt beside him on the pavement. His pant leg was soaked with blood. Noticing the large number of onlookers that had materialized along the road, the bowler yelled: "You got to get out of here!" He found the car keys in Slade's suit coat pocket and shoved them quickly into Jensyn's hand. "Go!"

The other teenagers lifted Jonathan to his feet. His face was dazed and he held the back of his head with his hand. Jensyn followed the group as they helped the hobbling American to the car.

"We have to get the police," Jensyn said.

"No," yelled the group leader. "They're corrupt. They'll hold you a long time. I'll tell them you were attacked and went to hospital. We saw it. You find a doctor instead. Now go!"

Jensyn got in quickly and started the car. She turned it around and headed fast toward town. "Are you okay?" she asked excitedly.

Jonathan struggled against the fog in his mind. "My head hurts ... bad ... I don't think ..." He looked down at his leg and ripped his trousers at the hole and gently felt the wound. Fortunately, it appeared to be a superficial wound and now wasn't bleeding as much. "Get us back to our car."

"No, Jonathan, I'm going to find you a doctor."

"No you're not, Jen. Do as I say!"

"And then what?"

"We'll find some dressings and head back to the Meikles to pick up our things. Then get us to the airport."

He turned over to the side and was out.

PART IV
LAKE GEORGE
(1993)

Chapter Forty-Four

Tuesday, August 24, 1993
Atlanta, Georgia

THE voice sounded like it was trapped in a drum, yet Kent Shaughnessy recognized the South African accent on the other end.

"Give it to me again, Doctor. But please be more clear."

A half-globe pause digitized over the transcontinental satellite connection. "Slade's dead. The bobbies were here not half an hour ago. They said there were two Americans, a man and a woman, at the scene of a street fight in Mbare yesterday. It's just south of Harare where a number of our experimental subjects live. Slade was killed in the fight and they escaped. Apparently, the man was wounded and took off for hospital, though nobody by his description ever showed up."

"Did they check the airport?"

"They didn't mention it. I told them I had no idea who the Americans were."

Shaughnessy thought about that. With what little the police had at the time they probably wouldn't have checked the airport yet before Sands had been able to catch a flight out. Or a train. Hell, he could have chosen any number of intermediate destinations.

"How'd the police find you?" Shaughnessy asked.

"Slade's company ID," answered the scientist. "He was carrying it on him, like a fool. They said they found the warehouse address in the city's commerce office records."

Shaughnessy knew the warehouse phone number was unlisted and that other records would have had to have been searched. "Did you tell them you knew him?"

"Of course not."

"Good."

Woods was silent a moment. His voice resumed woefully. "They know, Mr. Shaughnessy. The Americans must know it all. Sands and the woman were here, in the warehouse."

"*What!*"

"Somehow they got in over the weekend. I don't know how," Woods lied, "but they were here."

425

"Did they break into the lab?"

"I don't see how they could have. But it's not good. They're probably well out of the country by now." Graham Woods paused again. "And I have other bad news. We have two more cases of leukemia in the sample. All the same type."

"*Damn it!*" Shaughnessy turned on his heals, pondering the information before speaking again. "Listen, doctor, I have to talk to Carpenter. I'll be back in touch with you."

"What do you want me to do?"

"How should I know? Hell, stop injecting yourself with the shit! You may still have a chance." He slammed down the handset.

* * *

Somewhere over the South Atlantic

The cabin pressure and temperature mixed in an uncomfortable way. With a blanket over her and a pillow resting against Jonathan's shoulder, Jensyn roused a bit from the turbulence. She looked up at him. His eyes were open.

"Can't you sleep?"

"Hmm?"

"Can't you fall asleep?" she asked again.

"No."

"How's your leg?"

"Still there." His hand and head hurt more than his leg. He wondered if he fractured his wrist when he slammed Slade in the arm. "Go back to sleep, Jen."

She settled down and closed her eyes. The cabin lights had been shut down, the movie was over, and darkness filled the windows. But the muffled drone of the jets and hissing of the pressurized air teased with her ears. Sleep teasingly hovered, occasionally touching ground though never really landing. Surrendering hope, she raised her head and noticed his eyes were moistened.

"What's the matter?" she asked.

"Nothing." He patted her hand. "I'm fine. You go to sleep, Jen."

"Jon?"

"Please." He kissed her forehead and turned away toward the window to his side.

"I can't sleep." She pulled herself up. "What's going on in that head of yours?"

"Survival," he said, turning to her. "Your survival, my survival. I brutally killed a man, and I enjoyed doing it."

"But you acted in self-defense."

"No … I found pure pleasure strangling the man's neck. I wanted to keep on going after he was dead. Doesn't that scare you?"

"No, he was going to kill us and wanted to rape me," she said in an energized whisper.

"People don't change, Jen. They can't. You have to know that."

She paused. "You mean your father?"

"Of course I do. I have his blood inside of me. I can't do anything about it."

Another period of silence followed his comment, which she eventually broke by uttering a single, lapidary word: "*Timshel*."

"What?"

"*Timshel*," she repeated. "Have you ever read Steinbeck's *East of Eden*?

"No."

"It's a Hebrew word that means 'thou mayest.' Which also implies 'thou mayest not.' Our behaviors are our choices to make, choices not to let our blood define us. It's what makes a man a man and not an animal."

"I have no idea what you're talking about."

She kissed his cheek. "When all of this settles out, I want you to read it. It might heal you of that kind of fatalist thinking, the notion you can't do anything about nature's bent and proclivities."

Jonathan retracted to the dark cabin window again, holding his silence for a long time. "I can't continue going on like this, Jen," he said finally.

"We have to go to the Justice Department," she answered quietly. "We have to give them all the information we have and—"

"And then what, Jen?" Jonathan reacted, breaking her off. "And then what? Don't you see with all that's been going on, I've just been ignoring the obvious? Hell, I can't even share my past with you." His face relinquished strength. "I just want it over with."

Jensyn squeezed his hand. "*We're* not over."

"I've ruined your life with this mess. They'll be searching all over for us and won't stop."

"Which only tells you we have no choice but to go to the authorities as soon as we get home."

He shook his head. "No, if I do that I won't be able to use what I have against Decker."

"But he won't confess to you. You've already tried. He won't give you what you want."

"If not him, then the FBI. I may go to jail, but he will too. Maybe I can get a reduced charge with all I have on him."

She stroked his arm. "I think you better talk to a lawyer when we get home."

"Boston's not safe. I'll call my lawyer, but we can't go home."

"Then where?" Jensyn asked.

There was only one place he could think of.

* * *

Atlanta, Georgia

Larry Carpenter's fist came crashing down on his desk. "How could this have happened? That's *twice*. I thought Slade was better than that."

Kent Shaughnessy and Joe Moran stood in front of his desk like obsequious serfs. "I thought so too, Larry," said Shaughnessy. "Who knows how it happened? Woods said something about a street fight."

"But Slade had a gun," frowned Carpenter. "Certainly *they* didn't."

"Maybe Sands found a weapon of his own," speculated Moran, "you know, a spear or something."

"Dammit, Joe," blared the CEO. "I'm in no mood for your idiocy at the moment."

Moran looked at his watch and sauntered over to the sideboard. "Mind if I help myself to a longneck, Larry?"

Carpenter dismissed the fat man with a wave of annoyance.

"You could use a stiff one yourself, Larry," said Moran from across the room. "Want me to suit you up with a nice double martini?"

"Yes, yes. And then shut up, Joe. Please, just shut the hell up."

The CFO grunted.

OPTIONS

"There's more, Larry," Shaughnessy said. "But I'll wait for Joe to get you that martini first."

"How the hell can there be more?" Carpenter squeezed his eyes with his forefingers and pressed his temples with his thumbs.

In a moment Moran was back at the throne. "Here you go, sir, down the hatch." He handed Carpenter his drink, who commenced gulping down a full mouthful, olive included.

"Okay, gentlemen. I'm not going to sit here and get drunk on bad news. What is it, Kent?"

Shaughnessy gave it to him measuredly. "And even with the small sample, two more cases of leukemia is far more than a simple coincidence."

Carpenter's face drained with the information.

It was all news to Moran as well. "Two more cases, Kent? How many does that make now?" He downed a long swig of his Budweiser.

"Eleven in total. And they're all of the same type."

"We wouldn't have a rat's-ass-in-a-propeller chance getting FDA approval," said Moran. "Good thing we're only trying to peddle the stuff off in Africa. They won't care."

"Like hell they won't care!" came back Carpenter. "We've sold them on the notion there are no side effects."

"We could always play dumb," Moran suggested. "You know, while we work out the bugs."

Kent Shaughnessy traipsed over to the window and looked out over the cityscape. "No, gentlemen, I couldn't be party to that. A loss of life here and there was one thing—which I've justified to myself was for a much greater cause." He turned around. "But I couldn't knowingly sell the stuff under this kind of specter."

Moran disagreed. "But it's only eleven out of four-hundred people, Kent."

Carpenter didn't interrupt. He wanted to hear both sides from his trusted minds.

"Eleven now, Joe, but who knows how many more cases are brewing out there? Leukemia isn't like a cold with symptoms that show up right away. It takes time."

"So what rate of complication would be acceptable to you?" pursued Moran.

"How can I answer that? What I do know is that we have to bring it back here to find out exactly what we're dealing with."

Carpenter couldn't let that statement go unchallenged. "You know we can't do that, Kent. We need human clinical data, which, as you very well know, requires years of animal testing first. We've been through all this before too many times."

They had indeed been through it all many times before. The likelihood of penicillin, or for that matter, even aspirin, getting approval under existing FDA protocols would be remote, since both drugs were poisonous to common laboratory animals. The more troubling problem, however, was that human HIV didn't comport with any known animal subject models.

"I'm sorry, Larry," resumed Shaughnessy, "but I can't do it. Not now. We have to know why the peptide is causing this chromosomal translocation Woods keeps mentioning. Maybe our scientists can modify the amino acid composition in a way that preserves what we want yet eliminates what we don't. That kind of research doesn't require animal testing."

Carpenter took a studied sip from his martini and set down his glass, looking up at the President of his company with an altered favorable expression. "That's what I like about you, Kent. You sift through the issues and make a sensible suggestion."

Moran spoke up. "What about me, Larry? I do that too."

"No, you don't, Joe," Carpenter said. "Outside of finance you're a blithering fool. But that's okay because you know your numbers so well. And you make me laugh. Though, not when I'm around you."

Joe Moran knew he was no fool. He also knew Carpenter knew that as well. It was all a peculiar version of humor the two men played between each other, even in their off moments.

Carpenter concluded with unequivocal sternness in his voice. "Okay, gentlemen, reel it back in. Harare, everything, sealed stateside and top secret. I don't want any trace of it left. Tsumbia and the other nation governments will have to be told we have some final tweaking to do on the product."

Kent Shaughnessy stepped back to Carpenter's desk. "What about our auditor problem? It could explode quickly and we don't have another Geoffrey Slade on the payroll."

"No, we don't. But we have alternatives. Hell, why not use those hoods we used back on the Maplefield case?" A key witness in a product liability lawsuit had to be eliminated cleanly; the guys were good. "Either way," resumed Carpenter, "it's not my problem to solve, Kent. It's your problem, and you better solve it quickly without any more foul-ups."

Carpenter sat back in his chair and contemplated the matter more as he stroked the shank of his martini glass. "Furthermore, I want you to give Mr. Moss a call. Don't tell him my decision about Harare. Play like everything's still a go, but let him know what his auditors have been up to. Perhaps he'll be able to play out his ideas and we'll get good news."

As Shaughnessy and Moran waited in silence, Carpenter lifted his drink and flushed down the last of it. "But you know what, gentlemen? We had no idea about any of it, did we? We just tell the feds the Camden thing must all have been Wolcott's doing."

"Your brother-in-law?" asked Shaughnessy, surprised.

"I never could stand the ass. Besides, Columbia needs new leadership anyway. Screw him." Carpenter chomped some ice from his glass. "And don't forget those licensing and purchase option contracts Moss signed over to us. We just may have to screw him, too."

* * *

Wednesday, August 25, 1993
Hague, New York

The small lakeside town of Hague was slightly less than a two-mile drive south of Moss's lodge. Although Decker pulled into his summer place the night before, it was too late to do any shopping at the time. After enjoying a morning cup of coffee on his deck that looked out over the lake, he drove the short distance to town for a two-week stock of groceries and supplies.

He hated spending his vacations alone. Over the years, however, he had become accustomed to bachelorhood. Hard work during the days, hard play in the evenings, and more often than not, cheap—or not-so-cheap—pickups on the weekends. Regrettably, Lake George offered little of either. Fortunately, a fresh acquaintance agreed to visit him the coming weekend. Not overly pretty, but still a nice body and decent time, he thought, and he looked forward to it.

The practical issues of singleness came no more to the forefront than in the grocery store. Buying for one might as well have been buying for four. He filled his cart with canned goods, produce, dairy products and prepared frozen foods. It was

431

inevitable he would end up giving away a good portion of his purchases to a neighbor when it came time to leave.

Following stops at the hardware and liquor stores, he pulled into the town's filling station. The owner was a weathered local Decker had known since he was a kid.

"So, my boy, how've ya' been?"

"Fine, Mr. Jarvis. Great to see you again." Moss handed the old-timer a twenty in payment for gas. He never knew Jarvis's first name and he never bothered to find out. It had always been Mr. Jarvis and would always be Mr. Jarvis.

"Have a good winter?" asked the proprietor, who was wearing the same dark gray cap and work clothes Decker always remembered. A partially-smoked cold cigar hung permanently from his lips.

"No, but what winters are good? Glad to finally be back home again, though."

The man made change and handed it to Moss. "Ain't seen your folks now in many years. They doin' okay?"

"Pretty much the same. Dad had a minor stroke this spring, and Mom's still got her arthritis thing. But they're holding in there pretty well down in Tampa."

"That's good. You tell them both I said hello and hope they can get up here again soon."

"I'll be sure to do that," Moss said. He was just about out the door when Jarvis called out to him. "Say, ain't it somethin' about that body they found out in front of your place?"

Decker froze in his steps. He turned around. "What did you say?"

"That body." The wrinkled gentleman gave Moss a quizzical look. "Why, you haven't heard?"

"No. What're you talking about?"

"Craziest damn thing. This past weekend they dragged out a sack with a girl's remains in it, east of your bay. It's been the buzz around town."

Decker shook his head and squinted at the man with unfocused eyes. "You're kidding."

"Wouldn't joke about something like that. You really haven't heard?"

"Who was it?" Moss was trying to hold himself steady at the news.

"No idea. They're still tryin' to find out, that's what the paper said. Just that it was a young woman. Must have happened quite a while ago." Jarvis came around the counter and grabbed a copy of the local paper, handing it to Decker. "Here, have a read for yourself. On me."

Moss saw the follow-up story, squarely on the front page. His mind was reeling. *Was it really possible?* Decker summoned composure. "Incredible. Thank you, Mr. Jarvis."

Moments later he was in his car heading for his place, driving fast beyond the speed limit.

* * *

Boston, Massachusetts

Sands and Chandler arrived in Boston a little past noon. On account of Jonathan's leg injury, the services of a courtesy cart were requested to shuttle them around the airport terminal. The driver took them to the baggage claim and then to convert plastic for currency at a cash machine. A generously tipped attendant helped them with their luggage to Jonathan's car.

Again they were exhausted. This time, however, the seven hour time change would be on their side. Unfortunately, they still had a three hour drive to his mother's home in Vermont—his idea for a place to 'hunker down' while they rode things out.

Painful as it was, Jonathan's right leg was still functioning enough to do the driving himself. Once on the interstate, he used his car cell phone to call his secretary. No news of importance or other needs requiring his immediate attention, she informed. She transferred him to his docked phone messages. There were 24 in all. Some he deleted, most he preserved for later reply.

The twelfth stopped him cold. It was from Decker Moss, recorded at *11:19* the previous morning: *Jonathan, we have to talk. It's urgent. Please call me as soon as you get in.*

He had Jensyn scribble down the phone number. A few messages later there was another one from Moss, delivered at *8:04* that morning: *Jonathan, I'm willing to negotiate.*

That was all it said.

"What do you think it means?" she asked.

"I don't know. But something's changed." Jonathan assessed the possibilities. "He may just be trying to flag me for another

433

Drexel-Pace hit. They've probably been in close contact with him throughout this whole ordeal."

"Is there any way they can trace your calls from that thing?"

"I don't think so." Though he wondered about that. The technology probably existed to triangulate the position of a cell phone, yet he doubted his pursuers' ability to do so. Then again, who knew what kind of resources Drexel-Pace was able to bring to their manhunt?

"So call him back and see what he wants," Jensyn said. "Maybe it's really your day."

"No, not yet. I have to call my mom first. I don't want to just pop in with a woman she's never heard about."

"You've never mentioned me?"

He tittered. "Jensyn, I've never even made good on a dinner date with you."

* * *

Albany, New York

Agent Edward Fitch sat at his desk reviewing the coroner's report showing a match on Karen Wyman's dental records. He received word of the positive identification that morning. Comparisons had been made to those on file of unsolved missing persons in the greater Vermont and upstate New York area, cases that went as far back as the range of estimates for the time of death. As he analyzed again the facts concerning the body's discovery, the cause of her death, and the other evidence found in the bag—in conjunction with his earlier finding showing a DNA match on the saliva found in her car—he concluded it was all very consistent with his long-held suspicion: Jonathan Sands.

But was it enough to charge him?

If it weren't for the location of the body and the fact that Sands was reportedly so drunk that night, he thought so. But how on earth could he have driven that far in the condition he was in? Middlebury is at least an hour's drive to the lake. And how would he have gotten out onto the water that night?

It wasn't that Fitch didn't have enough for a grand jury indictment. He would just feel far more comfortable if those pieces tied together better before making a formal charge. There was also the problem of motive. He suspected rape, but of course there was no way to make such a determination.

OPTIONS

The agent grabbed a file on his desk and withdrew a folded map of the northern section of Lake George. Laying it out flat, he contemplated. His pencil rested on an existing red hash mark—the exact location of the body—a good half mile from shore. Then he compared the marked spot to the one on the map mailed to the dive shop owner about the sunken carriage. If not an exact match, it was extremely close. *Coincidence?* He seriously doubted it. Unfortunately, there was no return address on the mailing, and the typed name on the brief letter wasn't at all familiar to the dive shop owner.

How could Sands have gotten her out there?

A rowboat perhaps?

Referencing the map, Fitch traced the main road that ran along the western shore. Earlier in the day he had a meeting with a state police detective who told him of two boat access ramps nearby. Just to the north was a camping park, Roger's Rock, which although closed at that time of year, was the detective's best guess as to where someone might put in a boat. According to him, the place was deserted in November and a person with a small boat, a canoe, for instance, could portage the thing at night through the woods—or just around the gate for that matter—and set it in without being seen.

His finger coursed the span from the park to the hash mark. Just about two miles. Fitch tried to imagine canoeing that distance in the dark with a body. Then he recalled something else about the night of Karen's disappearance. It was foul weather … probably far too rough on the lake for a small boat.

The other boat launch was to the south, in the town of Hague, about the same distance out from where the body was found. It was a public access ramp right off the main road. A larger boat could be put in. But the reason the state police detective couldn't imagine it being used was that a motel was located right next door, not twenty feet away. With that and the road traffic, he couldn't believe anybody would take the risk. Fitch tentatively agreed with the detective's reasoning.

He studied the map's stretch of shoreline along the western side of the lake. Reportedly it was dotted with homes and summer camps.

Wouldn't the owners have boats? For year-round residents maybe it was still early enough in the season for them to keep their boats in the water.

435

A check of the names associated with the addresses on the shoreline would have to be made. He wondered if the post offices in the area could fax them to him. Crediting the idea as his next logical step, Fitch picked up the phone.

* * *

Hague, New York

It was just before three o'clock in the afternoon and already Decker Moss was working on an overdose of Scotch. He was reclined in a chaise lounge, looking desolately out at the lake from his back deck when the phone call he had been anxiously awaiting finally came in.

"You want to talk?"

"*Sands! Where the hell have you been?*" Decker knocked over his drink.

"Out and about. You want to talk?"

"Damn right we have to talk. You don't have much time."

"I've got all the time in the world."

"Jon, they found her. *Karen's body*! Sunday afternoon."

A pregnant silence.

"Jon?"

No response.

Decker's breathing was heavy. "I don't know anything other than that. But if they haven't gotten in touch with you yet, they certainly will. We have to get together before they do."

Sands detected the thick-tongue of drink. "Why's that?"

"Because she was found out in front of my place! I'll be connected with this along with you."

"Gee, that's too bad, Decker," Jonathan intoned sarcastically.

"Look, Sands, stop with the games. I'm willing to negotiate."

"What are you willing to give me and what's it going to cost?"

"It's a quid pro quo."

"Right," said Jonathan. "I'll pay the quid, what's your pro quo?"

"No, not on the phone. I have an idea, but you have to come here. I can help you and you can help me. We have to get our stories straight. Do you understand?"

"No, Decker, I don't. Help me understand."

"*Dammit, Sands!* I'll tell you what you want to know, okay?"

"I mean Middlebury."

"I know what you mean."

"All of it, Decker. I want every bit of it, and don't screw with me. If it's believable enough with no holes I just may be willing to forget about that eleven million bucks of yours. But you'll only have one chance with me, do you understand? You color it up or slip in one of your lies and I'm out of there. And just in case you think I might be expendable, there's someone else who has everything I have. Anything happens to me, and they'd like nothing more than to take this to the Justice Department and see you all hang."

"Yeah, yeah, just get here as soon as you can. I'll tell you everything if you just get here fast."

"Two o'clock tomorrow."

"*Tomorrow!* No way, Sands! It has to be tonight."

"Sorry, Decker, that's not possible. I'll see you at two, tomorrow."

"*Jon!*" Decker yelled. "They've identified her body! It was on the radio this morning. There may not be a tomorrow. You have to get here right away!"

The phone clicked.

* * *

Interstate 89N

Retreating into himself, Sands held impassive at the wheel of his convertible while Jensyn waited for him to speak. "Aren't you going to tell me what he said?" she asked anxiously.

Silence.

"Jon?"

His taciturn manner when upset was something she had come to learn about him. It was also intensely annoying. "I hate it when you get this way."

There was a long period before he finally spoke. When he did, it was absent emotion. "They found Karen's body."

"What!"

"It won't be long now. You'll probably have to visit me in jail."

"Stop it. How can you joke at a time like this?"

"Who's joking?" He turned on the FM, hitting the auto signal search button.

"Where'd they find her?" she asked. But he didn't answer.

Jensyn pulled a torn glance out her side window and then shifted back to shut off the radio. "This is just too incredible! I can't believe they just happened to find her now. Why now?"

"*Now* may be exactly the right time."

"What are you talking about?" She stared at his enigmatic expression. "Why are you being so cavalier about something as serious as this? Please tell me."

"I can't tell you, Jen. They can force you to testify. You'd be incriminated as an accessory after the fact, and that's not something I'm willing to do."

He switched on the radio again and turned down the volume, thinking it all through. Everything Decker does from this point forward will reveal more than his words, Jonathan knew. Such as the fact Decker called him in the first place. Why would he want to help me? He would like nothing more right now than for me to be tagged with this. With the medal and the contrived break-in of his boathouse, why not just let the police come after me and let me hang?

She was found three days ago, yet there was no message on his answering machine concerning the matter. The fact the police hadn't yet tried to contact him about it was more than curious. *Was the medal gone?* He concluded they were probably simply waiting to gather additional evidence before making a formal charge.

Sands lifted his cell phone to call Lake George information and requested the number for the local paper. After a few minutes and several connections later he spoke to a reporter who was working on the story. Yes, a body had been found Sunday in Lake George. Yes, also to his other question, off the record—following notification of family members that morning, a formal announcement of her identity had been made: *Karen Henley Wyman.*

"Lake George!" Jensyn exclaimed when he told her about the announcement. "My God, Jon, that answers all your questions right there! Decker must have done it!"

"Not necessarily. It's a big lake."

Jonathan pushed in a cassette. It was the one she had fallen in love with: Barber's *Adagio for Stings.* The top was down, blowing a warm August air, and she nervously rested her head against the backrest. The music could barely be heard over the rushing breeze.

The I-89 north into Vermont routed through the Green Mountains, a saddle that furrowed the state, east to northwest.

Interspersed in the median, where construction required blasting, tall monoliths of stone ledge were left standing.

"I have to go tonight, Jen."

She came up.

"Decker's vulnerable. He's as vulnerable now as I'll ever find him. I can't wait till tomorrow."

"But you're dead tired and you need to see a doctor."

"That can wait until tomorrow."

Jonathan picked up the cell phone and dialed Decker's number. In a single statement he informed Moss of his revised plans. If Moss replied it must have been quick, Jensyn gathered, because Jonathan immediately disengaged to dial his mother. When she answered he told her that he would regrettably have to leave right after dinner on an emergency business trip.

* * *

Hague, New York

Upon hearing Jonathan's change of plans Decker immediately called Kent Shaughnessy. Moss had been in contact with him frequently to discuss a "clean solution" to their problem, and now the pharmaceutical executive informed him of his progress.

"We've got some trusted contractors in New York City," said Shaughnessy reservedly. "I should be able to get someone there tonight, but I'm not sure what time it'll be. Do you have a gun just in case?"

Moss grimaced at the question. "I happen to have one, but *I'm* certainly not going to use it!"

"No, just to hold him off if you have to. To buy time until our contractor arrives. We can't afford to let him slip away again."

Decker understood and gave Shaughnessy directions to his place. It would take three to four hours to drive from the city, Moss informed him. Shaughnessy terminated their conversation by saying: "Good luck."

Yeah. Good luck.

Decker tried to think clearly through his Scotch. It was Green something. Greenberg, Greenwood? ... The surname was a common one, and it had some obvious—some symbolic—connection with Vermont. And she now lived in Stowe. That was all Decker could recall from the conversation he had with Jonathan about his mother the night in the restaurant. Decker correctly deduced that Vermont was Jonathan's most likely destination; his mother's home, specifically, was the most logical hiding place. Boston was too obvious. Moreover, Vermont would be close enough to easily make the trip that evening, which Decker now knew Jonathan would be doing.

He pulled out a local phonebook as a perchance prime of his memory. *Greenberg, Greenfield, Greensmith, Greenwood.* Damn! What was it? Greenfield and Greenwood were the best-sounding possibilities. They sounded "Vermonty" enough.

He dialed for directory information, requesting Stowe numbers for the two names.

A moment later of waiting he hit pay dirt. Greenfield was listed and Greenwood was not. He wrote down the number. The more he thought about it, the more convinced he was that Greenfield was in fact the name Jonathan mentioned.

Then he dialed another number.

* * *

Stowe, Vermont

Somehow in the little time she had, Cheryl Greenfield set about putting together preparations for her guests that were of the highest order. A roast beef dinner was in the oven, complete with Yorkshire pudding, fresh summer vegetables—and Jonathan's favorite—her recipe for twice-baked garlic potatoes.

She couldn't stop staring at Jensyn. The fact Jonathan had finally found someone, and such an obviously special woman, caused her more joy than she could conceal. Feelings were apparently mutual. The two spent much of the time before dinner getting to know each other, gabbing away in the kitchen while Jonathan lounged in the living room. The white lie he told about a racquetball injury explained his limp.

Frank Greenfield arrived home early from work, and the four of them came to sit out on the front veranda before dinner. It was a large country farmhouse with a sprawling lawn. Mount Mansfield stood tall in their view. The couple accepted some port sherry, though Jonathan's glass ended up sitting untouched.

The meal was as delicious as it smelled, Jensyn thought, a dinner as good as any he had never made good on.

OPTIONS

Crickets and peepers now chirred a late summer symphony as Jonathan sat in his convertible, ready to leave. Jensyn reached for his hand. He leaned up to kiss her.

"You better tell me directions just in case something happens," she said.

"Nothing's going to happen. He'd never do anything to me with all that you know, not with you safely tucked away here." Nonetheless, Sands ripped a small sheet from his pocket calendar and jotted down some directions.

"Please be careful," she said, pocketing the piece of paper.

"I will."

Her eyes narrowed. "I mean it, Jon, I want you back."

As she watched him drive off, a wave of nerves rose in her stomach.

Chapter Forty-Five

Albany, New York

IN response to Edward Fitch's request, the faxes came in slowly from the three post offices. Earlier on the phone, apologies were made by all three postmasters that their rural carriers had gone home for the day. Their mail clerks had to first finish casing their afternoon mail before compiling the list of lakeside residents the FBI agent wanted.

The first two faxes arrived just before five. The entries covered the region of the lake along the western shore, and up and over the northern part to the eastern side. They were lengthy listings, amounting to several hundred addresses for each office.

Fitch combed through the handwritten pages looking for any standout names. He had a short list of Karen Wyman's male acquaintances in Middlebury, given him years earlier by her roommate, Susan Cabot. It was a long shot, of course, and predictably after many minutes scrutinizing the lists, nothing matched. He wondered if he should have asked for a composite listing, including post office boxes and hold mail, thinking there were probably plenty of seasonal residents—vacationers—who probably preferred to pick up their mail in town. He would call the postmasters again in the morning.

After poring over the final page he got up, stretched, and went to check for the remaining fax. The machine was in an alcove just off the hallway, next to the copier and office coffee maker. The latter gave off the pungent smell of burnt resins. He poured the last ounces from the decanter.

A beep sounded from the fax machine.

Following the header page nine sheets of single-spaced typed names and addresses scrolled out. Beyond the fact that the mail clerk typed the entries, Fitch noted that the dates of seasonal delivery were included as well. He frowned at the amount of time needlessly wasted on such detail. Probably some postal worker trying to impress the feds.

Grabbing the output he checked his watch, which showed a quarter past six. He returned to his office and progressed methodically through the names, looking initially for last names beginning with S—as in "Sands." As with the previous faxes the entries weren't in alphabetical order but in delivery sequence. When he had finished culling through those he focused on the first letter of the other names on Susan Cabot's list.

It was the end of the day and he'd been at it for more than two hours, now exhausted. It was the type of mundane detective work he deplored.

And then one shot up and slapped him in the face.

Moss!

He stared at it, disbelieving. But there it was in black and white. He took his pencil and circled the name several times.

Sands must have used Moss's boat, he thought. *Or maybe Moss himself ...?*

Fitch concluded it was definitely time to have a sit down talk with the owner of the property. He knew Decker Moss lived in Manchester, New Hampshire. It would have to wait until tomorrow.

Then, peering down at the faxed page again and seeing what he saw, he wanted to kiss the postal worker who took the time to provide the detail they did. *The seasonal delivery dates.*

* * *

Hague, New York

Decker dialed the number he had written down earlier. It was answered after two rings.

"Hello?"

He recognized the voice right off as belonging to Jonathan's mother. "Is Jonathan there?" he asked. He knew she wouldn't recognize his own.

"Jonathan?" she repeated, surprised. "Why, no. He had to leave on a quick business trip. May I give him a message when he returns?"

Moss concealed his excitement. "No, that's okay. I'll call him back later."

Before she could get off another question Decker terminated the connection by depressing the cradle button.

Smiling, he called Kent Shaughnessy with Jensyn Chandler's confirmed location. A second 'hood' was definitely needed.

* * *

Burlington, Vermont

Sands took I-89 out of Stowe, headed west to Burlington, and then got off at the exit for Route 7 south. He stopped at a service station to fill up. While waiting for his charge card to be processed he asked the attendant if he knew of an electronics store in the area.

The attendant informed him that a Radio Shack just happened to be up the road, not more than a quarter mile away.

His purchase at the electronics chain store was brief. The request probably sounded odd to the salesman, but after several minutes Jonathan walked out of the store with a rather expensive slim-profile tape recorder that had a built-in low impedance mic. Yes, the salesman assured him, it was the best available for picking up "ambient conversation."

Sands traveled the remaining two hours to Lake George on two-lane roads.

* * *

Stowe, Vermont

"Someone called for Jonathan?" Jensyn asked. She tried to conceal her alarm.

The two women were sitting on the living room couch where Cheryl was sharing a family photo album, pictures of her son when he was growing up. Frank Greenfield was in a corner recliner reading the paper and digesting his dinner.

"Yes," answered Cheryl. "Why dear? You look upset."

"No, it's nothing," Jensyn fibbed. She flicked to the final page of the album: Jonathan's high school graduation picture. "I'm just surprised someone would call for him here, at this hour." She had been certain no one possibly knew where they were. "And they didn't give you their name?"

"No, he just said he'd call back," said Cheryl.

Closing the album, Jensyn perfunctorily flipped through the pages of a coffee table tome, feigning interest while she thought about the situation. *Vermont: A State of Mind.* It was filled with glossy pictures and short vignettes of the state's landscape and historical attractions.

OPTIONS

What could it mean?

"Has anybody ever called for him here before?" Jensyn asked.

The Greenfields now gazed at each other, their curiosity raised by the question. "No, but why would they?" Jonathan's stepfather asked.

Jensyn didn't answer. She closed the book. "Would you mind if I used your phone?"

"No, of course not," answered Cheryl.

From the kitchen Jensyn dialed Jonathan's car cell phone. It rang on and on without answer. Eventually, she replaced the handset, hoping her failure to get through was just due to a cell repeater problem in the mountains.

Decker Moss had experienced the same problem many times on his trips through Vermont. Unknown to Jensyn, it was, in fact, a problem he was now relying on.

After a few minutes thinking of the worst possible scenarios, Jensyn said to the Greenfields: "I know you two haven't known me long, but could I possibly ask you for a huge favor?"

* * *

Hague, New York

Jonathan recognized the old routed wooden sign along the side of the road: *Mossy Rocks.* He pulled into the gravel driveway. The sun had just set beneath the mountain ridge to his back. As he passed through the stand of conifers he saw the log lodge down by the lake in front of him.

Memories percolated up from the dregs of his mind and his stomach tensed.

He quietly pressed his car door shut and walked over to the spot where they had parked that awful night, half a life earlier. *She was just here.* His eyes traced the pathway from the driveway down to the boathouse off to the right. *And then he dragged her down there.*

It all looked the same. Different was the weather and the time of day, but the place all looked hauntingly the same.

Decker emerged suddenly from the rear entranceway to the house. "Jonathan, thank God! Come on in." He reached for his visitor's arm.

Sands pulled away and limped up the stoop and into the foyer.

"What's wrong with your leg?" Decker asked.

Sands didn't answer.

The sight and smell of the great room coaxed stale reminiscences from his college summer visit of the place. Decker directed him to the couch in the center of the room, whose backside faced a set of French doors that went out to the patio. Two armchairs sat directly opposite with a full view of the lake behind.

"Have a seat," Decker said. "Want a drink? Beer? Scotch?"

"No thanks." Jonathan detected the scent of whatever his host already consumed that day on his breath.

Moss strolled to the kitchen area behind the stone fireplace. Sands pulled the tape recorder from his blazer pocket. He thought of placing it between the cushions of the sofa but worried about it impeding a clean mic pickup. Noting the couch's pleated ruffle went fully to the floor, he set it beneath and activated the record button.

Then he surveyed the room.

The Moss family lodge was as much an engineering feat as it was a contradiction in architecture: rustic yet modern, spacious yet cozy, earthy yet comfortable. Its golden urethane floors and rough-hewn log walls—all accented with brightly-colored Native American throw rugs and tapestries—filled the air with the resinous smell of pine. An arched two-hearth stone fireplace bifurcated the kitchen area and the great room. Connecting the first floor to the balcony of the second was a spiral stairway whose steps were also made of logs, cut lengthwise, and bolted to each other with wrought iron rods that went the full height to the ceiling. The place was huge and the lake was everywhere. A full wall of picture windows took up the entire front of the house and gave entrance to the out-of-doors.

Decker returned with a tall glass of Scotch. "Sure you don't want something to drink? Water?"

Jonathan shook his head and sat down on the sofa with his back to the lake.

Decker took a seat in one of the facing arm chairs.

For long moments the two men just stared at each other, saying nothing. Decker finally broke the silence: "Why couldn't you just leave Harare alone, Jon?"

"I'm not paid to leave things alone."

"You've made a big mistake."

"Was Camden a mistake?" asked Sands.

"Camden was different. I told you that. I didn't know a thing about it. And that's the God's honest truth."

"But you know about it now."

"Yes I do, and I have to say I think it was brilliant."

"Killing people is brilliant in your mind, right Decker? As long as it made the buyout of your firm possible and lined your pockets with millions, that's all that's important to you, isn't it?"

"Look, Jon, if you're talking about that excavator, he committed suicide. Carpenter assured me they had nothing to do with that."

"He's lying."

"I'm just telling you what he told me." Decker pulled a generous sip from his drink. "And you've got no proof it happened otherwise."

Sands shifted in his cushion and changed the subject. "Tell me about Harare."

A trace of a smile formed on Decker's lips. "I thought you said you already knew about Harare."

"I know all that matters. I want the details."

"I'll bet you do. And then what?"

"And then, possibly, we negotiate."

Decker knocked back another gulp and set his glass down on the coffee table. He stood up. "Seems to me a man who wants to negotiate might want to have something to negotiate with."

"I told you, Moss, I want everything, and no crap, or I'm leaving. I have enough to rip you and Drexel-Pace apart."

Decker stared down at him, anger spreading in his eyes. "Yeah, that's right, Sands, no shit. You, who always thought of me as some dumb-ass jock who'd never amount to anything. Well, Harare proves you wrong." He jabbed at the air in Sands's direction. He stood like that for a while, his finger pointing menacingly yet totteringly at his foe, and Jonathan knew he was drunk. Then, faster than a chameleon, Decker's expression changed and he sat back down in the second armchair. "But you know what, Sandman? Despite what you think about me … despite that, I still think enough of you to treat you as a friend."

Jonathan turned and draped his sore arm along the back of the couch to look out at the display behind. The suffusing pinks and reds of the setting sun lit up the shoreline across the lake.

"You always hated me, Decker. Jealousy or whatever, you always hated who I am, haven't you?"

447

"I hated being judged," Moss replied straightly. "If you think that means I hated you, then you're wrong. But you always had a way of making me feel inferior. I could never measure up to your prissy vanilla standards."

Jonathan turned, assessing his old roommate. For some reason Jonathan actually felt pity for him. "We were an odd match, weren't we, Deck? So little in common yet still as close as can be at one time. At least I thought we were. But you were always using me, weren't you?"

"Using you?" Decker threw back. "What the hell are you talking about now? How could I have been *using* you?"

"Those tutoring sessions? Those times you wanted to pay me to help you cheat?"

"My God, Sands! You used *me*. My parents paid most the rent, or do you forget that little detail?"

Jonathan felt he was wasting time with the argument. "Tell me about Harare, my friend … if that's really who you'd have me believe you are."

Moss cocked his head with a smirk as he sat backward. He knew he had nothing to lose now by summarizing the matter, and if for no other reason than to impress the one whose favor had always eluded him, that's what he did. From Drexel-Pace's discovery of the peptide reaction on a critical HIV protein; to the Threonatrix metabolizing agent that made subcutaneous delivery possible without immune system rejection; to the human trials in Harare that had unequivocally established disease treatment efficacy. Jonathan listened intently as Decker expounded, raising an eyebrow once or twice, but otherwise offering no interruption or comment.

"So, Jon, other than for the current field research they've been doing there's really nothing illegal about it. And even that's not unethical. The drug works. *Miraculously.* People are being cured with a one hundred percent survival rate. And the FDA, with all their bureaucratic hoopla and regulatory nonsense, is completely shoved out of the picture. The African governments will produce and dispense the medications themselves from the production secrets we share with them. Our real profit, however, comes later, once the drug's success is proven. You'll like that part, Jon."

Decker waited for a reaction. Sands offered none.

Frustrated, Moss continued: "The profit installments to us are linked to special income tax receipts their governments take in from businesses and the upper-class. All tied to the cumulative change in GNP numbers—official sector figures that can't be played with. Think of it, Jon. We get compensated for the drug's trickle-down economic success. People healed of AIDS re-enter the workforce and prop their economies back up like crazy … exponentially. What follows is a throw-off of cash by the capitalist engine, siphoned by the taxing machinery of their governments and all back into our pockets."

"Somewhat like taking an equity position in a promising start-up," said Sands. "Only here the start-up happens to be an entire country—an entire *cartel* of countries."

Finally, a reaction, Decker thought. "That's right, Jon, and we're not just talking about millions, or even hundreds of millions of dollars. Over five, ten years, with the certain boost in their economies, we're talking about billions."

Jonathan silently marveled at the cleverness of the plan. *Except the drug doesn't really have a perfect result at all. It causes leukemia. But you don't even know about that, do you, Decker?*

"Jon, the problem we have is that you're on the cusp of screwing it all up. We, of course, don't want that. Nor should you. Think of the good you can do—the good for mankind—just by walking away and playing dumb about any sins we may have committed. I'll even cut you in on my take."

Of course not. Drexel-Pace wouldn't share that untidy fact with you yet, would they? It would compromise your loyalty to their secrets. And when it all hits the fan, they'd fear you'd turn on them, pleading ignorance about everything they've set up with your chemical products and patents.

"Jon, you've got to see reason."

What would Drexel-Pace be planning at this point, given what they know? How would Decker fit into any plans they have?

"Dammit, Sands, talk to me!

He wouldn't fit in at all. They're using him.

"What would you like me to say, Decker?"

"That you'll stick with us on this thing!"

"And if I do? Then what? Do you really think I have any interest in your blood money?"

"It's not blood money. I told you. People are being healed! And it's big money, Jon. You'd never have to work another day in your life."

Sands did nothing to suggest he was impressed. Instead, he changed the subject a final time. "Now, Deck, I want you to tell me about Middlebury. You tell me all about Middlebury and then we'll see what I might be willing to do for you. If not, I'm leaving and you're all screwed."

* * *

The man eventually found the driveway on Route 9N. It was a little farther north along the lake road than he expected, yet he was certain of the location from the sign. He pulled his car off onto the shoulder of the highway and then took the rest of the way on foot through the tall hemlocks.

Dusk had come and gone and deep shadows melded in the trees.

A couple hundred feet ahead was a log home. Exterior sconces lit up the parking area in front of the garage, where sat two cars: a white Ford Explorer bearing New Hampshire plates, and a sleek black Mercedes from Massachusetts. The latter's convertible top was down and he opened the glove compartment. In it was a leather-bound document folder, which he carried over to the garage light.

Sands.

Withdrawing his gun, he skirted around the side of the lodge, and quieted to the back. Tall casement windows were cranked open and voices could be heard.

* * *

"Hell, you've always been too virtuous," said Decker, rattling the cubes in his glass.

"You sound as if I should apologize."

Decker stood from his seated position, his depleted drink in hand. "I love you as a brother, you know." He walked off around the walled fireplace and into the kitchen. "I never had one and wished I did." Jonathan heard the clinking sound of ice and the pouring of another drink. "Yes, I loved you more than a brother, Jon, if you can hear that coming from another man." His words were loud and slurred. Then he peered from around the fireplace. "Sure you don't want a drink? I bet you've never had 40-year-old Scotch before."

"No, to be honest, I haven't had strong drink since that night you got me wasted."

Decker bellowed a laugh. "That was sixteen years ago, Sands. My God, have you ever frittered your life away!"

Jonathan stood and limped over to the French doors. But there was only blackness out there now. He thought of the sixteen years she was out there. "I have to know, Decker," Jonathan said lowly. "It's time."

Moss was now occupied at a pine credenza along the back wall, in the shadows beneath the spiral staircase.

"It's time," Jonathan said again, turning around in the direction of his old roommate.

"I know, Jon." Decker emerged from the shadowed area into the light. "It's time."

The two men stared at each other. There was no emotive air to their conflict, no reaction whatsoever from either. For Jonathan, it was as if another consciousness was now being lived outside of him, one that no longer felt fear or pain, staring down from above, seeing him as he always wished he could be. And Decker Moss as he had always been—his old friend now with a pistol in his hand.

"I'm sorry, Jon. I hoped I could buy you off, but I knew I probably wouldn't be able to. You're too fucking virtuous to see the practicality of things. As I told you a long time ago, there's nothing after this life. You chose to do with it what you did, and I've chosen to do what I've done. Unfortunately, only one of us will be left because *I'm* not going to be the one to go down for this. For the thousandth time, *I* did not kill her."

Jonathan came around the couch. "Using that would be an incredibly foolish thing to do, Deck. I told you, there's somebody else who has all the information I have."

"I won't need to use this. Someone will be visiting us shortly. And I know who your 'somebody else' is. Her name's Jensyn Chandler, and she's staying at your mother's place in Stowe as we speak."

Sands's face went pale.

"See, Jon? I'm really not the dumb-ass jock you think I am. She'll also be running into a tragic accident soon."

"*You bastard!*" Sands started to race at him but stopped as Moss raised his gun.

"Sit down, Jon."

Sands thought of his promise to Jensyn to return. Slowly, he sat down. His mind shrouded over. Eventually he looked up.

"Before you do what you're going to do, Deck, just tell me. It's the least you can give me."

Moss preferred to buy time, not that it was necessary, but in his drunken thinking there was also nothing to be lost by giving his old friend his last wish. "My God, Sands, you're so naive! You have all the book smarts in the world but you're so incredibly naive." He reached into his blazer pocket and withdrew a set of car keys. He tossed them over to Jonathan.

Sands caught the keys but didn't know what to make of them. They looked like an older pair.

"It was her *keys*, dammit!" Still pointing the gun in Jonathan's direction, Decker seated himself on the spiral stair tread where he had placed his drink.

Jonathan fingered the keys some more, staring at them, realization fomenting.

"You can come out now!" Moss yelled into the air with a slur.

In the shadows beneath the stairs, to the side of the credenza, a bedroom door opened.

The identity of the fair-haired man entering the room was unmistakable. Older yes—pockmarks where once there was acne—but unmistakable nonetheless. And he stared at Jonathan with ragged hatred in his eyes.

Decker handed the gun to him. "You remember Peter Roy, right Jon?"

Moss wiped his forehead and took down a final long draw of his Scotch, finishing it. "We couldn't move her car without the keys. When I got home that night, I saw Roy standing next to Karen's car in the driveway, wondering what the hell he was doing there. Wondering what *she* was doing there. He was beside himself and eventually pointed toward the vestibule. When I went over and looked in, there she was, lying on the floor."

Decker got up from the stair tread. "Peter, tell him what he wants to know. It still makes me sick to think about it, and I need another drink."

Roy sat down on the stair tread Decker gave up, and with his arms on his knees he kept the gun leveled on Sands. "Long fucking time, Sands," he nodded, "although I can think of better ways to spend my evening. Deck wasn't going to do this alone, and to be honest, he doesn't deserve to. He saved my life that night. I've always owed him for that. We've stayed close over the years, being the only bachelors left in the group. Closer recently because of all this, ironically." Roy turned his head toward the kitchen. "Isn't that right, Deck?"

"That's right, Little Bro," returned Moss with a holler.

"Anyway, when he called me this afternoon, to tell me what happened, I drove over. I live just over in Rutland. You should know we've planned for this possibility long ago." Roy paused, seeming unaccountably at ease. "To be honest, Sands, I've wanted to square this out with you for a long, long time. You fucked with me that night, shamed me in front of the whole place. I was humiliated in front of the best friends I had—*have*—in the world. Choking me; punching me when I was only kidding around with you; calling me 'acne-boy.' I'm not going to go into some psychological explanation for all that happened that night. Let's just say you represented everything I wasn't. I despised you before that night, but especially that night ... your cocky attitude about school, and guys like us who like to party, and that great job offer you got. And your great looks the girls always talked about. You always thought you were so goddam better than everybody else. Such a prick."

Decker returned to the room with his drink and handed a beer to Roy. After taking a large swig, Roy resumed. "A while after you left I took off as well. I had to get out of there. The whole place was staring at me holding a bag of ice to my face. My throat hurt too much to drink anymore, thanks to you, not that I was in the partying mood any longer. I was too wiped to know really where I wanted to go at first, so I just wandered around the streets for a while. But it didn't take long to decide to head over to your place, to find you and finish the thing off with you—fairly, not like you did with me by knocking me down and pinning my arms under your legs. And I would have.

"When I got to your apartment, there she was ... coming down the back stairs ..." Roy's eyes were dark, unreflecting, and he seemed to set them on autopilot, staring vacuously at the darkened lake vista to Jonathan's back while he recounted the story.

"She was beautiful, Jon. I always thought she was so fucking beautiful. Decker told me early on that she liked you, and I admit I was jealous about that, too. Just one more thing, you know? I don't know why I did what I did, but I was drunk. I grabbed her, and she yelled out a bit, trying to get loose. I guess that's when she must have thrown her keys. Decker told me he finally found them in the pile of leaves down the staircase. Anyway, she slipped on the stairs, and when I kissed her she didn't put up a fight. I thought she wanted me to. She just froze in my arms, and I thought she liked it, like she wanted more. I got her down on the floor. She just held there, locked up, and I kept telling her to relax. She looked up at me and I lifted her sweater. When I tried undoing her pants she started to freak out. I kept telling her to relax, but she began to cry. I didn't know what to do. I just wanted her to relax, to quiet her down, that's all."

Decker was now sitting next to Jonathan on the couch. Sands's body was vibrating. Tears streamed down his face as he listened to Roy's seemingly shameless reiteration of events.

"She just kept on crying and then she started to scream, and I got worried someone was going to hear her. I grabbed for the only thing that was there. The iron doorstop. I didn't mean to hurt her. It just happened."

Jonathan shot up from the couch in Roy's direction, and just as fast Decker grabbed his arm and pulled him back. "You wanted to hear this, Sands!" he yelled. "We never wanted you to know. Now sit down and listen!"

"She wouldn't wake up," Roy continued, "but she was still breathing. I didn't know what to do. I searched for her keys but she didn't have them on her. I had to get her and her car out of there. Your apartment door was locked. She must have locked it when she left. So I checked all over her car, but they weren't there either. And as I stood there freaking out a long time, that's when Deck showed up."

Jonathan's face was cradled in his hands, tears flowing through his fingers.

"Don't worry, Sands, I never got inside her," said Roy.

And then Jonathan crumpled over the arm of the couch and retched on the floor. He peered up with filled eyes, wiping the mess from his face with his arm, the key ring still around his finger.

Moss thought it was all very pitifully remindful of that awful night sixteen years back. He took his arm to Jonathan's shoulder, which Sands immediately threw off.

"When I went to her I found she was dead," said Moss grimly. "That's when I went up to check on you and saw you were totally passed out, with your clothes on the floor. Roy was frantic and we had to do something. I admit my idea was somewhat diabolical ... based on knowing your past ... but it was the only thing I could think of. I had to save Roy. To save all of us, really. I didn't know you didn't have sex with her, and who knew what a court would find in the end? Hell, I couldn't rat on Roy since it was an accident, and I obviously couldn't make a thorough search of your room because I'd wake you up. I really had no choice, Jon. Don't you see? After we quietly carried her up and left her and her clothes in your room, Roy locked your door and rode out the rest of the time in the attic."

Jonathan's face came up. "*He was up in the attic the whole time?*"

"Yes, Jon, the whole time," Decker said. "We had no choice but to do it that way."

Jonathan shook his head from side to side. "But the night Fitch interrogated us, nobody said Roy left Smitty's earlier. They acted like he was with you guys all the time."

"They covered for me," said Roy.

"They knew all along?" Sands screamed. "They knew you killed Karen!"

"Of course not," exclaimed Roy. "They just didn't think Fitch needed to know I left earlier than the rest. They knew damn well I had nothing to do with Karen's disappearance, and the fact I left beforehand would have only led to more irrelevant questions for him. You messed up my face and neck pretty badly that night, and that's all Fitch needed to start sniffing at my ass."

"So they knew you weren't at the frat house when they got home?" pursued Sands.

"No." Roy stood up to stretch his legs and back. "Nobody actually checked my room before going to bed." Then he looked down at his nemesis with a smirk. "Fraternity brothers don't play mommy and daddy with each other, Sands. Not that you would know anything about that." Roy sat down on the step again. "I got back much later. And even if they did see me coming in after they got home, I would have just said I was out walking. They knew how fucking depressed I was."

A pause. "I'm sorry, Jon," said Moss, "I really am. You never had to know. But it was you who wouldn't push off. With her body found we have no choice. You had 'plans' that night, remember? After your crazy attack on Roy in the bar? The guys will be only too happy to come clean with Fitch about that detail. And the fact I told him about your room being locked? Well you locked it because you weren't in your room and you didn't want me to know. I'll just say it was the pushbutton kind you can lock from the other side. Fitch never knew what kind of lock it was. And then you drove Karen here to Lake George. You knew about it from your visit that summer, which my parents will vouch for. You broke into our boathouse to use our boat. Then you drove back, ditched her car and ran back to our apartment. They know you're a runner. And they'll find the police records verifying the boathouse was broken into."

"They'll never believe you, Decker."

Moss got up and circled the room. "Oh, they'll believe me. Why wouldn't they? Don't forget I've had as much time to think about all of this as you have. You came here tonight, after all. You came here when you heard her body was found. You had to get rid of me because I'm the only one who could finger you." Decker looked down at Roy and gestured at the gun he held. "And if you think that's traceable, it's not. Dad bought it years ago in a private sale. It won't be hard to explain. Roy just happened to be my house guest when you arrived with your gun, and during a fight between us he ended up having to shoot you instead." Decker continued pacing the room and pointed at the keys still in Jonathan's hand. "We'll make it all look good, Jon. When it's over tonight, those will be found in your house with your fingerprints on them. A puzzle for the police, perhaps, but pretty damning evidence in the end, you'd have to admit."

Hearing it all, Sands now knew it was over. He threw the keys on the floor and struggled with the last question he still had. It was an enduring question he had wrestled with for years, but never had the leverage to find out. "And the iron doorstop?" he asked falteringly.

Decker was counting on Shaughnessy's contractor to arrive by now. A professional was certainly better suited to take care of the problem in a clean way, especially since Chandler now made it double duty. He worried if Roy would actually have to carry out the dark deed himself.

"Your medal, Jon," Moss continued and then paused. "... I couldn't have thought of such a thing that night. I was too drunk. When I cleaned your room the next day, I found it next to your bed. I threw it away when I got the idea. But what did go down with her would tell you for sure you couldn't have been the one responsible for her death. And there's no way in hell I can have that now." Decker paused again. "The iron doorstop. That's what I put in the bag, Jon. Not your medal."

Sands flew off the couch and tackled Moss to the floor. Roy stood up and took careful aim at Sands.

"HOLD IT! FBI!"

Peter Roy quickly pivoted in the direction of the unseen voice, seeing movement at the side casement window. He fired.

The impact of the bullet slammed Fitch to the ground. Roy ran over to the window, and with the light spilling from the room, he peered out at the fallen and immobile figure. Then he quickly turned around and aimed the gun squarely at Sands, who was still on the floor. Decker stood up and Roy came to his side, next to the stairway.

"So it's finally all over, Sands," said Roy with a sick smirk. With no more than a few paces separating them, the casement window to Jonathan's back as he sat up, Roy aimed the pistol down at Sands's forehead, his finger tightening over the trigger. He paused a few moments, calculating how their story would still hold. Staring at the dark blue eyes with thick lashes he hated with all his being, he uttered his final words to Sands: "Fuck you, you prick."

Then, in quick succession, three gunshots rang out across the lake.

Chapter Forty-Six

"ARE you alright?"

He was sitting on the floor, dazed, and looked up at her.

"I ... *how'd you*—?"

"Your mother's car," she managed to say through excited breathing. "Someone called for you, and when I couldn't reach you on your cell phone ... I knew something was wrong."

"But—" Jonathan pointed to the window behind him. *"The shots ..."*

Jensyn knelt down at his side. "I heard a gunshot just after I pulled into the driveway. I ran down and saw that man lying outside. I had no choice but to use his gun."

She got up and went into the kitchen to wet a towel for his face. Handing it to him, she said: "I'll call the police." She went to look for the phone.

"No, Jen! Wait!"

"Huh?"

"Let me think."

"But, we have to—"

"No, give me a moment." His halting hand was raised to her as he looked around at their surroundings. Then he stood. Roy was on the floor where he fell—a shot to his chest. He kneeled down and felt his jugular. No pulse. He then moved over to Decker. The bullet had gone through his neck, but he was still breathing, barely. Blood oozed from the hole in his flesh with each struggled breath.

Jonathan quickly limped to the back door and exited the lodge. A minute later he returned with Fitch's gun. Jensyn watched him as he took a dry towel from the kitchen, carefully wiped it off, and exited with both.

Another gunshot fired through the screen and into the ceiling of the room.

"What are you doing!" she yelled when he returned.

"I placed it back in his hand and fired another shot so there'd be gunpowder on him. For forensics." He threw the towel onto the kitchen countertop. "We're getting out of here."

"No, Jon, we have to call the police."

"No we're not. We have to leave right away."

458

OPTIONS

"Why? It was in self defense! They were going to kill you."

"I'll explain to you later!" he shouted. "Someone's coming! Get to the car!"

She did, and in the time he feared he didn't have, he quickly moved about the area, panning for any evidence that remained of his or her presence. He used the wet towel Jensyn gave him to wipe up the vomit next to the couch and went to the sink to wash it out. After picking up Karen's car keys from the floor, and then the tape recorder from beneath the sofa, he grabbed the dry towel from the counter again. He was about to wipe the doorknobs, but caught himself.

No, doorknobs have fingerprints.

He brushed a bit at the knobs, hoping they wouldn't yield any ascertainable prints by him or Jensyn that might have been left behind. Then he re-entered the great room a final time and nervously looked about the area. Seeing nothing, he exited the house and veered off in a fast limp for his car.

Jensyn was getting into hers, parked several lengths of empty space behind his. Jonathan briefly wondered where Roy's and Fitch's cars might be. He threw the tape recorder and Karen's keys onto his passenger seat, and just as he was about to get in he looked up. "Jen!" he yelled, pointing out beyond her to faint headlights that appeared in the distance. They broke faintly through the trees at the top of the driveway. "Quick, into the woods!"

They watched the car slowly pull off to the side from their reclined position behind a mature hemlock tree. It was close to the main road, up several hundred feet away from where they lay. The headlights went dark and a lone figure emerged. Although the image was faint and broken through the trees, Jonathan was comforted by the fact no one else appeared to be with him. But what was unfortunately also very clear was that he held a pistol, a long barreled one—one made that way by an attached silencer.

"Jen," he whispered, "you have to listen to me. Do exactly as I say. When he gets into the house, I want you to run as fast as you can to your car. Don't start it right away. Wait for my signal. When I do, tear out of here as fast as you can."

"*And leave you here!*" she said in hushed exasperation.

"We have to get you out first."

"*But he'll kill you!*"

The thug made his way down the driveway holding a small flashlight, shining it for footing and along the sides.

Sands quietly spoke his fomented decision. "I have to stay behind until I can come up with something. A diversion. He'll be fast on us if we try to head out of here together."

As the man came down the driveway, his profile now almost in their perpendicular line of sight, Jonathan mulled over their situation. He wondered about heading back for Fitch's gun. But how many rounds did it still have left in it? And even if he could get to Fitch, then what? The whole scenario he had hastily contrived minutes before to erase their presence from the scene would all be for naught.

The hit man was now at the side window of the house, looking inside and then down at the body next to it.

Except for a slight breeze rustling in the trees and the gentle lapping of waves against the shoreline, there was no sound to the evening. Jonathan felt spent, physically and mentally. In the few moments he had left, he tried to think through his options. Unfortunately, whatever he came up with outpaced his ability to think through completely. There were simply too many of them, with too many potentialities, and most had likely bad outcomes.

As the man made his way around to the back entrance of the lodge, the sound of the lake carried Jonathan's attention in that direction. Then his gaze down to the boathouse. Perhaps a hundred feet away, though out of view from their position, it provoked his thinking.

A fire perhaps? There would certainly to be plenty of gasoline inside—in the boats or cans or whatever. But a fire, while a distraction, would only provide a few moments for him, not the kind of time he needed to get back to his car and safely out. And a pursuer would certainly follow him if he tried to escape on foot.

The man entered the backdoor.

"I have an idea," he whispered excitedly. "Turn left out of the driveway. A few miles down the road is a marina. Wait for me. If I'm not there in an hour, I want you to hide out someplace, somewhere up in the Adirondacks. When I start the boat, you'll hear it and he'll hear it. As soon as he comes out of the house he'll head down for the boathouse. Then take off as fast as you can."

"*But—?*"

Before waiting for her broken-off response, Sands was quickly on his feet, feeling his way through the trees in the evening's dim lighting. He looked back only once to make sure Jensyn headed off for her car. Thankfully, she did.

OPTIONS

As he felt for the light switch, his recollection of the boathouse arose darkly, vividly. The petroleum/pine smell of it aroused a slumbering olfactory memory ... a vestigial reminder of their horrific deed. The larger Sea Ray on the left had been replaced with a more modern version. But the smaller Boston Whaler on the right was the same. Its mahogany wood appurtenances had been re-varnished over the years, but it was the same boat, he knew. The scratches on the gelcoat of the bow were still faintly apparent from the rocks dropped on it by Decker that night.

He got into the Whaler and pocketed its lanyard key from the console. Then he went over to the larger cuddy-cabin Sea Ray and found its key was also in the ignition—a tradition of trust adhered to by most of Lake George's shoreline residences. He untied the dock lines.

The inboard/outboard fired immediately to life. Quieter than its older versions, the Sea Ray's engine was still loud enough to travel a ways. He got out and peered from the doorway up at the lodge.

Nothing.

Then he heard the sound of Jensyn's car starting. And then her tires squealing, spinning furiously atop the loose gravel. It quickly brought the man out the of the house. He chased after her, heading in a sprint up the driveway for his own car. Jonathan retreated back into the boathouse to the Sea Ray, and without getting in, revved its throttle to full. It screamed and he returned to the doorway to see if it caught the man's attention.

It did. The man did a double-take and started fast towards the boathouse.

"I know it's you, Sands!" he yelled, his back now against the exterior rear wall of the building. "And I know you don't have a gun, or you would have certainly tried using it by now."

Silence.

The contractor peered into the doorway and entered slowly, but saw no one inside. He panned his flashlight across the space, across the rafters, below the work bench and under the tarps strewn along the sides, but there was nothing. Getting into the Sea Ray he searched the cuddy cabin and the boat's anchor hold beneath the floor. Then he directed his light at the water, under both boats' hulls and their sterns, and along the cribbing beneath the U-shaped dock that served as the boathouse's foundation. Flummoxed, he headed out and looked along both sides. No side docks and no sign of movement. From there he went to search the surrounding woods and outbuildings.

Jonathan took the immediacy of the moment from his hiding place to swim to the Sea Ray's stern ski platform. He had been clinging to the dock cribbing at the front of the boathouse, a hidden position made possible by the limited angle of sight permitted by the liftgate opening. Pulling himself aboard, he threw the engine's gearshift forcefully in reverse, taking the cuddy cabin at full throttle out of the boathouse.

The man was back in seconds, standing on the platform in front of him, gun raised. Sands ducked behind the protection of the cuddy cabin's bulkhead just as he got off his shots. Spits from the silenced weapon splashed into the boat, splaying shards in all directions.

With his body tucked low, Sands reached for the gearshift along the gunwale and pulled it fully forward. The boat roared back into the boathouse, crashing powerfully against the front docking, splitting its planking. It sent the man into the water.

Sands then abruptly pulled the Sea Ray into reverse and out of the boathouse again.

Finding his footing and balance in the waist-deep water, the man came up, but without his gun.

Jonathan veered the boat around in a 180 and revved it backwards through the liftgate. The man was now between the Whaler and the front platform. The stern was coming in on him, and as he moved behind the smaller Whaler's bow to protect himself from the oncoming crash, he reached down into the shallows for his gun. He came up with it.

It was an easy shot. Certainly for a professional. Sands had his back to him, and even in the fury of the moment, the assassin capably lined his sights on Sands's head. He knew full well that his Sig Sauer worked fine when wet—indeed, many in his craft preferred a slightly-wetted silencer for improved muffling.

But what he hadn't anticipated was an important detail of internal ballistic physics. Travelling at over 800 miles per hour, a round fired through a flushed barrel clogged with muck didn't comport with relied-upon functionality. The baffled chambers of the suppressor, now filled with soot, created a vacuum, a sucking action that impeded proper rifling action of the barrel. It wasn't a squib shot—one that literally lodged in the barrel—but it was enough to buck his aim off several inches from target, into the left windshield.

Jonathan thrust back and forth on the gearshift, throwing the inboard/outboard hard against the Whaler in repeated blows, which pinioned the man in a daze between the Whaler's bow and docking. Sands pulled back a final time in full reverse thrust, thumbing the hydraulic trim on the UP-position as he did so. The outdrive lifted, and the high-RPM strength of the propeller, half in water half in air, caught him ... first his pants leg ... then his flailing protecting hand ... then ...

Blood filled the water.

Completely unintended by its manufacturer, the 250 HP MerCruiser sterndrive ground his lower half into pulp, like so much mincemeat in a food processor.

* * *

Thursday, August 26, 1993
Schroon Lake, New York

It was dawn and Jensyn was asleep. Jonathan quietly got up and got dressed.

They had taken a room at an obscure motel located in Schroon Lake, a half hour north of Decker's place on the interstate. He gambled that whatever pursuers might be after them at this point wouldn't have the time or resources to comb all of the area's many motor inns. Nevertheless, Jonathan paid cash and registered them under a fictitious name. He left his Mercedes at an all-night convenience store and then they returned to the motel in his mother's car, now secreted along a side road a couple blocks away. A brief call the night before calmed his mother's concerns. It was a believable story about an emergency business issue he needed to tend to in Albany. Jensyn's unexpected request to borrow her car was relegated to a woman's "sometimes over-reacting to irrational fears." At that, Jensyn shot him a look, but understood the need for his quick contrivance.

Sands exited the motel room and walked across the street to a park bench that looked out over Schroon Lake. It was calm and serene with a coral sunrise. A flock of gulls squalled in the distance, working a rocky shoal to the north. He pulled the miniature tape recorder from his coat pocket and pressed the play button.

Although the quality of the audio pickup wasn't what the Radio Shack salesman had sold him on, the captured dialog was enough to sink Carpenter and company for good. The confession from Decker Moss and the evidence concerning his and Roy's guilt in Karen Wyman's death was also all on tape.

Then something very intriguing about it struck him. Just to be sure, he listened to the entire recording again.

Incredible as it was, there was nothing in the first half—prior to Peter Roy's abrupt entrance—to implicate him. Nothing explicit about his involvement in Karen Wyman's death or disappearance whatsoever. Perhaps a few hints of fact or statements that might be inferred to suggest otherwise, but even those could be alternatively explained. Or edited out. And as he thought about it more, the second half could be erased altogether.

Sands pocketed the recorder and pulled the key ring from his other blazer pocket. Holding it in his hand, fingering the keys, he knew that he had a very important decision to make.

He had always been willing to do time for what he had done. But not for what he hadn't. And now he could be free of it all. Roy was dead. Fitch, his antagonist, was dead. And the gaping wound in Moss's neck meant he was also surely dead by now. Sands could walk away from everything right now and the secret would remain his forever.

And what really was his guilt? Accessory after-the-fact? Obstruction of justice? Yes, both. But he was drunk. And he tried to stop Decker from doing it. All could be explained by his being drunk and Decker's manipulation. All, that is, except for his silence over the years. That couldn't be explained so readily now that he knew the engraved medal was never in the bag. It would be an unlikely jury that would ever buy his true motivation—to protect his mother.

A year? Two years, at most? Even if he confessed, he suspected a good lawyer would be able to get him off altogether. Jonathan contemplated again about all the pieces—pieces he had only too many years to ruminate about.

Karen Wyman had dried blood on her cheek. His belt was wrapped around her neck. He knew people don't bleed after they're dead. She would have had to have been struck with something to knock her out before being strangled. Otherwise she would have put up a fight. Yet there was nothing on the bedroom floor other than his clock and their clothing, nothing blunt enough to strike her with. And there were no bloodstains on his bed. Whatever was used to kill her had to be elsewhere, outside his bedroom.

He remembered staring at her long that night before Decker covered her with a sheet, not really comprehending any of it at the time. As he recalled her pale skin and absence of markings on her neck, however, he reasoned much later on that the belt had to only be a ruse.

The missing iron doorstop was always a lingering possibility in his mind. The fact their landlord used a kitchen trashcan to prop his door open their final night in the apartment together became increasingly prominent in his thinking. The vestibule was where Decker found Karen's keys. If it was indeed the blunt instrument used, then it went down with her in the bag.

It was actually that suspicion, along with Decker's lie about not seeing Karen's car in the driveway, which drove Jonathan to exercise his last desperate option. The fabricated story of a horse-drawn carriage was necessary to raise her body in a way that wouldn't point back to him. The depth of her sunken remains ensured that a fractured skull, if it existed, would be preserved enough to prove that a blow was the cause of her death. And from his brief research on the issue, freshwater divers were always in search of intriguing new dive sites.

Ironically important to his confession strategy, however, was the presence of the medal in the bag. Before they told him about the damning evidence they found pointing to him, *he* would tell them what they found. Why else would he tell them? Certainly he wouldn't have placed it in her hand. No, Decker had framed him by placing the medal in Karen's hand, and because of that, he always felt he could never confess to his lesser culpability.

Probabilities and rationality: the requisite elements of any game. The only thing that never fit was the chained door. Improbable as it was, he concluded Decker had somehow been able to pull it off, possibly with a coat hanger. In Jonathan's notional thinking, Peter Roy's involvement never even rose as a possibility. Why would it? His whereabouts that evening were always accounted for by the frat brothers. At least that's what he thought all these years.

"Still sorting out your ghosts?"

Jonathan turned. She came down from the bank and sat at his side, wrapping her arm around his. She sniffled.

"Thanks, Jen."

"Thanks?"

"For saving my life last night. For saving my life … period."
He grabbed her head to his shoulder and stroked her hair.

"Three shots, two were blind luck. I've never even held a gun
in my life." Tears were in her voice, as they had been periodically
throughout the night. "Will I ever be able to live with it?"

"Jen, we can both live now, *because* of it."

They sat quiet there like that for a long time, her head resting
against his shoulder. He eventually broke the silence. "Are you
ready to hear the rest of the story?" he asked. "About Karen, I
mean?"

"I've always been ready. Not that it's ever really been
necessary."

He stood from the bench and looked back at her.

Her nose was red and she forced a smile: "Though, finally
taking me out to a nice restaurant one of these nights might be
necessary."

"That sounds about right." Then he turned back to the lake.
Looking down at the keys he held in his hand one last time, he then
threw them out as far as he could.

Time already served.

EPILOGUE
(1993)

OPTIONS

JONATHAN Sands and Jensyn Chandler were placed under the protection of the U.S. Marshals Service. Preliminary inquiries were underway at the Department of Justice, with a long list of likely indictments under the federal and state securities laws. Separate criminal investigations against the Drexel-Pace team of chief officers were also pending, along with injunctions being sought under the Foreign Corrupt Practices Act. Sands surrendered his tape to the authorities. It was an easy matter to erase the second-half portion subsequent to Decker's elaboration of the Drexel-Pace conspiracy. Sands couldn't admit the recording was made in Decker's summer house, so he testified that he surreptitiously recorded it when he met with Moss at his office the week earlier. The date of the meeting was a matter of record with Moss's secretary. Dr. Graham Woods had agreed to turn state's evidence, personally concluding that the drug had no hope of achieving formal approvals for disease treatment efficacy. It helped that the evidence concerning his role as a key participant in Zimbabwe's covert experiments clearly implicated the chief management team of Drexel-Pace.

Conceivably, it would take years to disentangle all the knots and to retie the ropes in their proper strangling places. But ultimately, in all likelihood, the merger would be reversed. Schoen shareholder restitution would come from the flush coffers of the Drexel-Pace pharmaceutical giant.

Jonathan willingly confessed to Geoffrey Slade's death. Jensyn corroborated every aspect of his story—all of it a simple matter of self-defense. Owing to the other verifiable information about the Harare episode, no charges would be filed on either side of the Atlantic. The only piece they concealed, of course, was Jensyn's role in Decker and Roy's shooting.

On that, it didn't take long for the Albany FBI office to satisfactorily piece together what had probably taken place. They knew Fitch was working on the Wyman case at the time. Indeed, the case file still rested open atop his desk in the Albany office. The fatal wound to Karen Wyman's skull precisely matched the tapered end of the antique iron. Moss's name was circled on the postal address printout found in Fitch's car, and Peter Roy was listed among the names of Susan Cabot's associations at Middlebury. Subsequent questioning of several of the other fraternity members in Fitch's notes corroborated the close affinity between Moss and Roy. And their affidavits also stated that Roy's presence in the fraternity house in the afterhours of the night in question could not be definitively established. Lacking such an alibi there was the very real possibility Moss and Roy colluded in the matter of Karen Wyman's death and disappearance. Forensic study confirmed the bullets that killed all three men were fired from their respectively positioned firearms. Forensic analysis also found that the trajectories were consistent with the location of the bodies. The only details the FBI investigators remained puzzled about was why Roy's car was parked hidden in the woods down the road and why the exchange of gunfire had taken place through the screened window—why Decker Moss and Peter Roy were inside and Edward Fitch was outside. And why Fitch shot *both* men when his subjects had only one gun between them. Most perplexing of all was the "who and why" of an armed man found chewed up in the boathouse by the propeller of Moss's boat. A man whose remains had yet to be identified, but whose ostensibly-driven car to the scene was later discovered to be on a stolen auto list from Queens, NY.

They were all pieces of a convoluted puzzle that would apparently remain a mystery for a very long time. Perhaps always.

In the end, Jonathan Sands never read *East of Eden*. He wanted to, but Jensyn wouldn't let him. She bought him a personal hardcover copy, embossed with his name on the front cover, and insisted on reading it *to* him. In the evenings, in bed, when she knew she had his undivided attention.

With that gift he finally got the richest gift of God to man, above his blood—an abjured misconception of the supposed dictates of one's provenance—embodied in the mysterious Hebrew word *timshel*.

Man is a victim of his genetics, his circumstances and happenstances … yes, a victim of them all.

But not of his choices.

And what was a man, really, but the sum of the choices he makes?

OPTIONS

About the Author

Stephen J. Dempsey, Ph.D., received his doctorate in corporate reporting and finance from Virginia Tech. A professor at the University of Vermont's Grossman School of Business, he is the recipient of numerous teaching awards and academic honors. Although most of his writing career has been technical in nature, one day when on a family trip to their summer place in Canada his children prompted him to write a novel. He enjoyed telling impromptu stories during the ride, and by the end of the trip he had the basic idea for *Options*. Aside from writing, his interests include cartooning, cooking, boating, scuba diving, and playing jazz saxophone. He lives with his wife in northern Vermont.

Photo by Lynn Dempsey